The
Belladonna
Maze

Sinéad Crowley is a writer and
broadcaster, whose three DS Claire Boyle
crime novels were all nominated for the
'Best Crime' category at the Irish Book
Awards, with the first two becoming
Irish Times bestsellers. She is currently
Arts and Media Correspondent with RTE
News, the Irish national broadcaster.

Sinéad Crowley

The
Belladonna
Maze

An Aria Book

First published in the UK in 2022 by Head of Zeus Ltd,
part of Bloomsbury Publishing Plc

9 7 5 3 1 2 4 6 8

A catalogue record for this book is available from
the British Library.

ISBN (HB): 9781801105637
ISBN (XTPB): 9781801105644
ISBN (E): 9781801105613

Typeset by Divaddict Publishing Solutions Ltd

Printed and bound in Great Britain by
CPI Group (UK) Ltd, Croydon CR0 4YY

Head of Zeus Ltd
5–8 Hardwick Street
London EC1R 4RG
WWW.HEADOFZEUS.COM

Conor agus Séamus, le grá mór

Chapter 1

1825

Lisheeha, Co Roscommon

'Come and find me!'

There was a giggle, and then a rustle of leaves as the small, sturdy figure disappeared around the corner of the hedge. Ciarán stared after her, the temptation to run tingling in his toes. But he had not come to the maze today to play, he had an important job to do and had spent so long begging his father for the chance to prove he could work as hard as his older brothers, it would be beyond foolish to let him down now. Dropping to his knees, he took out the small, sharp knife he had been given that morning and began to prune the brownest leaves at the bottom of the thick, strong branches.

'Come on, Ciarán!'

Moments later, and clearly bored of her own company, Deirdre appeared beside him again, hopping from foot to foot in her heavy navy skirt.

'I'm bored, do come and play!'

'I have to work today.'

The English words felt thick and dull in his mouth and they made Ciarán feel dull too, and far older than his ten years. He looked down at his hands, already calloused and now itching from the mud that caked the palms and fingers, and felt once again the temptation to run and give chase – and then the decision was taken away from him as the smaller child bent down and grabbed the knife out of his hand, waving it gleefully before turning and sprinting down a long, leafy corridor.

'You have to catch me now!'

And Ciarán O'Mahony was a little bit annoyed, but mostly delighted at the excuse to turn and run after her. His bare feet slipping on the mud, he rounded a corner and then jogged along a narrow passageway. The light was dimmer here, the air thicker, somehow, and he slowed his steps, ears straining as he tried to figure out which way Deirdre had gone. He took a right turn and then a left and then stopped dead, hemmed in by the leafy wall in front of him. Turning, he retraced his steps, but he was at a junction now, the corridors to either side of him equally silent and equally empty. He had been a fool, he realised, to think that catching up with her would be easy. Deirdre Fitzmahon might have been a full two years younger than him – and a girl! – but the maze had been her playground ever since she was old enough to walk and Ciarán was sure that, by now, she could find her way around blindfolded. Of course, not many girls of her station would be allowed to run around alone at all, much less in the company of the gardener's son, but there was plenty about the way Deirdre Fitzmahon was being reared that was far from typical. Ciarán shared a truckle bed with one of his brothers, across the room from his parents, and he knew from listening to them late at night that the master had been disappointed when his first-born child was a girl, and sadder still when he and his wife were not blessed with other children. And now, although it could not be said that the Fitzmahons mistreated their only daughter, they seemed to care little about how she spent her days. Meanwhile, Deirdre herself was quite happy to have the youngest son of the gardener as a playmate and she and Ciarán had been as close as brother and sister for as long as he could remember. To take his knife, though? Ciarán's heart seemed to tighten in his chest when he thought of it. That knife belonged to his father, a man who was never reluctant to use a belt on one of his offspring.

And then the giggle came again, from the left this time, and so Ciarán chose his path and ran down it, his bare feet pounding against the mud and dust. He rounded a final corner and then emerged, panting, into the clearing at the heart of the maze to find the source of the merry laughter sitting on a large stone plinth, her feet dangling off the edge. The plinth itself formed the base for a statue of an angel, its blank stare taking note of everyone who entered the space. Deirdre had lost a shoe, Ciarán noticed, and her stockings were muddy and torn.

'I knew you wouldn't catch me!'

The child's voice, despite her mocking words, was warm and her eyes sparkled as she looked down at him. Ciarán shook his head. He did not want to argue with her, but his fear of his father was stronger than their friendship.

'Give me my knife back!'

'Here!'

Deirdre stretched out her hand and flung the small instrument away from her, angling the throw carefully so it sailed past Ciarán and landed safely on a patch of grass just behind. He turned to pick it up and then froze as a pair of shiny black boots appeared from around the corner and stopped in front of him.

'What's this?'

The man, which was how Ciarán always thought of Paul Fitzmahon, even though he was barely a year older than he was himself, bent and picked up the knife before Ciarán had a chance to grab it.

'What the hell do you think you are doing, boy?'

Ciarán opened his mouth to speak but the words dried in his throat. Behind him, he heard Deirdre jump down from her stone platform and in a moment she was standing between them.

'You leave him alone, Paul!'

'Leave him alone? I don't think so, cousin. I wonder what Uncle Richard would think if he knew the gardener's boy had been chasing you with such a weapon!'

'He wasn't chasing me...'

But Deirdre's voice suddenly sounded very young and very high pitched and the wobble at the end of the sentence told Ciarán she was fighting back tears. Paul, who was both a head taller and several stones heavier than he was himself, gave a sharp, barked laugh.

'Uncle Richard will want to dismiss his father, I shouldn't wonder, when he finds out what this ruffian has been up to.'

'Oh no, please...'

Ciarán found his voice, at least, but it sounded almost as weak as Deirdre's and he swallowed the rest of the sentence as Paul narrowed his eyes.

'Are you arguing with me, boy? Do you want to fight, is that it?'

And before Ciarán could ready himself Paul punched him in the stomach, sending him crashing painfully to his knees. Winded, he bent double, clutching his midriff, and then froze as he felt the point of the knife against the back of his neck.

'Leave him alone!'

Although his eyes were closed, Ciarán could feel the rush of air as the little girl darted past him and heard a succession of dull thuds as her small fists rained blows down on her cousin. But Paul Fitzmahon's arm did not shake and the blade of the knife remained exactly where it was, not quite breaking the skin at the nape of his neck but with a promise in the pressure that it could do so quite easily.

'Leave him be!'

The sting suddenly disappeared and Ciarán raised his head slowly to see Paul take a step backwards, the knife now glinting in his hand.

'You stay out of this, little girl.'

'You can't speak to him like that!'

Afraid even to breathe audibly, Ciarán tipped backwards until he was sitting on his haunches. His friend was gazing up at her cousin, her fists clenched, shoulders shaking with rage.

'You can't! Ciarán is my friend and I asked him to play with me, I took the knife; if anyone should be getting into trouble it should be me! Oh, Paul...'

Ciarán could see the physical effort Deirdre was making to calm her breathing, drop her shoulders.

'Why don't you play with us?' She waved her hand around at the maze. 'It would be much more fun with three, we could hide and you could find us…'

Paul's gaze flickered from the girl to Ciarán and then back again, and Ciarán could see an expression akin to longing cross the plump, spoiled face. For a moment all three were silent and then, as quickly as a cloud crossing the sun, the look of desire disappeared, to be replaced by sullen bad humour.

'Baby games! I have better things to do, and so should you, Deirdre Fitzmahon, look at you! Running around like a gypsy with the gardener's boy, and who knows what else you've been getting up to? You're a disgrace, that's what I'll tell Uncle Richard when I see him.'

He turned, the knife still clasped in his hand, and jogged out of the clearing towards one of the six identical exits. Ciarán's stomach twisted so suddenly, he thought he might be sick. He was in trouble now, for sure – the loss of the knife alone would earn him a beating – but if Paul told the Fitzmahon family that he had been threatening Deirdre with it, or worse… The breath left his lungs as he tried to contemplate the horror of how bad things could get. Deirdre's parents might give their daughter an unusual amount of freedom but even they would surely be horrified if they thought the son of a servant had put her in any sort of danger. Ciarán's father, Tom, had been gardener at Hollowpark Hall for years but never tired of telling his children that the job and the home they lived in were fully dependent on the Fitzmahons' goodwill and if one disappeared, the other would immediately follow. And then Deirdre sank down beside him and put her small pale hand on his grimy one.

'Don't worry.'

'How can I not?' Ciarán wanted to say but he knew that if he spoke, the tears that were building behind his eyes would spill out and only increase his misery and shame.

But Deirdre continued as if he had answered her anyway.

'Because you're my friend, and Hollowpark will look after you.'

Her face was suddenly so calm, and so trusting, that Ciarán almost groaned aloud. Of course, he had heard the stories about Hollowpark Hall, the belief held by the family that no harm would come to them as long as there was a Fitzmahon in residence. But it was just a story, and there was no shortage of strange stories on the estate, nor indeed in the village of Lisheeha itself. Around here, people traded tales at night, calling from house to house and swapping legends of the Púca and the Bean Sí, whispering the darkest of details as firelight flickered across their faces. But those stories were fairy tales, no more than that, yarns told to amuse children and old people and certainly no defence against bullies like Paul Fitzmahon. But even as Ciarán was thinking this, Deirdre closed her eyes and when she opened them again she looked, he thought, suddenly much older than her eight years. When she spoke her voice was steady.

'Hollowpark looks after its own, Ciarán. And you live here, and that means it will look after you too. Wait...'

She sat stock-still, a small smile now playing around her lips. Then she jumped up and motioned to Ciarán to follow her.

'This way!'

It took a second for him to clamber to his feet and by the time he had recovered his balance she had disappeared back into the body of the maze. Despite the encumbrance of her heavy skirts she was swift as a deer and it took Ciarán all of his strength to keep the small navy figure in his sights as she disappeared around one corner after another. And then Deirdre pulled up so quickly he almost ran into her, and she turned to him and raised her finger to her lips.

'Listen. Can't you hear?'

It took a moment for his ears to decipher what he was listening to but then the sound crystallised into sobbing, loud, harsh and uncontrolled.

'Come on!'

Deirdre darted away again and it must have been later in the afternoon than Ciarán had realised because the sun had almost completely disappeared now, and some trick of the gloom was making the passageways feel much narrower. But no, no, it wasn't just a feeling, this arm of the maze really did seem to be different from the others, the branches were so close together they were scratching at his face and he was forced to stretch his arms out in front of him to keep the leaves out of his eyes. Ciarán followed Deirdre around one final corner and found that it led to a dead end. And there, hunched at the base of the hedgerow, was Paul Fitzmahon, his face buried in his hands. And Paul was just a boy after all, Ciarán realised, a very upset young boy, and as they approached him, he lowered his hands and looked up at them, mud and tears staining his face.

'I can't get out.'

He was breathless, his words coming in sharp gasps.

'I turned and turned and there is no way out, I can't find it, I...'

'That's a shame.'

Deirdre took a step forward and Paul jumped to his feet and grabbed her by the wrist.

'It's not a joke, you stupid girl, there's no way out, I've been in here for ages, we're trapped—'

And then his eyes widened as he looked over her shoulder to where Ciarán was standing, a long passageway clearly visible behind him.

'That doesn't make sense...'

'Would you like us to show you the way?'

Deirdre's voice was light but pointed.

'Or we could just leave you here?'

Ciarán could see resistance flicker across the boy's face and then a shudder rippled through him as he dropped her wrist and gave a quick abashed nod.

'Take me with you. Please.'

'And the knife?'

Paul dug his hand into his pocket and handed it to her.

'You can have it, please, I was always going to give it back, I was just joking. I didn't mean anything...'

Deirdre took the knife and nodded at her cousin to follow her. As the three of them travelled in silent procession through the maze, the sun emerged again, making the passageways feel bright and airy, and it only took three turns for them to find themselves safely at the entrance. Paul darted away without a word and Deirdre handed Ciarán the knife, its handle mud-stained but otherwise unharmed.

'He won't say anything now, don't worry. Hollowpark

looks after its own, Ciarán, I told you that. You don't have to worry about anything while I'm here.'

And she, too, scampered away. Ciarán stood for a moment, looking after her, and then he cleaned the handle of the knife on the tail of his shirt before dropping to his knees and resuming his work, pruning and shaping and caring for the Belladonna Maze.

Chapter 2

2007

Zakynthos, Greece

The world tilted. Slack-jawed faces stared up at me as I hit the water, hard. For a moment I hung motionless, shocked by the sudden cold and anchored by the water pooling in my clothes, but then my survival instinct kicked in and I struck out against the bottom of the pool. My head broke the surface of the water and I could hear, above the pulsating music, some cheers.

'Ladies and gentlemen! Give it up for Gorgeous Grace!'

I gave the wave they all expected then swam to the side and hauled myself out. Mindful of outstretched phones, I tried my best to look dignified but sodden clothes made elegance difficult and I ended up flopping onto the deck like a dying fish – that was if a fish could wear a yellow Kidz Klub T-shirt and unflattering navy shorts.

'And now it's time for BINGO!'

Dave was still shouting, caressing the microphone as if he was on stage at Wembley, not poolside at a family hotel on an Ionian island, but for once I was grateful for his over-the-top bellowing, because it was diverting attention away from me. It was an unwritten rule that every rep in the resort got dunked at least once every season, usually after losing some random challenge against a hotel guest, and we were supposed to be good sports about it, but I couldn't help feeling it was all a bit, well, beneath me. I was a qualified nanny, after all, not some teenager on a gap year.

I squeezed water from my hair, then squelched into my flip-flops and checked the digital clock that sat high above the pool. Twelve noon and thirty-one degrees, a temperature gauge set to perfection. The morning shift complete, I still had plenty of time to shower and even grab a decent lunch before the afternoon 'Klub' shift started at two, I might even—

I don't know what caught my eye from the centre of the pool. Instinct maybe? Experience? The water was packed with guests, screaming kids, laughing parents, inflatable toys, everybody appeared to be having fun, letting off steam after the structured games of the previous hour. But one flash of pink just didn't look right. A blonde head rose, then sank and didn't rise again. There was no time to second-guess myself, I just ran forward and dived in, forcing swimmers out of my way as I struck out for the far side of the pool. A deep breath, and I was underwater again. I saw more pink, then my fingers closed on a soft shoulder and I yanked it upwards.

There were no cheers as I emerged this time, just the music and above it, one single piercing scream.

'My baby! My baby's in the water!'

The child was pulled from my arms. She was screaming now too and as I stood upright and wiped water from my eyes I realised that had to be a good thing. If she was screaming, then her lungs must be clear. If she was screaming, then she hadn't... As the full realisation of what might have happened hit me, my vision clouded. An ashen-faced Dave took my hand as I clambered shakily out of the pool.

'We just can't thank you enough.'

'Honestly, it's fine, I was just doing my job.'

I took a sip of orange juice then settled myself awkwardly on the bar stool. After the hotel doctor had checked me over I'd been all set to go back to work, but the little girl's parents had been waiting for me outside the first-aid room and insisted I join them for a drink, to thank me, they said. A drink that was now starting to feel like the most awkward first date I'd ever been on.

'If there's anything – anything we can do...'

The man fell silent then looked across at his daughter who was now sitting on her mother's lap, fiddling with a doll and looking as if she couldn't even remember the drama she had been at the centre of.

'I mean it – we're incredibly grateful.'

My mother would love him, I decided. He had one of those posh public-school voices that make people sound like they are giving orders even when they are only saying hello, with another layer on top of it that I couldn't quite place. He turned to his wife and daughter again and I snuck a proper look at him. He was a good-looking guy, tanned and leaner than most of the other dads in the hotel who tended to look like they only tore themselves away from their cars and computer screens for one brief fortnight every year. The tan showed off his deep brown eyes too, although his hair was too long, flopping all over his forehead, and every few minutes he pushed it away in a manner that was almost, but not quite, annoying.

'I think you can let Skye down now, darling. She's fine.'

His wife started, then looked at him as if she couldn't quite process what he was saying. After a moment, she released the little girl who immediately jumped down and began to bounce on a nearby sofa. Her mother kept her eyes fixed on her face, while her father turned to me again.

'I'm sure you see this type of thing happen all the time?'

He was clearly looking for reassurance and I did the best I could.

'Sure, kids run off, of course they do. It's a big hotel, people get distracted and...'

But then my voice trailed off because, the fact of the matter was, although I had worked in family hotels all over Europe, I had never had to fish a kid out of a hotel pool before. I'd seen accidents, of course, plenty of them, and put my first-aid skills to the test on many occasions with broken wrists and cut foreheads, all the usual tumbles you get when overexcited children meet slippery pool sides. But no, I hadn't ever seen an accident like this one before. Most of the parents were pretty vigilant, even if they did get stuck into the all-inclusive wine at lunchtime. Hang on though, was that... but the woman beside me didn't look drunk, nor hungover. She just looked – shattered. As if the worst thing in the world had happened to her, was still happening to her. She was attractive too, or could have been, with long, fine blonde hair bleached almost white by the sun and one of those broad, strong faces that look best with a tan and no make-up. But right at that moment, all you could see on her face was unhappiness. She picked up a beermat and began to tear it into small pieces, her eyes still fixed on the small girl.

Her husband cleared his throat. 'It was my fault, of course, I got distracted by my book and—'

'Don't, Patrick. It was my fault. I was looking after her, or was supposed to be.'

Well, there was no mistaking that accent anyway. Skye's mother was what used to be called a 'Sloane', with a voice that could have cut the glass tumblers behind the hotel bar, the good ones they keep for imported drinks that aren't part of the all-inclusive deal. It was a voice full of money all right, but also full of despair and I couldn't imagine what they were doing here, this handsome, anguished couple in this nice but mainstream hotel on a touristy Greek island, when they looked like they'd have been far happier on a yacht anchored offshore.

'My eyes closed – it was only for a minute. I thought, here, things would be OK...'

A tear ran down her cheek, making her resemblance to her daughter unmistakable. Her husband ran his hand through his hair, his fringe flopping perfectly back into place afterwards.

'No harm done, darling, I told you. It's all fine now. Isn't it?'

He looked to me again for support but this time I stayed silent and drained my juice. Time to go. My part in their little family drama was at an end and besides, I barely had time to eat before my next shift started. Saving the little one would get me a clap on the back from my supervisor, but that didn't mean she would find anyone else to lead Art Attack at 2 p.m. I scraped my chair back and knelt in front of the kid – Skye, I heard them call her – to say goodbye. Sweet little thing. Her parents were bloody odd, but that didn't matter. She wasn't registered with the Kidz Klub, I'd never seen her before and there was no reason to think I ever would again.

Which explains why I'll never make a living as a psychic – or a professional gambler. It was in fact less than an hour later when I heard a knock on the Kidz Klub door and opened it to see Skye's bright blue eyes looking up at me. Letting go of her dad's hand she wriggled past me and dashed towards a box of toys in the corner of the room.

'She's making herself at home!'

Her father ran his hand through his hair again in a gesture that was becoming familiar, and gave an almost nervous smile.

'I do hope it's OK – for her to join in?'

I shrugged. 'It's fine.'

It wasn't, actually. Guests were supposed to register their children at the beginning of their holidays if they wanted them to take part in organised activities; it was one of the reasons our hotel was a bit more expensive than others on the strip. We, the children's reps, were all fully trained and qualified in childcare and were not, as my boss was fond of saying, a fallback babysitting service for people who overindulged on the lunchtime retsina. But I was glad to see the little one had recovered from her earlier ordeal, so I simply took a step backwards and grabbed the clipboard that was hanging from the wall.

'Can I get her full name, please?'

'Skye Uprichard Fitzmahon.'

Skye's father gave what looked like a practised shrug.

'I know, it's a mouthful, isn't it?' He extended his hand. 'You can just put down Skye Fitzmahon. And I'm Patrick – I'm sorry I didn't introduce myself properly earlier. It was all a bit – well, mental.'

I returned his handshake, which was dry and firm despite the heat of the day, and picked up my pen again to scribble down their room number.

'My wife is Isla. We're both incredibly grateful for what you did earlier.'

'That's fine,' I muttered, flustered by his effusiveness. To change the subject, I looked across at his daughter who was now chatting animatedly to a little boy and trying to persuade him to race a pair of toy cars.

Patrick followed my gaze and gave a smile of obvious pride.

'She's been asking us for days to come here. It's the main reason we picked this hotel, to be honest with you, I wanted her to have other kids to play with. Skye starts playschool next term and I thought it would be good to get her used to other children, you know? But when we got here, Isla decided to keep her with us after all. I think that might be why she ran off, earlier. She was getting a bit bored hanging around with her old pair, poor kid.'

There was something very endearing about his obvious concern for his daughter, so I nodded at my colleague to start giving out the colouring books and decided I could afford to stay listening to him for a few moments longer.

'She hasn't been well. Isla, I mean, Skye's mum. She's had a tough few years.'

'Right,' I said and looked down at my clipboard again, unsure of how to respond. I had been working as a kids' holiday rep for eight years now, but rarely said anything to the parents other than 'hello' and 'will you be back tomorrow?' at drop-off time. It was totally different back in the UK, of course, where I worked as a nanny during the winter months. There, I had to hand the mothers – it was almost always the mothers – a long list of what their kids had eaten, drunk, played with and pooed out every evening when they returned from work. But on holiday things tended to be very different. We only had the kids for a couple of hours each day and the mums and dads tended just to mutter 'thanks, off to have a nice lunch' before they legged it. I suspected most of them used the time to have sandy sex on the narrow beds in their apartments, maybe squeezing in a bite to eat afterwards for the sake of appearances, but whatever their destination, they certainly didn't want to waste precious minutes talking to me. This guy, however, seemed to have all the time in the world.

'Yeah, it's why we really needed a holiday this year—'

'He's stolen my pencil! Miss – he's nicked it!'

Ryan, a tall, gangly child who I was convinced was at least a year older than the 'six' his mother had written on his registration form was, as usual, at the centre of the drama. I whirled around, ready to defuse the row, and Patrick took the hint, pausing only to blow a kiss in his daughter's direction before telling me he'd pick her up in an hour and disappearing down the corridor.

'Enjoy your break!' I was tempted to say, but didn't. Something told me that Patrick and Isla wouldn't be one of the sandy, sexy couples that afternoon.

Chapter 3

1840

'Meet me outside.'

The whisper was so soft, it was barely a breath against her cheek and Deirdre was worried she hadn't heard him correctly.

'Outside?'

'The maze. Five minutes.'

Laurence brushed his lips against hers then disappeared back down the hall and into the Great Room. Heart thudding in her chest, Deirdre touched one finger to her lips as her cheeks flamed. It was ridiculous, that her husband could provoke such a reaction, her lawful wedded husband. Ridiculous – but couldn't the same be said about their marriage? Their wedding had been six weeks ago but the kiss they had shared in front of the altar was still the closest they had come to intimacy. Maybe tonight, all of that would change.

She pulled at her skirts, taking a moment to compose herself before walking quickly down the shadowy passageway, away from the buzz of noise that leaked from the partially open door of the Great Room. The heat in there would be oppressive, with flames from the huge fire mingling with the smoke from the men's cigars, and just thinking about the fug and the scent of the women's perfume caused a headache to thrum in Deirdre's temples. It was that smell, and the lack of air, that had driven her from the room just minutes earlier, intending to retire with a book, as she had done almost every night since the wedding. Until she realised that Laurence had followed her. Laurence, her new husband. Her love.

The night before they married, Deirdre's mother had taken her aside and told her exactly what to expect once she and her new husband were alone. Deirdre had neither been shocked nor surprised at the details. Hollowpark Hall was a working estate, and she had picked up enough details about breeding dogs and horses to have figured out that human reproduction couldn't be that much different from the animal kind. But she had reacted as was expected of her, blushed prettily at her mother's words and told her solemnly that yes, she would do her duty as a wife. Had hidden the feelings that had welled up inside her, the sparkling realisation she was excited by, rather than fearful of what was to come. But the wedding night, when it came, was nothing like she had expected. After the meal was over and the guests had departed, Deirdre's parents had yawned and, with a clumsy but well-meaning attempt at discretion, announced they going to retire to 'their own quarters' – in reality, the suite of rooms they had occupied since their own wedding day almost thirty years before. And Deirdre, emboldened by the glass of wine she'd had with dinner, had placed her hand on her new husband's shoulder and asked him if maybe it was time for them, too, to go upstairs. Laurence, however, had simply smiled at her, removed the hand and told her that of course she should go up, that she must be exhausted after the day's events. She should get a good night's sleep, he told her, and he himself would sleep in the dressing room to make sure she wasn't disturbed.

Tears had welled up in Deirdre's eyes as she walked up the stairs, alone. Tears of embarrassment, at first – was she wrong about everything, had she misunderstood what her mother had told her? But by the time she reached her bedroom her sadness had changed to fury. What right had he, to send her to bed like a little girl, to tell her what to do?

She couldn't remember slamming the door, but she must have done, because her next memory was of sitting on the floor, blood running from a cut in her finger, broken glass from the picture that had fallen from the wall scattered in chunks around her.

It must have been a draught, she told her maid, Kitty, who came running when she heard the noise and helped her dress her wound. A draught that had caught the door and slammed it, shaking the painting from its hook. The fact that she couldn't remember the exact details of what had happened was easily explained by the wine, the excitement of the day, the lateness of the hour. Deirdre pretended not to see the look of fear on Kitty's face, or the way the maid's hand shook when she wrapped Deirdre's in a bandage. Kitty was a fool, a young fool, too easily frightened by ordinary, everyday things. Sometimes candles flickered, sometimes lamps went out at the wrong moment, sometimes objects turned up in the place you least expected them, that was just the way life was. There was always an explanation, Deirdre found, if you looked hard enough.

She and Laurence had gone on honeymoon the next day but had remained in separate bedrooms the entire time. On board ship there was an excuse of sorts as Deirdre had felt queasy as soon as they left port and, although she was quite recovered by dinnertime, her husband told her it would not be 'gentlemanly' to disturb her for the rest of the journey. Then, when they got to London, he said he had business to attend to and left her to amuse herself. Deirdre didn't mind that part too much, she had relatives to visit and their babies to coo over and she enjoyed the vague but knowing comments that she'd 'know all about motherhood, soon'.

But even after they left London and started what she felt was their proper honeymoon, her new husband never spent a night in her bed. Not in Paris, nor in Rome where she spent her evenings in a stifling warm bedroom, unable to sleep because of the shouts and roars from her husband's card game drifting up through the hot night air. Every evening it was the same: they would have dinner alone and then Laurence would kiss her on the cheek and tell her how much better she would feel after a good night's sleep, even though she hadn't been feeling sick to begin with. Sometimes Deirdre wondered if she was in fact ill, and if Laurence was keeping her condition a secret from her. Other nights she simply felt sadness and then, one evening, great anger.

When she woke the next morning in the tiled bedroom of the Italian pension, she couldn't explain the crack that had formed across the gilt-framed mirror on the wall, or the fact that the heavy wardrobe had moved six inches across the floor. Her husband would pay for the damage, she told the servant who brought her morning coffee on a tray. He would *pay*, she insisted a second time, and something in her voice had made the maid leave without saying another word. Deirdre returned to Hollowpark Hall a week later, as virginal as she had left it, and she didn't tell her mother what was troubling her because she didn't understand what had happened and couldn't shake the notion that it was all her fault anyway.

She walked into the vast hall, the heels of her new shoes clacking against the flagged stone floor. When she and her mother had travelled to Galway to shop for her trousseau, Helen Fitzmahon had led Deirdre to a row of low-heeled slippers, assuming without asking that she would not want to be as tall as her new groom. But Deirdre, who had inherited her father's height and broad, strong shoulders, had proudly chosen three pairs of heeled boots and shoes. Laurence always assured her he loved the way she looked, had stroked the wide palms of her hands and had even, in the moments following their proposal, murmured that it pleased him that he could place a kiss on her cheek without having to bend towards her. And then he had placed that kiss and had touched and smoothed a lock of her dark hair and Deirdre had shivered, her mind racing to other ways in which they could be together. There had been no further kissing, not yet. But maybe tonight, things were going to change.

Emboldened by the thought, Deirdre picked up her pace as she strode across the hall. It was dark, in comparison to the well-lit room she had left behind and, as she blinked her eyes to get them to readjust to the dim surroundings, a sudden blast of cold air caused her to shiver. Her mother must have left open a window upstairs. Helen Fitzmahon was a great believer in 'fresh air' despite Brigid's constant refrain they would all die of consumption – Brigid! Deirdre took a step to one side and concealed herself in the large hollow under the staircase. The last thing she wanted now was to meet the elderly servant on her way to bed, and to have to explain where she was going. It was silly, of course, to feel so shy, she was twenty-three years old, after all, a married woman, and if she and her husband wanted to walk outdoors after dark then there wasn't anyone who could stop them. But Deirdre knew the servants gossiped among themselves, just as she knew her aunt and her mother had taken note of the tight-waisted dress she had worn that evening. She was tired of being gossiped about. Maybe tonight, normal life would begin.

After determining she was alone, Deirdre pulled back the latch on the heavy oak front door and let it close gently behind her before slipping out into the autumn night. Moonlight bathed Hollowpark Hall and its grounds in a soft, milky glow as she darted across the gravel path and onto smooth grass. Dew tickled her ankles as she strode across the grass towards the hedge that signalled the end of the formal gardens, then found the gap she was looking for and wriggled through, emerging into the wilderness beyond. Her mother loved the blocks of garden that adjoined the Hall, separated from each other by paths that gave them the appearance of a chessboard, but Deirdre much preferred the informality of the meadow on the far side of the driveway where weeds and wildflowers bloomed in disordered clumps. No part of Hollowpark or its grounds had ever been out of bounds for her, but as soon as she was old enough to roam around on her own, her friend Ciarán, the gardener's son, had warned her about the deadly nightshade that poked its way through the friendlier plants, and made her promise that she would never pick its bell-shaped, purple flowers, or taste the berries, no matter how enticing their sheen. Deirdre had heeded the warning, but it hadn't dampened her love for the grounds and now she was grown she valued the meadow as much as she ever had, both as its own destination and because of where it led her – to the maze.

Deirdre lifted her skirts over a small clump of gorse and then paused in the shadow of the giant, manicured hedges. Planted by her grandparents, the structure was now over eight feet tall and as much a part of Hollowpark as the Fitzmahon family themselves. Here, too, the nightshade – or *atropa belladonna*, as her father insisted on calling it, having searched for it laboriously in one of his beloved leather-bound reference books – here, too, the belladonna had taken hold and a trail of black berries glistened at the entrance to the structure, as if to entice her in. This was her place. And tonight, she was going to share it with the man she loved.

A cloud crossed the moon and she tightened her shawl around her shoulders. But where was Laurence? Far more than five minutes had passed – and then a bolt of excitement shot through her. Maybe he, too, wanted to play a game. Well, if he did, then she would have the advantage. Deirdre took a deep breath then walked forward and hurried down the first shaded passageway. Foolish man, if he thought he could trick her in there, she knew every false turn, every diversion. She rounded a second corner, then a third, then stopped as she heard a rustle in the bushes. Was it her husband? Was the game to be won this easily? She paused, then a nervous laugh escaped her as Prince scrambled through a patch near the ground where the leaves grew less densely and emerged at her feet. Deirdre bent down to allow the little terrier to lick her hand, then ruffled the coarse hair between his ears. But after a moment, she pushed him away. She, who had never had a sibling or, indeed, once Ciarán had grown too old to play with her, a close friend, adored the little terrier but Laurence had made it quite clear that 'hounds', as he called them, belonged outside. One advantage of their marital chill was that he had no idea the animal still spent every night asleep on his mistress's bed. Tonight, however, Deirdre wanted her husband there instead.

'Home now, darling, go.' The little dog didn't move, and Deirdre gave him a firmer shove.

'Go home, now.'

The animal whined, his head cocked to one side. He regarded her for one more moment then turned and left, leaving Deirdre alone again. Or was she? She heard another rustle as the smell of cigar smoke seeped through the thick foliage. Ah, so Laurence was here, and looking for her. Well, if it was a chase he wanted... Pretending not to have noticed his presence, she turned, and began to weave her way through the dark, leafy paths. Right, left, right, there was no need to count steps and certainly no need to double back, her feet carried her without hesitation right to the centre of the maze.

Here, all was quiet. The stone angel who guarded the centre gazed impassively down at her from his wide stone plinth. Above him, moonlight winked through the window of the large stone tower which stood on the far side of the maze, its exterior weathered to a ghostly white. No one could remember the tower's original purpose. Although it had a set of stone steps at its centre and a round room at the top, its windows were permanently open to the elements and it was too cold to be used for guests. Sometimes Deirdre suspected that it was merely a folly, a guide to navigating the maze itself, because once you reached the centre it was simply a matter of keeping it in sight in order to find your way out again.

Deirdre loved the tower, had played in it as a child and even now used it to read in, or to sew in, or to be alone. There was a rage inside her which sometimes surged and overwhelmed her, frightening those around her. Over the years she had learned to control it, sometimes by retreating to her room, other times by walking in the gardens or through the maze, finding refuge in the quiet companionship of its passageways. But even now there were still days when the anger threatened to boil over, to consume her, and it was on those days that Deirdre Fitzmahon climbed into the tower and allowed its cool stone walls to drain the fury away.

Ignoring yet more movement in the bushes behind her, Deirdre looked up at the nearest moonlit window, and smiled. Even if Laurence hadn't suggested going outside tonight she would have made her way to the tower anyway, to sit for a while and get rid of her headache. She heard another rustle, closer this time. Then again, maybe she wouldn't need the tower and its quiet magic any more, now that she was a married woman, and had found her true love. She smiled, as a hand fell on her shoulder.

'I knew you'd come.'

Then the moon disappeared behind the cloud, and the tower with it, and Deirdre Fitzmahon and her husband were, for the first time and in total darkness, completely alone.

Chapter 4

2007

The next time I saw the Fitzmahons, they didn't see me. I had chosen my spot on the beach carefully – close enough to the water to allow me to keep an eye on my belongings when I went for a swim, but not too close to the rented sunbeds, which even at that hour of the morning were occupied by families who had scattered water bottles and inflatable toys in a semicircle around them, creating a slice of their own living room on the hot Greek sand. It wasn't that the proximity to children annoyed me – I'd have been a pretty useless nanny if I couldn't put up with the odd bop in the head from a beach ball, or spray of sand – but that morning I needed to gather my thoughts and to be alone. I didn't want to run into my fellow reps either, but at ten o'clock in the morning there was little chance of that; they were all either working, or asleep from late shifts or even later partying the night before. They were nice kids, most of them, but we had nothing in common, I had no interest in discussing hangover cures and uni options with Greg from Glasgow or Libbie from Leeds. I just wanted to sit, and look at the sea, and think about what I was going to do at the end of the summer.

I pulled my hat down further over my eyes and checked that the back of my neck was covered by my T-shirt. I worked outdoors in thirty-degree heat; I didn't need to sunbathe. But I loved the beach, treasured the feeling of swimming in lukewarm water and drying out almost immediately afterwards. It was one of the reasons I kept working as a rep, year after year, even as my co-workers grew younger and the nagging voice in my head, that told me I needed to find a permanent base, grew louder. Most of the families I worked for in the UK would have loved to keep me for the summer, some even offered to take me on holiday with them, presumably to stay in hotels far superior to the ones I ended up working in. But I always refused. I liked my life the way it was, the intensity of full-time nannying during the winter months balanced out by less well paid but more informal work in the resorts every summer. Or at least I had liked it. This year, for the first time, I was starting to wonder if I needed to make more long-term plans.

I first ran away to Greece when I was nineteen. There's no easier way to put it, I was desperate to get away from my parents and when some girls at school told me about jobs they'd picked up on a holiday island I'd filled out the application forms and hopped on a charter flight without a second thought. We spent three weeks on Zante selling cheap blue cocktails to tourists our own age but, while my classmates slipped straight into holiday mode, working till daybreak and staying in bed till it got dark again, I quickly discovered that I hated cleaning up blue vomit and got a headache if I slept past noon. I was all set to head home when a friendly barman told me about another resort on the far side of the island which, he claimed, attracted more families than stag and hen parties, so I hopped on a local bus and decided to give my summer adventure one last try. It cost three quid, that bus journey, and it changed my life for ever. When I got to the village I found a waitressing job in a family run taverna. I was terrible at it and dropped more plates than I cleared but the owner took pity on me and sent me to supervise the small playground he had built out the back to keep his youngest customers happy while their parents enjoyed their meals. The other waitresses hated that part of the job – three-year-olds don't tip – but I surprised myself by really enjoying hanging out with the kids. When their parents began making return trips to the restaurant – caring less about the quality of the moussaka than the fact that they could order a second carafe of wine in peace – the owner decided he could always hire another waitress and sent me to work in the play area full time. Three happy months later I headed home to Ireland, turning down my university offer and enrolling on a childcare course instead. My dad was quite enthusiastic about my choice, actually, once he found out how much fully trained, English-speaking nannies got paid, but my mother thought I was wasting my life and took great pleasure in telling her friends, when I was well within earshot, that she 'didn't think you needed to go to college to learn how to clean a baby's arse'. But I just ignored her. I'd had plenty of practice at that.

I grew up in a coastal village just outside Dublin, the only child of a father who earned lots of money and a mother who knew how to spend it. My parents lived in a large, red-brick house with a view of the sea from the back windows and my father's collection of cars from the front, and anyone who knew us reckoned our lives were pretty much perfect. Everyone loved my mum, and why wouldn't they? She was pretty and charming, witty and welcoming and liked nothing more than hosting dinner parties that ran into lunchtime the next day. She had a wicked sense of humour, a huge capacity for gossip and filled our home with original art, overstuffed sofas and a dining table that could fit twenty people, and frequently did. She was, in fact, the perfect hostess and the worst possible mother for a person like me.

My schoolfriends constantly told me how amazing it must be to grow up in a house with no rules, where no one cared if you smoked or put your feet on the furniture and where anyone from a struggling actor to a rock star on the up could arrive for supper and end up spending the night in the spare room. But I hated it, every inconsistent, noisy moment of it. I like long walks and longer baths, restful silence and gentle conversation and there was nothing like that to be found in my childhood home. Mum had worked for an advertising agency in her twenties and, when she married the boss, decided he earned far too much to justify her sitting behind a reception desk every day. And so she gave up the hard graft but brought home the bits of the job she liked best: the entertaining, the banter, the rivers of booze. I wasn't ever mistreated, at least not in the traditional sense of the word. I lived in a huge house in one of Dublin's most expensive suburbs, attended a private school and had plenty of money for clothes and outings and any extra-curricular activity I wanted to do. But what I didn't have were regular meals, or quiet nights in, or the ability to go to bed without being woken by shrieks of laughter or blasts of music coming from the stereo located just underneath my room. I got on fine with my father, but he was rarely around – for all Mum's exuberance, she was happy to be a traditional wife in the sense that he worked long hours while she kept the house and didn't bother him with any domestic details. The only problem was, she didn't bother herself too much with them either. By the time I was eight, I could take my own temperature and dose myself with Calpol if I felt it was too high, and at twelve I told my teachers it would be easier if they spoke to me about my work instead of expecting Mum to remember the time and place of pupil–teacher meetings.

'She's so glamorous, your mum!' the other girls would whisper to me at school sports days as we watched her trip across the grass in wedge heels, her blonde hair piled on top of her head, fixed in place by massive sunglasses while another pair of gold-framed reading glasses dangled from a chain around her neck. They happily accepted invitations to my house but they had no real interest in hanging out with me, they just wanted to meet her, to quiz her about her clothes and her latest big night out. I didn't tell anyone how much I hated being her daughter. What was the point? They wouldn't have believed me anyway. I was living the dream, I had a mother who didn't nag me to study, encouraged me to bring boyfriends home and told me to wear more make-up, not less, even when I was in school uniform – or especially then. But all I really wanted to do was curl up with a book in a quiet space, and there were precious few quiet spaces in that house.

Mum had always wanted a girl, she told me once, and had

been thrilled when I was born, imagining me in a patterned dress, handing around canapés at parties and singing a few charming verses of a ballad before heading off to bed when the adult part of the evening really got going. But instead she got me, who preferred jeans and Doc Martens to party clothes, hated crowded rooms and felt my face burn like a comet if anyone paid any attention to me, let alone asked if I 'had a song in me'. Mostly I just crept away but there were other times when I felt my anger at her, my humiliation and my hatred of all of their stupid drunken faces bubble up inside me and I'd run off and lock myself in my room, almost afraid at what I would have said if I'd stayed around them. It was then, in my late teens, that I became aware of something I used to describe to myself as 'absences'. I would wake up in bed, or in my father's attic study, or even in the shed at the bottom of the garden, with absolutely no recollection of how I had got there, or how long I had been away. Most of the time I was able to sneak back to my room without my parents noticing but on one occasion the guests must have left early and I found my mother sitting alone in the kitchen when I eased open the door, dew from the grass staining the bottom of my jeans. When she asked me where I had been I told her 'out for a walk', even though it was two in the morning and I was supposed to have been in bed for hours. And for just one moment I was sure she was going to ask me if I was OK, if there was anything I wanted to tell her or was worried about. If she had done, maybe I would have joined her at the table and maybe I would have made a pot of tea and we might have talked properly in that quiet kitchen with the moonlight streaming in through the windows. But then the moment passed and my mother shook her head, and laughed, and called me a 'chip off the old block' and said if I had been meeting a boyfriend that I should just ask him to call in the next time. We never had a conversation of any substance after that night and I never expected one.

And so, when I decided to head to London to complete my nanny training, and stay on afterwards to work, my decision was less based on a desire to travel and more on the need to get the hell away from home. Looking after other people's children made sense to me. I could bring order to their lives, create those gorgeous routines I'd always longed for myself. The first year I worked away from home, I took an expensive flight back to Dublin on Christmas Eve out of some innate sense of duty, only to find that my mother had turned my bedroom into yet another guest room and thrown away everything of sentimental value from my childhood: my books, my scented writing paper, the pictures of ponies I put on my wall instead of the pop stars she thought I should have crushes on. I didn't bother much about Christmas after that. The families I worked for were always enchanted when I told them I didn't need time off for the holidays. Instead, I wrapped their presents on Christmas Eve and took the kids and their new toys to the park on Boxing Day to give them a lie-in. I kept in touch with my dad, calling him on Sunday mornings when my mother would be playing golf. But one morning, when I phoned, she was still in the house and he tried to get me to talk to her, so I just stopped calling altogether and just sent them a postcard every time I started in a new place, to let them know I was still alive. That probably suited my mother, actually, having a card to display on the mantelpiece so she could tell her friends I was doing well without having to do any actual mothering. And it suited me, too. By the time I met the Fitzmahons I had learned to operate without my own family and my life was better for it. I cuddled new-born babies, chased toddlers around hundreds of playgrounds and drove so many children to so many after-school activities that I reckoned I'd have no problem getting a London taxi licence if I ever wanted to change career. My only rule was that I only worked in Britain during the winter months and spent my summers abroad. I told my clients that I wanted to see the world, and there was an element of truth to that. But mostly I moved around because I valued my privacy, and my solitude. I didn't want to be part of anyone's family, I had spent enough time getting away from my own. That summer, however, I was about to turn twenty-nine and was wondering if it was time to make more permanent plans. And that was what I was doing on the beach that morning. Staring at the waves as if a plan for my future would suddenly emerge from the sea.

And then the Fitzmahons walked past and interrupted my musings. I was wearing sunglasses and a large floppy hat but that didn't actually matter, I was sure they wouldn't recognise me. No punters, not even the nice ones, really took any notice of us reps, we were just generic Chloes, Emmas or Sarahs, whose job it was to call out bingo numbers, organise volleyball games and look after their children twice a day. I'm not bad-looking, objectively speaking. I mean, I'm not glamorous like my mum but I'm slim, because I never stop running around, and although I keep my hair short for convenience rather than fashion, I know the blunt pixie cut suits my high cheekbones and slightly slanted green eyes.

But not even a Greek Eurovision contestant could have made our uniforms look attractive, consisting as it did of knee-length navy shorts, which managed to make our legs look stumpy and our arses huge, and a bright yellow Aertex shirt with *'Kidz Klub'* printed on one boob and our name badges pinned to the other. And so I sat invisibly on the beach and watched the family who looked like they should have been on the front of a holiday brochure and not simply buying what was inside.

Patrick was holding Skye by her right hand and in the other she clutched a pink bucket and matching spade. He selected a clear patch of sand and she plonked straight down onto her bottom and began to dig while Isla, who had been following a few paces behind, gently deposited a large green and blue striped beach bag down beside her, sand puffing out gently from under its leather base. Isla then lifted out two large beach towels, blue and green to match the bag and, with a flick of her wrist, unfurled them and set them down neatly, side by side on the sand. As Patrick flopped down onto the nearest one I found myself suppressing a smile. Skye's dad was dressed like someone from a Sunday afternoon movie, one of those British ones from the 1950s – he was sporting knee-length black shorts, a white T-shirt and a straw hat with a black band around its narrow brim. The only person on the beach wearing more clothes than him was the elderly Greek man who collected the rent for the sunbeds and, no matter how hot it got, walked around every day in a long-sleeved denim shirt and jeans. 'I'm not a beach person' was what Patrick's outfit told the world, loudly and confidently. His freckled limbs were golden in some places, reddened in others and the overall impression was of a man who would rather be working outdoors than lying around. His wife and daughter, however, looked as though they had been born on a beach. They were both wearing sundresses – Skye's was pink while Isla's was a 1970s, dropped-waist, brown affair – and, as I watched she pulled it smoothly over her head to reveal a matching bikini underneath. I knew I had crossed a line from casual spectator to voyeur but couldn't stop myself from drinking her in. She was beautiful. Tall, athletic, slim but not skinny with broad swimmer's shoulders, Madonna's upper arms and a thin concertina of skin on her midriff the only sign that she had ever given birth. Fully dressed, Isla Fitzmahon wasn't the type of woman you'd pick out of a crowd – her face was too broad, her nose too long. But here, surrounded by over-oiled people with peeling skin and sweaty bodies, she was glorious. She rested her hands on her waist for a moment, looking out to sea, then beckoned to her daughter and led her to the water's edge where they laughed as the wavelets tickled their toes. They were too far away now for me to hear what they were saying but I saw Skye giggle as Isla grabbed her under the arms and lifted her over the bigger waves. I watched them for a moment, then turned my attention to Patrick who had pulled his wife's bag under his head for a pillow. He had tipped his hat over his forehead but left a gap between brim and nose big enough to peep through and I knew he was watching them too. The sun was high in the sky and I lay back, feeling the sand underneath my own towel mould itself around my body.

And then I blinked and, in that instant, the colour drained from the sky. I sat up and shook my head but nothing else had changed: Skye and her mother were still standing in the shallow water and Patrick seemed to have dozed off. No one else seemed to have noticed that we were in a black and white photograph now, our bodies casting menacing shadows on the grey sand. I jumped up, looking around at the rows of tourists who were turning themselves under the white sun like chickens on a spit and no one was moving, nobody was reacting. I tried to call out but my voice had frozen in my throat and my legs seemed locked in position. And the sea was swelling, swelling... I looked past Isla and her child and saw with increasing horror that a wave was rising, gaining mass and momentum as it approached them. Under their feet the grey sand was swirling, grabbing at their toes and pulling them forward and why was no one moving, why could no one see what was happening? I made one final effort to move but my feet were like stone and I fell forward heavily on the sand, my hand grazing the jagged edge of a seashell, and all I could do now was watch, motionless, voiceless, as the wave grew, rolling relentlessly towards them. And somewhere in my mind I knew I was dreaming but it didn't matter because the horror was real, the terror was real, and finally Isla noticed what was happening too, and screamed but it was too late, Patrick was standing now too, running towards them but they were gone, his women were gone, the water had claimed them, they had been ripped from the shore...

The water was gone. The grey was gone. I opened my eyes and colour dazzled me. I was lying flat on my back, my heart racing. The sun was high in the blue sky, that particular shade of Greek blue that had never looked so beautiful to me before. I hauled myself up, still shaking. I had had panic attacks before, sitting on a crowded Tube, or once, in my early days as a rep, when I was hungover, dehydrated and rushing to work in forty-degree heat. And there had been those absences too, although I hadn't experienced them since my teen years and assumed I had left them at home along with my school reports and sense of daughterly duty. But this? This was nothing like I had ever experienced before. My chest and back were dripping with sweat and there was a low, nauseating buzzing in my ear. I took a bottle of water from my bag and tried to calm my breathing as in front of me Isla and her daughter – both of them healthy, well, happy – walked back to Patrick and showed him the seashells they had collected. Patrick jumped to his feet and swung the little girl into the air as Isla lifted their towels, flicked the sand away and repacked her bag with care. They didn't look in my direction as they left the beach. But there was a sharp pain in my hand and I saw a seashell on the ground and a cut on my palm, blood dripping from it onto the golden sand.

Chapter 5

1840

All was dark and, apart from the sound of Laurence's breathing, all was still. Was she supposed to feel scared? Deirdre wondered. Alone, with her husband in the centre of the maze? But she wasn't afraid; instead, all she could feel was bubbling, burning excitement. She reached out and touched the coarse material of his coat and, emboldened by the darkness, pulled him towards her.

'Sssh.'

It could have been a reprimand, but his tone thrilled, rather than subdued her. This was really happening, after all this time. Laurence had come to find her, he wanted her... and she wanted him. The words appeared in Deirdre's mind like living things. She wanted him, wanted to kiss him and be kissed by him, to hold him and be held by him, to feel him pressed against her and for it to be just the two of them, alone. She had never felt quite like this before, yet there was a familiarity to the sensations rushing through her body, and a feeling of being exactly where she wanted to be. Of being at home.

'Not here.'

He kissed her, not on her lips but lightly on her cheek, then drew back again.

'Where then?' she wanted to ask, but the question was answered when he reached out and grabbed her hand, causing anticipation to ripple through her.

'This way.'

Laurence was whispering, although there was no real need to do so. Deirdre's parents and their guests were still in the house, and the servants would be in bed, bar the unlucky few dozing on their chairs in the kitchen, waiting to see if they would be needed. Deirdre herself had said she was going to her room, there would be no reason for anyone to think she had done otherwise, or to go looking for her. And if Laurence's absence was noted, well then, weren't they newly-weds? Weren't they supposed to be together? But still he whispered, and still she answered him in low tones. Maybe it was part of the game. It felt right, she realised. Deliciously dangerous. And then he tugged her by the hand and led her through the maze, this way and that, stumbling and tripping at the wrong turns. Deirdre stifled a laugh – why on earth did he feel he had to lead her? She, who could have found her way around with her eyes shut tight. But Laurence, it seemed, expected to be in charge.

It had been that way since the very first day they had met. Deirdre had been introduced to Laurence by her cousin Paul, who had brought Laurence to Hollowpark Hall with a mare he felt Deirdre's father would have an interest in buying. Deirdre, who had accompanied her father to the stables, noticed that the animal was nervy, even allowing for the unfamiliarity of its surroundings, and feared she might have been ill-treated in the past. But she had been fascinated by the easy way Laurence had in the saddle, the light touch of his slender fingers on the reins and the confidence with which he answered her father's questions, while retaining, at all times, a note of deference towards the older man. Laurence was a thin man, and not overly tall, a fact which only became evident when he dismounted. But he had an open, pleasant face with bright, intelligent blue eyes and when those eyes locked on hers, Deirdre found her reservations about the horse somehow melting away. He appeared to have the same effect on her father, who bought the animal and invited both Laurence and Paul to dinner at Hollowpark that evening to mark the deal. Deirdre had never considered her father a romantic man but he had taken care to seat her beside Laurence at dinner and, when their conversation dipped and became private, amused the rest of the company with loud stories, almost as if he was giving them intimacy by design.

As Deirdre had feared, the mare had never settled at Hollowpark and Father sold her, less than six months later, at a loss. But by then Deirdre and Laurence were engaged. It was his second engagement, he told her, insisting there could only be honesty between them. Agatha Mulhearn was the younger sister of a school friend, they had grown up together, and it had been assumed for a time that they would wed. But then – Laurence grasped Deirdre's hand as he spoke, and kissed its palm before looking into her eyes – then Laurence had met Deirdre and realised his previous feelings had been nothing but childish infatuation. He had broken the engagement and proposed to Deirdre the very next day.

Of course, Deirdre thought to herself as she followed her husband through the narrow corridors of the maze, so far their union had not been anything like what she had been expecting. But tonight, at least, they were together and alone. And after all, it couldn't have been easy for Laurence to move into her parents' home, to be asked to share his wife's childhood bed. Maybe, she thought to herself, maybe that was the cause of the distance between them – it was that simple. If leading her through the maze was what he needed to act like a husband to her then she would willingly acquiesce to that.

Leaves and branches tore at her face as they turned one way, then another but Deirdre batted them away and was smiling when they emerged, more through luck than through the power of Laurence's navigation, at the exit on the far side of the maze. It was a bright night but very cold, and Deirdre looked up at her husband hopefully.

'We could go back to the house, now?'

She tried to put everything she couldn't say into those few words – take me home, take me to my room, to our room, to our bed, let us be man and wife for the first time and I promise you it will be everything we have both been waiting for – but Laurence simply shook his head and turned to the tower.

'In here.'

'But Laurence—'

And then he lifted her hand to his mouth and kissed the back of it, and kissed the palm of it and then the fingers of it and as waves of pleasure rippled through her Deirdre knew she would have followed him anywhere. Up and up the stone steps they climbed, stopping occasionally to kiss, and her breath came in quick gasps as she wondered if her legs would carry her all the way. This was nothing like the married love her friends had spoken about, muttered asides about how it 'wasn't too bad, once you got used to it' and 'if you were lucky, it could be over quite quickly.' This felt alien, and exciting, and utterly right. Finally, they emerged into the room at the top of the tower and Laurence led Deirdre to the window, holding tight to her hand all the while. As they looked over the grounds she took a moment to catch her breath and then, feeling a heady mixture of bravery and anticipation, rested her head gently against his shoulder.

'It's very beautiful.'

His voice purred through her and she rested for one more delightful moment and then pulled away slightly again.

'I can't imagine living anywhere else.'

'It was your grandfather who built Hollowpark, wasn't it?'

Deirdre shook her head slightly.

'My great-grandfather built the house but his son, my grandfather, built the maze as a wedding present for his new wife. We have ledgers in the library that give all of the details, I'd love to show you some time—'

'There's no need.'

Laurence released her hand and took a step away from her. Maybe he was trying to get a better view? But the movement released a blast of cold air between them and Deirdre shivered suddenly. She turned to him and, when she saw the expression on his face, found herself having to force a smile.

'But I'd love to show you, Laurence. After all, it's your home now too. And one day...'

She felt a blush rise from her throat but was determined to say the words, to recapture the intimacy she had felt below in the maze.

'One day, with the help of God, it will be our children's home too.'

'Was that always your father's plan? That your husband would inherit the estate after his death?'

Deirdre nodded, a little puzzled as to the direction the conversation had taken.

'Well, if he'd had a son, things would have been different, of course. But yes, now we are married, Hollowpark belongs to us, to you. To our family.'

'And if you were to die, I would still inherit? And if I were to marry again, Hollowpark would still be mine?'

'I suppose so… but Laurence—'

But before Deirdre could continue Laurence pulled her towards him again and she felt her body grow limp. A breath of wind pushed away a cloud and his face was icy blue in the moonlight as he looked at her and then he kissed her there, and there, and there and Deirdre wasn't thinking at all now, Laurence was holding her by her waist, he was lifting her—

The hardness of the window ledge against her back broke through her pleasure and she smiled and pushed on his chest slightly.

'My love. If we could just—'

'You were never my love.'

There was no mistaking, this time, the look of distaste in his eyes as he stared at her.

Deirdre's voice cracked as she searched his face, confused by his change of tone, but her husband was not looking at her now and he was not kissing her. She forced another smile, waiting to understand this new part of the game, but her husband was not playing with her, instead he was lifting her and placing her on the window ledge, no, he was pushing her…

The kick was instinctive, she lashed out with her foot and scrabbled for balance as Laurence loosened his grip on her waist and staggered backwards, clutching his groin.

'You little bitch.'

Deirdre's heart thudded in her chest as she gazed at him, confused and desperately anxious. But the pain on Laurence's face had turned to anger and he darted forward again. His hands were on her throat now and she was struggling and gasping for breath. Laurence was not a large man, they were almost the same height, but Deirdre was encumbered by heavy skirts and her own confusion…

And then a sudden blast of cold air struck the back of Deirdre's neck and brought her to her senses. She jerked away from her husband, it was a slight movement but enough to distract him for a second and as he sought to reestablish his hold her hand reached for and then closed on the small figure that sat at one end of the window ledge. It was a paperweight, a replica of the Egyptian Sphinx, an 'ugly thing' her mother had called it, brought to the house by a relative and moved from room to room until Deirdre had claimed it for her own. She had always dreamed of travelling to Egypt one day. As Deirdre's grip tightened on the small bronze ornament with its rigid wooden base, she felt that familiar rage rise inside her. Who was he, to treat her like that, to lead her on, to tell her he loved her – how dare he! She lifted the little Sphinx high above her head, and brought it down, and down, and down, and Laurence, that man she had been so thrilled to call her husband, released his grip and fell forward onto the window ledge. The strangest thing, Deirdre thought afterwards, was the look of astonishment on his face as he made one final attempt to escape her anger and then tumbled out into the air.

Chapter 6

2007

I still wasn't myself when Patrick picked Skye up from Kidz Klub later that afternoon. I didn't tell him what I had seen on the beach, of course. It would have been beyond weird to admit I had been watching his family, let along dreaming about them – or nightmaring or whatever it was you wanted to call it. But I couldn't shake the feeling that something was terribly wrong. I was probably overtired, I told myself as I handed him the clipboard so he could sign out his daughter; overtired and more shaken than I had realised by the incident in the swimming pool. I needed a break, a proper holiday. Being a rep was good fun, most of the time, but it was hard work too. We worked six days out of seven and I was sharing a room with two girls who were much younger than me, just the right age to be able to fall in the door at three o'clock in the morning and still be ready for a day's work at eight. I'd try to get an extra early night tonight, I decided, and would hopefully be fast asleep when they got in. And if that didn't work, well then I'd pay for a couple of nights of peace in one of studios for rent down the road. I was so wrapped up in my plans I barely heard what Patrick was saying but he seemed to be in the mood for a chat and hung on at the door even as his daughter hopped from foot to foot, anxious to get going.

'Do you – do you have a moment?'

I didn't bother to mask my sigh, and gave a long look around the room but for once, blast them, all of the parents had turned up on time to collect their kids leaving me looking like I had all the time in the world to shoot the breeze.

Patrick took a deep breath.

'I just wanted to let you know we're leaving tomorrow.'

He ran his hand through his hair and then it hit me – he wanted to give me a tip. Now, that was a pleasant surprise. Parents at the resort rarely bothered singling us out but given the whole 'saving his daughter's life' thing Patrick Fitzmahon must have decided I deserved a bit extra. Well, that would be very much appreciated. I dropped my shoulders and tried to make my face look a little friendlier. Around here, fifty quid would buy me several nights of blissful, uninterrupted slumber.

Patrick coughed, awkwardly.

'You see, Skye has had a great time here…'

I was considering holding out my hand, just to put him out of his misery, when the next thing he said drove all thought of euros or anything else completely out of my mind.

'Isla is back at work now and we need a nanny and I was wondering, well, we were wondering if you'd be interested in the job? You know, if you'd like to mind Skye on a full-time basis.'

He must have mistaken my look of shock for an expression of interest because he continued to babble, his tone becoming more enthusiastic as he spoke.

'We'd pay you well and you wouldn't have to pay rent or anything, there's plenty of space in the main house. You'd have access to the car whenever you wanted it, we'd put you on the insurance – you do drive?'

I found myself nodding and Patrick grabbed at my first visible reaction.

'Great, because we're in the sticks, really, you'd need a car to get around. But other than that, Lisheeha is a great place to live, well, I would say that, wouldn't I? It's where I grew up. But it is, it's beautiful and you'd have the use of the car if you wanted to go the cinema in Carrick-on-Shannon, or up to Sligo even, you'd have plenty of time to yourself.'

'Hold on.'

I needed to make sure I had heard him correctly and put my hand up to stem the flow of chatter.

'Did you say Roscommon?'

'Yeah.'

'County Roscommon?'

I could hear my Irish accent, somewhat neutralised by years in the UK, coming roaring back even with those few words.

Patrick nodded again and pulled a small piece of cardboard from his pocket.

'That's right, yeah. I don't know if you've ever been, but it's a gorgeous part of the world and there's plenty of room in the house, honestly we'd make you feel so welcome—'

But I had stopped listening. Suddenly that weird bit about Patrick Uprichard Fitzmahon's accent was starting to make more sense – it was Irish I'd heard in there, a softness at the edge of the crisp public-school vowels.

'You'll have to think about it of course.'

Patrick pushed the card into my hand then backed away, clearly relieved to have said his piece.

'There's no rush. But my email is on there, and my phone number, and…'

I turned the card over in my hand.

Patrick Uprichard Fitzmahon

Estate Manager

Hollowpark Hall, Lisheeha, Co Roscommon, Ireland

The words were written in flowery gold script and there was a line drawing of a stately home just below them. Ireland. Home, although it hadn't been that for many years. It could just be the perfect place to live, and breathe, and make up my mind about the future.

'You'll think about it?'

Patrick touched my hand, briefly, as if he wanted to shake it, then took it away again and smiled.

'It would be lovely to hear from you.'

'I've thought about it.'

The words were out of my mouth quicker than I planned but I'd never been more certain about anything in my life. A brand new job with no need to register with agencies or do interviews, a family and, most importantly, a child I already knew. A few months in what looked like gorgeous surroundings, with time to think and plan and breathe.

Skye was a lovely kid; I'd enjoy spending time with her. And Patrick seemed sound, and I was sure Isla would be too, once I got to know her.

'I've thought about it, I'll do it.'

A slow grin spread across Patrick's face as I continued.

'I've four weeks to run on my contract here though – is that early enough for you?'

'Yes!'

He was smiling broadly now and moved forward as if to hug me before shaking my hand vigorously instead.

'That's fantastic news – Isla will be so pleased!'

His excitement was infectious, and I was starting to feel seriously excited myself, but then I gave a sudden, violent shiver. It didn't make sense; we were outside the play room in an un-air-conditioned corridor that must have been at least thirty-five degrees but I was trembling now and had to stick my hands in my pockets to stop Patrick noticing. Everything was grey. Patrick's mouth was moving but I couldn't understand what he was saying. I looked around, but there was no one to help me and I—

I blinked, and everything returned to normal. I removed my hands from my pockets and tried to control my breathing. Christ, I must have been more tired than I thought. Maybe the nine years of constant moving, constant planning and not really settling anywhere had caught up with me.

Patrick, who was gabbling about flight times and contracts, hadn't noticed a thing and I forced a smile as he continued.

'I'll send you an email, yeah? When you get home? And we can sort out the details then. Oh, it's just brilliant news! Come on, Skye love, let's get you fed.'

And then they left, hand in hand, almost skipping down the corridor. I leaned against the wall, utterly exhausted. I needed a break all right; it was definitely time for a change. I looked down at the card, now squashed and slightly sweaty in my hand. Hollowpark Hall. It sounded – romantic was the wrong word. But exciting and new, yet familiar, at the same time. An Irish adventure. It couldn't have come at a better time.

Chapter 7

1840

Sitting, back pressed against the wall, Deirdre measured the passing of time by the movement of the moonlight around the stone floor. Head bent, she listened out for a sound, a cry or a moan that would indicate Laurence had survived the fall from the tower window. A sound, she had to admit, that she did not want to hear. She owed herself honesty, at least.

But no sound came and so, as the cold from the stone walls transferred into her bones and the light continued its steady revolution, Deirdre began to make a plan. There was no doubt in her mind that her husband had meant to kill her. That had been his aim from the moment he had asked her to meet him in the maze that evening, or perhaps much earlier than that. Maybe, she thought as the light on the floor blurred and she had to close her eyes against a sudden wave of dizziness, maybe their whole marriage had been leading up to this night, to the moment where he grasped her roughly around the waist and lifted her onto the window sill... and then Deirdre Fitzmahon opened her eyes, to find her vision razor sharp once more. How dare he? How dare Laurence Foster violate her family, her home, how dare he try and claim Hollowpark for himself? She could have been a good wife to him, *would* have been a good wife; she would have loved him, borne him children – instead, he had tried to take it all. She stretched out her hand to ease a sudden ache in her back and her fingers connected with a small, hard object that was lying on the ground. The Sphinx was undamaged, yet covered in blood and grey matter and Deirdre knew, although her mind slipped and skidded over some of the details, that it was her hands that had clasped it, her hands that had dealt the blows that had rendered Laurence almost insensible and allowed her to push him towards the window and then...

Here, her thoughts faltered and her memory faded, but for a flickering in the corner of her mind. Laurence leaning. Her husband falling.

Had it been murder? Deirdre supposed it must have been. But there had been no other option open to her.

Suddenly resolute, she raised herself into a standing position, wincing as the blood flowed back into her limbs. Laurence Foster had tried to take her life, but he had not succeeded and she could not let him take her freedom now. She wiped the little ornament carefully on her underskirt and then replaced it on the window sill. Tomorrow was laundry day, Kitty wouldn't ask any questions, it wasn't seemly to enquire about women and their monthly flow. And when she was asked about other matters? She would simply tell them all that she didn't know.

She didn't know because she hadn't been here. Deirdre stood still for a moment, feeling the ache in her back swell and then ease, keeping her eyes fixed on the door on the other side of the room. That was the only way forward, now. She would tell them she knew nothing, would convince herself that she knew nothing, that she had not been here at all.

She walked towards the door, careful to keep her eyes away from the window. There was no point in looking out, there was nothing important to see out there. Growing stronger and steadier with every step, she headed down the stairs, calmly and steadily, pushed open the heavy wooden door at the bottom of the tower and strode forward into the moonlight. She didn't look to the clump of bushes to her left, because there was no reason for her to do so. There was nothing there to see. She made her way through the maze, her feet leading her along the familiar paths, head and heart fixed on home. The moonlight had softened to a grey dawn haze and Deirdre began to move more quickly, anxious to get back to the safety of her bedroom, the bed she had slept in since she had left the nursery, that place of ultimate safety. Just one final corner and then she'd reach the exit, she was nearly there now, could almost feel the softness of her bedsheets around her – and then she had to stifle a scream as a shadow loomed over her.

'Is it yourself, ma'am?'

'Ciarán!'

Deirdre gasped the word, then clapped her hands over her mouth to prevent any further sound from escaping.

The young gardener raised his hand in apology.

'I'm sorry if I disturbed you, ma'am, I thought I saw someone in the maze, an intruder maybe…'

He slurred the final word and, as Deirdre looked more

closely at her childhood playmate she could see that Ciarán's eyes were glassy and that he was swaying slightly, from something stronger than tiredness. They were not friends any more, of course – the difference between them became too acute as they grew older and Ciarán began working full time with his father and, although she had once bristled at the word, Deirdre no longer took any notice when he called her 'ma'am' and dipped his head slightly any time they passed each other in the grounds. But her maid, Kitty, had an interest in one of his older brothers and had told Deirdre that the O'Mahony boys played cards in the village some nights, and that their mother fretted when they did not return home until dawn. Deirdre hadn't paid much heed to the story, at the time, Ciarán's interests were no longer any business of hers. Until tonight, when he had found her somewhere she was not supposed to be.

'Are you all right Dee— ma'am?'

Seeming surprised by her sudden appearance, Ciarán moved closer, a quizzical look forming on his blurred features. He smelled of whisky, Deirdre realised, but there was no roughness about him, none of the menace the alcohol roused in Laurence. Deirdre's husband, so polite in company, could be both cutting and aggressive when he had drink taken, and there had been many evenings Deirdre had been secretly relieved when he had chosen to sleep alone. But Ciarán O'Mahony just seemed tired tonight, and somewhat confused.

'Was it out walking you were? Because...'

And then in an action that seemed to take both of them by surprise, he reached out and touched her cheek, gently, and when he took his hand away Deirdre was horrified to see blood on his fingertips. She raised her own hand then and felt for the first time a bruise under her eye and a long scratch across her cheekbone. But Deirdre didn't have time to worry about the pain – if she didn't leave right now the rest of the household would be stirring and her secret discovered. And so she reached out again and placed her hand on her old friend's elbow. Held his gaze until his eyes sharped into focus.

'We didn't meet this morning, Ciarán. You'll go home now, and we won't speak of this. Do you understand?'

And she prayed that this was not the gardener's assistant she was talking to, but her friend, Ciarán, a boy who had once been as close as a brother, who had chased her around these very hedges and helped her choose Prince from a neighbour's litter. A boy who had suffered at the hands of Paul Fitzmahon, and a young man who knew, because gossip at Hollowpark flowed in both directions, that Laurence Foster and Paul were close friends.

Ciarán returned her stare and then inclined his head slightly, and sighed.

'I'm so sorry, ma'am. I was supposed to cut back the branches at the entrance yesterday, but I didn't finish the job. It must have been one of those that hit you in the face.'

It was a statement, not a question, and Deirdre remained motionless as he continued.

'I'm away to bed now. I was out too late the night and drank too much, forgive me, ma'am, I'm not myself. I'll have no memory of this night when I wake.'

And then Ciarán turned and walked away. His home, Hollowpark's gatehouse, lay on the opposite side of the meadow to the Hall itself and Deirdre gave him a few minutes to cross the lawn alone before exiting the maze herself. Moving quickly, she ignored the large, imposing hall door and crept around the side of the building instead, entering the Hall through the boot-room and creeping up the back stairs. When she reached her bedroom she realised she had been holding her breath all the while, but she released it when she slid between the sheets and encountered Prince's warm body. The faithful little dog had waited for her all night.

Sleep must have come then, without her knowing it, because she was startled awake sometime later by the arrival of tea. Clear eyed, Deirdre sat up, greeted Kitty cheerfully, and agreed that yes, it looked like it was going to be a beautiful day. She was downstairs having breakfast with her parents when she heard a commotion at the front door and then the shuffling and scraping of heavy boots along the flagstones of the hall. But despite the disturbance Deirdre kept her eyes down and continued to eat her meal as her father was called away, and did not show alarm even when he returned, grey-faced and shaken. It was only when he told her that she would have to be a very brave girl, and explained that her husband's body had been found, that Deirdre allowed herself the luxury of tears.

Chapter 8

2007

Hollowpark Hall

'Sorry about the mess. You know how it is – it's more an office than a car, really.'

I didn't, actually, as I'd never worked in an office but even if I had I didn't think I'd have decorated it with empty crisp packets, sticky Coke bottles and – I looked more closely – was that a half empty packet of Haribo's? Ha. Back in Greece Skye's mother had been vehement – a more judgemental person might have said borderline obsessive – about not giving her daughter anything other than fresh food and had even sent in packets of organic snacks for use during breaktime at the Klub. So, I had to conclude that the debris in Patrick Fitzmahon's car was his, and his alone, and that little glimpse of human slobbishness made me like him even more.

Patrick grabbed a handful of rubbish and I remained on the path beside the battered Nissan as he looked at it for a moment as if deciding where to put it, then flung it onto the back seat. His faded U2 T-shirt rode up over an impressively flat stomach as he moved and I turned my gaze away, suddenly self-conscious. That's the funny thing about holiday resorts – all those women's magazines bang on about the need to 'Get beach body ready' but after a few days in a busy hotel all those beach bodies start to look the same. I'd had full-on conversations with Patrick while he was wearing nothing other than swimming shorts and hadn't batted an eyelid, but right now, climbing into the front seat of the car beside him seemed like a far more intimate prospect. And then I rubbed my eyes. I was being ridiculous. Despite all the clichés, and millions of words wasted on parenting websites, I had never so much as fancied one of the dads I worked for, let alone contemplated an affair. The truth was I didn't think of them as 'men', not really, they were bosses, plain and simple. Besides, I usually saw them at their worst, rushing out the door in the morning leaving cornflakes strewn across the counter, or coming in the door with their ties askew, smelling of beer and expressing surprise that they had arrived just too late for bedtime. Romantic heroes, they were not. So, taking a final breath of fresh air before climbing into the newly cleared front seat, I decided any discombobulation I was feeling about Patrick Fitzmahon must surely be due to lack of sleep, and nothing more exciting.

It was no wonder I was exhausted, anyway. The last few weeks had been a blur of activity, between finishing my contract in Greece, alerting my UK agency that I wouldn't be returning for my usual winter stint and then organising to have the belongings I'd left behind in London put into long-term storage, I'd been working around the clock, and now that I'd finally arrived back on Irish soil my body was telling me in no uncertain terms that it had run out of juice. I was hungover too, which was unusual for me but the other reps had insisted on bringing me out for drinks on my last night at the hotel and for once I'd let myself be led astray. Drinks in the hotel bar had led to shots at a beach party and I'd ended up going straight from the bar to the airport, planning to snooze all the way home. My flight to Dublin had been delayed, however, and any residual good humour had drained out of me along with the alcohol during the long, sticky wait at the airport. A stag party, all of whom had spent the delay tucking into their duty free, had put paid to any hope I had to sleeping on the plane and by the time I landed in Dublin and made my way to the Sligo train I was a dehydrated, sweaty and, not to put too fine a point on it, grumpy mess.

Stifling a yawn, I fastened my seatbelt as Patrick pulled out of the car park. It was September in Ireland, which meant we were driving under leaden grey skies through which the occasional patch of blue could be seen peeping through. It could rain torrentially in the next few minutes or we might need to wear sunglasses all the way back to Lisheeha, it was impossible to tell. The station walls were grey too, their traditional stone contrasting with the dull but surprisingly modern road on which we were now travelling, lined by a mixture of brightly painted terraced homes and newer, less attractive, apartment blocks.

I had never been to this part of Ireland before; in fact I was disgracefully ignorant about my native country. We holidayed in France most years when I was a kid, usually to a massive gîte owned by one of Mum's schoolfriends, and most summers turned into a Mediterranean version of her regular Saturday night gatherings with friends coming and going, bodies asleep on every available surface and meals that consisted of little more than bread, cheese and vast quantities of local wine. My dad used to fly over for the first week in August and I think even he found the vibe a little over the top, finally cracking the morning he walked into the kitchen to find an unwashed folk singer serenading my mother through a wreath of pipe smoke while I fed myself on out-of-date cornflakes. He took me to Paris the following day, telling Mum it was for a business trip, but I don't actually remember him doing any work at all. All I do recall is being given my own room in a small, spotlessly clean hotel and taking a blissfully long, uninterrupted bath before heading out with him for steak and chips in a restaurant across the road. We visited the Eiffel Tower the next day too, and the Louvre. It was like Dad wanted to pack an entire holiday into two days, and even after he left for the airport and I took a train back to the south the sense of calm, of being rested and well cared for, lasted for the whole journey. But no, other than the odd school tour we had never done family trips around Ireland, so this job at Hollowpark Hall was going to be as alien to me as any other new place I'd ever worked in.

Patrick steered us onto a roundabout which offered more destinations I'd never visited, Galway and Ballina among them, and I decided that this was the year I would finally discover my own country. Then my view was obscured by tall trees and I allowed my eyelids to droop and my head to flop back against the headrest. I hoped that shutting my eyes would send out a strong signal that I didn't have the energy to chat but, after tutting at a talk show, and dismissing several pop stations, Patrick snapped off the radio and cleared his throat. I forced my eyes to open again. We were well out into the countryside now, green fields flashing by the window and a light drizzle speckling the front window.

'You're probably looking forward to a bit of rain!'

'Yeah well, you'd get a bit bored with all that sun.'

You wouldn't, actually, at least I never had, but I didn't want my new employer to think I was some sort of hungover, silent weirdo so decided to make the best effort I could to keep the conversation going.

'There'll be no need for factor forty around here anyway!'

'Indeed!'

Patrick laughed.

'No place like home. Where is home, for you anyway, Grace?'

'My parents live in Dublin,' I told him, which was my stock response to the question. But his pause indicated he wanted more information, so I named the suburb, then noted the usual eyebrow raise. It was true, nannies didn't usually come from addresses like mine, or from families like mine. But I didn't feel like going into details and instead turned the question back on him in what I hoped was a friendly way.

'So how about you then? Where are you from originally?'

Another eyebrow raise.

'Well, I'm from here, of course! Lisheeha, born and bred.'

But I wasn't going to let him get away that lightly.

'That's not a west of Ireland accent,' I teased, and was surprised to see him blush in response.

'I suppose not, no.'

He pulled out to pass a tractor then steadied the car again before answering.

'Not in the traditional sense, anyway.'

He paused and then, when it was clear I was waiting to hear more, continued.

'I mean, I am Irish, I was born here, literally born at home, in Hollowpark Hall. Mum says they called the ambulance, but it didn't make it in time. I'm sure she'll bore you with the story herself before long. But yeah, I lived there till I was twelve, went to primary school in the village and then secondary school in the UK.'

He named a public school that several of my London clients had dreamed of sending their children to, and suddenly his la-di-dah accent started to make a lot more sense.

'I stayed over there then for university, Cambridge...'

He paused and, when he continued, his voice had taken on a clipped, almost off-hand air.

'Worked in the City for a few years, it was fun, for a while. But I always loved Lisheeha and when I met Isla – well.'

Patrick cleared his throat.

'It's all about kids, really, isn't it? When they come along. Lisheeha is a wonderful place to raise a child, you'll see that for yourself soon enough. Isla and I met in London, but we came back here four years ago and when Skye was born it turned out to have been the best decision we possibly could have made.'

'And will you be sending her away to school then? When the time comes?'

'Christ no.'

Patrick shook his head, clearly horrified at the thought.

'I wouldn't wish it on the poor kid. I hated leaving home myself – you end up not being from anywhere, you know? I had friends from the village when I was younger but then I went away to school and when I came back in the summer they had all moved on, or had some stupid idea that we'd have nothing in common any more. And at the same time the guys in London called me 'Spud' and teased me about the potato famine. I guess that's why I ended up sounding like this, it was easier, you know? To fit in. University was fine, and I enjoyed working in London for a while too when I was younger, but to be honest with you I never really felt settled anywhere until I came back here for good. This is home now; this is where I'm staying.'

He glanced across at me, his expression softening.

'And I really hope you'll feel the same way, Grace.'

Home. I'd have to send a card to my dad, I reminded myself, to let him know I'd moved on again – and then I was astonished to find tears welling up in my eyes. That was ridiculous, I didn't get homesick, I didn't have a home to miss, not any more. But something about the sincerity in Patrick's voice when he spoke about Lisheeha and, let's face it, the Greek brandy from the night before, were doing strange things to my emotions and so I lowered the window, hoping some fresh air would clear my head. Time to change the subject, fast.

'Skye is in playschool now, Isla said. I think she mentioned she's there in the mornings?'

'That's right.'

Patrick nodded again and I felt that he too was happy to move the conversation to a less sentimental area.

'The school is in the village, less than two miles away. We'll ask you to drop her in in the mornings, please, and collect her again at twelve. You'll be looking after her then until five thirty, or whenever Isla finishes up – I'm not sure how much she told you about her work?'

'Very little,' I responded, which was an understatement. I had in fact had very few dealings at all with Skye's mother other than the odd 'hello' when we passed each other by the side of the pool. All of the drop-offs at the Kidz Klub and indeed all of the information about my new job had been handled by Patrick.

'Isla is a sculptor.'

Patrick gave what I could have sworn was a reverential pause before continuing.

'She's incredibly talented, but she hasn't worked full time for a while. We've been – busy. With Skye and everything. But she's really getting back into her stride again now, I'm incredibly proud of her.'

I stifled a yawn, and this time it wasn't just from lack of sleep. An artist, how predictable. My mother used to bang on about how she'd love to write a novel 'if she had time' and held regular book clubs which consisted of gangs of her friends leaving the books in their handbags and giggling over wine. Once they'd even asked an author in for a 'question and answer session', and I'd overheard them quizzing the poor woman about how much money she made, and how she researched her sex scenes. Later on, one of my employers in London had called herself a 'poet' and took several weekend trips away to 'artists' retreats', then made me read her terrible, unpublishable verse when she got home. I didn't, to be honest, hold out much hope that

Isla would be any more talented, but her husband seemed to think she was up there with Michelangelo and if he needed me to go along with that for the sake of family harmony then I was happy to oblige.

'I'm sorry, should I have heard of her? I mean I travel a lot; I don't go to many exhibitions or...' My voice trailed off. Exhibitions. That was it, that was the sum total of my ability to converse about art. Thankfully Patrick jumped in before I had a chance to embarrass myself further.

'Oh, she hasn't exhibited in a while. I mean she should – I think her stuff is beautiful, although I know very little about it. But she's looking forward to getting properly stuck into it again and it'll be great to you have around while she's in her studio.'

'Is it in the village then? Her studio?'

I had only a vague idea of what being a sculptor entailed, most of it based on this old movie I saw one Sunday where Demi Moore got frisky with a dead guy and a potter's wheel, and I had a sudden image of Isla in a large, airy building, maybe with other artists floating around, eating cheese and drinking wine. In fact, it was starting to sound like fun, but Patrick soon shattered my illusions.

'No, she'll be working at home. There's a tower, near the main house, we've converted it into a studio. It was empty for years, in fact we are not quite sure why it was built in the first place. There's a local guy, a bit of an amateur historian, and he's been looking at papers and things, but I don't think he's ever got to the bottom of it. But it's perfect for what Isla needs, just one room at the top of the stairs, loads of light, obviously. We'll have to sort out some sort of heating when the weather turns but it has been so mild this year she's looking forward to working up there for as long as she can. So yeah, basically she'll be up there all day and you can shout if there is an emergency. But I'm sure there's no fear of that!'

'Not at all.'

I smiled, my reassuring manner as easy to slip on as the old fleece I wore when bringing children on mucky days out. The truth was I was quite disappointed to hear that Isla would be around the house during the day, as I have learned from experience that kids tend to be much easier to manage when I have them on their own. But this tower place sounded like it was a bit away from the main house, at least, so once Isla wasn't in permanent earshot, we'd all be fine. Either way I'd cope, I always did. I yawned again and felt my body relax into the seat. Everything was going to be fine.

'We'll be there in about twenty minutes.'

We had left the main road now and Patrick dropped down a gear as the car rounded a hairpin bend, then sped up again.

'We're about a mile outside Lisheeha now. It's a nice village, tiny obviously, but it has everything we need. I'll show you where the playschool is. That's where you'll have to drop Skye and then...'

But lack of sleep was gaining the upper hand. My eyes closed and this time they didn't open again. I couldn't wait for my bed. No, a bath first. Then bed, and supper, and clean pyjamas and...

'We're here!'

I jerked upright. God, I must have completely passed out, how embarrassing. I hoped I hadn't started to snore, or—and then all my self-consciousness drained away as I looked out of the front window of the car. Well now, this was far in excess of what I'd been expecting. We were driving up – no, *sweeping* up a long, twisting driveway, lined by trees that here and there afforded us glimpses of baled hay in the endless green fields beyond. I glanced at Patrick, noticing how the leaves cast dappled shadows on his angular face and then suddenly, after rounding one final corner we were out in the sunlight again.

Patrick heard me gasp and smiled at me.

'Welcome home, Grace!'

But I couldn't answer him. This wasn't a home, this building was a mansion, an extravagant expanse of butter-coloured stone that shone softly in the afternoon light. I turned my head from side to side but simply couldn't process the size of it, the grandeur... Patrick guided the car to a stop, then jumped out and opened my door, but still I didn't move.

'I'll show you around, later.'

Still silent, I climbed out of the car, barely registering the ache in my back and legs, and kept my hand on the door frame as I continued to drink in my surroundings. How big was this place, anyway? My head swivelled as I tried to count the windows, but it was impossible, there were too many and besides, there was clearly more to the house than what was visible from the front. I could see an L-shaped extension to one side and roofs of outbuildings behind that again... I looked back at the house then and blinked as sunlight flashed against the windows, and then my eyes were drawn to one pane in particular, and the figure of a woman standing behind it. I squinted and looked closer. It was impossible to see what she looked like, all I could make out was a knot of dark hair framing a pale face. It can't have been Isla, then – I took a step forward, trying to see more, but it was as if the ground itself had swum away from me and my foot connected with nothing but air.

Chapter 9

1840

The policemen arrived at Hollowpark Hall later that afternoon. There were two of them, a tall man with a narrow face and long, grey whiskers and his younger, stouter companion who didn't take the seat Deirdre's mother offered him but stood instead by the library window, rocking forward and backwards on his heels. The older man eased himself into one of the two high-backed chairs on either side of the large stone fireplace and then waved at Deirdre to take the matching one, as if he himself was the master of Hollowpark and she merely a guest, and an unsettled one, at that.

'It would be best if we could speak to Mrs Foster alone.'

Grey Whiskers – he had offered her both of their names, but Deirdre just couldn't seem to retain them – glanced at her mother who nodded and then left, shutting the door gently behind her. She sat awkwardly balanced on the edge of the chair, until Prince appeared from the other side of the room and dropped down onto her feet, forcing her to move into a more comfortable position. The policeman looked down at the little dog and then up at his mistress.

'When did you last see Mr Foster?'

She would take a moment before answering, Deirdre decided, long enough to make her answers sound genuine, not so long that he could accuse her of uncertainty.

'At dinner, last night.'

Grey Whiskers nodded but didn't speak, clearly waiting for her continue.

'I left the room before the end of the meal, I had a headache and needed air.'

'And what time was that?'

'It would have been around half past eight.'

He was probing her answers, Deirdre thought, like a dentist working on a sore tooth, proceeding slowly and carefully, seemingly aware that at any moment he could cause great pain. But she was ready for him, and was careful not to stumble over any answers. All the while his companion rocked, and stared.

'And where did you walk?'

'I walked in the grounds.'

'Alone?'

The younger man stopped rocking and spoke for the first time. Deirdre glanced across the room.

'Yes, alone. The others were still eating when I left.'

He was looking at the scratch on her face, but Deirdre was ready for him and touched it lightly with one fingertip.

'I went as far as the maze, intending to go inside, but there was an overhanging branch and I walked straight into it. It was so stupid of me, I wasn't looking where I was going. I wasn't badly hurt but I was startled and went straight back to the house.'

The stout man nodded.

'And did anybody see you?'

Deirdre kept her voice low, but made sure to meet his gaze. 'No. I was alone.'

At her feet, Prince raised his head, then settled back down again with a small sigh.

The stout man raised his eyebrows. 'Your husband didn't join you on the walk?'

Deirdre shook her head. 'No. He hadn't finished eating when I left the dining room, I didn't want to disturb him. And I was only outside for a matter of minutes.'

'And later? Did you see him after you returned to the house? In your bedroom maybe?'

She blushed, and, moving her head, addressed her answer to the marble fireplace. 'Laurence usually – often – slept in his dressing room.'

Grey Whiskers nodded, and took up the questioning again. 'So you didn't see Mr Foster again last night.'

'No.' Deirdre shook her head to hide the lack of tears in her eyes. 'No. I came down for breakfast this morning and the first I heard of what had happened was when…'

And then her voice really did falter and Grey Whiskers offered, for the first time, the ghost of a smile.

'Would you like me to call for some water?'

Her throat was dry to the point of pain but she didn't trust her hand to hold a glass without shaking, so Deirdre simply swallowed, and continued to speak.

'No, no thank you. I just want… I want to help you find out what happened to my husband. In any way I can.'

Grey Whiskers nodded.

'We will try not to detain you much longer.' And the probing began again.

After they had finished, and when their heavy boots could be heard receding down the driveway, Deirdre's mother joined her in the library and offered to keep her company but she insisted she needed time to grieve and retired to her room. There, she drifted in and out of a half sleep until Kitty appeared with tea. Exhausted, Deirdre tried to wave the little maid away but the girl was positively quivering with excitement and could not be stopped from discharging her news. The police were questioning everyone on the estate, she told Deirdre, setting her tray down with such force that tea spilled all over the bedclothes. Everyone, yes, the household staff, and the groundsmen as well...

But Deirdre couldn't hear any more through the sudden roaring in her ears. It was too hard to breathe, somehow, and the walls of the bedroom were moving towards her...

She was vaguely aware of the tray being taken from her lap and her mother arriving and, sometime later, a doctor too, and a spoon of sharp-tasting medicine and then came darkness and stormy, unsettled sleep.

The inquest was held a week later, in the Great Room at Hollowpark. Deirdre had expected to be brought to the courthouse in Sligo but that was not used, her father told her, in cases like this one; instead, the coroner and the jury would travel out to the estate to see the scene for themselves. The scene. Even language itself had changed, since Laurence had died. Her beloved tower was a scene, now, and her

76

husband, the deceased. Deirdre was in her bedroom when she heard the crunch of wheels on the driveway, and looked out of the window to see the coroner, a small, florid man with sandy hair parted neatly in the middle and mismatched coat and trousers, jump down from the carriage and shake her father's hand. A jury had been assembled, respectable men, some from Lisheeha and others from as far away as Sligo and, as Deirdre watched, the little coroner led them in a slow, almost stately procession through her beloved meadow and towards the maze. When they returned to the Hall they had mud on their shoes and three of them, Deirdre noticed, had the same kind of chalky residue on their coats that she often found on her skirts after a day spent in the tower. But before she had time to fret about what they had seen, her father tapped gently on her door and told her it was time to go downstairs.

The Great Room had been rearranged for the day, with the large dining table pushed to one side and chairs brought from all over Hollowpark to form neat rows in the centre of the floor. Deirdre had only time to see Laurence's mother, grim and grey-faced in a shabby black gown, sitting beside her daughter in the back row before she herself took a chair next to her parents in the front. The coroner sat at the head of the room and beside him had been placed a chair for witnesses, of whom the local doctor was the first to be called. Laurence Foster had suffered significant head injuries, the doctor told the gathering, and when he said the words, Deirdre's mother reached out and clasped her hand.

'And were those injuries consistent with a fall?'

Deirdre withdrew her hand from her mother's, feeling suddenly the ghost-weight of the Sphinx in her palm.

The doctor took off his glasses, and looked around the room for a moment.

'Yes, I believe they were.'

When her own turn came, Deirdre approached the coroner's questions as if giving them great thought although they were, in fact, no different to the ones the policemen had put to her. Yes, she had been in the garden for a brief period after dinner but no, she had not seen her husband at any time. There was a cough then from the other end of the room and Deirdre looked up to see the young, stout policeman lean forward in his chair, balance his elbows on his knees, and stare at her intently. But she did not falter, did not change her story. And it was her story, she suddenly realised. She had told it so many times, she believed it now.

Her mother was called then, and her father and her aunt who had been their guest at dinner that evening and person after person told the same tale, that Laurence had been his usual cheerful self and had drunk a lot of wine, and had been speaking about a new horse he was thinking of buying and a trip to Galway to see the sire. As their stories filled the room, Deirdre felt the stone that had been sitting in the middle of her chest shift and shrink a little, allowing her to breathe more easily. And then the door at the far end of the room opened and Paul Fitzmahon slipped in, accompanied by a fair-haired woman Deirdre did not recognise. He did not look at her, but grasped the woman by the elbow and guided her towards two vacant seats on Deirdre's right-hand side, murmuring, just loud enough for her to hear, 'This way, Miss Mulhearn.'

The name triggered a memory, a flash of those final moments in the tower, and Deirdre felt a sudden stab of pain in her temples. Agatha Mulhearn, a woman who had once hoped to be Mrs Laurence Foster herself – and then, even that thought was driven from her mind as the coroner raised his head and called the next witness, and Ciarán O'Mahony moved forward from the centre of the room. Deirdre's old friend was a stranger today in tight breeches and a starched white shirt and he did not catch her eye as he took the Bible in his hand. Her own hands began to shake then and she sat on them, and tried to ignore Paul, who was staring at the young gardener, his brows drawn.

The coroner offered Ciarán a brief smile and unfolded a piece of paper in front of him.

'Your full name?'

'Ciarán Thomas O'Mahony, sir.'

Ciarán's voice was gruff in the elegant room, it seemed to bounce off the polished floorboards, and Deirdre felt a sudden pang of sympathy when she noticed he was rounding his shoulders, trying to make himself smaller, daintier, better suited to the elegant space.

'And you are employed here at Hollowpark Hall?'

'I work for my father, sir. He's the head gardener here.'

The coroner gave a small nod and scribbled a note on his page before continuing.

'And did you see Mr Foster, Mr Laurence Foster on the night in question?'

'I did, sir.'

Even sitting on her hands was not enough to stop them

shaking now and Deirdre pressed the full weight of her body down into the chair, trying to ignore the fact that Paul was looking from her to Ciarán in turn. On his other side, Agatha Mulhearn took out a large blue-edged handkerchief and pressed it to her eyes.

'What time did you meet him?'

'It would have been around eleven, sir.'

'You were out late?'

'My brother had gone into the village to play cards, sir, and I was unable to sleep and decided to follow him.'

'And did you speak to Mr Foster?'

'I did, sir.'

The stone in Deirdre's chest was back now, larger than ever, and Agatha Mulhearn let out a soft, but audible sob.

'And what did you speak about?'

'We spoke about the maze, sir, out in the garden. We often spoke about it.'

The coroner paused another bout of scribbling and looked up at him.

'You often spoke of it? What do you mean? Was Mr Foster interested in gardening?'

An image of Laurence's long, thin, clean fingers came into Deirdre's head and she had the mad feeling she might laugh. Instead she turned her hands around and began to pinch at her skin through her skirts, praying the pain would steady her. Across the room Ciarán shook his head.

'Mr Foster was interested in the maze, sir, how it had been planted and how a man could find his way through.'

'Is that right?'

The coroner cocked his head, as if giving Ciarán the opportunity to continue.

'Yes, sir.'

Ciarán cleared his throat before continuing. He had grown handsome, these past few years, Deirdre thought, and she forced herself to look at his long, tanned neck and to think about sunshine and long walks and not to panic and not to scream.

'He used to ask me, sir, how a man could find his way through the maze. And I told him the tower would show him the way, if he allowed it.'

'The tower?'

The coroner's eyebrows rose again.

'Yes, sir. There's a tower, at the far side of the maze, it helps you find your way if you are lost inside. And if you climb into the tower and lean out, well then, sir, you can see clearly how the maze was designed. That is what Mr Foster said he was going to do, climb up there, to look for the way. And that's the last I saw of him.'

It was as if Deirdre was floating above herself, looking down on Ciarán and hearing his words and, at the same time, seeing the scene in the tower, just the way Ciarán described it. Laurence, alone, his head muddled by wine, leaning out to trace a pathway through the maze… Beside her, Paul was muttering something under his breath but she couldn't make out what he was saying, and when she gathered the courage to turn to him, he fell silent again. When Ciarán returned to his seat, he took the route on the opposite side of the room.

It took less than an hour for the verdict of accidental death to be returned. Grey Whiskers smiled, and the stout policeman lifted his head from his hands and sighed but did not speak. Paul Fitzmahon escorted a sobbing Agatha

Mulhearn from the room and Ciarán O'Mahony stood aside and allowed them to exit before him. And Deirdre Foster, née Fitzmahon, told her mother she was feeling tired, but quite well, thank you, and would clear her head by going for a walk in the grounds.

Chapter 10

2007

'I can't believe he didn't feed you. Fecking eejit.'
Pain shot through my temples and I let out an involuntary groan.

'Take it easy there, my darling. That was quite the bang you took.'

The voice was so gentle, yet somehow so in control that I kept my eyes closed and felt a cold cloth being placed on my forehead. The pain receded almost immediately, and I sank back into the pillows. The pillows? I was in bed then.

'I could strangle Patrick, but what use would that do? He's the image of his father, he'll never change.'

Curious now, I peeled open my eyelids. My first thought was that there was a dormouse sitting on the end of the bed. My second was that I wasn't quite sure what a dormouse was, I'd only read about them in kids' story books but it was the first word that had come to mind because the woman *was* like something out of a kids' story book, the hardback type bought by well-meaning aunts and uncles when the child in question would much rather a *Paw Patrol* TV tie-in.

The woman had a sensible haircut, greying locks tucked back behind her ears, rosy cheeks, no discernible make-up and striking navy eyes and she was wearing a faded pink and white checked apron over a pair of sensible jeans. An apron? I blinked and felt the headache twang at my temples again. I could remember fainting all right but wasn't sure why I seemed to have ended up back in the 1950s.

'Here, take a sip of this.'

The dormouse handed me a glass of water, then pulled a blister pack of paracetamol from her apron pocket.

'And two of these. Then I'll bring you something to eat if you feel up to it.'

The mention of food made my stomach growl, and the dormouse gave a satisfied smile.

'I've a feeling that's all that's wrong with you, my darling. Paddy said ye didn't stop for grub, you're not dieting, are you? You don't need it. Oh, I hope you're not going to be a vegan like my niece, are you? She stayed here for a while last year, lovely girl, but there are only so many ways you can cook a bean casserole and it was very difficult trying to keep all of the things separate in the fridge…'

'I'm not vegan.'

My voice sounded faint and most unlike myself and I coughed before trying again.

'Food sounds lovely… Thank you.'

The woman gave a sudden grin. She was probably only in her late fifties, I realised, despite the old-fashioned clothes and hair.

'And sure, even if you were a vegan that would be fine too! We just want you to be happy here, Grace.'

She reached over and patted my hand.

'You relax there, and I'll bring you some tea and toast. I'm sure you could do with a breath of air, too.'

She stood up, straightened her apron then walked to the window and drew back the curtains. But I couldn't help wincing as the late afternoon sunlight streamed in and, noting my reaction, she closed them again straight away.

'So sorry, my love, your poor head. We'll leave them shut, so, and I'll be back in two ticks with the tea.'

As the door closed behind her I fixed the pillows under my head, feeling better by the second. I was utterly embarrassed, obviously, for having arrived at my new job literally unconscious but I was also fairly sure the woman had been right, and that there was nothing wrong with me other than exhaustion and hunger. In fact, right now, simply being horizontal was making me feel very happy indeed. I sighed contentedly and took my first proper look around the room I assumed was now my bedroom. It was enormous, bigger than the holiday apartment I'd been sharing with two other reps in my last job, and beautifully decorated, with polished wooden floorboards and a dark red rug which matched the throw at the end of the bed. The bed, too, was massive, antique, I reckoned, and definitely king size, but there was still space in the room for a Narnia-style wardrobe on one side and a gorgeous writing desk on the other, both polished to the same sheen as the floorboards. I'd worked in enough posh houses to know that they hadn't skimped on the linen either; that was a serious thread count I could feel under my bum. Meanwhile, the duvet I was lying under must have been made from real feathers. I'd never slept under anything other than polyester before and I couldn't get over how wonderful this felt, soft and yet heavy at the same time, and pressing down on me in the most delicious way...

'Now, love, your tea.'

I opened my eyes, completely disoriented. I must have dozed off again. God, I really was exhausted. I pulled myself up in the bed, delighted to find my head almost totally clear, and smiled at the dormouse, who placed a large wooden tray on my lap.

'Milk? I wasn't sure.'

A heavy mug had been filled almost to the brim with tea and she added a drop of milk from a bone china jug, then handed me the drink and nodded towards a plate of thick white toast which was dripping with butter and honey.

'You can't beat toasted batch when you're not feeling the best.'

I was too hungry to respond to her, just took a huge bite from the toast before washing it down with scalding tea. The mixture was heavenly, and I continued to eat as the woman nodded towards the window, through which the sun was now streaming again.

'You decided to throw a bit of light on the subject after all, did you?'

I wasn't sure what she meant, in fact I was a bit annoyed that she had obviously decided to open the curtains again. Was she trying to hint that I should get up, or something? But she didn't look annoyed with me, in fact the way she settled herself at the side of the bed made it look like she would be happy to shoot the breeze all day.

'Take your time now, there's plenty more where that came from. You gave my son a right fright anyway, he won't be forgetting to feed you again!'

Her son, of course. Patrick had mentioned his mum also lived at Hollowpark Hall but in the confusion of the journey and my light-headedness I had forgotten some of our conversation. I took another bite of the delicious toast and wiped honey from my chin as she continued.

'I'm Delia, by the way, Paddy's mam. But sure, you'll have figured that out yourself by now.'

I swallowed my food, and attempted a smile.

'I'm Grace. It's lovely to meet you. Thanks so much for the food, and I'm sorry about all – this.' I gave a vague shrug which I hoped would cover my rather unorthodox entry into the household, and was rewarded with another smile.

'That's no trouble at all darling, and you're very welcome to our home. Himself was all set to give you the grand tour but I told him that could wait till later – am I right?'

I drained my tea, all set to reassure her that I was fully fixed and ready to leap into action, but was then ambushed by a huge yawn. The sugar and carbs combo had hit me like a bullet and suddenly, it was all I could do to keep from crashing out right on top of the tray. Delia smiled, and took the mug out of my hands.

'No nausea, anything like that? I don't think you hit your head when you fell?'

'I don't think so,' I managed to mutter, between yawns.

Delia bent closer and extended a finger in front of my eyes.

'Follow that across – and that way – grand.'

She sat back and looked at me, suddenly serious.

'If you're in any way worried, love, we can call a doctor. The surgery in the village will be closed by now but Paddy could run you into town if you feel you need to get checked over. I think you're grand though. I trained as a nurse, I wouldn't take any chances if I thought you had a concussion or anything. But the colour is well back in your cheeks now you've had a bite to eat.'

She laid her hand gently against my forehead again. There was something incredibly reassuring about her touch. Lucky Paddy, I thought to myself, and then wondered where the thought had come from.

'I'll be fine.'

Delia nodded, then strode to the windows and shut the curtains tight.

'You doze off now and I'll call you when dinner is ready – around six, if that's OK with you?'

'Sounds great.'

I was already drifting off as she carried the tray through the heavy bedroom door and shut it behind her. Drifting, floating… it was a wonderful feeling, lying down, being warm. Being mothered, I supposed. And the luxury of space! After three months of sharing a room with younger colleagues, spending every night either too warm or too cold depending on who had control of the air con, it was nothing short of blissful to be at exactly the right temperature in a bed that could have doubled as a cloud. All I wanted to do was sleep – but then two glasses of water and a large mug of tea nudged my bladder and told me not to get too comfortable. I kept my eyes closed for a few more moments but it was no use, I was going to have to find the loo. I allowed myself one more delicious second of comfort then sat up gingerly and swung my legs out of bed. The dizziness had entirely subsided, proving Delia had been right in her diagnosis. I was still wearing the tracksuit bottoms and T-shirt I had travelled over in so I picked my hoodie off a chair where someone – Delia again, I guessed – had hung it and made my way towards the door on tiptoe. It felt foolish to be so quiet in a room all by myself but I still didn't know the layout of the rest of the house and I didn't want anyone to know I was up and about, not when I still needed time to recover. I didn't want any more conversation either, just wanted to find a toilet, pee, and get cosy again.

But when the bedroom door shut behind me, I was plunged into darkness. I stretched out my hand, puzzled, then realised that my room was located down the end of a dark corridor. I felt around for a light switch, to no avail, and then walked forward, hands stretched out in front of me. A couple of steps later, I had to muffle a squeal when my outstretched fingers connected with thick, heavy velvet. I gave the material a gentle tug – it was a curtain, covering the end of the corridor, something to do with draughts, I guessed, and at least it explained the blackness, but I could have done without feeling like I was in a tacky haunted house at a fairground this early on in my stay. Then I pushed the material aside and gasped again, only this time, with pleasure. This was more like it.

I had emerged onto a large, semi-circular landing, encased by highly polished mahogany banisters. Directly across from where I was standing, a wide, richly carpeted staircase swept down into the hall below. I peered over, catching sight of what looked like a stone-flagged hallway – and then a wave of dizziness passed over me. I could jump now. The feeling was piercing, and immediate. I could jump now, it would only take a moment – steady on, Grace. I took a step backwards, my legs trembling. I'd had this feeling once before, during a clifftop walk near a hotel I'd been working at, and although I'd had no intention of actually jumping, then or now, it was a disconcerting feeling, the undeniable sense that I could, if I wanted to, take one simple step into mid-air.

A twinge from my bladder brought me back to my senses and I turned and looked right and left along the landing. There was no shortage of doors but no signs to indicate where the toilet might be and the first two I opened revealed what presumably had once been bedrooms but were now crammed with more boxes, bags and crates than the storage facility I rented back in the UK. Feeling like a trespasser, I walked a little further along, my need to pee getting more urgent by the second. Thankfully, the next door I tried opened smoothly into a large, sunny bathroom, with a window to show me I was back at the front of the house again.

I used the loo, then remained seated to take a better look at my surroundings. This space was stunning, like something from a boutique hotel, and a million miles away from the dusty, cluttered rooms elsewhere on the corridor. There were yellow tiles on the floor and the walls had been painted a soft yellow too, which made the whole place feel both bright and incredibly soothing. To my left sat a roll-top bath, the base of which had been sprayed gold, and to my right was a double sink, set into a large cabinet that could have contained all of my toiletries several times over. And even then, there was still enough space in the place for a stand-alone, ultra-modern shower. I stood up and walked to the basin to wash my hands, then looked into the large, gilt-edged mirror that hung over it, and cringed. My hair was greasy, my eyes bloodshot and even my tan appeared to have faded as soon as I hit Irish soil. I would have given anything for a toothbrush but there didn't seem to be any spares lying around so I settled for a quick wash, bending down and splashing water on my face before backing away and, keeping my eyes shut, reaching for the towel I'd seen hanging alongside the sink. I returned to the mirror, patted my face dry, then took the towel away to see if the wash had made any difference.

And that's when I saw her, sitting on the edge of the bath. A teenage girl, dressed in black, dark eyes set deep into her wan face. I stared at her through the mirror, too terrified to move. She was utterly still but her eyes sought mine and held them and I found myself powerless to look away.

'What do you want?'

I was too scared to say the words but it was as if she understood me anyway and opened her mouth to speak, and the thought of this, of hearing her speak, of having to acknowledge that she really existed, galvanised me and I shoved myself back from the sink and forced myself to turn around, to confront her, to confront whatever was happening – there was no one there. The bathroom was yellow and sunny and I was alone. I stumbled forward until I too reached the side of the bath, then sank down on to it. Jesus, O Jesus. I dipped my head until it was resting on my knees, my heartbeat thudding in my ears, then took one, shuddering breath and exhaled shakily. Inhale, exhale – there was nobody there. There had been nobody there. Inhale, exhale – I stared at the soft yellow floor tiles, willing my breathing to return to normal. Inhale – I was alone

– exhale – I was just exhausted. Tired, confused, sick after days without proper food and sleep. There was nothing in the room with me other than a shadow, or a dream.

Moving slowly but with grim purpose I raised myself up off the bath and forced myself to walk back to the mirror. And saw only my own reflection. I was dazed and distressed, with a greenish hue to my tan and bags under my eyes, but I was alone. Of course I was. I gripped the side of the sink and forced myself to keep staring in the mirror, allowing my eyes to rake over the reflection of the room, the ultra-modern bathroom fittings, the shine from the freshly cleaned tub. I needed to get a grip – mysterious girls did not coexist with Villeroy and Boch mixer taps and power showers. I needed sleep. Legs still shaky, I tottered back out onto the landing, stumbling slightly as I headed for the corridor that led to my bedroom. I just needed to rest and reset my brain which I'd clearly left on a Greek island somewhere. I reached my room and pushed open the door then stopped as a breeze hit my face. Someone, Delia I assumed, had opened the curtains again, and the window this time. What was she, some sort of fresh air freak?

And then, from the garden outside, came a shaky scream.

'Skye? Where are you, honey? Mummy doesn't want to play hide and seek just now. Please, Skye!'

There was no way I was going to be able to sleep now, so I might as well make myself useful. Zipping up my hoodie I headed, once again, for the door.

Chapter 11

1843

Cold air swirled around Deirdre as she swept through the entrance hall, leaving the door wide open behind her. Hollowpark Hall needed the air, she decided. She was tired of stuffy, overheated rooms, weary of deferential silences and grieving servants. Removing her coat and then her hat, she laid the garments on a side table for a maid to collect later. She scraped mud from her boots and then, after examining them more closely, left them to be cleaned too. Her mother was waiting for her in the blue drawing room and would be angry if she tracked dirt in there. Too impatient to call for slippers, she walked on her stockinged feet towards the back of the hall, opened the heavy wooden door and then paused to admire the cornflower blue wallpaper she had chosen for the rear passageway. It was not a pattern her parents would ever have chosen, too bright, too modern. Too young, probably, for a widow's home.

'Mrs Foster, relict of the late Laurence.' Deirdre wished she could discard her late husband's name as easily as she had done her coat but there was no prospect of that without remarriage and she had no desire to supplant one man's name with another. In her head she was still Deirdre Fitzmahon and she was content to remain that way. The widow of Hollowpark Hall. But now, not the only one.

Deirdre allowed the door to swing closed behind her and made her way along the passageway. Two widows, sharing a home. It was such a flat, dark sentence that if Deirdre had read it in a book she would not have wanted to continue with the story. But the truth of the situation was, of course, far more complicated. Three years after her husband's death, she herself was as content as it was possible to be. She never spoke and seldom thought of the accident that claimed her husband's life, but it had been an accident, and if an alternative thought ever came into her head she pushed it firmly away. What had happened was in the past now and she herself was utterly at peace within Hollowpark's walls.

Her mother, however, had had her own happiness ripped away from her just two months previously when Deirdre's father, Richard, had died at the age of fifty-seven. The only thing Deirdre had to be thankful for was that it was she, and not her mother, who had found him, lying just yards from the stable, on his way back from a visit to his favourite horse. Brigid had described the sudden death as a 'wonderful way to go' and Deirdre could see past the clumsiness of the sentiment to recognise the truth underneath. Richard's palms had still been warm from stroking the mare, his mind during those last few moments presumably occupied by nothing more taxing than whether to turn her out the following day. There would have been a flare of pain, little more, the doctor had told them, before the end. A very easy departure. But there was no ease for the wife of thirty years he had left behind.

An only child, Deirdre hadn't much experience of other people's families and it was only since her father's sudden death that it had dawned on her just how unusual her parents' relationship had been. She knew, because he had never hidden the fact, that her father was sorry that his first-born child had not been a boy, and knew too that he had hoped for other children but they had not arrived. But leaving that sorrow aside, he and his wife had always seemed utterly content in each other's company. In fact Deirdre had a suspicion that her parents would have survived quite well as a childless couple, and sometimes, when she entered a room unexpectedly, they had looked up from their conversation with a vague sense of wonder, as if they had forgotten she was in the house at all. Maybe that's why she had been so eager to marry Laurence, she thought to herself sometimes. To create a unit of her own.

Enough, now. Deirdre shook herself lightly. Widowhood and tragedy and loneliness – it would do her no good to dwell on these matters any longer. It was just herself and her mother left at Hollowpark now and she owed it to Helen to make their lives as comfortable as possible. Her mother was fathoms deep in sorrow, it was true, but surely time would bring some consolation and there would be a day in the not-too-distant future when Helen would walk the grounds of the estate again, and maybe even welcome some of their beloved guests once more. Cheered by the thought, Deirdre pushed open the door of the Blue Room, but was surprised to find that her mother was not sitting, as she had expected, by the fire, but was standing instead by the window, staring out into the garden. Deirdre felt a dart of pleasure to see her up and moving about – maybe she was already starting to recover? But when Helen turned to look at her, there was no look of peace or acceptance in her eyes; in fact, Deirdre was startled to see that her mother appeared as distraught as she had done the morning her father had died.

'Has something happened?'

'Deirdre, daughter, I need to tell you something.'

And then the story tumbled out, and this time it was the mother who had to comfort the daughter, the younger woman who could not comprehend the news. Hollowpark Hall was to be taken from them. Their family solicitor had called that morning, he was sorrowful, Helen said, but there was nothing he could do. Deirdre's father had followed the path laid down by his father, and his father before him, and had willed the estate to his eldest male heir. When Deirdre had married, Laurence had become that heir and would have been Master of Hollowpark even if Deirdre herself had not lived – she felt a stab of pain, when she heard this, and had to force herself not to cry out – but when he had died, Richard had not changed the terms.

'Maybe he intended to,' her mother told her desperately, frightened by the look on her daughter's face. 'But he did not. And now Paul…'

Deirdre sank into a chair as the full truth of the situation was revealed to her.

Hollowpark was to pass to her father's eldest nephew, her cousin, Paul Fitzmahon. Deirdre and her mother would be forced to leave their home.

'I'm so sorry, darling.'

Helen dropped to her knees and clasped her daughter's

tightly joined hands but Deirdre found herself unable to move or speak. Paul had called over earlier that morning, Helen told her with an uncharacteristic flash of anger, uttering empty words of consolation while looking like he was already imagining how comfortable he would be in the blue armchair by the fire. Despite his rigid belief in tradition, Helen did not really think this was what Richard would have wanted for his beloved wife and daughter. But they were alone now, with no man to speak for them.

They would not be homeless, Paul had told Helen with a wide smile. The gatehouse, currently home to the head gardener and his family, would be converted for their use. There would be no space for servants, of course, but the women would have a roof over their heads and they could even take a walk around the grounds on occasion – perhaps one morning a week could be put aside for that purpose. His wife was looking forward to making Hollowpark Hall her home, he had told Helen, and by the way – he threw the next words across the room with light disinterest – maybe it would be best if Deirdre didn't walk in the maze or climb the tower any more. He and Madeline were expecting their first child, and it would be nice for their own family to have somewhere special to play.

Deirdre did not remember leaving the Blue Room, did not hear her mother's voice calling after her, did not feel the cold of the flagstones under her stockinged feet as she ran towards the front door. She did not remember running through the maze but she must have done because her feet were muddy and bleeding by the time she came to her senses, standing by the window at the top of the tower. She leaned out then, felt the maze calling to her, saw the speckling of purple belladonna in the foliage below and wondered if it would be simpler, after all, just to let go...

But she would not give him the satisfaction. Instead Deirdre picked up the little Sphinx that kept watch on the window sill and hurled it at the wall, letting rage replace sadness, allowing fury to billow like steam inside her. From outside came a thunderclap and the terrified whine of a dog and then the clouds split, and a sudden shower of hailstones came pelting down on Hollowpark, on the tower and on the maze below. The storm was so violent that some of the hailstones shot through the window and struck Deirdre on the face but she couldn't feel them, couldn't feel anything other than burning anger and the determination that she could not, would not leave this place. There was a crack, and the room was lit up by lightning. Deirdre staggered back from the window and stretched out her hand to where a jagged tear had appeared in the smooth plaster of the wall. And then she placed her hand on the fissure and felt herself grow calm. It was cracked, but not broken, the tower would not fall. It would stand and so would she, and anyone who tried to separate her from this place would live only to regret their actions.

'Hollowpark Hall protects its own' – it was an old saying, passed down through generations of Fitzmahons, and Deirdre had no idea where it had come from or what it really meant. But she was a Fitzmahon, wasn't she? And she was of Hollowpark, and it would be up to her to protect it now. Hollowpark Hall was her home. Hollowpark Hall protected its own, and she would never leave.

Chapter 12

2007

'You need to calm down, Isla.'

The soles of my trainers made a slapping sound against the large grey flagstones as I followed the voices down into the hall and out through the open doorway. Delia was standing at the bottom of the wide, stone steps, holding her daughter-in-law firmly by the shoulders.

'I thought she was with you!'

'Ah, listen to me now!'

Delia was rubbing the tops of the younger woman's arms, the way you'd dry a child who had just stepped out of a cold sea. There was something very soothing about the gesture and I could see her daughter-in-law's shoulders relax under her touch.

'Skye is with her daddy, love, they've gone down to feed the cattle, they're grand.'

'I thought...'

Isla shuddered and then, seeing me walking towards them, made a valiant attempt to smile.

'Grace! It's good to see you! I'm sorry for all this fuss. It was just a stupid misunderstanding, that's all. I thought... I didn't know where Skye...'

She stepped away from her mother-in-law then scrubbed at her eyes with her fists with a strangely childlike gesture, before continuing.

'What must you think of us! I'm sorry for shouting, it's just I thought Skye was playing out here and when I couldn't find her... well. I panicked, that was all. I was convinced Patrick was still in Sligo, I had no idea you two were back already..."

Before I could say anything, Delia gave her daughter-in-law a final, reassuring pat on the arm, then turned to me and gave me the ghost of a wink.

'Sure Paddy came back hours ago, and then Grace here went for a lie-down. You know what you're like when you're working, Isla, you lose all track of time. Paddy took Skye with him for the walk, they'll be back soon.'

'I see. Well. I suppose – I might as well get back to work, then.'

'And isn't that a great idea!' Delia gave her a great, beaming smile. 'You do that and I'll text Paddy, tell him not to take too long. I'll have the dinner on the table for the lot of us at six, how does that sound?'

'Oh, there's no need—'

But her mother-in-law ignored Isla's murmur.

'It's no trouble, I was going to get something for Grace here anyway. Now!' She turned to me cheerfully. 'Paddy's gone off with the car keys, Grace, the big eejit, and your cases are still in the boot but he won't be long. Would you like me to show you around a bit? You'll hardly be able to sleep now, and you can sit with me then while I'm making the dinner.'

She was right – the surge of adrenaline caused by my dash downstairs had done a better job of waking me up than any power nap could have done. Besides, even though I knew I had only imagined the face in the bathroom mirror, the fright had unnerved me and I didn't particularly want to go straight back to that large room at the end of the long, dark corridor.

'I'd love to,' I told my hostess, and when I followed her back up the stone steps and into the house, the front door shut behind us with a soft sigh.

'Is Mrs Fitzmahon—is Isla OK?'

I followed Delia across the entrance hall to a long, low table just to the left of the staircase and, when she reached it, she turned to me with a smile.

'Ah, she's grand. She gets very caught up in her work sometimes, a bit distracted, I suppose. That's the artistic temperament for you.'

There was the faintest chuckle in her words and I couldn't help but return a slight smile. 'Distracted' was a good word for Isla, I felt, thinking back to the first time I'd seen her at the swimming pool. She seemed like a lovely person, yes, but was clearly a bit of a dreamer and nothing like her practical, cheerful mother-in-law. I knew from experience that nervy mothers didn't make my job particularly easy and I was becoming increasingly glad I'd have the solid Delia around to back me up at Hollowpark.

'We'll start here so: this is where we greet all the visitors.'

Clearly ready to move on with the conversation, Delia pointed towards an old-fashioned cash register, a pile of black and white leaflets and, rather incongruously, a credit card machine.

'We get most of our bookings through the tourist office in town. Patrick is talking about getting a website done up – I don't know anything about that side of things but maybe, when we're ready to open properly, that will take off too. There's more about the history of the place here.'

She rooted around on the table, or reception desk as I supposed I should call it, then picked up one of the black and white pamphlets and handed it to me.

'You can have a read of this later. I wanted nice glossy ones, but you should have seen the price of them; maybe next year when we're back on our feet a bit. But it gives you the opening hours, and a price list.'

I took the pamphlet and stared at it. Delia must have noticed the expression of confusion on my face.

'You do know we're planning on running tours, don't you? Lord above, has Paddy told you anything?'

'Not really,' I replied cautiously, not wanting to land my new employer in trouble with his mum but rather irritated, at the same time, that during the entire journey in from the train station he hadn't thought to mention that there would be tourists tramping through my new home. It looked like Hollowpark Hall wasn't exactly going to be the deserted rural idyll I had imagined, but then again – I walked across the hall, the echo of my footsteps only emphasising the emptiness – it didn't look like they were beating the tourists away with sticks either. Still though, I thought, as I stuffed the leaflet into my pocket, I would have appreciated a heads-up.

Delia tutted. 'Never mind, I'll explain as we go. 'Tis early days anyway, we've a while to go before we are fully open.'

'It's no problem,' I reassured her, then turned to check out the rest of the cavernous hall. On the wall opposite the table, a giant marble fireplace contained only a vase and some dried flowers while the mirror above it reflected the countless paintings and portraits that lined both the hall and the staircase. They were mostly standard issue, country house stuff, women in long dresses and men puffed up by wine and their own importance, and there were plenty of pictures of animals too, dogs and horses, many of which had been placed closer to eye level than their human counterparts. But as I looked closer I could see gaps as well, rectangles of brightness on the wallpaper indicating where paintings had been removed while the paper itself, moss green with a raised gold pattern, was torn in places.

The hall was cold too. The flagstones I'd first noticed from the upper storey were dramatic to look at but I doubted underfloor heating had been invented when they were first laid, while the ceilings were so high, I had to crane my neck to see the elaborate cornicing and huge, dusty chandeliers. I lowered my gaze again and continued my look around. A scuffed pink sofa, or a chaise longue I supposed I should call it, stood in front of a glass-fronted cabinet, empty apart from what looked like rolls of old wallpaper. The whole place, in fact, gave off the vibe of a large but rather rundown hotel but I could tell by the look on Delia's face that she wouldn't have appreciated the comparison and instead made pleased noises about how authentic everything looked, which elicited another beaming smile.

'Come this way, so.'

I followed her across the hall and through a door, twice as high as one you'd find in a suburban house and—

'Bloody hell.'

It wasn't the most dignified response I could have come up with but judging by the grin on Delia's face, she found it flattering.

'Quite something, isn't it? I'm glad you like it. This would have been the drawing room, back in the day.'

'It's incredible.'

I fell silent then and allowed myself to simply wander around the room, occasionally reaching out my hand then snatching it back when I saw the many 'Do Not Touch' signs. I wouldn't be bringing little Skye in here on rainy days, anyway. Every surface, from the grand piano to the display cabinets, was crammed with stuff: ornaments, candlesticks, even leather-bound books that looked like they belonged in the Long Room in Trinity College or somewhere equally prestigious. Although generously proportioned, this room was much warmer than the hall, thanks to the sunlight streaming in through the floor-to-ceiling windows, while the selection of brightly coloured rugs on the restored and polished wooden floor gave it a cheerful and much more welcoming air. There were plenty of paintings here too, including a vast canvas that covered most of one wall and showed a tall, fierce-looking man with greying hair curling gently over his ears. He had been painted in partial profile, leaving one side of his face almost completely hidden, and he was looking through a window – possibly, I realised as I looked closer, the one in this very room.

Delia noticed my interest.

'That's Paul Fitzmahon,' she said, walking over to join me. 'Handsome man, wasn't he? He'd be Paddy's great-great – oh, I can never remember how many greats – great-grandfather. Don't you think there's a look of my Paddy about him?'

I squinted, but could see nothing in the haughty bearing and thin, rather weak mouth that reminded me of my new employer. However I had dealt with enough mammies to know what they liked to hear so gave Delia an enthusiastic 'yeah, totally' before turning to take another look around the room again. A fireplace caught my eye and I walked over to it. Now this *was* gorgeous, almost as tall as I was, and made from black iron with winged angels depicted on each side and an ornate flower design across the top. Beside it sat the cosiest armchair I had ever seen, green velvet with a high back, padded arms and a deep seat that practically demanded you sank into it with a book in one hand and a glass of something ruby-coloured in the other. Delia noticed my interest and smiled approvingly.

'You have good taste, Grace! Well spotted. That's an original piece from the house. It has been re-covered a good few times, of course, but I'm pretty sure the ladies have been plonking their behinds on there for hundreds of years.'

I could stay here for hours, I realised, examining ornaments, looking at pictures, just nosing around. The room contained no trace of the spookiness I had felt upstairs either, it was a museum rather than a home and despite the antiques and original furnishings, contained no real echo of the people who must once have used it for afternoon tea.

Delia ran her fingertip along the top of a sideboard and frowned as she scrutinised the dusty residue.

'When we are up and running, we'll give the tour groups a history of the family in this room. Maybe you'll be able to take a group yourself, Grace!'

I gave what I hoped was a non-committal smile. Delia seemed lovely, but Isla and Patrick were my employers, and I'd only be taking instructions from them. Time to change the subject.

'Do you think you'll have many visitors?'

Delia shrugged. 'I hope so. I used to give tours on an informal basis, I'd show anyone around if they gave me a bit of notice, but it was only when Paddy came home for good that we decided to make a real go of it. This was the first room we worked on and in here...'

I follow her through a connecting door into the next room while she continued talking.

'Is the second. It's a work in progress really, but this will always be my favourite.'

I could see why. This room lacked the wow factor of the first, it was smaller, with fewer items of furniture, but it was incredibly elegant, with flower-print paper on the walls and a dainty writing desk and chair in the corner. There was another, smaller, fireplace here too, on top of which perched a gorgeous blue-patterned vase.

'This would have been the lady's sitting room,' Delia told me, lifting the vase, blowing away more dust before setting it down again. 'The women would have retired here after dinner, to play the piano maybe or just have a chat away

from the men. And this' – she opened yet another door – 'is
what they used to call the Great Room.'

'I can see why,' I responded, immediately struck by the
room's massive proportions and heavy velvet drapes that
blocked any sense of a sunny September afternoon and
plunged us straight back into a far more formal era. But
Delia checked her watch and kept on walking, and I had
only time to clock a massive shiny dining table and another
dramatic chandelier before she turned on her heel and
beckoned me to follow her back through the interconnecting
doors and out into the hall again.

'And now I'll show you the work in progress.'

I had to trot to keep up as she headed to the back of
the hall, opened yet another heavy wooden door and strode
through, allowing a steady stream of chatter to flow over
her shoulder.

'We don't bring the tours back here yet, for obvious
reasons, but it's very exciting – are we OK to come in, Jack?'

There was a smaller, newer door at the end of the
corridor that had been propped open with what looked
like a wastepaper basket, and Delia hopped over it without
breaking stride.

'Are you decent?'

She turned to me and gave me a surprisingly lascivious
wink.

'Sure, whether you are or not, we're here now. Come on,
Grace, I'll introduce you to the professor.'

I followed her inside, but I was only able to take a couple
of steps before my nose began to prickle and I gave three
violent sneezes in quick succession. Well, it was inevitable
in a house like this, I supposed. I don't have the type of

allergies that make you carry an EpiPen or anything serious like that but I don't do well with dusty carpets or house pets. In recent years my sensitive nose had been kept in check by hot, dry Greek summers and lots of salty sea swimming but here in Lisheeha it was clear that the piles of artefacts – or let's face it, junk – coupled with the damp Irish weather could make me very miserable if I didn't do something about it. I wiped my eyes, which had already begun to stream, and looked around the room. No, I should really avoid rooms like this altogether, the place was literally crammed with boxes and files, some stuffed onto shelves, others stacked haphazardly on the floor, and you could actually see the dust mites float in the air and resettle themselves around us as we moved. But my quick tour of the house had only ignited my curiosity and at that moment all I wanted to do was nose around, even if my respiratory system would pay for it later.

'Good afternoon, Delia.'

The tall man unfolded himself from his perch on the side of a large wooden table and walked towards us, hands outstretched. He was a little older than Patrick's mum, I thought, and had an impressive shock of white hair, but he held himself as erect as a soldier and there was a definite look of strict schoolteacher about his frown.

'Jack, meet Grace.'

I returned the handshake as quickly as I could before rummaging in my pocket for a handkerchief. Delia smiled at us.

'Grace is the new nanny; I was just giving her the grand tour. And Jack here is our resident historian.'

'Ah now, Delia...'

He shook his head in mock humility but it was hard to ignore how his chest had swelled with pride at her words.

'Strictly amateur, I'm afraid, my background is in science – I taught in the boys' school in Lisheeha for over forty years.'

I silently congratulated myself on my guesswork as he continued.

'But I've always been fascinated by this house and we – that's the Lisheeha historical society, by the way' – he gave the words as much weight as if they were an Oxford College – 'we're a small group, we meet once a week in the library, but we have made it our business to document the history of Hollowpark Hall and Delia here has been more than generous with her access to documents.'

''Tis you that is doing us the favour, Jack.' Delia reached out and patted his arm, then turned to me. 'My in-laws were awful hoarders, God bless them. You should see the stuff we took down from the attics when Paddy's grandmother died. Some of it was pure useless, the poor woman must have kept every bill since the foundation of the State. But there was some amazing stuff too, maps from when the house was built, receipts from the purchase of cattle going back hundreds of years. Jack is going to write a book, aren't you?'

'Oh well now, I don't know about that...'

By now his chest had expanded so far, the historian looked like a budgie my grandmother had kept in the corner of her sitting room and I was grateful for another sneeze as an excuse to hide my grin. Fair play to Delia, I thought. She might have looked like the presenter of a 1980s cookery show, but she knew how to turn on the charm all right.

'You'll have a cup of tea?'

Jack beamed.

'That would be lovely. I'll just finish up here.'

'Take your time.'

Delia wriggled past a large pile of boxes and brushed dust from her jeans.

'You know where to find us. We're almost finished ourselves anyway – now, Grace, tell me what you think of this!'

She flung open an interconnecting door I hadn't noticed before and I followed her through then gasped, in genuine admiration.

'Oh. It's beautiful.'

Now it was Delia's turn to grin.

'This is the library, of course. You should have seen the state of it last year, but Paddy and I almost broke our backs getting it ready and, to be honest, I think it was worth it.'

'Oh, it was, it really was.'

Leaving Jack and his manuscripts behind us, I walked in after her and began to move slowly around the gorgeous, light-filled room. It was just that sort of place: you couldn't dash through it, it demanded attention, even reverence. Bookshelves stretched from floor to ceiling, creating a warm womb of dark wood and leather bindings. There was even one of those amazing ladders that could be slid across the floor in order to access the highest shelves and when I touched it, it moved forward gently and noiselessly under my hand, clearly restored and oiled to perfection. There were chairs everywhere too, proper deep leather ones designed for sinking into, as well as several modern-looking sofas.

'You're welcome in here any time you like,' Delia told

me, pointing towards a smaller, neater bookshelf filled with paperbacks including, to my delight, what looked like a complete Agatha Christie collection.

'Hollowpark isn't a museum, I want this to be a proper working library and it needs to be used. I'm hoping overnight visitors will really enjoy it. When the house is finished, we'll encourage them to relax in here in the evenings... Oh yes!'

She must have noticed my look of surprise.

'Paddy is full of ideas, Grace! We're just doing daytime tours at the moment but the eventual plan is to rent out the house to groups at weekends, maybe even for weddings if we get it all up to scratch. I mean, we're a long way off that yet, we've made a start upstairs, there's your room, obviously, and the bathroom down the corridor, but other than that we haven't really made much headway. But we'll get there eventually. Let's go out this way, so...'

I followed her across the room and out a set of French doors that led us into a section of the garden I hadn't seen before, then down a set of steps which led to a manicured lawn. Ahead of us was a wild field and in the distance, what looked like a tall hedgerow. But my mind was still on what Delia had just told me.

'Are you saying mine is the only finished bedroom in the main house?'

'So far!'

Delia gave a cheerful smile.

'Isla and Patrick have been talking about getting an au pair or a nanny for a while, so they worked on that room first. Isn't it lovely! It's not en suite, of course, that wasn't a priority back when this house was built, but you have that bathroom on the landing all to yourself, the fittings are very high spec, they ordered it all from Dublin.'

But I had more on my mind now than power showers.

'So where do you live? And Isla and Patrick?'

Delia pointed to her right, to where what looked like a newer wing of the house had been attached to the original building.

'I've a flat over the kitchen. Paddy and Isla live in the Gate House, you can't see it from here but it's quite near the driveway where you came in. Don't worry! You'll get the lie of the land soon enough.'

But I was only half listening to her. Instead I was thinking of a long, dark corridor and a face in the mirror that, even though I knew I had imagined it, was still flickering at the edge of my mind.

'So I'm alone? Upstairs, I mean – in that part of the house?'

'Yes, my darling!'

Delia gave me a cheerful smile.

'Sure, that's not a problem, is it? You'll be over in the Gate House most of the day anyway, minding little Skye, you'll probably be dying for a bit of peace come evening time. We'll get you a telly and we'll insure you on the two cars too, you'll be able to come and go as you please.'

Her positivity was infectious, and I shook off any lingering doubts about my new accommodation. That was what I had come to Ireland for, wasn't it? A bit of peace and quiet, time to think? After all, I had lived in every sort of room over the past eight years, converted attic bedrooms, brand new en suite guestrooms, and rooms beside nurseries where crying babies were just that bit more audible to me than to their parents on the other side of the landing. Here, it seemed, I was about to have the entire first floor of a stately home to myself and it would be idiotic, surely, to complain about that.

'Yes, it will be—'

But before I could respond properly, the sky darkened and within seconds a fat drop of rain had splatted onto my nose. Delia pulled her cardigan firmly around her.

'Right so, I think that's enough sightseeing for one day. We'll go back and make dinner – the others will be here soon. It'll take you a while to get your bearings all right, but I do hope you will be happy here. We have great plans for the place, and I do hope you will be part of them. I know you have tonnes of experience, but you won't have worked in a haunted house before, I'll bet!'

'I'm sorry – what did you say?'

Despite the rain I stopped short, and Delia burst out laughing.

'A haunted house! Ah now, you don't think a place this size would be without a few spooky stories, do you? Your face, Grace, you're a tonic, you really are. Sure, there's plenty of stories I can tell you about this place, and we'll have plenty of time to do it this winter. But come in now out of the rain and I'll get you some tea.'

The rain was hitting us squarely in the face now and we both put our heads down and began to sprint for the nearest door.

Chapter 13

1847

A fat flake fell on the ground in front of him, and Ciarán lifted his head to allow the snow to fall onto his face, then extended his tongue to absorb the moisture. He hadn't stopped to drink all day and, as the water filled his mouth, he felt briefly invigorated. But within seconds his thin shirt was soaked through and misery overwhelmed him again. He had been walking since daybreak and was in no way sure he would be able to reach his destination. And then he reached the crest of the hill and saw below him the tall oak tree that marked the entrance to Hollowpark Hall, and suddenly his steps became lighter, the cold that had seeped into his bones a little more bearable. He could keep going now, surely. He was nearly home.

The bundle in his arms was feather light but he was so weak it still took effort to hold it close, and when he occasionally shifted it upwards to further secure his grip, each movement sent stabs of pain through his joints. But pain was part of him now and, as he staggered along, Ciarán found himself almost wondering at it, examining it dispassionately to see

how bad it would get and how much more he could cope
with. Keep going. Nearly home. Ciarán bent over the damp
bundle, afraid of what he would see when he pulled back the
cloth, but although the small face was milk pale, almost grey,
his daughter's lips were moist and rosy and her tiny chest still
rose and fell. Keep going. If the daughter could keep going
then so too could the father. He lengthened his stride, the
increased movement bringing fresh tears to his eyes, but at
least the discomfort drove everything else out of his mind, at
least it kept him from remembering—

'Maa.'

And then the baby's soft, lamb-like bleat brought those
memories flooding back, as sharp and painful as the stones
beneath his bare feet.

It had been four years since Ciarán O'Mahony had last
seen Hollowpark Hall, but the sense of desolation he felt on
the day he left was still fresh and sharp in his mind. When
Mr Fitzmahon, or Deirdre's father as he had always privately
referred to him, had died, his nephew Paul had moved onto
the estate. While it wasn't perhaps surprising that he chose
to bring some of his own staff with him, Ciarán's father,
who had provided almost a lifetime of loyal service to the
Hall, had been heartbroken to be told that he would have
to leave the only home his family had ever known. Ciarán,
his brothers and his parents wheeled their possessions away
in a cart less than a week later and, when Ciarán caught
sight of his childhood friend Deirdre moving into what he
had always thought of as 'his' gatehouse, it was hard to say
which of the two of them looked more unhappy.

For a while, however, the O'Mahonys managed to live,
if not as comfortable a life as they had in Hollowpark,

then a relatively contented one. Ciarán's eldest brother was already married by the time they left the hall, to Deirdre's former maid, and he moved to live near her family while Ciarán's father bought a small plot of land in his own home village to be subdivided between his other children when their time came to settle down.

In fact, when Ciarán met Mary Sullivan, it seemed for a while that the move from Hollowpark had been the best thing that could have happened to him. They were married within weeks and, for the next year lived not in luxury but surrounded by love and happiness.

And then one day Ciarán sliced a spade through the small potato patch at the side of his cabin and all that emerged was a sodden, reeking mass. He rushed to the shed, a small wooden construction that divided his home from his parents', but the unearthly fog that hung over it told him, before he even opened the door, that those potatoes were rotten too. How quickly life could be drained from a place when there was nothing substantial to sustain it! Ciarán and his family had not been wealthy, but they had had a home, and neighbours, food, warmth and companionship. Less than a year later they were worse off than the animals in the fields, and competing with them for whatever sustenance they could forage. Ciarán's brother and sister-in-law had been the first to die, and then his mother, famine fever ripping through their homes as quickly as the blight had ripped through their fields. His father had left then, taking his third son with him, on a journey ostensibly to find food but mostly, Ciarán believed, because he felt that walking for as long as he could bear was easier than sitting and waiting for death to find him. There had been no time for goodbyes, and no emotion left anyway because by then his own world had shrunk to Mary and the child growing in her empty belly. His foraging grew more desperate and he ventured further from home, following rumours of bread in one town, public works in another... It was all for nothing, in the end.

The child in his arms gave another whimper. Or almost nothing. Ciarán shook his head, gathered whatever scraps of determination he could find and clutched them to him. His daughter lived, and he still had a chance to save her.

He had left them alone, that was the thought that haunted his every waking moment. Following the birth of the baby, and driven almost beyond reason by hunger and fear, Ciarán had left Mary and the infant behind in their tiny cabin and gone in search of food, returning less than a week later with half a loaf of bread in his pocket and the glow of hope that it would be enough to save them. But when he opened the door and announced his return to his wife there had been no answer, just a stench so thick it was almost tangible, which sent him stumbling backwards into the yard. He had stayed there for a moment, afraid to go back into the house because to do so would make the horror real. But then not knowing became worse than knowing so Ciarán had pushed open the door again and walked across the rush floor to the tall bed, hoping against all reason that it was the smell of illness and not death that permeated their home. That hope had been extinguished when he saw his wife's face and then, dear Jesus, the space at the side where the rest of the face should have been, and heard the satisfied squeak of the rat as it raised its face from its meal and looked at him with a squatter's insolence before giving its tail a lazy flick and lowering its jaws again—

'Maaa.'

The sound had been so tiny he almost missed it, and then it had come again. Ciarán had held his breath, reached over to that terrible figure in the bed and drawn back the covers. And she had looked up at him, not another corpse but a living thing, his baby daughter, her eyelids flickering as the light hit them. A scrap of humanity tethered to the earth by embers of heat from her dead mother's breast. Ciarán had lifted the little body away from his wife and made a promise to both of them there and then that, even if he hadn't been able to keep the mother safe, he would cherish the life of their child.

Keep going. A stone dug into Ciarán's big toe and he stumbled, but his grip on the baby in his arms was so tight she didn't move. Keep going. He rounded the corner and, when the shadow of the Big House fell over them, felt for the first time in a long time a flicker of optimism. Home. Ciarán had never set foot inside Hollowpark Hall itself yet had always felt he belonged there. As a child, he and his brothers had been free to roam the estate, climb the trees and, best of all, explore the large maze to the west of the main building, the maintenance of which caused his father pride and heartache in equal measure. It was there he had played with Deirdre and, although they had grown apart as they grew older, he had always felt he was just as much a part of the estate as she was. Surely some element of that bond remained?

The child in his arms whimpered again and there was a desperation to the sound now that had not been there before. She needed food, and Ciarán sensed an anger in her, a rising indignation that pulled from him a sense of pride.

She had fought so hard to stay with him, he would not, could not let her down.

Hollowpark Hall protects its own.

Ciarán remembered Deirdre's words as he approached the huge wooden door of the house, as familiar and comforting as his own mother's face. That was why he had come here, that was why he had walked for miles, on ripped and bloody feet. He had thought it was a fairy story but there was nothing left in the land but fairy stories to sustain them now. Paul Fitzmahon was not known to be a generous man, it was true, in fact Ciarán had a memory of a day in the maze long ago, a childish fight and a strange resolution – but they had only been children, then. Surely all of that would be forgotten, when Paul saw how desperate he was? Surely no Fitzmahon would turn an O'Mahony from the door...

He was at that door now and, as it opened with a creak, Ciarán lifted his head, reminding himself to look friendly, not threatening. He was a visitor, that was all, a friend in need but a friend, nonetheless. He had planned to go around the back to see if any of the servants would take pity on him but now the front door was fully open and maybe that was a good thing? Look, here was Paul Fitzmahon himself coming towards him, it was a sign, it must have been, that help was now on its way. Reaching out his hands, Ciarán spoke in English.

'Please, sir, and can you help me, sir, the baby—'

The pain from the kick was worse than any other pain because it brought with it shock and, immediately afterwards, stinging disappointment. Ciarán kept the bundle clutched tightly in his arms, forcing his limbs into an awkward position to save her and, in doing so, scraped the skin from his knees and ankles as he tumbled down the unforgiving stone steps. He lay at the bottom then, winded and heartbroken, and glanced up at the man who had struck out at him. The look of distaste on Paul Fitzmahon's face was unmistakable and, in that second, Ciarán saw himself as the bigger man saw him, a stinking skeleton in ragged clothes. And then he saw something else behind the anger – fear.

'Get off my land.'

There was a shake in the voice but then the man rushed downward and kicked out again, and Ciarán groaned and curled up into a ball, trying to protect the child. But maybe the man didn't fully remember him?

'Mr Fitzmahon, Paul, I'm Ciarán O'Mahony, I...'

But his words had deserted him and so Ciarán opened his shirt and, still lying on the ground, held the infant out towards the man. The hard eyes flickered. And then Ciarán saw in Paul Fitzmahon's face an echo of how he himself had felt when he saw the rat: hatred, disgust and overwhelming urge to be rid of a monster. Without giving the young master the chance to strike again he hauled himself up off the ground and began to run back down the driveway, stumbling and weaving, only dimly aware that Paul Fitzmahon was yelling at him and warning him never to return. He did not stop running until he rounded the corner and then, Hollowpark now no longer visible behind him, Ciarán sank to his knees and pulled the bundle away from him, knowing that she and she alone could give him the courage to continue. But when he eased back the blanket he saw that, although the blue eyes were open, the little chest had fallen still.

Chapter 14

2007

'So, this is where I "hang out" as the kids say.'

There was a massive Aga pumping out heat from the corner of the kitchen and I exhaled happily as blood started to flow through my veins again. Welcome back to Ireland, Grace! In the space of six hours I'd experienced warm sunshine, thick cloud and heavy rain and whatever about Kansas, I certainly wasn't in Greece any more. Delia nodded towards the heavy wooden table that stood in the centre of the room.

'Sit down there now and I'll put the kettle on.'

Part of me wondered if I should be offering to make tea myself – I was there to work, after all, and most of my London employers would have thought nothing of making use of me straight off the plane. There was one couple who started giving me orders before I even took my jacket off. He was a forty-five-year-old, outrageously rich and notoriously tight-fisted banker and she his twenty-eight-year-old second wife. When she left him – and her stepchildren – just a month into my contract I took great pleasure in doubling my fee to 'save him the inconvenience' of finding someone new. But Delia seemed pretty fond of the whole hosting business, so I decided to do what I was told and sank down onto one of the kitchen chairs that sat on either side of the table, which had been covered with an oilcloth that reached almost to the ground.

Other than its size, this room couldn't have been more different to the rest of Hollowpark Hall. There were no oil paintings here, no antique furniture and no flagstones. In fact, we were sitting in a surprisingly modern kitchen lined with what looked like brand-new appliances and a tiled floor that, judging by the rate at which my feet were thawing out, had some very non-traditional underfloor heating installed. Directly across from where I was sitting was a living space complete with squashy red sofa, a reclining chair and an impressively large wall mounted TV, and I could tell that when Delia said she 'hung out' here, she really meant it. And I liked her style.

'I redecorated when I knew Paddy was coming home,' she said, as if reading my mind. 'I thought he and Isla might move in here, and that they'd need a bit of comfort, coming from London and that. But Isla prefers the Gate House, so they've set themselves up over there. They'll bring you over later, no doubt; that's where you'll be looking after Skye.'

Delia filled the kettle, plugged it in then opened a cupboard over her head but was interrupted by a scrabbling sound at the door. Opening it, she was nearly knocked over by a pack of dogs who pushed against her, nibbled at her apron, looked pleadingly at her and did everything to ask for food short of sitting down at the table with napkins tucked into their collars.

'Ah, would ye ever give over.'

Delia shoved the dogs aside, but gently, as if this was a pantomime they had gone through many times before.

'Ye just had to get in on the act, didn't ye! Get DOWN!'

But she couldn't keep the smile off her face as she lifted what looked like a bowl of scraps off the kitchen counter and waved it at them.

'You'd swear ye weren't fed from one end of the day to the other. Get DOWN, will ye?'

She opened the back door again and emptied the bowl into a number of smaller containers that were lying in the yard, then came back in and pointed the dogs towards them. As the bigger ones did a comedy-style scramble to see who could get out of the door first, one little guy detached himself from the pack, slid under the table and sat down beside my foot. I could actually feel him shake with nerves, poor fella – he was tiny in comparison with the rest of the hounds. There were actually only three of them, I realised now, four if you counted my little pal, but the others were huge, lolloping things and even though the tone in Delia's voice told me they were completely harmless, I was guessing my little buddy often lost out when it came to dinner time. I put my hand down under the table and he gave it a tentative lick, then cuddled in, close to my ankle.

''Tis like a mad house here at the best of times, Grace.'

Delia shook her head in mock indignation.

'The dogs would live in your ear if you let them, but we do try and keep them outside. This is a working house, always was. We love our animals, but they belong in the yard, or the fields. I don't like dogs in the house, never did, and the smell! Lord have mercy. You can see how hard we're working to get the place up to scratch, and I just can't be dealing with dog hair everywhere, I'm sure you'll understand. Back in Paddy's grandfather's day, you couldn't lower your backside on to a chair without sitting on some sort of creature, but times have changed.'

My nose prickled in sympathy, my allergies meant I could never live with animals which was a pain in the arse when it came to choosing live-in jobs, although one family were so desperate to get an English-speaking nanny they'd offered to get rid of two cats and a hamster just to secure my services. I'd turned them down, figuring anyone who could get rid of their pets that easily mightn't have much sympathy when it came their children either – or, indeed, their staff. But the little warm body at my feet felt so comforting, I figured I'd let him stay for a little while and pop an extra antihistamine before bed. I'm solitary by nature – I've had to be, moving around so much – but it might be nice, this deep in the countryside, to have a friend.

With a grunt Delia shoved the oldest and slowest dog out of the door, closed it behind him and went back to the sink to rinse her hands. Then she made tea and carried my mug and a packet of biscuits over to the table and as she turned back towards the fridge again I slid out a HobNob and dropped it down to my new friend. I was rewarded with another lick, then felt him settle down at the top of my foot, his breath warming my ankle, his little body completely hidden from the lady of the house by the long tablecloth. Delia was still at the fridge, fussing about finding a milk jug, and I took the opportunity to sneak a look at him. He was a gorgeous little mite with short bristly hair and soft brown eyes that looked up at me, practically begging me not to throw him out in the rain. I scratched his head, signalling he'd be OK, for a while anyway. I shouldn't have done it, of course. It was Delia's house, Delia's rules but something about the little animal made me want to mind him, and maybe be a little bit minded in return.

Finally abandoning her search, Delia brought over a carton of milk and came to sit opposite me. The kitchen was so cosy, it was easy to forget we were sitting in a stately home and I felt comfortable asking a few more questions.

'Have you a lot of animals, then? You mentioned cattle earlier, I think?'

She nodded, then took a large drink of tea.

'That's better! I was parched. We do indeed, we've a small dairy herd, nothing to what it would have been like years ago, of course, but Paddy is talking about building it up again. He loves being out on the land, he used to spend hours out there with his granddad, God be good to him. Patrick senior was no farmer, mind, he had a manager to do all of the hard work, but he liked keeping an eye on things. To the Manor Born, we used to call him down in the village, and young Paddy was like his shadow at times.'

She sipped her tea again. The warmth of the kitchen seemed to have softened her and I couldn't resist the opportunity to do a bit more digging. I'd be living with the Fitzmahons for months, maybe more, and I knew from experience that forewarned was forearmed when it came to even the nicest families.

'Are you from around here yourself, then?'

'Oh yes, Lisheeha born and bred.' Delia flashed a rather wicked grin. 'We caused quite the scandal back in the day, you know! Rory was supposed to marry one of his own crowd, a nice Protestant lady from Dublin, or London even, but instead he ended up with the girl next door. Well, from across the fields, actually, but as far as his mother was concerned it was the same thing, and she wasn't a bit pleased about it.'

My ankle received another lick and I decided to keep her talking, not least to protect my new buddy who clearly didn't wanted to be turfed out into the cold with his older, hardier companions. Delia, meanwhile, settled into the story in a way that implied she had told it many times before.

'The way Mrs Fitzmahon went on you'd swear it was *Upstairs Downstairs* or something and that I was the scullery maid. I mean fair enough, a lot of the girls from the village did help out up here from time to time when they needed a few bob but the fact of the matter was, my father was the local chemist and I would have been considered quite the catch myself back in the day! But unless they had three surnames and didn't pronounce their haitches, nobody was going to be good enough for Ruth Fitzmahon's blue-eyed boy. Rory got his way in the end though.'

She gave a snorted laugh. 'He usually did.'

Delia looked down for a moment, a flicker of some emotion I couldn't quite place passing over her face. And then her expression cleared again and she gave me one of her warm, generous smiles.

'You should have seen the place in those days, Grace! It was gorgeous. Rory's parents, Patrick and Ruth, really loved Hollowpark and they knew how to make full use of it. You remember the Great Room, where I brought you earlier? Well, they could have had thirty, forty people in there for a sit-down meal. Other times they'd have a Hunt

Ball, or a New Year's Eve party – there would be up to a hundred guests then, even more sometimes, they'd come from Dublin, London, all over. Rory, that's Paddy's dad, he was away at school, of course, but he came home for the holidays and that's how we met. He was a beautiful man.'

Her smile dimmed for a moment and she grew more thoughtful.

'We don't call men beautiful usually, do we? But Rory was. Paddy is like him, but Rory had a slighter build and these long fingers – I used to think he could have been on television, could have done anything really, if he'd pushed himself. But that wasn't his way.'

She lifted a hand and patted down a stray hair.

'I was nineteen when we realised Paddy was on the way. Oh God, there was war when the parents found out. Mrs Fitzmahon, Ruth, was horrified, I mean she was too much of a lady to say anything to my face, but I could tell she was disgusted. All that money spent sending her son away to school in England and then he comes home and knocks up a girleen from the village! And to be honest with you my own parents were just as cross. I was a bright girl and I was supposed to go to university, maybe even follow my dad into pharmacy or something and take over the business. But sure lookit, we were kids and we couldn't be told. We got married straight away, the parish priest must have owed my father a huge favour because I was out to here' – she indicated a space halfway down her lap – 'and marrying a Prod too! Disgraceful behaviour altogether! But when young Paddy arrived they were all pure cracked about him and that was that. I got on a nursing course in Galway and my parents helped mind him while I was away. So it all worked out, really.'

I was leaning over the table now, completely drawn into the story.

'And you lived here?'

'We did indeed, in the Gate House, where Paddy and Isla are now.'

Delia stared out the kitchen window for a moment, marshalling memories.

'Ah, they were marvellous days. The parties! Rock stars and show jumpers – we had them all here, oh yes!'

She laughed at the look of shock on my face.

'I'm serious! They all loved coming here. I shared a joint with a chap once who told me he was just back from *Top of the Pops*. I can't say the joint did much for me, only made me feel sick, but I wasn't going to say no to him now, was I? Rory even talked about building a recording studio in one of the stables at one stage, maybe that would have been a smart thing to do, but sure there wasn't the money in the end.'

'Bloody good thing too.'

We both started as a door that I hadn't noticed before, at the opposite end of the kitchen, was flung open and Jack, Delia's pet historian, walked in. She patted her hair and looked over at him.

'Did your mammy never tell you not to be listening at doors? Come in here now and have a cup of tea. I have poor Grace bored to tears with all my old yarns.'

'Quite the opposite,' I reassured her as Jack pulled up a chair. 'I'm dying to hear more. So...' I turned to Jack, who was vigorously stirring sugar into his drink. 'You don't think the recording studio would have been a good idea, then?'

'Absolutely not!'

He gave a theatrical eye-roll.

'There were enough oddballs hanging around the place in those days, you didn't want to be drawing any more of them down on top of you.'

'Could have made us a fortune though,' Delia muttered, looking at him over her mug. Then she sighed.

'You're probably right though, Rory would have loved every minute of it but there would have been no question of him collecting bills on time or anything like that. Anyway – his dad died then and sure, that was that really.'

She paused, and I muttered, 'I'm sorry to hear it,' more to fill the gap than anything else. After a moment Delia shook her head and seemed to pull her thoughts back from the past.

'It was a shock all right. My Paddy was only eight years old when it happened. Patrick senior took a massive heart attack, just out the front there, on the lawn. The Fitzmahons all have weak hearts, a good few of the men have gone that way, well before their time. I've told my Paddy several times to get himself checked out but sure, he thinks he's invincible. He was devastated when his granddad died, though. Patrick senior was only sixty-three, but he'd enjoyed life, if you know what I mean.'

She waggled her wrist, the international sign for heavy drinking.

'My mother-in-law was glad to have me around then, I can tell you. There was no more talk of Rory having married beneath him. Poor woman, Ruth was a lady but she had never done anything for herself, Patrick senior had handled all the money – not particularly well, as it happened! And as for Rory...'

She flashed Jack a look.

'I'm not giving away any secrets when I say that Rory Fitzmahon was not the type to settle down. You won't remember it, Jack, you were a married man at that stage, but the parties got wilder when Rory was the man of the house.'

'Oh, I remember all right.'

Jack gave a sudden grin that showed too many teeth. I didn't like him, I realised, although I wasn't quite sure why.

Delia continued.

'I loved the bones of that man, but he hadn't a clue how to be a grown-up. It was exhausting, to tell you the truth, Grace. I had a small child and I was getting up for work every morning but sure you wouldn't know who you'd find on the sofa when you came down to make a cup of tea!'

It was all starting to sound a bit too close to my own upbringing for my liking and I gave Delia a sympathetic smile.

'We had people arriving for the night and staying for a week, or longer. Fellas escaping from their wives and young ones looking for a bit of freedom. It's hard to believe now, Grace, but you couldn't even get condoms in Ireland until the 1990s, and even then only in the big cities. Hollowpark was a place where people felt they could do whatever they wanted. Oh, it could be great fun, we met the most extraordinary people and young Paddy ran wild in the middle of it. He had the most marvellous childhood, he went to school in the village and his friends used to come up here and ride the ponies, play football, watch TV. They had so much space, you see, in comparison to their own houses. So even though he was an only child, this place was always full of kids and life and fun. But it was exhausting, trying to keep the show on the road, and then one day I found out all the money was gone, and that was the end of that.'

She put her mug down on the table with a decisive thud, and the little dog at my feet twitched, then settled down again.

'Gone?'

I'd been listening so intently I had almost forgotten that these were real people she had been talking about – real people, living in this real house. But the look on Delia's face now told me that it was no fairy tale.

'Every penny.' She smiled, wearily. 'Rory spent the lot. They were great hosts, the Fitzmahons, but bloody useless businessmen. Patrick senior had a few investments, which Rory inherited, but he hadn't a clue how to manage money. Hadn't the wit to ask for help either, the big eejit. He financed half the daft schemes in the country and didn't get a penny in return.'

'You kept this place going.'

Jack looked across at her, admiration clear in his voice. Delia tucked a strand of hair behind her ear.

'I did, I suppose.'

She smiled at him, then looked at me again.

'I had to ask my own father for a loan in the end. He had retired at that stage and had sold his business. It wasn't easy, but I asked him, for Paddy's sake, not my own. Hollowpark is Paddy's home, his birthright, I suppose you'd call it, and I couldn't stand the thought of it having to be sold.'

I was surprised at the stricken look on her face.

'Were things really that bad?'

She nodded. 'Rory was gambling, too. I only found out how bad things were towards the end. You know, Grace, people talk about drinking being a curse, and indeed it can be, but at the end of the day you can only drink until you fall over, whereas you can gamble till every penny is gone and then move on to the roof over your head.'

She held up her hand, finger and thumb a nail's breadth apart.

'We were this close to losing everything. So I took Dad's money, and I paid off the debts and we moved in here.'

She waved her hand around the kitchen.

'This used to be the main kitchen for the house, with staff accommodation upstairs, but the staff all had to be let go, of course. We shut up the Gate House, and most of the main house too, and the four of us moved in here, me and Rory, Paddy and Ruth, Rory's mam. All of us in the three upstairs bedrooms.'

She jerked her head towards the ceiling.

'Paddy went off to England then, a grand-uncle of Rory's paid for the school fees. I hated seeing him go but it was a damn sight better than him being squashed in here with us. And poor Mrs Fitz didn't last long after her husband, she got cancer, poor woman, and died before her seventieth birthday.'

'Oh my God.'

I looked around the kitchen again. Forget about the main house, this room alone had seen more drama than any other place I'd ever lived in. Delia was lost in thought now, seemingly determined to see the story through to the end.

'We had offers to buy Hollowpark, of course, but I didn't want to sell, I couldn't do that to Paddy. It was his home, I wasn't going to be the generation who let it go. So I took what was left of Dad's money and I started to claw things back. We did up the Great Room first and then we got a small grant to do the driveway as well and I started the tours, just locals at first, school visits, that sort of thing, coach parties that were travelling this way anyway. I did everything myself, showed the house, made tea, sorted the paperwork. I sold some of the paintings, a few bits of furniture – I hated doing it, as you can imagine, it was like selling Paddy's heritage. But I did what I could to keep the place going. Then we had a stroke of luck – I heard that a film company were looking for a place to make a movie. A ghost story, can you believe it?'

I could believe it only too well, I thought, thinking back to the long corridor that led to my bedroom and the face in the bathroom mirror that had absolutely, definitely not been there.

'You and your ghosts.'

Jack snorted and Delia reached out and tapped him on the hand.

'Now listen here! Those ghosts helped build that lovely library you are so fond of working in, and paid for that flat screen telly over there too!'

She grinned at me.

'I never even saw the film in the end, it was only on one of those cable channels in America, but one of the women in the village saw it on her holidays and she reckons you'd know Hollowpark all right, she said they made the place look incredibly spooky. The main thing is, by the time they had finished I'd saved enough to do up two more rooms in the main house. After that it was just a case of more grants, more hard work. And then Paddy came home, and he and Isla decided they wanted to settle here with little Skye. And that's where we are now. We'll do one last push on the renovation this winter and I'm hoping that by next summer we'll have people coming from all over again to stay in Hollowpark Hall, only this time they'll have to stick their hands in their pockets.'

She looked straight at me, a mixture of pride and determination in her eyes.

'We're not there yet, but we're getting there.'

I sat back in my chair.

'You've done an amazing job.'

Delia gave a bashful smile, but I got the feeling she was quite happy to accept a bit of verbal applause.

'It was worth it, especially now when I see young Skye running around. Another generation of Fitzmahons will grow up here, and I'm delighted. Speak of the divil!'

The kitchen door flew open and Skye ran in and headed straight for her grandmother's arms. Her father followed, accompanied by a cacophony of barks and whimpers as the dogs tried once again to get in from the cold.

'Away with ye!!'

The little bundle at my feet started at Delia's roar and, clearly realising he'd pushed his luck as far as he could, gave my foot one last lick then darted out to join the other dogs as Patrick pushed them out the door and closed it firmly in their faces. His mother looked up from over her granddaughter's blonde head.

'Isla not with ye?'

'No.'

Patrick made his way towards the sink.

'She's gone back to the Gate House for a rest, she's exhausted.'

'Oh, she must be tired all right, sitting up in that tower all day.'

I shot Delia a look but she was cuddling her granddaughter, her face as cheerful as ever, and I reckoned I must have imagined a certain sharpness in her tone.

'So, how are you finding the place, Grace?'

Filling the kettle, Patrick threw the question over his shoulder, but I was prevented from answering by a huge yawn.

'Mam's been boring you with the history of the house, has she?'

Delia didn't look offended, instead she stood up and patted me on the arm.

'You look done in, pet. I was going to make you dinner but would you rather have a nap instead?'

My answer was smothered by another yawn and the others laughed as I stood up from the table. Jack drained his tea, and came to stand beside me.

'I have to head off too. I'll show Grace the way back to her room, if you like?'

Delia pushed Skye gently off her lap and stood up too.

'That would be great, Jack, if you don't mind. And you can help me get the dinner, Paddy?'

Exhaustion certainly didn't seem to be an issue for Delia, I thought, but was too tired myself now to even contemplate staying to help so I just bid them all a muttered goodbye as I followed Jack to the back of the room. The tea and biscuits, combined with my sleepless night, had hit me like a cosh and it was all I could do to walk in a straight line as he held the door open for me and I followed him down a long, wood-panelled corridor. A small, unshaded bulb on the wall didn't do much in the way of illumination but, when I hesitated, Jack gave me another of his wide smiles.

'Don't worry, my dear, I know all the nooks and crannies around here.'

There was something really seedy about him, I decided, despite Delia's obvious affection for him, and I felt a sudden pang of sympathy for generations of secondary school students who I suspected had to put up with a lot more than 'my dear.' We reached the end of the corridor and when he pushed open a heavy wooden door I blinked as light spilled in.

'You've fallen onto your feet here, you know. You're a very lucky young lady.'

'Yeah,' I muttered and followed him through the doorway, relieved to find we were back in the familiar surroundings of the main entrance hall again.

'I'll just head off so...'

But although I turned my back on him and headed for the stairs, Jack continued talking.

'Delia is a marvellous woman.'

I was so tired I was practically weeping but politeness made me turn around again.

'Yes, she seems to be.'

'Oh she's a treasure.'

Jack's gaze took in the entirety of the hall.

'You know, this house was built in the 1700s but

sometimes I think Delia put more work into it than any of the original labourers. She really is incredible.'

He bid me good night then, and disappeared out of the front door and, as I began to drag myself up the stairs that now looked far more challenging than they had earlier on, I couldn't help wondering if Jack had a notion that he might be a good lord of the manor himself. Really, I thought as I finally reached the first-floor landing, this place couldn't be more interesting if the film makers were still in residence. And then I put all of the thoughts of the Hollowpark Soap Opera out of my mind as I stumbled down the corridor that led to my bedroom, too exhausted to do anything but remove my shoes before flopping onto the bed and passing out where I fell.

When I woke up some hours later, I found myself in a pitch-black bedroom, freezing cold, dry-mouthed and disorientated. Still fully dressed, I clambered properly under the covers but a rumble from my gut reminded me I hadn't eaten anything approximating a proper meal in days and that, despite Delia promising to include me in the family dinner, I had fallen asleep before it materialised. I rolled out of bed, pulled on my trainers, opened the door then tripped over my bags which had been left right outside. Stubbed toe aside, I was delighted to be reunited with my belongings and I rooted through the bag to find my phone and charger before plugging them in and heading off into the night again.

If Hollowpark Hall had seemed large by daylight, it was positively cavernous now and I was shivering as much from nerves as from the cold as I felt my way down the vast staircase and tried to remember the route back to the kitchen again. Thankfully, there were 'Emergency Exit' signs here and there, something to do with the grants Delia had mentioned, I presumed, but it still took me three attempts to locate the correct door. Once back in the kitchen, the clock on the microwave told me it was midnight, earlier than I had assumed, but the room held the silence that comes with everyone in earshot being asleep and I stayed on tiptoe as I moved, first towards the sink for a glass of water and then back to the fridge. I would have eaten dry bread at that stage, if not the leg of the kitchen table, but Delia, bless her, had left me a plate of sandwiches, wrapped in cling film with my name scribbled on a Post It note in case there was any confusion. Within minutes I had demolished the lot and, feeling much happier, I made my way back to my bedroom with the minimum of wrong turns, thinking of nothing other than climbing into that gorgeous bed again.

When I got there, however, I walked into the room and then paused. The room was bright, but lit by moonlight rather than electricity, even though I was sure I had left the light on and the curtains closed when I'd headed out looking for food. Then again, I'd been so sleep deprived and, let's face it, bloody ravenous when I'd set off, it was hard to remember exactly what I had done, so I shrugged off my vague sense of unease and headed over to the window, intending on drawing the curtains again. When I looked out, however, it was to see stars twinkling above my head and the thought suddenly hit me that, just twenty-four hours ago I'd been dancing up a sweat under those same stars and paddling in the Mediterranean Sea to cool down. It felt like a world away but they were the same stars, the same sky – and just like that, the vague feeling of displacement that had been nibbling at the outer edges of my consciousness disappeared, to be replaced by a sensation of intense peace. I liked Hollowpark Hall, I decided, I could make a home here. I'd been on the road for such a long time, it was time to settle down. As I continued to look out the window my gaze was drawn to a large black shape at the far end of the garden and beyond it, a tower. There was so much to see, to explore, to like about this place. Maybe I could even grow to love it in time.

I took a step backwards and then I saw, reflected in the window, a girl sitting on the edge of my bed. A pulse pounded in my temple as I stood, frozen in fear, unable to look away. It was the same girl that I'd seen in the bathroom, her shoulders slightly hunched, her hands clasped loosely in her lap. She was younger than I had first thought but it was unquestionably the same person, with a fuzz of dark hair and a solemn expression on her pale face. My hands leapt to my throat but, as if to prove I wasn't looking at some corruption of my own reflection, the girl on the bed in the window did not move. My throat dry, I found myself unable to scream, even though I desperately wanted to; instead I just stood and looked at her through that inky window, my eyes taking in what my brain refused to accept. She was there, God damn it, yet she *couldn't* have been there – and yet she was. Did ghosts – did spirits wear jeans? This one did, and a black T-shirt, and as I stared at her, her head rose slowly, slowly and as she lifted her eyes to meet mine a chill unlike anything I had ever felt before ran the length of my spine. All I wanted to do was look away but I couldn't move, not my head, not even my eyes and my skin was on fire now, nerve endings screaming, blood pounded in my head and my vision was greying...

She was gone. I blinked and, using courage I did not know I possessed, turned from the window and forced myself to look directly at the bed. It was empty. Of course, it was empty. I was alone. Of course I was. I flexed my fingers, willing the blood to begin to circulate again, and then rubbed my eyes vigorously. Of course I was alone.

But I saw her.

I saw nobody.

I turned again, pulled the curtains tight then marched towards my bed with a determination I did not feel. Sleep deprivation caused hallucinations, everyone who has ever spent time around new babies knew that.

But I saw her.

I'd make myself ill, I'd be seeing pink elephants next if I didn't get some sleep.

But I saw her.

You saw nothing, I told myself firmly as I climbed into bed and pulled the covers towards my neck. There was nothing to see.

I forced myself to go to sleep and did not dream.

Chapter 15

1848

'Sebastian, you demon!'

But the child didn't answer, just laughed and ran even faster, taking just one quick look over his shoulder before disappearing through the gap in the hedge. Paul Fitzmahon wiped sweat from his forehead then lumbered after him, last night's wine sloshing uneasily in his stomach. If only he had been able to walk alone this morning as he had planned, everything would have been fine. He could have taken the air – and a quick nip of brandy from his hip flask – then returned to his study to 'go over his accounts' and emerge when lunch was ready and his hangover napped away.

But because Nanny was busy with the twins, and the other servants occupied with that evening's dinner plans, Madeline had insisted Paul deal with their eldest child. And Madeline, lying in bed with her eyes shut tight and a sheen of sweat on her forehead, was not a woman to be crossed that morning. So Paul had removed Sebastian from his mother's side and allowed him to follow him through the Great Hall from where, dogs yapping at their ankles, they headed out into the morning drizzle. As the rain grew heavier, even the dogs had given up on the idea of a walk but Sebastian had been like a prisoner unleashed from chains and darted away from his father, straight across the lawn and into his beloved maze.

That bloody maze. His son's blond curls bobbed in front of him as he took one turn, then another but no matter how loudly Paul shouted the child refused to slow down.

'Catch me, Daddy!'

'You'll get a beating if I do,' was what Paul wanted to say in response but despite the pounding in his head he resisted the urge. Sebastian was his mother's pet and anything his father said to him would be relayed straight back to her and, given her pallor that morning, Paul would do well not to upset Madeline further. His wife had told him, vehemently and frequently, that she did not want another child but they were man and wife, for God's sake, and men had certain needs – Paul paused and coughed out an acidic burp before continuing at a slower pace – men had certain needs and now Madeline would take to her bed and those needs would not be met again for several months, if at all. Really, the whole morning could not have been more depressing.

'Catch me, Daddy!'

The boy's voice was fainter now but Paul didn't have the energy to run, instead he yelled at Sebastian to slow down but his voice was so muffled by the foliage he had no way of knowing if he had been heard or not. To be fair to her, it wasn't just Madeline's condition, nor indeed his own hangover that was causing his rotten mood. No, Paul admitted to himself, it was the meeting with his aunt and cousin the night before that had truly left him on edge. Paul had been riding home from a neighbour's house, full and mellow after a game of cards and an excellent dinner, when his horse had reared on her hind legs, almost dislodging him, then stood, trembling and reluctant to walk any further. He had coaxed, cajoled and then whipped the animal until she began to walk forward again and it was only then he had seen what had disturbed her – two black-clad women, walking arm in arm. It was his aunt and his cousin, shuffling like old women even though Deirdre was a full three years younger than he was himself and her mother barely sixty. It was no wonder the animal had been spooked, Paul thought to himself as he watched their long black skirts catch in the muddy stones of the long, winding driveway.

He had ridden past them and bade them good evening, but the older woman had ignored him and the younger had turned such a baleful gaze on him that he half expected the horse to shy again. It had taken several glasses of a very good Burgundy to get rid of the memory of it. Ungrateful witches, Paul thought. He had been more than generous to his relatives – the gatehouse was a fine building, dry and warm, and more than fulfilled the terms of his uncle's will. Yet those bloody women insisted on acting as if he had thrown them out onto the road. Madeline hated them, she dreaded other visitors seeing their long mournful faces and, perhaps, believing the commonly held view in Lisheeha that they had been treated unfairly. Paul could not stop the women from walking up the driveway, it was a common entrance from both of their homes out onto the main road. But he could and had asked them not to wander in the gardens any more. It disturbed Madeline, to see them there.

'Sebastian!'

He could do with Deirdre's knowledge of the maze now, however, he thought bleakly, as he lumbered around another corner, branches tearing at his face.

'Papa!'

The child's voice came from behind him – entirely the wrong direction to the one he had been taking – and Paul groaned.

'Come back here, stupid child!'

He turned and made his way back the way he had come, his feet sliding beneath him as the rain turned the ground to mud. This bloody maze – he'd tear it down, by Christ he could. Small black berries crunched under his feet as he trudged onwards. Tear it down, burn the branches, bloody waste of space. He had always hated it, had sore and embarrassing memories of Deirdre running around it as a child, tanned as a gypsy, and him following her and getting lost – a memory washed over him suddenly, the gardener's boy and a feeling of utter terror – damn it anyway. Paul stopped for a moment and leaned over to catch his breath. He would tear the bloody thing down. Why was he keeping it anyway? His uncle was gone, he was owner of Hollowpark now, he could do what he wanted. Once the twins were big enough, there would be three children running around here soon enough, or four, judging by Madeline's incapacitation, and what if one of them got lost in here, or injured? Madeline would blame him, of course. Yes, Paul thought as his sleeve snagged on a branch, he'd rip the bloody thing to pieces next chance he got. Encouraged by the thought, he lengthened his stride to a run and then his ankle caught a stone and twisted beneath him and he stumbled, then fell face down, his hands out in front of him, mud splashing onto his face and hair. Tear it down, by Christ he would. Blood oozed from a cut on his finger and Paul lifted it to his mouth and sucked it, trying to remove the worst of the mud and mulch. Then he rolled onto his side and groaned. The cut was deeper than he had first realised, and filthy, and he sucked at it again, the beginnings of panic fluttering in his chest. If it got infected, there was no telling... God damn it, Sebastian! He raised his head and shouted at his son.

'You can find your own way home!'

And then Paul Fitzmahon's voice cracked and a feeling of intense cold swept over him. That cursed brandy – but this was no ordinary hangover, he thought to himself as his throat dried and he scrabbled at his neck, gasping for air.

'Sebastian...'

He was shouting for help now but his voice was slurred and weak, and he knew there was no way the child would hear him through the dense foliage that surrounded him on all sides. His head drooped and he was face down into the mud now and the dirt was everywhere, filling his mouth, and choking him. He pressed his hands on the ground again but the wound in his finger burned and his limbs were weakening; it was useless, he could not breathe. Desperate for air, he twisted his head this way and that, then screamed as a small branch pierced his eyeball, the pain extending all of the way through to his brain. And Paul Fitzmahon, Master of Hollowpark Hall, tried one final time to call out for help but his mouth was completely clogged with dirt now and blood from his ruined eye drained into the dirt on his face as he sank further into the mud, his screams of pain muffled by the hedges that loomed over him from all sides.

Chapter 16

2007

A chirrup from my phone woke me the next morning. I had left it to charge overnight and when I peered at it, saw that I had been welcomed back to the Irish network. Or had I? Even as I stared at it, the bars disappeared again, proving that what Delia had told me about Hollowpark's dodgy signal hadn't been an exaggeration. No matter, there was no one I wanted to call anyway; I'd send my dad my usual postcard when I next visited Lisheeha. I pushed the covers off, walked over to the window and looked out onto a bright, sunny morning. I was still exhausted, it would take several more days to catch up on my sleep, but even though climbing back into bed was tempting, I knew I needed to start the day, to take some time for myself before meeting Skye and beginning my new life in earnest.

The bathroom was lit up by the morning sunshine and as the final grains of Greek sand washed off my toes and disappeared down the Irish plughole, I felt any lingering fears about my new home disappear with them. Everything was going to be OK. The house was stunning, the family pleasant, the location close to ideal. Everything was going to work out, I could feel it. And there had been no girl.

I had been keeping my fair hair cropped short for years, it made the hot summers far easier to deal with, so my shower only took a couple of minutes and, following a blissful reunion with my toothbrush, I returned to my luggage and some fresh clothes. There had been no girl, and plenty of reasons to explain what I had seen, or thought I saw. A dark night, clouds drifting across the moon, a bellyful of cheese sandwiches had all been behind my nightmare, there was no mystery there.

But I hadn't been asleep.

Enough! I grabbed my hoodie, zipped it, and came to a decision. This was what I had wanted, wasn't it? A fresh start, a place to clear my head. The fact of the matter was, this wasn't the first time in my life I had 'seen' things, or imagined things that weren't there. When I was a kid I used to wake screaming – night terrors, the doctor had called them, when my mother eventually called in the experts having been woken from her precious sleep one too many times. He hadn't come up with any real solution though, just prescribed exercise, no TV in my bedroom and no eating just before bed. That seemed to sort the problem out, or so my parents thought. The truth of the matter was I still woke sometimes in the night, heart hammering, convinced I had lost something precious or seen something in the corner of the room that couldn't possibly have been there. I just didn't bother telling my parents about it any more and, since I left home, had coped with it alone. One of the women I'd worked for in London had been into psychic phenomena, mind-reading, all that malarkey, she had shelves full of books about it and I'd thought about asking her if she had ever heard of someone like me. But that would have been ridiculous, and possibly dangerous for my employment prospects – there was no way she was going to entrust her children to someone who sometimes woke in the middle of the night, convinced the glass on her bedside table had been in a different position when she had fallen asleep. And so I ignored those things when they happened, wrote them off as vivid dreams, because, after all, what else could they be?

I looked towards the window again. Speaking of dreams, this was a dream job, a dream home and it would be beyond foolish to let something I thought I had seen, late at night in a darkened room, ruin this incredible opportunity.

I took the stairs at a gallop then slid back the bolt on the massive front door and added 'get keys' to my long mental 'to-do' list. For the moment, however, I simply pulled the door shut behind me, trusting that even the most enthusiastic of burglars would be unlikely to be roaming a ramshackle estate in rural Roscommon before 7 a.m. The fresh morning air felt wonderful against my skin as I jogged down the steps and across the gravel driveway. I'd been wearing factor fifty sunscreen for months and, as much as I loved the Greek sun, I knew my skin would appreciate a few months away from its relentless glare. I kept going till I reached the flowerbeds then turned and looked back at the house again. Given my rather embarrassing collapse the day before, this was the first chance I'd had to really stand and look at it and I was thrilled to find Hollowpark Hall even more impressive in the morning sunlight. I'd have to do a bit of research to get the dates right – surely there was a proper history book somewhere in that wonderful library? – but right now it was enough to know that the house was very old, very big and very, very beautiful. The main building, in front of which I was now standing, was sand coloured and symmetrical with – I counted them – fourteen windows across the top and ten on the bottom, the massive wooden door dividing the ground floor neatly in two. The stone steps at the entrance looked even steeper when viewed from this angle and matching pillars supported a stone portico. I directed my gaze towards the first floor again, trying to see which window was my bedroom, but even though I knew from the view that I had to be looking in roughly the right direction it was impossible to tell from this distance which room was mine. There had been a woman looking out that first day, I remembered, it must have been Delia – and then that thought disappeared as I stepped backwards and almost fell over the little dog, who had trotted up behind me without my noticing. If anyone *had* been looking out the windows, I realised, they would have been highly amused by the windmilling motion of my arms as I fought to retain my balance, but I was too delighted to see the little guy to feel cross and, once I'd gathered myself again, bent down to say a proper hello.

'There's a good boy!'

I didn't know his name, of course, and hadn't been able to ask Delia yesterday, given that he wasn't supposed to be in the house in the first place, but the terrier seemed happy enough with just 'good boy' and stuck closely to my heels as we set off together across the garden. I took a lungful of fresh air and smiled. Delia had obviously been speaking the truth when she said the dogs were not allowed in the house as I hadn't had a hint of my usual allergic reaction since

I'd landed here. I looked down at the little figure skipping beside me and found myself grinning. Maybe Hollowpark Hall would be the first place I'd be able to have a canine companion of my very own.

Moving briskly, the dog and I passed a sign for a children's playground – good, that would be somewhere to entertain Skye on fine days – then kept walking, first across a manicured lawn and then over a much wider patch of wildflowers. And then my steps slowed as we reached a bank of large, carefully groomed hedges. A maze! I'd never been so close to one before – but my friend didn't give me much time to contemplate it and, giving a little bark, scampered through the entrance and disappeared inside. After a moment I followed him, it was only a hedge, after all, how complicated could it be? For a few minutes I enjoyed simply jogging after him, following his tail as it bounced around corners, enjoying the twists and turns, the shade from the leaves and the crackle of branches under my feet. Then, as those branches grew thicker and the sound of my feet grew louder in the gloom, I started to wonder if I shouldn't have dropped some breadcrumbs or something, or maybe told someone where I was going. Before I could get too worried, however, I heard a bark up ahead, turned one final corner and emerged into a clearing where my little buddy was sitting beside a large stone statue, looking as pleased with himself as it was possible for a terrier to be.

'This is lovely!'

That was another nice thing about dogs, they let you talk to yourself without any embarrassment. The statue, a rather twee little angel, was sitting on a long stone plinth which made a very useful bench after a long walk, so I sat on it and took a look around. All that fresh air and exercise had made my nose run but when I dug inside my hoodie pocket for a tissue my fingers found the edge of a piece of paper instead. I pulled it out and looked at it. Of course, Delia's 'brochure'. I glanced at my companion but he seemed quite happy to sit at my feet for a while, and as my legs were complaining after the fastest trot they'd had in a while, I unfolded it fully and began to read.

And almost immediately began to yawn. Delia was, as I knew, a terrific storyteller in person but she had a long way to go before replicating that talent in print. The first page of the pamphlet was packed with dense text about Hollowpark Hall's opening hours and entrance fees and enough confusing information about single entrance and family passes to make the average tourist feel the visit might not be worth the hassle. Meanwhile, the 'Where To Find Us' section was a map that seemed to have been copied from a smudged original, and could have been of Lisheeha or indeed of the Greek island I'd just left, it was impossible to tell. I had reached page three before I finally found something of interest.

Hollowpark Hall – a History

The curly font bore all the hallmarks of someone having fun with their first word processing package, and Delia hadn't been able to resist throwing in another smudged image either. This time it was a line drawing of a young woman, which looked like it had been photocopied from a 1970s romance novel, standing at the window of what I assumed was supposed to be Isla's tower and staring into the distance. I began to read out loud, figuring the little dog would like the company.

Built in 1779 by the Fitzmahon family, Hollowpark Hall is a fine example of Palladian architecture, and a house about which many legends and stories exist.

Ah yeah, this was more like it. But the next sentence made me snort out loud and disturb the little dog who had made a comfortable perch for himself on my right foot.

'Sorry, dude,' I muttered and waited until he had settled down again before continuing to read. Honestly though, it was awful stuff.

A member of the Fitzmahon family has always lived at Hollowpark, indeed, it is said that the house will always stand while a Fitzmahon is in residence, and that the house protects its own...

Come on, Delia, you can do better than that. I mightn't have travelled much around Ireland, but I'd spent enough time on enough touristy Greek islands to recognise a fairy tale dressed up as history and a yarn about as authentic as imported 'local' beer. Still though, I might as well see where she was going with it.

Over the years, strange lights and unexplained noises have been experienced in sections of the grounds, including in the tower which stands some distance from the main house. Locals say this may be linked to a tragedy which occurred in the mid 1800s when a young man, Laurence Foster, just recently wed to Deirdre, the daughter of the house, fell to his death from the tower. Devastated by his passing, Deirdre never remarried, and it's said her spirit haunts the corridors of the house as she desperately tries to be reunited with her lost love...

Oh, for God's sake. Irritated, I folded the pages and returned them to my pocket. Drivel, all of it. I loved a good ghost story, I'd read *The Haunting of Hill House* and a good few Stephen Kings and I was always up for a horror movie, the more jump scares the better. This, however, was not a good ghost story. 'It's said her spirit returned' – keeping it all nice and vague, eh, Delia? And then I thought back to our conversation in the kitchen the previous day and the truth of the situation suddenly dawned on me. Delia was trying to monetise her ghosts! One of my most recent London employees had been a big deal in marketing, and 'monetise' had been a big buzzword of his. I'd hated it at the time, but it seemed most appropriate here. It made perfect sense – Delia herself had said she'd made a small fortune letting the house out to a film company for a while, so it stood to reason she'd try and use the spooky atmosphere in the place as a more permanent revenue stream. I'd watched enough cable TV to know there was a lucrative paranormal tourism market out there and I reckoned the lady of Hollowpark Hall had come up with a great way to give her house – now, what was that other term my former boss kept using? Oh yeah, a USP. There were plenty of Big Houses in Ireland, some of them in far better repair than this one, but I was willing to bet not all of them came with a decent ghost story, and a nice romantic one at that. I shoved the leaflet back in my pocket, admiring Delia's ingenuity. She needed to work on her design skills though.

Or indeed write about the real ghost. The thought popped

into my mind but I banished it immediately. There was no ghost, Grace! Teenage girls in jeans weren't ghosts, they were the unpalatable offspring of low lighting and mature cheddar. The stone bench was starting to feel cold under my bum so I nudged the dog off my foot then stood up and stretched, looking for the exit. And then felt my heart do a weird, double beat. From where I was standing, I could see six gaps in the hedge but I hadn't a notion which one I had entered through, let alone which one would lead me out to the other side. I began to walk around the space, looking from one gap to another but I was starting to panic now. What the hell had I been thinking, coming in here without even telling anyone where I was going? It wasn't yet 7 a.m., no one would be looking for me. I began to jog, running from one entrance to another, but each route led to such immediate twists and turns that I was afraid to do anything other than turn and make my way back to the centre again. Tension built in my neck and I rolled my head from side to side, then forward and back trying to ease it. And it was then that I saw, out of the corner of my eye, the edge of a tall stone structure. The tower. I walked back towards one exit and it disappeared, then forward again and there it was, at the edge of my vision. Forward – there; back – gone. The dog wagged his tail and yapped encouragingly as I walked towards the only exit from which the building could be seen.

'This way, is it, dude?'

My voice was shaky but the dog didn't judge me, just scuttled down the leafy path then looked back, waiting for me to follow. My nerves still jangling, I followed him down several identical passageways, realising I would be hard pressed to even find my way back to the centre now. But at every turn I looked up and saw that the tower was still above me. We had been walking for at least fifteen minutes and I was starting to wonder if I'd have to tunnel my way out of the damn hedge when I finally followed the dog around two more sharp bends and emerged, scratched, breathless but unharmed, into the daylight again.

I bent down and rubbed the dog vigorously behind his ears then straightened up to catch my breath. As my heart rate returned to normal my anxiety drained away, to be replaced by a feeling of utter foolishness. What the hell did I think was going to happen, anyway? That I'd be trapped inside the maze for ever, like an aging princess from a cut-price fairy-tale? It was just a hedge, presumably planted as a piece of entertainment, and besides, if Delia and Patrick had their way, this garden would soon be a tourist attraction with hundreds of people tramping through it every week. It was hardly dangerous, there were probably several ways out; in fact it was quite possible all paths eventually led to the end if you followed them for long enough. Having succeeded in talking sense into myself, I decided I might as well get on with the exploring and looked up at the tower that now loomed directly over my head. It must have been eighty feet tall and was built in the same stone as the house, but it was nowhere near as well maintained, with moss growing in the cracks in the stone and, here and there, gaps where large chunks had been weather-worn away. The wooden door was weather-beaten too but, when I pushed it, I was surprised to feel it swing open easily under my hand. The small lobby inside was lined with ancient wood panelling and strewn with leaves and other debris but the stairs themselves were relatively clean and, without thinking any further, I began to climb. After only a few steps my calves began to ache and I was struck by the uneasy thought that I might be trespassing, but I'd come too far to give up now and besides, having conquered the maze I was anxious to see the layout of the gardens from the air. The dog's little legs weren't built for the steps, however, and although he panted and scrabbled with all his might, he gave up after a few attempts and bounded back down again. Feeling surprisingly lonely once he had left, I began to climb more quickly. The air inside the tower was chilly, the heat of the day completely blocked by the thick stone walls, and as I put my hand out to steady myself it was hard to tell if the brickwork was damp, or just freezing cold. Small slits had been fashioned at seemingly random intervals but they were so narrow they barely relieved the gloom and I was almost climbing in darkness by the time the stairs came to an end and I emerged onto a landing, and was confronted by a door identical to the one at the bottom. Part of me was hoping this one would be locked and that I'd have an excuse to go back downstairs again but it too swung open when I pushed and I blinked as I walked into sudden sunlight.

'Hello, Grace!'

'JESUS!!'

For the second time in less than twelve hours my hands flew to my throat. This time, however, my unexpected companion let out a peal of laughter.

'I'm so sorry, I didn't mean to startle you!'

Isla wiped her hands on a cloth, then dropped it onto the floor.

'I was waving at you out of the window, I was sure you

saw me! You're welcome anyway. I hope you're feeling better today?'

'I was,' I told her weakly. 'Between the climb and that fright, I might need a defibrillator now though. I'm so sorry, I had no idea you'd be working this early or I wouldn't have just barged in.'

'Oh, it's the best time.'

Isla nodded towards the nearest window.

'Especially at this time of year, the light is extraordinary. And up until now I've had to work while Skye was asleep. It'll be different now you're here, of course – please, have a look around!'

My new boss waved vaguely around the wide, airy space then took a seat at a kitchen chair, one of several which surrounded an elderly table on which various tools had been arranged, including what looked like an ordinary builder's trowel. She picked it up and I bit my lip.

'I don't want to bother you.'

'Honestly, it's no trouble.'

Isla's hair was tied up in a ponytail, emphasizing her broad, handsome features, and she tucked a strand back against her ear before picking up another cloth and beginning to wipe the plaster from the surface of the trowel.

'I was just finishing up here anyway. I'll be about another ten minutes or so but it's fine, you're not disturbing anything.'

I hesitated for another moment, but the invitation to explore was too tempting and I walked slowly across the circular room. Large, whitewashed and flooded with morning light, it was easy to see why Isla had adopted it as an artist's studio. Walking towards one of the windows

I saw on the wooden ledge a small gold Sphinx, tarnished with age and sitting on a faded and scruffy base. The windows themselves, in contrast looked brand new and had been fitted with large glass panels that opened outwards to allow air in, but not wide enough to pose a safety hazard.

'I do yoga up here as well sometimes.'

I turned to see Isla pointing towards a rolled up blue mat which was resting against a wall.

'You should join me some morning, it's incredibly peaceful up here. I keep trying to get Delia to try it out, but she's not interested.'

There was a flicker of amusement in her eyes and I almost giggled as I tried and failed to imagine Isla's mother-in-law pushing her sensible apron aside and having a go at the downward dog. But then I felt a sudden stab of guilt. Delia, after all, had been nothing but kind to me.

'It looks like the perfect place to work all right,' I told Isla, as neutrally as I could, and she looked at me for a moment and then nodded.

'It's incredible. I tried a few different places in the main house, it's not like they are short of rooms over there. But it's not just about the size, or even peace and quiet. When I'm working on a piece, I need the space itself to work for me.'

She put down the trowel and started to clean what looked like a collection of palette knives, and I could see that she was blushing slightly.

'That sounds terribly arty-farty when I say it out loud! But it can be intense, what I do. And over in the main house…'

Her hand stilled, and she seemed to be staring at her own reflection in the knife's blade.

'What, too busy?' I prompted. 'I guess it must have been hard to work with Skye around...'

But Isla shook her head.

'No, it wasn't that. Delia and Patrick were great, gave me all the time I needed. No – it was something else. I tried to work in one of the rooms near the Great Room – I don't know if you've seen it, it would have been a gentleman's drawing room I think, but it's empty now, Paddy hasn't got around to figuring out what to do it with. It's a lovely space, big windows, wooden floors that haven't been sanded yet, so it didn't matter what damage I did to them. But sometimes – oh, this is going to sound so stupid.'

She squared her shoulders and looked at me.

'Sometimes I thought I heard noises.'

I tried, but must have failed to hide the sceptical expression on my face because Isla nodded, ruefully.

'I know. Mad, isn't it? I mean, I tried to tell Patrick about it one night but it just sounded ridiculous. It was small stuff. I thought I heard a rap on the door, or that I could hear Skye crying somewhere else in the house, that sort of thing. It sounds bananas when I say it out loud. Hollowpark is ancient, you'd be hard pressed to find a floorboard that doesn't creak, or a door that shuts properly. But I just couldn't settle, you know? It was like I wasn't welcome in the house. It's hard to explain but I couldn't work at all down there, couldn't block out the world the way I needed to. And then one day I climbed up here.'

Isla rose from her seat and came to join me at the window, and I could see the tension ease from her shoulders as she moved.

'I found this space and it was perfect. It cost quite a bit, getting the windows in, and we had to hire people to carry everything I needed. And as for getting the work down again!'

She grinned, a genuine smile this time.

'We had to hire in specialist removers in the end. I was afraid Patrick would think it a waste of money but once he saw how much I loved it he was incredibly supportive.'

'And no funny noises?'

I kept my voice light-hearted to show her I was joking.

'Nope, just the odd bird.'

Isla reached out her hand, clearly keen to change the subject.

'The views are incredible, look!'

Cold air rushed up against my cheeks as I moved closer to the window. The view was indeed spectacular. From here I could see the entirety of Hollowpark Hall and its grounds, while the maze, that had so freaked me out just twenty minutes before, had been reduced to what looked like a child's puzzle. Isla reached past me and tapped lightly on the window.

'That's our house over there, can you see it?'

I squinted and then saw a brown roof rising from behind a clump of trees. So that was the famous Gate House. It was further from the main building than I had expected, practically on its own grounds.

'And your room is fourth from the left – see?'

Isla was pointing towards the main house again, and I realised I'd been looking in entirely the wrong place earlier that morning. Delia needed to do a lot more work on the brochure, I decided – a good map and a floor plan would be worth a million ghost stories and complicated opening hours. I pressed my nose against the glass, trying to get a sense of the geography of the maze underneath the window, and as my eyes raked the green pathways a rush of vertigo washed over me. The ground was just there, I could see it, if I jumped I could be...

'Oh yes!'

Forcing my voice to remain steady, I stepped back from the window, took a final, exaggerated look at Hollowpark Hall then turned towards the centre of the room again. I didn't know what was going on with me, but if I got wobbly in front of another member of this family they'd send me back to Greece before I could say moussaka and, to be honest, I wouldn't blame them. Maybe the flight had messed with my inner ear, or something? Whatever it was, I needed to sort it, and fast. Isla didn't seem to have noticed anything, however, and simply returned to the table.

'Don't worry if you don't get the layout straight away, it's a big place, Hollowpark, and imposing. It certainly took me a long time to get used to it. In fact, I'm not sure I'm quite there yet.'

She dipped her head and began her cleaning routine again, scraping material from each knife, dipping it in clean water poured from a bottle and then polishing it with a soft cloth. There was something almost meditative about her actions and I watched her in silence for several minutes before allowing my gaze to wander around the room again. It was a large space, with no furniture other than the table at which we were sitting, but several of what I assumed were her art works, spaced at intervals along the walls.

'You can take a look if you like.'

Isla hadn't raised her head but seemed to have noticed something had caught my gaze. Not needing further prompting I walked to the nearest… I didn't even know what to call it, sculpture, I suppose? Work of art? From a distance it looked like a figure of eight but when I got closer I could see the piece was a torso with smooth, elegant arms folded over a slender trunk. There was no head, but I knew just by looking at it that it was a woman's body.

'That's one of the twins.'

This time Isla did look in my direction and smiled.

'I sold her sister last year; it was the first piece I made here in Hollowpark. A dealer in Sligo looked after it for me; it paid for the flights to Greece, actually.'

'It's beautiful,' I told her, and meant it. Other than the paintings some of my London employers hung on their walls and tried to impress me with during job interviews, I knew bugger all about art but this piece was attractive in its simplicity and if I couldn't quite imagine plonking it in the corner of my living room I could certainly see it being appreciated in an art gallery or even here in Hollowpark Hall, in one of the bigger rooms.

'And what are you working on at the moment?'

It felt like the type of question you asked an artist. Isla paused before continuing.

'I'm not sure. That was going to be a series but now I've completed the two – no, I don't think there is another one there. So I'm just looking around really. Playing, you could call it. These last few months, since moving up here, I really feel like things are coming together, you know? Like I'm myself again. I'm proud of the work I'm doing and selling the piece meant an awful lot, it was a way of giving back, do you know what I mean? Patrick and Delia have been so kind…'

Isla's voice faltered for a moment.

'They have such plans for the place and I want to help them, I really do, but I don't have any business background or anything, and I'm not practical like Delia. But if I can sell my work, well then I'll really feel like I'm making a proper contribution.'

Isla stopped suddenly and grinned at me.

'Good lord, Grace! You're a good listener.'

She wasn't the first person to say it. Growing up at the centre of a perpetual party had taught me to be silent, and still, and it was a skill I'd often used with my families. If someone wants to tell you about problems with their children, or any problem within the home, then it's best not to ask them directly. If you stay still, I find, it all comes out eventually. And this family fascinated me, it was no sacrifice to hear their stories.

Isla checked her large man's wristwatch and raised her eyebrows.

'Skye will be up by now, why don't you come back to the Gate House with me? We'll have a proper chat then; we were hoping you'd be able to bring her to playschool this morning if that's OK. Patrick has business on the farm and I'm looking forward to getting stuck in here.'

She dried the knife she had been cleaning then replaced it neatly on the table and prepared to leave.

'You can see why I love it, can't you?'

'Because of the peace and quiet?' I asked her, as I followed her outside.

'Yes.' Isla paused, and then looked around the room once more before shutting the door behind us. 'That, and the safety. You can see for miles from up here.'

Chapter 17

'**L**et's get you strapped in, eh?'

There may well be a way to lean over and buckle a small child into a car seat without displaying your backside to the world but, despite a folder of childcare qualifications, I certainly hadn't learned it. Thankfully, Skye wasn't one of those kids who reacted to her restraints like a prisoner being sent to the electric chair, so I secured her with a minimum of fuss before backing out and climbing into the front seat of Patrick's Nissan, which was by far the best car on the estate. There was a tractor too, but you couldn't exactly bring it on the school run, and Delia drove some sort of hairdryer on wheels which she promised I could borrow any time I wanted, but I needed to be far better acquainted with the Lisheeha roads before I tried it out.

I put the car into first gear and guided it down the narrow path that linked the Gate House to the main Hollowpark Hall driveway.

'Now, me dear!'

I looked at my young charge in the rear-view mirror.

It was our first journey alone together and I was looking forward to us getting better acquainted.

'I can't wait to see your school.'

She nodded at me, then broke into a smile.

'Music, please, Gwace?'

'Of course, my love. Wheels on the bus?'

I hummed a few bars but the three-year-old gave me a disdainful look, then pointed at the car stereo.

'No! Music please, Gwace.'

'You're dead right, Skye, who'd want to listen to me?' I told her and flicked on the radio. But the warbling of a guitar strumming megastar didn't seemed to impress her any more than I had and I could see through the rear-view mirror that her blue eyes had filled up with tears as she pointed to the stereo again.

'MUSIC! Daddy's music!'

'I don't...' I began, before finally realising what was bothering her and pressing the car's CD button. 'Mr Brightside' roared out of the car's speakers and Skye kicked her little legs against the back of my seat with pleasure.

'Daddy's music. Thank you, Gwace.'

'You're welcome,' I told her, but kept my face serious. Kids hate to think you are laughing at them and besides, her taste in music – or, rather, Patrick's taste – seemed to be pretty similar to my own. I checked the mirror again and saw that she was now happily singing to herself while looking out the car window. I hadn't been wrong in my initial assessment – my charge was a little doll and it would, I decided, be a pleasure to spend time with her. Which was a good thing as I had now discovered we'd be existing in fairly close quarters a lot of the time.

The end of the driveway dipped suddenly – maybe this was the hollow that had given the house its name? – and I turned left onto the road that Isla had promised would take me straight to Lisheeha. It was more a track than a road, really, with a strip of grass down the middle and huge hedges on each side, and only an occasional break in the greenery to allow cars to pull in and yield to traffic coming in the opposite direction. It was the type of road where you instinctively held your breath going round corners and I remained in second gear as I felt my way along, the morning's events spooling through my head as I drove.

As promised, Isla had brought me back to the Gate House for breakfast but although the exterior of the old stone cottage was straight out of a child's fairy tale, with ivy climbing up the walls and flowers lining the narrow path, the inside of the house veered more towards a nursery rhyme, specifically the 'Old Woman who Lived in the Shoe.' Rather than the fry-up I'd been hoping for, Skye and I had breakfasted on own-brand Weetabix – there was a new German discount supermarket in Lisheeha, Patrick had informed me with no small amount of pride – while he and Isla had chewed toast while standing at the kitchen sink, as there wasn't room for three adults at their tiny, wood-effect table. After he'd done the washing up – no room for a dishwasher either – Skye's dad had shown me around the house, which was essentially a holiday cottage with two bedrooms and a bathroom upstairs and the open plan kitchen–living room comprising the entirety of the downstairs space. Lovely, if you had rented it for a weekend with a gang of friends, but as a family residence it was crammed to bursting with toys, books, piles of clothes and a smelly kitchen bin I was itching to disinfect. It was no wonder Isla had taken the tower for herself, I thought, as Patrick tried to locate the car keys under a pile of raincoats that had slithered from the banisters onto the floor.

'Sheep!'

'Good girl, Skye! Do you see four sheep? I see four sheep!'

We waved at the animals out of the windows and then I blushed as a farmer, dressed in grey corduroy and a green jacket, waved solemnly back at us. We were passing houses now, two on one side and three on another, bungalows of varying shapes and sizes that looked like they had been dropped from space and bore no relationship to each other or to the landscape around them. The local architects must have watched a lot of *Dallas* as they were growing up, I decided, driving past huge white pillars, each one topped with a grey eagle, which guarded a two-storey mansion, with three cars and a speedboat taking up most of the space in the front garden. I'd worked for top London lawyers who had far less living space, but I guessed the price of houses were slightly less in Roscommon than they were in Richmond.

I turned another corner, agreed with Skye that there were indeed sheep AND HORSIES in the field we were now driving past, then let the car creep up to just below the speed limit. After years spent tackling hairpin bends on Greek islands, Irish roads held no fear for me, but I still wasn't going to take any chances, particularly not with Skye in the car. It drives me mad when I see people driving dangerously or even checking their phones with kids in the back seat. Take your own life into your hands, mate, but leave the children out of it. People like my mother might scoff, but I take my job very seriously, just as seriously as those masters of the universe in designer suits who can't stand in a coffee queue without checking their Blackberries to let the world know how valuable their time is. I never ever take the safety of my little clients for granted. Nor their happiness either.

'My daddy has horsies,' Skye informed me, solemnly.

'He does indeed, Skye! And cowsies.'

A withering look pierced the rear-view mirror.

'They cows, Gwace.'

'They are, indeed, Skye,' I answered, smothering a smile.

The driver of a car travelling in the opposite direction raised one finger off his steering wheel in salute and I returned the gesture, feeling my mood lift even further. Patrick had said that he and Isla's move back to Ireland had been prompted by Skye's arrival and right now it was easy to see what he had meant by that. Sure, London had art and theatre and all of the food and drink and adventure you could wish for, but on a day like this it was hard to beat the view of the hills I could see in the near distance and the stunningly fresh air that was flowing in through the open car window. It was strange, actually, how much at home I felt here, how quickly I was slipping into the rhythm of the place. Maybe it was Delia's soft accent, or her home-made brown bread, maybe it was the way that just being on the island had brought my accent to the surface again, causing me to slip 'grand' into almost every sentence. Whatever the reason, my new life in Lisheeha was starting to feel remarkably like coming home.

The road ahead opened out suddenly and I obeyed a yield sign before allowing myself to speed up slightly. The grey exterior of the giant supermarket Patrick seemed so proud of loomed out of a field on my right while, to my left, an extraordinarily urban-looking housing estate looked like it had been assembled from flatpack. We must have been nearing the village, I reckoned, and sure enough, within minutes we passed a sign which read *Fáilte go Lios na hOíche / Welcome to Lisheeha* in formal black and white. That was another thing I enjoyed about being home: seeing the odd word of Irish here and there and, although I hadn't spoken a word of it since I'd left school, it was starting to come back to me. 'Oíche', pronounced ee-ha, meant night, I knew that much, and although I wasn't sure what Lios na hOíche meant, precisely, at least the name of the village now made a bit more sense to me. Town of the night, village of the night, something like that? Then again, maybe I was completely on the wrong track, and I made a mental note to find out more once I was back at the house.

The main street was narrow and I took my time navigating my way down it, passing a bizarre combination of shops that included several pubs, two shoe stores, a 'gentleman's outfitters' and, most strangely of all, three Chinese restaurants. I wouldn't be stuck for Peking duck anyway, but the depressing number of boarded up outlets told me that Patrick wasn't the only person buying in bulk from the new German retail overlords. I pulled into the car park at the top of the town, killed the engine and climbed out. There was a nice library across the road, as well as a decent-looking café.

'My school!'

I lifted Skye from her seat and followed her outstretched finger to the large white community centre adjoining the café which, I could now see, had a sign outside with *Ladybird Learners* written in bright red paint. I set her on her feet and grasped her hand. A tractor trundling slowly down the road waved at us to cross but I'm pretty strict about road safety so I shook my head and led Skye in the opposite direction to our destination and towards what looked like the only set of traffic lights in the town. I allowed her to press the button, and then we waited. And waited.

'Hi, Skye!'

The woman, who was pushing a massive double buggy, only one seat of which was occupied, grinned at me.

'Honestly, you can chance it. You could be here ten minutes waiting for these lights to change.'

'Oh.' I hesitated, still not keen on breaking the rules, but with Skye squirming by my side and at least a kilometre of clear road either side of me, I decided to take my chances. As we crossed, Skye bent down and began an animated conversation with the child in the buggy who, I could now see, was around her own age. The woman caught my gaze and rolled her eyes.

'I know, I should be letting him walk, but it could take an hour at his pace and I don't have the patience for it.'

'Right.' I nodded, blandly. I hadn't in fact had any opinion on her parenting at all, but the woman seemed keen to chat and ploughed cheerfully on.

'You must be Skye's new nanny? My dad met you up at the house – I think he said you were from Greece?'

'Er, no. Well, yes, I'm the nanny, but not Greece, no.'

We reached the other side of the road and, as I helped her pull the tank of a buggy up onto the pavement the woman smiled her thanks.

'Sorry, Dad can be awfully vague sometimes. Well, you are very welcome to Lisheeha anyway. Where are you from, so?'

Yep, I was back in Ireland all right.

'I'm from Dublin originally, but I've been living away for a while.'

I could see she was dying to ask what part of Dublin, but I was focused on getting Skye sorted and didn't have time for the inevitable 'who do you know' conversation which would end with her discovering she had once dated my cousin in Irish college, or something, an occurrence that would have been bizarre in any other country and utterly unremarkable here. Instead, I bent down and waved at the little figure in the buggy who was now straining against his straps.

'And what's your name, dude?'

'Eamon,' the child told me and lifted his arms to his mother. She opened the straps, but he'd been bundled up in so many layers it took him a while to roll out, then he ran up the street after Skye, leaving his mother lumbering after him. By the time we caught them they were standing at the door to the community centre, and Skye was leaping up and down.

'Now, Eamon, it's Skye's turn today,' said the woman, who lifted the little girl up and allowed her to ring the bell.

'They have quite the routine going.'

She grinned at me.

'Doesn't matter who drops her off, Delia, or Patrick or indeed her mum, you can't forget whose turn it is to ring that bell!'

Still in her arms, Skye waved vigorously at a camera

mounted just over the doorbell before the woman set her down again and turned to me.

'Maura, who runs the place, is very conscious of security. I mean you'd have to be, wouldn't you? Even in Lisheeha, you can't take any chances.'

After a moment, the door buzzed open to allow us entry and Skye and her buddy ran down a long, bright corridor without a backwards glance. The next few minutes were taken up by a chat with the ferociously efficient Maura who was extremely put out by the fact that Skye's parents hadn't filled out the requisite form to allow me to drop her off and collect her. After quizzing me with more vigour than a blind date – and phoning Patrick – she grudgingly accepted that I was the new nanny and was allowed to drop off and pick up Skye, if I and the Fitzmahons promised to fill in the official form she handed me. Once back outside the door again, Eamon's mother smiled at me.

'That's us free now for a little while! I'm sorry, I didn't even introduce myself, what am I like? I'm Evelyn, Jack Sheehan is my dad.'

She stuck out her hand and, as her coat fell open I noticed her bump for the first time.

'Yeah, Eamon is getting a little sister in a few months' time, that's why I'm pushing around this tank.'

She nodded at the buggy.

'I swapped my old one online and the other woman wanted it straight away. Won't be long till I have the two seats filled, I suppose, and it can't come quick enough, to be honest with you. I don't suppose...'

We were walking away from the community centre now and she looked longingly at the café next door.

'I don't suppose you'd be interested in a cup of coffee, would you? I've a few bits to do in town but I'd love a sit down first, my back is killing me.'

I hesitated but the woman was clearly both lonely and friendlier than her father and apart from some unpacking I didn't have much calling me back to Hollowpark Hall. Besides, although Delia had the Irish mammy's knack with a teapot, I hadn't had a decent cup of coffee since I'd left Greece.

'Go on then.'

I opened the café door and helped Evelyn park the massive buggy near the loos, then told her to grab a table while I ordered drinks. A woman, with what I was pretty sure was a Polish, rather than an Irish, accent took my order for two lattes, decaff for Evelyn and a skinny vanilla for me, and I paused before selecting two slices of what looked like home-made apple tart to go with them. I carried them over and, by the time Evelyn had gone through the whole 'oh I shouldn't, oh go on then maybe half a slice and is that cream in that jug? Might as well be hung for a sheep as a lamb I suppose' dance, our coffees had arrived and we settled down for a chat. Or at least, Evelyn did. My new friend, it transpired, had been on early maternity leave for a month already and, not to put too fine a point on it, was going out of her mind with boredom.

'Blood pressure.'

She swallowed a mouthful of tart, then washed it down with coffee.

'It's the maddest thing – you walk into the hospital feeling fine and then they announce you have to give up work straight way. And to be honest with you, I'm not sure I'll be able to go back after this one is born, either.'

She stroked her bump with a frown.

'Colm, that's my husband, he works in Sligo, he's on the road at six most mornings and doesn't get back till after seven most nights. It was hard enough when Eamon was small, but at least we had Mam to help us out then. But she's waiting on the new hip now and I can't see her running after two of them.'

The apple tart tasted as good as it looked and, sleepy now after my early start, I was happy to eat and drink and let her words flow over me.

'We live in the new housing estate, just outside the village, you might have seen it on the drive in? But Mam is five miles further out the road again, and she can't drive because of her hip. And you've met my dad, I mean, he's not exactly the childminding type, is he? He and Mam split up years ago, there's no bad feeling or anything but I can't imagine him changing a nappy. God knows, he never changed mine!'

The shop bell jangled and Evelyn's stream of consciousness stuttered to a halt as a shadow fell over us.

'Ah, Evelyn, you're blooming! You can't have much longer to go?'

I arranged my face into a neutral smile but was puzzled to see the garrulous Evelyn looking nervous, rather than welcoming, as the newcomer stared down at us.

'That's right, Angela. Beginning of November, all going well.'

'Is that right? The size of you, I thought you were ready to pop. Isn't she looking marvellous?'

The woman's eyes swept over me, clearly anxious to

include me in the conversation. She was being a bit rude, I thought, but other than that there was nothing about her that justified how uncomfortable Evelyn was looking. To me she was just the village gossip, standard issue, aged in her early seventies, I guessed, and dressed for chat in pastel slacks, a waterproof anorak and grey orthopaedic shoes. I waited for Evelyn to introduce us but, when that clearly wasn't going to happen, reached out my hand.

'Hi, I'm Grace.'

The woman gave a faint smile.

'Is that a Dublin accent I hear? Friend of yours, is she, Evelyn? Down for a visit?'

A look of even deeper strain passed over Evelyn's face. Maybe she was feeling unwell, I speculated, and decided to keep the conversation going to give her time to recover.

'No, I'm working up at Hollowpark Hall. Do you know it? I'm the new nanny—'

It was as if a light had been switched off. The woman stepped back and inhaled, sharply. Across the table from me Evelyn shot me an apologetic look but before I could say anything the older woman bent towards me and hissed into my face.

'Bad luck to you so, and bad luck to anyone who crosses their door. May God forgive Patrick Fitzmahon, bringing a child to that cursed place. If you have any sense, my girl, or indeed any compassion, you'd get the hell out of there!'

And then she turned and left, the shop door slamming behind her, the jangling of the bell an affronted afterthought.

'Jesus.' I turned back to Evelyn, amused at the over-the-top reaction of what I assumed was the local fruitcake. 'Lisheeha would want to work on its welcoming committee.'

But Evelyn wasn't laughing. Instead she looked close to tears and blew her nose on a napkin before continuing.

'That was Angela Clancy. I don't know if any of the Fitzmahons mentioned...'

The blank look on my face made the answer obvious, and she groaned.

'Oh God, I thought maybe my dad might have told you – feck. Look, Grace, I don't want to be the one to tell you, maybe if you ask Delia...'

But I shook my head. 'Please, Evelyn. I only landed yesterday, if there's something going on I'd really like to know.'

I put down my fork, seriously concerned now. I knew enough Irish history to know there would have been some tension between the 'Big House' and the locals in an area like this but that sort of thing was all over hundreds of years ago, wasn't it? Sure, Isla might come across as a bit standoffish, but Patrick clearly loved the place and his mum was as down to earth as you could get. I couldn't imagine anything about the place that would warrant such a violent reaction from the local busybody. Evelyn, however, was still looking upset. Then she pursed her lips and seemed to come to a decision.

'OK, I'll tell you. If I don't the rest of the village will be queuing up to fill you in and I'd rather you heard the straightforward version. But don't tell the Fitzmahons I told you, OK? They might have their own way of handling it.'

She began to stroke her bump in long, low circles and took a moment to herself before continuing.

'That lady, Angela? Her daughter Catherine went missing

over thirty years ago. She was only fifteen, God love her. And the last place she was seen was up at Hollowpark Hall. It was awful, no one around here has ever forgotten it. I mean I wasn't even born when it happened but it was held over us kids for years. Any time we wanted to stay out late or if we forgot to phone home it was all "remember poor Catherine Clancy and what happened to her!"'

I wrapped my hands around my cooling coffee cup, both fascinated and appalled by the unfolding story.

'So what did happen?'

Evelyn paused for a moment, as if to gather her thoughts, then continued.

'It was Hallowe'en night.'

She clocked the look of disbelief on my face, and grimaced.

'I know, you couldn't make it up, could you? Lisheeha's own horror movie. Dad will tell you more, he was there that night, actually, he'd brought my two older brothers. But every kid around here was told the story when they were growing up.'

She took a sip of her coffee, relaxing into what was clearly a familiar tale.

'The Fitzmahons used to have parties up there every year – that's Skye's great-grandparents I'm talking about. It was their way of getting involved with the community, I suppose. The Fitzmahons have been living in Lisheeha longer than most but they were still seen as outsiders back then, not like everyone else. And although most of their parties were for their own friends, they used to invite the locals up at Hallowe'en, to try and give a bit back to the community or something. They had games, apple bobbing, sweets for the kids, that sort of thing. And sometime during the night, Catherine Clancy went missing.'

Evelyn sighed.

'Everyone is fairly vague on where she was last seen. That's part of the problem, you see, almost every child up there would have been dressed the same that night. It wasn't like now, with shop-bought costumes and the like, back in those days you got a black sack if you wanted to be a vampire and a white sheet if you were a ghost and that was as good as it got. So, you'd have had twenty-five, maybe thirty kids all wearing the same outfits, you know? Which made it much harder for people to remember what happened to one young girl.'

I remained silent, utterly gripped by the story now as Evelyn continued.

'No one remembers seeing Catherine leave. There was so much going on, every group assumed she was with someone else, and when they couldn't find her, her friends assumed she had just gone home. Things were different then, there were no mobile phones or anything, and Catherine was fifteen, she would have been considered pretty grown up. Kids were able to roam freely. It changed after that, of course. But by then it was too late for the poor girl.

'Her mother got worried around ten o'clock when there was no sign of her. Not everyone was on the phone in those days so she got into the car and started driving around. But Catherine wasn't with any of her friends. She even called out to Hollowpark but all of the locals had gone back home at that stage, it was just the Fitzmahons and their friends and they were all well-oiled and hadn't a clue what she was talking about. Angela, God love her, kept thinking Catherine would just turn up and she didn't call the guards until the following morning. Things got serious quickly then, but they never found the poor young one. They searched every inch of the village and Hollowpark, the maze and that tower too. But there was no sign of her.'

It was my turn to shiver now, remembering how eerie the maze had been that morning, in broad daylight, and then imagined how panicked I would feel on a cold October night if I thought my child was lost inside. Evelyn caught my eye and gave a wan smile.

'I know, it doesn't bear thinking about it, does it? Lisheeha had never seen anything like it, the newspapers were down, and a TV crew too, and that would have been a massive thing in those days. You still see the pictures on the TV the odd time when they do shows about unsolved mysteries and missing girls. Because, you see, they never found her. The guards questioned everyone. There had been rumours going around that my cousin Declan was dating her but sure that was all codswallop, they were only kids. But the guards questioned him twice anyway, and I don't think he ever really got over it. He was very cut up about it for years afterwards, said she was a beautiful girl, big head of black hair and blue eyes. He moved away as soon as he turned eighteen and I often wondered if that was the reason...'

But I had stopped listening. A big head of black hair. My heart began to hammer in my chest as I thought back to a girl I had been determined to forget, a girl I had been determined to put down to my imagination. A girl of around fifteen years of age with long dark hair who had been sitting on my bed, staring at me. Asking for help, maybe?

Evelyn looked at me. 'Are you all right, Grace? You've gone awful pale.'

But I couldn't answer her. I pushed my chair back from the table and made some excuse about having left shopping in the car and needing to bring it back to the house. I could tell Evelyn didn't believe me but that didn't matter, nothing mattered except getting the hell out of this awful place. There had been a girl, I knew it. I climbed into the car and, barely bothering to fasten my seatbelt, began the journey back to Hollowpark Hall again. I had to get out. Maybe I could get a flight from Dublin tomorrow? My job in Greece was gone but I had some savings, I could head back to the island for a while and make a plan... I checked my watch, it wasn't yet eleven, I'd have time to repack my things and then return for Skye before handing in my notice. I'd miss her but I'd have to get over it, I couldn't stay. I couldn't stay. There had been a girl. Catherine Clancy. And now I knew her name.

The car must have known its own way down the narrow country roads because I can't remember navigating my way back to Hollowpark, only coming to as I crunched up the driveway and abandoned, rather than parked it, and dashed towards the house, half-formed plans tumbling around in my mind. I'd stay for another day, no, I'd leave that night, or maybe I should... My brain was frazzled, I needed my things around me, to gather my thoughts. But when I ran up the steps and pushed against the heavy wooden door it was shut tight. The keys, I still hadn't asked anyone for a spare set. Christ.

I stood back, hands on my waist, panting. Delia and Patrick had taken her tiny car into Roscommon town for the day; he had told me their plans over a breakfast that now seemed like days, rather than a couple of hours in the past. Isla. Isla was still here, surely she would help me. Turning, I ran back down the steps and across the garden in the direction of the tower, avoiding the maze and taking the path around the outside instead. Tears welled in my eyes as I jogged, Evelyn's story had completely rattled me and I felt a ferocious need to do something rather than just think about it, to find Isla, to pack my stuff, to go. I reached the tower and pushed open the door at the bottom but something was blocking it. I pushed harder and the wooden structure moved just enough for me to see a pile of material lying just inside. I dropped to my knees and saw then that it wasn't material. I reached in and touched clothes, soft skin, a face. Then I grabbed onto her shoulder and shook it gently. But Isla did not respond to my touch.

Chapter 18

1853

It was as if the maze had been waiting for him and Sebastian allowed himself a shout of laughter as he darted across the meadow and ran inside. His foot caught on a root and he almost stumbled but didn't care, simply righting himself and running on, delighting in the feel of the fresh air on his cheeks, the scent of earth in his nostrils.

Sebastian was rarely allowed to wander the grounds of Hollowpark on his own, but that morning his father had gone into town – had been driven there, because he didn't ride on his own any more, didn't do *anything* on his own any more – and his mother had been too distracted by his feverish younger brother to care where he went as long as, she said, he kept far away from her. Mama's voice had been sharp, but Sebastian knew her anger hadn't been directed at him, nor at his brother nor even at the twins, red faced and fretful in the care of a new and inexperienced nurse. Mama was just angry all the time now, and when she wasn't angry she was sad, and Sebastian wasn't sure which mood frightened him more.

He rounded first one bend and then another and another, feeling the familiar and delicious thrill of being so deep inside the maze that there was no point in turning back now. His parents would be shocked, Sebastian knew, if they thought he still played in here but they had never expressly banned him from entering, presumably assuming that no child who had seen what he had seen would ever want to enter the structure again. But, five years after that dreadful day, Sebastian didn't blame the maze for what had happened to his father. He rounded a final bend and emerged in the clearing in the centre, where the stone angel was waiting for him. Sebastian didn't blame the maze because he couldn't, he loved it too much, felt too happy in here.

He perched himself on the long stone plinth and rested his hand on the soft curve of the angel's wing. Everything about this place, from the thick hedges to the stone walls of the tower, made him feel safe and secure. Sebastian had always hated living at Hollowpark Hall, hated the huge, cold rooms and the echoing corridors and hated, too, the comments his father occasionally made about how one day the Hall would be his and he could fill it with children of his own. Ugh. The very thought made Sebastian's stomach churn, he didn't want children, there were enough of them around the place already. And he didn't want to 'own' Hollowpark Hall. It was a sad and cold place that would never, he felt, feel like home.

He picked a leaf off his shirt collar, brushed it onto the ground. As long as he remembered to clean his shoes when he came home, none of the servants would guess where he had been. His mother would be too distracted to ask him any questions and his father? His father would not notice, or care. Sebastian's father was not blind, at least not in the way Sebastian understood that word. He still had one good eye and he didn't use a stick or feel his way down long corridors. He had an eyepatch, true, but so did the pirate captain in one of Sebastian's favourite books and he could command men and plunder ships and do all sorts of exciting things. But Sebastian's father didn't seem to want to do anything, other than sit in his study and drink whiskey in front of the fire.

The Accident was how his mother referred to what had happened to his father that day in the maze, and an 'accident' was the only explanation that had made sense. His father had tripped, and fallen awkwardly, and had injured himself horribly, losing the sight of one eye. There had been berries in the maze that day too, the poisonous fruit of the deadly nightshade plant that grew, entangled in the hedgerow, and the doctor thought his father might have eaten one, or even sucked the juice from his fingers after he fell, and that the effect of the poison had left him unable to save himself. It had been a terrible accident, but an accident nonetheless, and one that could be easily explained.

Sebastian stood up from his perch, gave the angel's wing one last goodbye pat then walked to the far side of the clearing and looked up, finding the tower and the exit next to it. That was the only trick you needed to find your way out of the maze and Sebastian had figured it out some time ago. He looked up again and blinked. It looked like there was a person in the window of the tower – but there couldn't have been. His parents never went up there, his brother and sisters were too young and the staff, he knew, avoided the whole area since his father's accident. He blinked again and the shape disappeared. It must have been a trick of the light, nothing more.

Putting his head down, Sebastian began to jog again through the green leafy passageways, reaching the far end of the maze within minutes, the tower guiding his way all the while. Then he ran to the tower itself, pushed open the door and began to climb up, because it wouldn't feel right to have come all this way without completing the journey. Sebastian liked completing things, he liked round objects, the number four, and always washed his hands twice, or even four times, even when his mother was calling him. He liked things to be round and simple and safe and, although he couldn't quite explain it, he only felt truly safe when he had climbed the tower, and looked out of each window in turn, moving anticlockwise around the cool space before climbing down again. When viewed from up there Hollowpark Hall looked small and neat and manageable and made Sebastian feel like he was in control. He reached the top of the steps and pushed open the heavy wooden door. He would start at the far window this time—

'Hello, Sebastian.'

Big boys didn't cry, and they certainly didn't scream, but Sebastian felt the air rush out of his lungs all the same and he had to clap his hand over his mouth to stop himself making a noise. His cousin simply smiled at him. It was a gentle smile.

'It's all right, Sebastian. You're welcome here.'

Deirdre was her name; he knew that from listening to his parents. Or 'That Dreadful Deirdre', which was how his mother always referred to her. Sebastian never asked why she called her that, it was one of those things that parents said, that children were not supposed to question because, if they did, they would be told they shouldn't have heard them in the first place.

That Dreadful Deirdre. She didn't look dreadful, Sebastian thought. She looked sad, but gentle. Old – older than his mother, with grey bits in her hair and lines on her face. But she had a kind smile. Her parents used to own this house and she had once thought she would own it too – Sebastian had learned a lot from listening to his parents when they thought a small child wouldn't understand what they were saying. They had nearly had to 'drag her from it', his father had said. But looking at her now Sebastian couldn't imagine Deirdre being dragged anywhere. She was too calm, too still.

Deirdre patted the window sill on which she was sitting, encouraging him to join her. He hadn't imagined the face at the window, Sebastian realised. She had been up here watching him all the time. When she saw how hesitant he was, she smiled again.

'It's OK, Sebastian. I was watching you play in the maze. You love this place, don't you? I do too.'

Sebastian nodded and walked over to join her. She was holding something in her hand and when he reached her side she held it out to him.

'It's called a Sphinx, it's from Egypt – look!'

She handed the ornament over and Sebastian stroked it gently with his fingers. It was like a lion, but it had a man's face, and it had been polished so smoothly that when he looked into it he could see his own, distorted reflection.

Deirdre touched the Sphinx's head gently with one long, pale finger.

'Do you like it? It brings me luck, a certain kind of luck. It lives here, to watch over us.'

As if in a dream he sat down beside her, the breeze from outside ruffling his hair as he smiled at him again.

'You're very good at finding your way through the maze. I was watching you.'

'I keep the tower in my sights,' he told her, and his cousin nodded thoughtfully.

'Yes, I could see you had figured out the secret. You didn't put a foot wrong.'

They both turned then and looked out across the maze, to the fields beyond.

'It looks like my toy farm set,' Sebastian said, suddenly, and Deirdre smiled at him.

'It does, doesn't it?' She reached past him and pointed. 'I can see my little house too, the gatehouse – can you? It's over there...'

He followed her finger and then without thinking, leaned forward, straining to see over the trees. Wind rushed up towards him and he felt himself sway, the ground was so far away and he was so tiny – suddenly he felt her hands on his back and his head started to spin...

'Careful!'

There was a sharp tug on his midriff and Sebastian tumbled off the window sill and onto the floor. Pain shot through him and he bit his lips to stop the tears as he looked up at her. His cousin looked almost as shocked as he did, and she hesitated for a moment before stretching out her hand.

'You have to take care, my love. These windows are extremely dangerous – you don't want to lean out too far.'

And the fright, coupled with the pain in his back and the softness in her voice, a softness he hadn't heard from any adult for many years now, pierced something inside him and Sebastian Fitzmahon found that he was not a big boy any more and started to cry. And before he knew what was happening his cousin had slid down onto the dusty floor beside him and was weeping too, and stroking his back gently the way his mother had not done for an awfully long time.

'It's all right, it's all right to be sad. It has been very hard on you, seeing your father's accident and everything...'

Tears and more tears; it was as if there was a tight ball of sadness inside him and somehow as he cried the ball deflated a little and made it easier to breathe. After a few more moments Sebastian wiped his nose on his sleeve and moved away from her.

'Do you like living in Hollowpark, Sebastian?'

He knew the polite thing to say would be yes, but Sebastian felt that he and his cousin were friends now and that he didn't have to pretend any more.

'No. I'm frightened of it.'

Deirdre sighed. 'That's a shame, my darling. It's a lovely place, once you get used to it. What is it that scares you?'

Sebastian sniffed again.

'It's too big, and it's cold. And there are sounds – in the middle of the night.'

Deirdre smiled. She looked much younger than his mother when she smiled, Sebastian realised.

'Ah, now that's just the house talking to you!'

Sebastian squinted at her suspiciously. He wasn't a baby and he didn't want to hear some stupid baby story. But his cousin didn't look as if she was making fun of him, instead she reached over and patted his hand.

'I mean it. The stairs are squeaky because they are old and not all the doors fit properly so they wobble in the wind and make all sorts of funny noises. It used to scare me too when I was your age. But then I realised it was just the house saying good night to me and I felt quite differently about it then!'

'And does the gatehouse talk to you too?'

His cousin took her hand away, letting it flop into her lap.

'No. It's quite silent there. Nothing like the Hall.'

'You should still be living there.'

The fierce determination in his voice shocked Sebastian and it must have shocked his cousin too because she paused for a moment before answering him.

'That's not how things worked out, my darling. Oh I know...'

She raised her hand to quiet his objections.

'I was very sad for a long time when we had to move away. But there was nothing I could do about it, so I had to make peace with where I am now. But you can do something for me, Sebastian.'

Right now, sitting on the floor beside her, the warmth of her embrace still resting on his shoulder blades, he would have promised her anything.

'I want you to love Hollowpark for me.'

Sebastian stared at his cousin, not sure what she meant. Deirdre reached over again and touched him on the shoulder.

'Your great-great-grandparents built that house for our family and it has kept us safe for generations. And it will always look after the people who live in it but, you see, Sebastian, the people who live there must love the house too. Those who are not kind to the house, or its people...'

Her voice trailed away and Sebastian thought he heard, from the maze below, a faint echo of his father's screams.

'Those who are not kind to the house, or those who live in it, will not be happy here. Do you understand what I'm saying?'

'My father hates it now.'

'Yes.'

Deirdre rose from the floor and went back to the window again.

'He does, and that won't change, but yet he'll be too stubborn to leave it. You'll have some difficult years, but I know, if you get through them, that you will be incredibly happy here. The house will take care of you.'

The pain in his back had receded and Sebastian Patrick Fitzmahon climbed up off the floor and went to join his cousin at the window. They stood for a moment together, looking down at their home.

'Don't tell your father that you saw me, please.'

Deirdre's voice was low. Sebastian was embarrassed that she, a grown woman, had to ask this favour of a child but understood and simply nodded.

'I like to come here sometimes, just to sit.'

'I hope you will always feel welcome here,' he told her. And then she handed him the little bronze ornament and he turned it around in his hands and the reflection of his face was clear, and smiled back at him.

Chapter 19

2007

'Isla!'

I called my employer's name, shouting the words through the thin gap in the heavy wooden door that guarded the entrance to the tower, but received no response. Then I sank back on my heels and forced my thoughts into some sort of order. Nannies are great in a crisis. People might think of us as wipers of bottoms and tyers of shoelaces – indeed I know for a fact my mother does – but we also tend to be qualified in first aid and very experienced at calming people down, whether that be tantruming toddlers, pushy parents or, if needs be, ourselves. And now I'd have to draw on all of that experience. I reached through the gap, moving my fingers around until they connected with Isla's cheek. Relieved to find it warm, I stroked it softly then guided my hand gently downwards until I found what I was looking for, a pulse at her throat, fluttery but distinct. Isla was alive, then, and that was something to be grateful for. But I also knew she was lying in a dreadful position, and that she needed help as soon as I could get it to her.

No signal. I knew that would be the case, but took out my phone anyway, waving it in the air as if I could conjure 3G from the trees. I called out to Isla that I was going for help – that, too, was a pointless exercise but it seemed important to say something out loud, to make whatever connection I could with her to let her know she was not being abandoned, then I sprinted away from the tower, in the direction of the driveway, checking all the while for a bar or two to appear. As I rounded the outside of the maze I heard a sharp bark, and then the little dog scrabbled out from under the bushes and ran to me.

'Good boy!'

My voice was shaky, but I didn't have time to panic, or feel sorry for myself so I just kept running, the terrier at my heels, until I reached the top of the driveway and finally saw a signal wobble into view on my phone screen. The handset vibrated and I had to swipe away a number of irritating messages welcoming me to the Irish phone network, and one informing of a sale at a nail salon in Highgate I'd last visited three years ago, before I could fumble for the keypad and dial 999.

'And where are you located?'

'H-Hollowpark Hall.' I paused, panic threatening to overwhelm me as I struggled to remember the proper address. If Isla died it would be my fault – but thankfully the woman on the other end could sense I was losing my focus and, with a mixture of kindness and efficiency pulled the word 'Lisheeha' from me and then the name of the nearest big town.

'I have you now, I'm sending a unit. Can you stay near the phone?'

'Yes...'

And with that my knees buckled, and I sank to the grass, trembling, finally giving in to my fear. Every shredded nerve was telling me to go back to Isla, to sit with her and hold her hand through the door, but my rational brain, my nanny brain, told me that the paramedics wouldn't be able to find her if my phone was out of range and that I should stay where I was. So, I forced myself to sit, damp seeping through my jeans as I stared at the handset as if by doing so I could summon help more quickly. Then I felt a nudge and looked down to see the little dog inching his way under my arm. He settled himself in beside me, quiet apart from the odd snuffle, and as his warmth spread through my body I found myself able to think in straight lines again. Patrick and Delia. Of course, I had to call them next. They were in Roscommon for the day, for some sort of meeting at the tourist office in the town, and as I dialled my new boss's number my hand shook slightly as I tried to figure out how best to tell him what had happened. But in the end, it was Delia who answered as her son was driving and, although I could hear his voice rise as he listened to her end of the conversation – Ambulance? Who? Where? How is she? – she herself stayed calm enough to take the information in and ask the important questions. There was no point in them trying to come back, she told me, instead they would make their way to the hospital and meet the ambulance there.

'And listen to me now, love.'

Delia's voice deepened and I pressed the phone closer to my ear, as if by doing so, I could bring myself even closer to her warm words.

'Isla will be grand. It sounds like you did exactly the right thing, so you're not to be worrying yourself, OK? The ambulance will be there any minute, she was lucky to have you around, she'll be fine.'

She couldn't possibly have known that, of course, but it was what I needed to hear and her voice calmed me down just enough to be able to discuss Skye and to agree that, yes, Delia would ring the playschool and arrange for Evelyn to take her for the afternoon. We said goodbye, and then it was just me and the phone and the dog again. And I'm not sure what I would have done if he hadn't been there because every time I let my mind drift Isla wandered into it, bruised and broken or, worse still, accompanied by a young woman with a fuzz of dark hair... but I couldn't allow myself to think of either of them, that would surely tip me into panic, so instead I forced my brain to stay blank and just sat, cuddling the dog, staring at the ground and clinging to my phone, the only thing tethering me to normality and Isla to safety.

It was around twenty minutes later when I heard the sirens. Sound travels for miles on those quiet country roads and I had enough time to dislodge the dog and straighten both myself and my thoughts before the ambulance powered up the drive then screeched to a halt in front of me. The paramedics jumped out and, after grabbing a stretcher piled reassuringly high with complicated equipment, followed me across the grass around the side of the maze until we reached the tower and the tall wooden door. I could have panicked then, I supposed, but I had grown used to staying calm so I just sat on the grass again and waited while they worked steadily and quickly to ease the door open. All the time the little animal remained by my side, silent, his hair standing on end as if he, too, understood the gravity of the situation.

'Is she alive?' I asked them when they finally lifted Isla onto the stretcher and wheeled it past me. Their nods told me that she was but the urgency of their movements made it clear that the situation was still extremely serious and within moments we were in the back of the ambulance and I was holding tight to Isla's hand as we bumped over the gravel and down the long driveway.

The journey to the hospital was a blur of blue light and activity. Evelyn texted to assure me she'd mind Skye for as long as was needed, and then my phone lost signal again which actually came as a relief as I could finally just sit, and hold Isla's hand and tell the paramedics that I didn't really know the answers to any of their questions, like how long she had been lying there and what the hell had happened in the first place. When we reached the hospital I kept hold of her trolley as it was pushed into the emergency department and it wasn't until I heard two familiar voices – Patrick's, taut with fear, and Delia's behind him, deeper and calmer and stronger – that I was finally able to step away. Doors clanged, Patrick disappeared, Delia guided me to a chair and asked more questions, what had I seen, what did I know? But she didn't pressure me for answers and finally we just sat there, hand in hand, until the door opened again and her son reappeared.

'She's going to be fine.'

It was only when Delia let go of my hand that I realised how tightly she had been clasping it.

Chapter 20

'Thank you so much for coming. We just wanted to explain a few things.'

'OK.'

I accepted a cup of coffee from Patrick and waited for Isla to continue. The hospital canteen smelled of disinfectant and burned lasagne and I couldn't imagine a more unappealing place for a chat. But when I'd arrived at the hospital to collect them, Patrick and Isla had insisted we go there rather than immediately hitting the road for Lisheeha. At first, I'd accepted the explanation that they were waiting to speak to another doctor, but now it looked like they wanted a heart to heart as well.

'It's complicated...'

Isla's voice cracked into a cough and tears leapt into her eyes as the action jarred her sore arm.

'I'm all right...'

She tried to wave Patrick away but only succeeded in causing herself more pain and he popped two tablets from their blister packet, then went to the counter to get her some water to wash them down. While we waited for him to return I sipped the coffee which tasted like someone had wiped down the machine, then wrung the dregs out into a cup of tepid water. After the past twenty-four hours I'd had, however, I just needed the caffeine.

Once we'd learned that Isla was suffering from nothing more than a dislocated shoulder and mild concussion, Delia and I had headed back to Hollowpark, collecting Skye from Evelyn's house on the way. Patrick stayed in the hospital to be near his wife and I offered to spend the night with Skye in the Gate House. Delia, clearly exhausted, had been happy to take me up on the offer, but I'd be lying if I didn't say I was acting less out of selflessness and more from the desire not to spend a night on my own in the main house, and to avoid any meeting with the girl, or ghost, or spirit who I was now convinced was in residence there. But although Patrick and Isla's bedroom was comfortable and Skye didn't stir all night, I still found it impossible to settle, seeing dark-haired teenagers in every corner and fearing what nightmares would emerge if I closed my eyes. In the end I managed a couple of hours of fitful sleep before Skye came in to wake me at half past six. She, bless her, had been her usual bubbly self, not put out in the slightest by the unusual events of the previous day and quite happy to accept my explanation that her mummy had hurt her arm and needed a night in hospital to get better. But even the nicest of children can be hard work at the crack of dawn and I was looking forward to dropping her to school and returning to the Gate House for a couple of hours' rest before collecting her again.

And then Patrick had called and upended my day's plans.

'Can you come into town and collect us? We need to talk to you about something.'

Skye had been nose-deep in a bowl of cornflakes, but I had moved away from her anyway, pressing the phone to my ear, taken aback by the seriousness of his tone.

'Please, Grace, it's important. You can ask Mum to do the school run, you'll think of something.'

'OK.'

I'd paused, then remembered something that had seemed so important yesterday and so inconsequential now.

'Actually, you hadn't signed the right form anyway, for me to collect Skye, I mean? So I'll tell Delia she needs to drop her off today and we'll sort it out later?'

'Grand.' Patrick, I had noticed, tended to sound far more Irish when he was under pressure.

Thankfully Delia, whose night had clearly been more refreshing than mine, accepted my explanation with nothing more than an eye-roll and 'that fella would forget his head if it wasn't attached to him', and headed off quite cheerfully with her granddaughter, the two of them singing pop songs as her tiny car bumped its way down the drive. I set off for the hospital myself then, leaving the car windows down in the hope the fresh air would compensate for my sleepless night, but in the end it was the scenery that distracted me and even lightened my mood. I had been too tired to appreciate my new environment when Patrick had collected me from the train station but today it was a salvation, emerald-green fields broken by traditional stone walls and the shimmering promise of a lake beyond the trees. Even the accents on the local radio station made me feel welcome. It was good to be in a place where my soft consonants were commonplace while the presenters' gentle jokes and, yes, even the Country 'n' Irish music reminded me that despite all of the strange things that had happened, there were still many things I loved about being home.

'Here we go!'

I jumped as Patrick placed two paper cups of water on the table, then watched him faff around, clearing up the spillage with paper towels. Both he and his wife were jumpy today and I had a feeling it wasn't just the night in hospital that had upset them. I waited patiently for them to steady themselves and then Isla took a deep breath and looked at me.

'We just wanted to let you know... You see, Patrick and I aren't actually married.'

'OK.'

So that was their big reveal? My first instinct was to laugh it off, after twenty-four hours in which I'd confronted the possibility of a ghost in my bedroom and had faced what had appeared to be the near death of my new employer, it would have taken more than that to cause my eyebrows to rise. But Isla looked fragile, and far from amused. I stole a look at the hand hanging out of her sling, the glint of gold on her ring finger. I had noticed way back in Greece that her wedding ring wasn't particularly expensive-looking, but had assumed that was simply part of the outdoorsy, arty look she had going on. Now it transpired it might be just a cheapo piece of costume jewellery after all. What I couldn't figure out though was, why they would bother pretending? Lisheeha might have been in the sticks but it was 2007, not 1907, and Ireland had come a long way from Magdalene Laundries and lone parents being labelled 'unmarried mothers', as if the fathers had no role at all in the proceedings. She and Patrick looked so upset, however, I figured there must be something behind the lie.

'It's a bit complicated. Well, a lot.'

Isla's face was chalk white and if I hadn't actually seen her being discharged by a doctor twenty minutes previously I'd have assumed she should have still been in a hospital bed. Patrick reached over and gave her good hand a squeeze as she began to speak.

'I was married before, you see. I still am, actually. To someone else.'

I nodded, but remained silent while waiting for her to continue.

'Patrick and I met in London. We – my husband and I – were attending a charity ball; his firm were the chief sponsors. Ethan and I – my husband... we didn't have a good relationship.'

She swallowed and it was clear that, despite her obvious injuries, the pain she was experiencing now was something more than physical.

'He'd had a lot to drink that night, and I was trying to persuade him not to drive home. And he—'

'I saw him assault her in the hotel car park.'

The chill in Patrick's voice made it almost unrecognisable. I looked at him, but his gaze remained fixed on Isla's face as he took up the story.

'He should have been arrested for what he did to her.'

'Patrick...'

Isla took her hand out of his and pushed her hair back from her face. Then she touched the skin under her right eye gently, and I wondered how many times she had been bruised there. Patrick continued in the same icy, almost dispassionate tone and there was no trace of the west of Ireland in his clipped accent now.

'I was on my way to my own car when I heard her cry out. He tried to tell me I'd imagined it, of course, but I could see the mark on her face.'

Isla flushed, tears springing to her eyes.

'I just wanted to get out of there. It's hard to explain, Grace, but when you are in that situation...'

'I know,' I told her, and we both stared down at the crumb-strewn table for a moment. And I did know, at least from a distance. I had worked for a family in Surrey for a while. There had been a strange atmosphere in the house from the very beginning but it was only when I saw the bruises that I understood why. He was a six-foot-tall bank executive, she was a size eight ex-model, but it still took me a while to cotton on to what was happening, because the bruises were on his face, not hers. I've learned a lot, living in other people's houses, and I've also learned not to show surprise at anything I hear.

'I told Patrick I was fine.'

Isla extended the index finger of her good hand and pushed a solitary crumb around the table surface.

'That's what I did all the time, back then. Told people I was fine, tried to make them go away. I was afraid, you see. Of what he... of what Ethan would do to me when he got home, of how bad it could get if he knew I'd confided in someone. I felt so trapped – we had lost a baby the year before and he persuaded me that I needed to give up work, concentrate on my health for a while. But that only made everything worse, it meant I had no money of my own and there were days when I didn't talk to anyone except him. Once, I tried calling a women's helpline, but he found the number on the phone bill...'

Isla's voice faded away and for a moment I could sense she was back there, reliving it. Then she blinked and when she spoke again she sounded stronger.

'But that night I got lucky. Patrick helped me pour Ethan into the passenger seat of the car and when I got home I found his business card tucked into my coat pocket. So I texted him my number. I deleted the sent text, of course, but I still spent days regretting what I'd done, terrified of what Ethan would do if he knew I'd contacted another man.'

She touched the skin under her eye again, the action butterfly light.

'And then I got a text from a hair salon.'

Isla looked directly at me for the first time and gave a watery smile.

'A number I didn't recognise, telling me I was entitled to twenty per cent off my usual blow dry. It was genius – where did you get the idea from? I never thought to ask.'

Patrick shrugged, looking equal parts proud and embarrassed.

'You weren't the only person ringing helplines. I asked one group for advice, they said it wasn't foolproof but that I could try sending a dummy message. And they also told me to be very careful, because if the abuser in question found out, things could get very serious for you. But I was desperate to help you, so I took the risk.'

Isla nodded.

'I texted Patrick back when Ethan was in the shower, told

him I'd meet him at eleven the following morning. I had a hospital appointment, you see, and I knew Ethan would allow me to go on my own.'

Her voice wobbled.

'I was due a check-up at the maternity hospital. The baby we lost – it had been a late miscarriage, it had been so awful, but Ethan told me it was all my fault, that my body had failed us and that he wasn't going to take time off work to make up for my mistake. I was so upset when he said that but it turned out to be the decision that saved me. Patrick met me after the appointment and I never went home again. If it wasn't for that baby...'

There were tears pouring down her face now but her voice remained steady.

'That little baby, that baby that was never born, she saved my life. If it wasn't for her I wouldn't be here, Skye wouldn't...'

Isla shuddered, and then wiped the tears away and what was left on her face was a strength that hadn't been in evidence before.

'I never went back. Patrick took me to one of those hostels, but it was horrible, so in the end he offered to let me sleep on his sofa. We were just friends in the beginning...'

They looked at each other in perfect silence for a moment, then Patrick took up the story.

'We called the police, they were terrific, and that meant we could go back to the house and pick up Isla's stuff, and then we went back to my flat. But Isla couldn't settle there, or anywhere in London.'

Isla had fallen silent now, tension pumping off her in waves, and she was holding herself so tightly her injured arm must have been agony. But she said nothing, just kept staring ahead as Patrick continued.

'And then I thought of home. And once the idea of Lisheeha and Hollowpark came into my head, I couldn't think of anything else. I mean, Isla had got away from Ethan but her life was pretty grim, you know? I'd go out to work and leave her sitting in my flat and she'd still be there when I got home; she was terrified of going out, terrified of meeting him. It was clear to both of us that she'd never really recover in London.'

He paused and Isla seemed to come back to the room a little and took up the story.

'He bundled me into the car and we took the ferry over. I swear, I can barely remember the journey. But I do remember seeing Lisheeha for the first time and then coming up the driveway to the Hall... It was the first time I'd felt safe in a long time.'

Isla gave the ghost of a smile.

'I never had a real home, you see, not really. My parents are both dead and I married Ethan when I was twenty-five. I had never even lived with anyone before then. That's why it was so hard to leave him, it wasn't like I had an old flatmate or someone I felt I could turn to. My only brother lives in France and he's a friend of Ethan's, he's the person who introduced us, as it happens, so I didn't feel like I could talk to him, he'd never have believed me. So you see, Grace, I'd never felt safe, not really. At least, not until Delia offered us the Gate House. I knew straight away it could be a perfect little home for the two of us. The three of us.'

Another look passed between them, and then Patrick gave himself a small shake, and smiled at me.

'Yes. We – Isla and I – were in a relationship, obviously, by then, and when we found out that Skye was on the way, well it made even more sense to stay in Ireland, long term. It was a difficult pregnancy, I mentioned that before, I think. And even afterwards, Isla was very unwell.'

She nodded her head before taking up the story again.

'The doctors just said it was post-natal depression, and that was part of it, certainly, but there was more to it too. It was like I just crashed, you know? That baby, leaving Ethan, moving to a new country – I fell apart.'

Patrick leaned over as if to hug her but remembered her injured arm just in time and had to be content with just patting Isla gently on the shoulder as she continued to speak.

'I had to be hospitalised in the end; I had a complete breakdown. Patrick and Delia were wonderful, they minded Skye when I couldn't. It was awful, I missed the first few months of my baby's life. But I came through it.'

She looked over at Patrick and he smiled at her.

'You did. You were amazing.'

I left a beat of silence and then asked one of the many questions on my mind.

'But why pretend to be married? It's not such a big deal, is it? I mean, Delia is cool, she'd hardly get hung up on something like that and you can get married eventually, once you have everything sorted with your ex...'

The faint smile on Isla's face disappeared.

'He doesn't know where I am, Grace. I'm still terrified of him. Ethan – he's a dangerous man. He says he's a businessman and that's true, but he does business with some very dodgy people. He's not the type to just sign divorce papers, you know. I'm terrified of what he'd do if he found us – found me.'

Another look passed between them, and I thought of little Skye's blue eyes, and Patrick's brown pair, and wondered if there was an important part of the story they were not telling me. But it wasn't my place to probe any deeper so I let the silence settle until Isla spoke again.

'In order for us to get divorced I'd need to make contact with him, maybe even meet him. Oh, I know I'll have to do it someday but I've been so ill, so tired…'

She started to cry and a canteen worker who was clearing a nearby table looked over, then studiously looked away again. They must be used to people sharing sad stories in this place but few, I guessed, as unusual as this one.

'I couldn't bear the thought of him finding me. I changed my name…'

I must have done a double take because Isla nodded.

'Yeah. I was plain old Lucy Atkinson when I was married to Ethan, Lucy Wallace before then. My mum was Scottish, and she gave me Isla as a second name so I just started using that.'

I must have looked confused because she dried her tears and gave me a sympathetic smile.

'I know it's a lot to take in. I'm Isla Uprichard Fitzmahon here, that's all you need to know, and Skye uses the same name. And the point is, Ethan would never think of looking for us here – for me, I mean. We told Delia we'd been married in London, a spur-of-the-moment thing when we found out I was pregnant. She was a bit put out we hadn't invited her but when Skye came along she was so besotted she forgot she had ever been angry. We've promised her we'll renew our vows when the Big House is ready and that is the plan, actually. I'll sort out my divorce, then we'll get married and start again, properly. Well, that was the plan. Until yesterday.'

Isla sighed.

'I was feeling better, Grace, really I was. The holiday was wonderful, and then starting work again… Even you agreeing to come to live with us, it felt like everything was starting to come together again. I was all set to contact Ethan, be a grown-up about it, you know? Set things in train. And then…'

She swallowed.

'Yesterday morning, I saw someone in the maze.'

She took a sip from the glass of water before continuing.

'I was taking a break from work, I walked over to the window, just to get some air. And that's when I saw him, walking through the maze.'

'Who?' My voice was sharp, and Isla took a moment to compose herself before speaking.

'I was so sure it was Ethan. I couldn't see his face, couldn't tell if it was a man or a woman, even, but I was so scared and so sure it was him, or that he'd sent someone looking for me, that he had tracked me down. I knew you had all gone out, that I was alone and I felt so vulnerable up there, if they came up the stairs I'd be trapped, I even thought about jumping.'

Patrick flinched, but Isla didn't seem to notice, and I could tell by the look on her face that she was back there again in her mind, at the top of the tower, cornered and frightened and desperate.

'Instead, I ran. I figured if I could get to the bottom before the person left the maze I could run around the side and get away. It was the idea of being trapped in the tower that terrified me, so I ran, but when I got to the top of the stairs I must have tripped because I don't remember anything else, just waking up here and Patrick being beside my bed.'

Isla looked directly at me, a watery smile on her face.

'They told me what you did. I'll never be able to repay you, Grace.'

'It was nothing.' Isla was chalk white now and Patrick pressed the glass of water into her hand again. As she drank it, I took the opportunity to try and get my own thoughts in order.

'Why are you so sure it was someone looking for you? That your husband had sent someone – there could be an innocent explanation, surely?'

Isla swallowed her drink and shook her head.

'A tourist? Maybe, but why would a tourist be wandering around the grounds like that? The house was locked up, we weren't open to visitors, and there's a big sign outside the maze saying no one should go in without a guide. No, I'm convinced the person, whoever it was, was looking for someone, for me.'

Or they could have been a ghost, I thought to myself, and immediately felt foolish.

Isla exhaled.

'And do you know what? Even if they weren't sent by Ethan, even if there was a perfectly innocent explanation, it just threw me, you know? I was so scared, Grace, it was as bad as if Ethan *had* found me, just the memory of him had ruined everything again. It was like he was right there in my home, my studio, the one place I felt safe. That's the sort of hold he had over me, or has over me. One fright, one unusual thing and look at me, my arm, I won't be able to work for weeks...'

She burst into tears, clearly exhausted and in serious pain.

'He ruined everything and he's still ruining everything—'

'Isla Up – Richard?'

The newcomer was small, with red hair pinned back off her face, pink scrubs and a quizzical expression on her face. A brown envelope was clutched in her outstretched hand.

Isla sniffed back a tear, tried to calm herself.

'That's me.'

'I have your X-ray here. You can give us a call tomorrow, make an appointment for physio.'

It was as if a spell had been broken. Isla dried her tears and thanked the woman while Patrick and I gathered her belongings and then the three of us made our way out of the hospital and into the car park. As Patrick busied himself getting a ticket and loading up the car, I helped Isla into the front seat, fastening the belt around her broken arm as gently as I could. Before I could finish, however, she reached out and grabbed my wrist.

'You might be wondering why we told you all this.'

I had been, of course, but remained silent to let her tell me in her own time.

'We need you, Grace, we need your support.'

Her gaze was fierce now, her eyes locked on mine.

'Delia has been fantastic to me but I just can't face admitting that we lied about being married or that I'm worried that my bloody ex-husband will come tramping all over the west of Ireland looking for me. I couldn't do that to her, couldn't bring that sort of stress into the house, it wouldn't be fair. And I'll sort it out, I know I must, but I can't even dress myself at the moment.'

She looked down at the white fabric sling.

'Patrick has been wonderful, but he has been dealing with this, carrying me for such a long time, he's exhausted from it too. I'm tired of being scared, Grace, and I'm worried about Skye too. She needs normality, someone to depend on. I was so ill when she was a baby and I need to protect myself to make sure that doesn't happen again. That's why I wanted to tell you everything, it's because we need you, Grace, to help us keep everything going. Skye needs you.'

She didn't know it, but she had only needed to say those last three words to make up my mind. Patrick returned and I folded myself into the back seat as he started the car.

Skye needs you.

I rested my head against the window, grateful that Patrick had put the radio on and that everyone was too tired for further conversation.

We need you.

It was a happy house, Hollowpark Hall, despite everything Isla had told me; the Fitzmahons were good people. But there was no doubt it was a rather chaotic one too, with three adults trying to start a business and one of them now physically incapacitated as well. They all loved the little girl, that much was clear, but Skye needed someone who could focus solely on her. As Patrick slowed down over a speed bump, taking care not to jar Isla's arm, I realised my decision had already been made. Skye needed me. Isla needed me. Even Patrick – I looked up at the tanned back of his neck and then turned my gaze away again, ignoring the sudden lurch in my stomach that surely linked only to the stress of the past few days. The whole family needed me. The young girl in my room, that face in the window – there was a lot to worry about, a lot, let's face it, for me to be scared of, and Isla and Patrick had no idea how close I had come to leaving them. But they needed me, and so I would stay.

Chapter 21

1864

Sebastian Fitzmahon was only nineteen years old the day he buried his father, but everything about the event made him feel as if there had been a rehearsal he couldn't remember but which had showed him exactly what he needed to do.

He had come down for breakfast that morning to find his mother already dressed, white faced and weeping yet calm and perfectly able to tend to his younger brothers and sister who were, as always, huddled around her and bickering among themselves. Her composure did not surprise him. Sebastian did not know much about how other people's families behaved behind their own closed doors, he had never made a friend close enough to invite him home for the school holidays. But he had always felt that there had been something rotten between his parents, something damaged beyond repair, and it was obvious now that this absence of genuine marital affection would, in fact, be of benefit to his mother in the weeks and months ahead. Oh, it was true that her life would be diminished by her husband's passing, widows were not wives, and Madeline Fitzmahon would now have to live in a world where her son, although not yet out of his teens, would become the owner of Hollowpark Hall and the head of her household. But other than that change in status Madeline would not miss her husband because, in every way that counted, he had already been absent for a long time. No, it was he, Sebastian, who would feel the loss of his father most keenly, because it was his life that was now utterly, irrevocably changed.

The head of the household.

As he followed the hearse on the short journey to the church and greeted the knot of mourners that had gathered outside, Sebastian felt his new title settle like a cloak around his shoulders, heavy and constricting but with a certain undeniable comfort in the weight. He shook hands and agreed with person after person that, yes, the loss had been beyond measure, yes, his father's death at the age of fifty had been a terrible tragedy. Had it though? As the vicar began the familiar words of the sermon and Sebastian was finally allowed a moment with his own thoughts, he found himself less than certain. The truth was that everything that had been vibrant about his father had passed away almost two decades before, when the maze had taken half the sight and all of the joy out of Paul Fitzmahon's world. It was the drinking, Sebastian supposed, that had been behind that final fall, the crack of the skull on the fireplace that had brought his father's half-life, finally, to an end. His mother called it an accident, blaming the incident on her husband's bad eyesight, and claiming that a discarded shoe on the floor had caught him by surprise. But the facts,

Sebastian knew, didn't really matter. His father had been missing for a long time, now, but at least the family had a body to bury. And he, having not yet turned twenty, had a house to run and no one to advise him how to do it.

Fear. It was only after the ceremony, when the mourners began to make their slow way back to the house for refreshments, that Sebastian allowed himself to acknowledge that fear, rather than sadness, was at the root of his dark mood. It was just not *fair* – he flushed at the word, which brought to mind the way his youngest brother fussed and moaned at the slightest inconvenience – but that was how he felt, it was just not *fair* that all of this responsibility had fallen to him, so early. Sebastian had hated school, and his holidays at home in Ireland had provided little relief, surrounded as he was by spoiled and fretful siblings and a father too gloomy to provide anything like good company. But he had made plans to travel after school and had indeed spent many happy hours planning the route he would take. He would start in Paris, of course, and then go on to Florence to visit art galleries and from there to Rome – maybe he would take art lessons too, far from his father's scorn. But now his father was dead and there would be no travelling, no art, no joy at all. Instead Sebastian had to take a much shorter journey, from the world of childhood to that of adult responsibility with no vacation in between. His father's final, miserable legacy.

Sebastian sighed, rose with the others as the vicar brought the ceremony to a close, then followed the coffin on its slow final journey down the aisle and into the adjoining churchyard. The well-maintained building and neat graveyard were in stark contrast to the surrounding land, still littered with scorched fields and abandoned homes. Sebastian was too young to remember the worst of that devastating period when the Irish potato crop had failed, but no one who grew up in Ireland could have avoided hearing stories of the crisis that had afflicted every corner of the country; the suffering and starvation that some called a tragedy and others, his father among them, the inevitable result of the native man's inability to provide for his family.

'Too bloody dependent on the potato,' his father had scoffed one winter, when Sebastian had commented on the beggars that had flung themselves at his carriage as it rounded the corner into the driveway, one of them narrowly avoiding being crushed under the wheels.

'It was a crop failure, no more than that. Bloody country is surrounded by water and the Irish didn't have the wit to fish for food!'

Sebastian's mother had smiled vaguely and although he hadn't really understood what his father had meant, Sebastian had nodded too, knowing even at that young age that to agree with Papa was to secure a more peaceful evening for all of them. It was only years afterwards that he allowed himself to think of how far Lisheeha was from the sea, and how difficult it would have been for a healthy man to walk there, let alone the skeletal figures he had seen at the gate. But by then he had grown used to letting any possible argument evaporate for the sake of peace.

Having pressed some coins into the vicar's hand and invited him back to the house for refreshments, Sebastian dawdled for a while in the churchyard, ostensibly to pay his last respects to his father but in reality to give his aching head a moment of silence before heading back to the house and assuming command of the day again. But his hopes of a solitary walk back to the Hall were shattered when he saw two figures a little way up the lane ahead of him: a tall, thin woman, dressed in black, and a man, broad-shouldered but stooped with age. Sebastian recognised his cousin Deirdre almost immediately and quickened his pace, afraid she had been accosted by one of the many destitute Irishmen who still roamed the country, but as he drew closer he saw to his astonishment that the older man was crying, and his cousin was gently patting his hand. As he drew nearer the man noticed him, pulled away and then, after a few quiet words with his cousin, shuffled back in the direction of the village. Deirdre herself merely adjusted the black shawl she had thrown around her shoulders and smiled at Sebastian as he approached.

'Your father would have been proud of you today.'

'Do you think so?'

Sebastian's question was genuine. Deirdre was the only person whose opinion he valued and the only one he knew, with utter certainty, who would never lie to him.

His cousin nodded. 'Yes, I do. Poor Paul appreciated formality, even in his later years. He would have wanted his funeral to be correct, and it was.'

The journey back to the house was less than half a mile and as they fell into step together Sebastian found himself wishing it were longer. There were only two places he felt completely at home, at the top of the tower and in his cousin's company, and sometimes he felt that it was only when the two were combined that he felt truly happy.

'Who was that man?' His cousin smiled.

'That man is called Thomas O'Mahony.'

The name meant nothing to Sebastian but he could hear the affection in his cousin's voice.

'Why was he weeping?'

'He brought me a letter. From his son.'

The tenderness in her voice was so vivid it almost stopped Sebastian in his tracks. There was a genuine intensity to it that had, he realised, been missing from the funeral that morning. There was a sadness to her tone too, a sadness that he knew was rooted in the years of suffering that had been experienced in this country, in the fields and villages around Lisheeha, although its tendrils had never sneaked into the house itself. The Hunger, as the native Irish called it, had happened a decade before but the tears on the face of the old man were a reminder that many still battled the hardship it had created.

'What happened to the man's son? Why was he writing to you?'

'That man, Thomas, was the head gardener here, once upon a time. He had five sons. The youngest, Ciarán, was around my own age. We used to play together, actually, in the maze when we were children. The family lived in the gatehouse, but they had to move away, when your father came to live here.'

It was a simple sentence, 'had to move away', but Sebastian heard the sudden edge in his cousin's voice.

'Did they fall on hard times?'

Deirdre sighed. 'The hardest. It was a bad time for a man like Thomas to lose his job and when the potato crop failed things got very difficult, very quickly. Ciarán came back here one day, looking for help.'

Deirdre's eyes flashed briefly with anger.

'You could actually hear the hunger; do you know that? Early in the morning, you could hear the keening of the women as they realised all of the food was gone, all of it, rotted in the ground or in their stores. And you could see it, a sickly green mist hanging over the countryside. They say it was a blight, a naturally occurring phenomenon, but the local people described the land as cursed and it was hard to see it any other way. Anyway.'

She blinked, then took up the story again.

'Ciarán's wife had died and he was half blinded with hunger himself but he found his way back here, to the place he had called home as a child, to look for help. He made it as far as the door, but...'

Her voice faltered but it was easy for Sebastian to fill in the rest.

'My father turned him away.'

Deirdre swallowed, composed herself, nodded.

'I found Ciarán just there.'

They had reached the beginning of the long driveway now and she pointed at the large oak tree that had guarded the entrance for as long as Sebastian could remember.

'He was no more than a crumpled pile of rags. When I bent over him I thought he was dead, that I would have to call someone from the Hall to bury him, but I thought I saw a flicker of a pulse at his throat and when I loosened his shirt to see if he was really alive I found the baby, clutched to his breast.'

She stared fixedly ahead.

'The child was dead but when I lifted the body away from him Ciarán tried to stop me and I knew he had some strength left in him. I helped him up then and brought him to the gatehouse.'

Sebastian could not imagine how his cousin could have carried a grown man, not even one as malnourished as Ciarán must have been, but he knew Deirdre well enough not to ask too many questions and allowed her instead to finish the story.

'I was sure he would die that night. It was three days before he could even keep down a little soup – my mother and I took turns to sit with him, poor man. He was raving, screaming about what he had seen, dreadful things.'

She gave herself a small shake and her voice was stronger as she continued.

'But he was a strong man, and a good man. He left us two weeks later, but I made him promise he would keep in touch. And that's what his father came to tell me today. Ciarán went to America, you see, and he wrote to his father to tell him he is married again and that his wife is expecting a child—'

'You saved his life.'

Sebastian blurted out the words. His cousin regarded him calmly.

'Hollowpark saved him.'

Her voice took on a cool, almost distant tone.

'He knew where to come, to find sanctuary. Your father wouldn't provide what he needed but he had come to the right place after all. I've told you, Sebastian, Hollowpark Hall protects its own.'

The trees were blocking the afternoon sunlight as they continued their walk up the long drive.

'He rested in the gatehouse, and he recovered, and he will have a good life now, a long life. And your father...'

Her voice trailed away. A sharp, sudden wind rustled the leaves in the trees above them and despite the stress of the last few days and his own exhaustion, Sebastian felt the breeze blow open his mind. His father had not been a good man, had not respected Hollowpark Hall nor those who sought shelter in it. And he himself had not had a happy life there. Sebastian's hands had grown cold and he flexed his fingers, trying to bring warmth to his limbs and clarity to his thoughts. It was all superstition, of course. He was an adult now and would have enough to worry about, running this large estate without paying heed to fairy stories. But his cousin was by his side, the woman who had been his friend for many years, and she believed those stories.

They rounded a corner and as the canopy of trees thinned, a shaft of sunlight warmed his face and he felt, as he always did in Deirdre's company, a deep sense of contentment. Despite the age difference between them they had remained friends over the ten years since he had met her in the tower and Deirdre had written to him while he was away in school, her letters often his only source of comfort. Once, a boy in his class had found him poring over the letter with its small, neat handwriting and had snatched it away, encouraging the others to jeer him about the mysterious Deirdre whose affection meant so much to him. But Sebastian had ignored the taunting and treasured every letter, every line. They were approaching the house now and he could see carriages pulled up near the stone steps, hear the murmur of conversation floating through the open front door. He would invite his cousin to join them in mourning his father but knew that she would not. Deirdre had not set foot in Hollowpark since Sebastian's father had moved in and, even though he himself was master now, he sensed that she never would again. Instead, as she stopped at the junction that would lead her back to the gatehouse, Sebastian reached out and touched Deirdre gently on her sleeve.

'Will you help me? To run this place, to protect it. I'm scared.'

Deirdre smiled up at him. 'Of course I will. But you won't need much help, Sebastian. You're a good person and you will do the right thing. And Hollowpark will shelter you.'

'You speak about the house as if it's a person.'

'That's how it feels to me. Do you know I was married once, Sebastian?'

Her voice was so low he had to move closer to hear it, and he shook his head.

'He was not a good man and he would not have been kind to me. But Hollowpark saved me, one night. No harm came to me within its walls. And no harm will come to you, not if you love this place and take care of it.'

'Please come inside,' Sebastian said again and his voice was that of a little boy's. But Deirdre shook her head.

'No, you don't need me today. It's your house, Sebastian, you march in there, hold your head high. Besides, you have business to do. Your father's land agent, McGarry, he is not a good man.'

Sebastian nodded, recalling the agent's reddish complexion and doughy features and the way his breath had smelled of brandy when he leaned over him outside the churchyard and entreated him to 'look after his beautiful mother, now'. The man had worked at Hollowpark for many years and getting rid of him would not be easy. But Deirdre was right, he needed to put his own stamp on the place.

'It won't always be simple.'

Deirdre pushed back a lock of hair that had fallen from under her bonnet. A shaft of late afternoon sunlight caught her face and for a moment Sebastian thought she looked close to his own age.

'But it will be a good life if you allow it to be. I look forward to seeing your family grow up here. Your mother is a strong woman. Let her take some of the strain tonight and tomorrow, talk to McGarry. You are well able for this journey, Sebastian.'

A thought occurred to him.

'You will still be here though? To help me? And we can meet? In the tower.'

Deirdre's smile blazed.

'I'll be here.'

She walked away, and then, as he watched her, Deirdre turned once again but the shade of the tall trees had fallen over her now and he could not see her face, could only hear her words as they floated back to him.

'I'll always be at Hollowpark, Sebastian. I will never leave.'

Chapter 22

2007

'Are they here yet?'

'Not yet, lovey, but soon. Why don't I give you a push on the swings?'

'OK, Gwace.'

Skye hopped up on the wooden seat and I stood behind her and gave the small of her back a gentle push.

'Higher!'

I offered a firmer shove, and then another, and we were both giggling by the time Skye reached a height she deemed satisfactory, her sturdy little legs soaring out over Hollowpark's fields.

'That one has no sense of danger!'

I turned to see Patrick striding towards me, two large dogs following close behind. His mud-encrusted wellies pointed to a morning spent on the farm but even if I hadn't noticed them, the broad smile on his face would have given me a good indication of what he'd been up to. It's amazing what you pick up about a family when living with them, even after a short space of time. I was already well aware that Isla craved the quiet time she spent in her studio, while Delia loved pottering around the main house, making plans. Patrick, however, was at his happiest out in the fields with his dogs and his cattle and if it was left up to him I reckoned he would spend pretty much all of his time outside patching up fencing and tending to animals. Hollowpark didn't have a massive amount of livestock, in fact I reckoned the animals on the estate would be of more use as a pet farm than as a money-making venture in their own right, but Patrick loved every single one of them and was never more content than when preparing food for one end or shovelling away what came out the other. Computers, on the other hand, were his idea of hell. I'd had the misfortune to drop Skye home one evening when he was trying to apply for a tourism grant on his ancient laptop and I'd had to clap my hands over the poor child's ears to stop her from learning some colourful new vocabulary.

'Push me, Daddy!'

'Do you mind if I take over?'

I shook my head, then stepped aside as Patrick slipped into my place and began swinging his daughter, who immediately upped the volume on her demands.

'Higher, Daddy! Into the clouds!'

As Skye's daddy attempted to keep her happy without actually launching her into orbit, I moved further out of the way and leaned against the frame of the swing. It was a beautiful piece of work, like the rest of the playground equipment. There were no rusty slides or death-trap climbing frames here, every item had been carefully chosen to suit the space and stood on a bed of soft bark. We were about five hundred metres from the main house and there wasn't even a clear path from there to the playground, just a muddy track across the overgrown meadow, but the facility itself was as good as anything I'd seen in the poshest parts of the UK. And given my profession, I'm quite the playground connoisseur.

Patrick seemed to read my thoughts and paused in his pushing for a moment.

'Do you like it?'

'It's absolutely gorgeous,' I told him. 'Skye's a lucky girl.'

'Well, she is, but it's not—'

'Push me, Daddy!'

The imperious cry came again and Patrick's next couple of minutes were taken up with pushing his daughter, then tickling her under the arms every time she swung back towards him, an action that soon reduced both of them to helpless tears of laughter.

'You're bold, Daddy!'

'I am, I suppose!'

He gave her one final push and then grabbed the swing by the seat and brought it gently to rest, lifting her off and placing her gently onto the ground.

'Now, madam! Why don't you go and try out the slide and give your poor exhausted daddy a break for a minute?'

'Will you watch me? And Gwace?'

'Of course we will.'

Patrick winked at me, then led me to a long low wooden bench at the side of the playground. He sat down and stretched his long legs out in front of him and the dogs, too, seemed to relish the opportunity for a rest and sank to the ground, their muzzles resting on their front paws. Patrick gave a happy sigh.

'That's better. I've been on the go all morning.'

They were incredibly long legs, I noticed, and his jeans, although filthy, fitted him extremely well around the thighs. And then I realised I was looking at his thighs so I jerked my head upwards, hoping that Skye would suddenly decide she needed 'Gwace' for something, and that I'd have to move away. But the little girl, blast her, seemed to have developed a sudden streak of self-sufficiency and was, apparently, perfectly happy on her own so I had no option but to settle myself back onto the bench, keeping my gaze, and the rest of me, an acceptable distance from my employer. My married employer.

'Mint?'

Patrick eased a roll of sweets out of his jeans pocket and handed them to me. They were warm and slightly crushed from his hip pocket but I took one anyway and crunched down on it, while definitely not thinking about his hips. Skye was standing right at the top of the slide now, not bothering to hold onto the handrails and I wanted to warn her to sit down but her father seemed completely unfazed by her gymnastics so I decided to follow his lead, and cast around instead for something intelligent to say.

'Nice bench! Really – comfortable.'

Wow. It was a good thing the Fitzmahons hadn't employed me for my conversational skills, I mused, but Patrick seemed to appreciate the sentiment.

'Glad you like it! I did a lot of research before kitting this place out. Skye and I toured quite a few playgrounds, last spring.'

We both looked over to where the little girl was now

zooming down the slide, landing with a squeal of pleasure on the soft, safe ground.

'Good girl!' Patrick called, before continuing. 'It's not just for Skye, either. I'm hoping this place will be full of families by next summer. The plan is to have an ice cream van over there...' He pointed to the nearest fence. 'I'm going to clear a space in that field. There's a couple of lads from the village interested in running it, they've put in for planning permission and everything, they'll maybe sell teas and coffees too if they think there's a demand.'

'Sounds good!' I told him, and we fell silent again, but not in an uncomfortable way. The sun had burned away the few remaining clouds, and the scent of fresh hay wafted towards us on the whispering breeze. I could almost imagine the scent of coffee mixed in with it, and the brightly painted van with a line of children queuing outside, arguing with their parents over whether to get plain cones or 99s. And suddenly I found I was visualising myself inside the van, wearing an apron with a mildly amusing logo, and asking Skye and her friends if they wanted extra sprinkles – but now I was being ridiculous. I swallowed the rest of my mint and told myself, firmly, to cop on. It would be the local lads in there, not me, maybe even Isla, on busy days, doling out cans of Coke and counting change. There was no guarantee I'd even be at Hollowpark next summer, let alone helping out with the tourist side of things. I'd never stayed a full year in a job before, it simply wasn't part of the plan.

The thing was, though, I just couldn't see Isla in that apron.

Patrick yawned and stretched and I was very conscious, once again, of the close proximity of his long ungainly limbs and of my need to keep talking.

'So you visited a few different places then? On your road trip?'

'That's right.'

He offered me another mint but this time I declined.

'Yeah, we took a few weekends away in the spring, when the more established places were opening up for the season. Most of the houses were much better maintained than Hollowpark, of course, and we picked up loads of tips. But what really impressed me were the places that catered for the whole family. It's easy, when you think about it, to get a coach party of retired people to come and look around a house like Hollowpark but that's all they do, you know – a quick tour and maybe a coffee and then they're off again. What I really liked were the places with playgrounds and picnic areas, you could see families making a day of it, kids running around, playing tag, eating ice cream. There was even an owlery in one place we visited, it was amazing! I could just see Skye with her own pet falcon, couldn't you?'

I couldn't help but grin at the thought of Lady Skye and her birds of prey.

'So when we got back I got this place designed and built. It was pricey, but I think it was worth it, and I'm hoping it won't just be for tourists, but for Skye's friends as well.'

'Swing, Daddy!'

Skye had finally grown tired of her own company and ran back to her father, grabbing him by the arm and dragging him back to the swings. I followed them as he continued to talk.

'I really want this one to have her friends around her when she's older and I figured a playground would give them all somewhere to hang out, tempt them up from the village. When I was growing up the other kids just came up on their bikes, you know, it was no big deal, but it's different now, isn't it? It's all organised playdates, that sort of thing. I figured with a playground here, she'll always have someone around.'

His love for Skye, and the home he was creating for her, was infectious and I nodded enthusiastically.

'I think it makes perfect sense. We're having a playdate today, actually – Evelyn is bringing Eamon over, they are due any minute.'

'Oh, excellent! I'm so pleased you two are friendly. Evelyn's a sweet girl, she would have been one of the kids on the bikes hanging around here back in the day.'

Then he paused, and I saw a glint of mischief in Patrick's eyes. He waited until the arc of Skye's swing was away from him before he continued.

'Her dad's a bit of a dick though.'

I snorted, and stole a look at Skye to make sure hadn't heard, before answering him.

'Now, now, that's Delia's *friend* you are talking about!'

Patrick immediately picked up on the emphasis I'd put on the word 'friend', and threw his head back in laughter.

'He does fancy her, doesn't he? I knew I wasn't imagining it. Jesus, maybe he has his eye on the house for himself? Awful old rogue.'

I was laughing myself at this stage.

'Well, I had wondered if there was, you know... a little spark.'

Patrick shook his head, still chuckling.

'Mum has the measure of him, she's only using him to get the paperwork sorted out. There's no flies on that one!'

Patrick gave his daughter another push and when he spoke again, his tone was a lot more serious.

'You don't think it's OTT, do you, the playground and everything? I just want Hollowpark to be perfect – or as close to it as it can be, anyway.'

'It's a gorgeous idea,' I reassured him. 'Anyway, what you're saying makes perfect sense – this playground will be a huge draw when the place is fully open.'

Patrick nodded. 'I'm glad you think so.'

He paused as if deciding how much more he could say, then turned back to the swing so he could speak without looking at me.

'It's just sometimes I think Isla reckons I'm a bit obsessed with the place, that I put too much time into it. Oh, I mean she loves Hollowpark, how could you not? But in terms of getting the place up and running, I know she gets bored sometimes, listening to me. It's just not her thing. Then again, she's an artist, isn't she? Creative people are different to you and me, maybe I can't expect her to be worrying about, you know, planning applications for ice-cream vans and how many public toilets we'll need...'

There was something about the way he said 'you and me' that just hung in the warm air and I paused for a second and allowed myself to savour it. The sun was toasting the back of my neck and I should have covered it up but I was enjoying the sensation too much to move. The sound of the birds overhead was competing with Skye's happy chatter and when I turned my head slightly I could see the sandy exterior of Hollowpark across the fields, watching over us benevolently. The larger of the two dogs came over and nudged at my hand and right at that moment I couldn't think of anywhere else on earth I would rather live.

'I don't think you could go overboard about Hollowpark, actually. It's the most beautiful place I've ever seen.'

Patrick was still staring at the back of his daughter's head.

'I'm glad you think so, Grace, but I'm not sure its everyone's idea of a dream lifestyle. Some people want theatres, galleries, restaurants...'

It was clear that by 'some people', he meant Isla. And I usually made it a rule never to discuss, let alone criticise one employer in front of another but something about the sunshine, or the blue sky or the soft breeze seemed to have unleashed a bit of madness in me. Or maybe it was the polo mint.

'You can get all that round here though,' I told him, my voice squeaking slightly with enthusiasm. 'We're, what, forty minutes from Roscommon, less than an hour from Sligo? And that's got a theatre, a cinema, some lovely places to eat...'

'I know!'

Patrick gave his daughter a final push and turned to me.

'That's exactly how I feel. I love a good film, actually, although I'm more a James Bond man than anything too arty. Isla dragged me to a subtitled thing a couple of months ago and she wasn't impressed when I fell asleep halfway through. But there's nothing you'd get in London that you can't get here, or at least a version of it. To be honest with you, Grace—'

'They're here!'

We both heard the rumble of the car on the driveway. Skye leapt down from the swing and began to run towards it and as we chased after her I realised I wasn't going to hear what Patrick Fitzmahon was going to be honest about, and maybe that was just as well.

Chapter 23

'Where's Skye?'

The blue Nissan Micra had pulled in haphazardly by the side of the track and I waved in at Eamon, who was tugging vigorously at his restraints.

'She's right here, sweetheart, she's really excited to see you! Let's just get your mummy sorted out first...'

After a couple of failed attempts to do it gracefully, Patrick and I ended up simply grabbing Evelyn's arm and hauling her out of the car with about as much finesse as extracting tuna from a tin and we were all laughing by the time she was standing upright on the gravel. But then, from inside the car came a deeper voice that immediately stifled our giggles.

'I don't remember your mother making such a fuss when she was carrying you.'

'Yeah, because she was afraid to open her mouth,' Evelyn muttered, before turning back to the car, a look of serene gratitude on her face.

'Thanks a million for the lift, Dad! I'll just grab Eamon and you can head off, OK?'

But Jack Sheehan was peering out at us, an expression of supreme importance on his face.

'Oh no, I'm heading up to the house myself, I have a lot of work to do today. Delia is expecting me.'

Patrick shot me a glance of pure mischief.

'Say hi to my mum!'

Then, moving quickly to hide the smirk on his face, he bent to kiss Evelyn on the cheek.

'You look great, darling!'

'I look like an elephant.'

My friend smoothed some wrinkles from her voluminous top before reaching in to hoist Eamon out of his car seat.

'But it'll all be worth it in the end. See you later, Dad!'

Having deposited her child on the ground she banged her fist on the top of the car, which trundled off in the direction of Hollowpark. Evelyn and I then walked back to the swings, the children scampering like puppies around our feet, while Patrick said goodbye and headed off back to whatever he'd been working on. Evelyn nodded after him.

'Paddy seems in good form!'

'Yeah.' I kept my tone as light as I could. 'I had forgotten you two knew each other.'

'Ah, this is Lisheeha, Grace!'

My friend made her slow way back towards the bench we had just vacated and sank onto it.

'If you sneeze in Hollowpark, someone in the village will ask you how your cold is. Paddy is sound, though, there's nothing stuck up about him, despite growing up in a mansion. I was surprised, actually, that he didn't marry a local girl, like his father. He could have had the pick of young ones around here, back in the day.'

A small part of me wanted to settle into a long conversation about Patrick Fitzmahon and what he was like as a teenager and, indeed, what sort of 'young ones' he had been interested in. But thankfully a larger, and far more sensible part intervened, so I left the bench and went over to lift the children onto a see-saw shaped like a caterpillar. By the time I had returned Evelyn had moved on from Skye's father to her mother.

'How is Isla's arm? On the mend?'

'She's doing OK, yeah.'

Evelyn knew the bare bones of the story, of course, that Isla had fallen in the tower and injured her shoulder, but she had, of course, also been told that the fall had been a complete accident. Any mention of ex-husbands had been left behind in that hospital canteen.

'The doctor says she'll be up and about in a few weeks.'

That was as far as I was prepared to go. Evelyn had become a good friend but it wasn't my place to tell her about the hours Isla spent lying on the sofa at the Gate House, or the meals Patrick prepared which I found later in the kitchen bin. I knew, from talking to both of them, that Isla had been told to take gentle exercise but every morning, when I picked Skye up for school, I found her lying on the sofa watching TV, and when we returned in the evenings she was almost always in the same position. The closest she had come to doing any artwork was analysing the paint colours on *Homes Under the Hammer*. It was clear the incident in the tower had left her badly shaken, but I was there to mind Skye, and it wasn't my place to interfere.

Across on the slide, Skye was laughing at Eamonn who was insisting on climbing up the slide via the ladder, the way the manufacturer had intended. I gave Evelyn a mock guilty look.

'I'm sorry, she can be very bossy when she wants to be.'

'God no, let her boss away. It'll do him good to get used to having other kids around, he'll be a big brother soon enough.'

She took a bottle of water from her bag then took a small sip and replaced it, an expression of distaste on her face.

'Ugh, I can't even drink water now or I'll be dying for a wee. God, I hate this bit! Just want it all to be over.'

I nodded sympathetically, but said nothing, because I knew from experience that there was nothing I could say. I'd lived with quite a few mothers who were coming towards the end of their second or subsequent pregnancies and, to a woman, they all made the third trimester sound like a pretty miserable place to be. I often winced when I heard their husbands trying to jolly them along, suggesting a 'nice walk', or something equally bracing, to a woman who had lost the ability to tie her own shoelaces, and I sometimes wondered if my proximity to pregnant women, and all the hard work I knew that new babies entailed, explained why I'd never had any particular hankering for a child of my own. But maybe that would change one day, I thought, looking across at Skye whose head was thrown back in laughter, cheeks bright red with sun and excitement. And I thought again of how hard Patrick was working to make her home a happy one, how good a father he was, and I didn't like the road those thoughts were taking me down, so I turned back to my friend and changed the subject.

'Your dad seems like a bit of a character anyway!'

'Indeed.' Evelyn raised one, sardonic eyebrow. 'That's one way of putting it. Mam kicked him out years ago, are you surprised?'

'Well, I...'

My friend laughed at my attempt at diplomacy.

'It's all right, you can say what you feel! I mean I love him, he's my dad, but I don't really like him, if you know what I mean? Even today – I asked him for a lift over here because Colm has the car, and sure, he said he'd help me out but he had to make it all about him, you know? Had to make it clear that he had work to do at the house anyway, and that was the only reason we could tag along. God forbid he'd actually put himself out of his way. It's fine, I'm used to him. But I'm surprised Mam lasted so long, frankly.'

'When did they split up?'

'They separated when I was eight.'

Evelyn called her son over and wiped his nose before sending him back to play and continuing with her story.

'My brothers say things were OK, actually, when they were small. Dad was a teacher, and he was around a lot in the holidays obviously, and the lads remember some nice bits – he used to take them to the seaside and they'd work together in the garden, that sort of thing. But I don't remember anything like that. All I can remember is my parents not communicating, and I mean not talking at all! Dad used to sit in the sitting room, reading or watching TV, and Mam stayed in the kitchen and honestly there were days when a word didn't pass between them. The boys say it started soon after I was born, which is a bit shitty for me to hear because it means I was either the last-ditch attempt to save the marriage, or the final nail in the coffin. But anyway, when she finally kicked him out, all I really remember is a huge sense of relief. It was the first time we could choose what to watch on the telly, for starters. Mam and I used to watch every soap, and I mean every single one of them, just because there was no one to tell us we were rotting our brains.'

Evelyn winced suddenly and stroked her bump for a moment before continuing.

'This baba is full of beans today! To be honest, Grace, the only reason I have any sort of relationship at all with Dad now is because he moved out. He lives in a flat in the village and I used to call in after school if I needed help with homework or whatever. We didn't become best buddies or anything, but it was a lot less difficult knowing I could just get up and leave if he was being a prick. And even though he loves to grumble about Mam kicking him out, he's much happier living on his own. He retired from teaching last year, but the history society keeps him busy; there's a gang of them that meet in the library on Thursday nights and they can be boring together.'

'I'm star-ving.'

Skye's complaint floated across the playground to us and Evelyn grinned.

'That's the bit they don't tell you in the baby books – that the three-hour feeds don't end when they are out of nappies!'

But the kids were indeed getting fractious so we gathered

up our belongings and made our slow way across the fields and back to Hollowpark Hall.

'Ye must have smelled the scones!'

Delia's kitchen door stood open and, as we approached, the steamy scent of fresh baking reached out and drew us all inside to where Evelyn's dad was sitting at the table, a look of intense concentration on his lugubrious face. A large cardboard box lay open in front of him and he pushed it to one side as Delia carried over first a teapot and then a plate loaded with cakes and sandwiches. Evelyn and I set about washing the kids' hands, feeding them and then doing the usual adult game of pretending not to want them to watch TV while actually dying for a break, and it was around twenty minutes later by the time we had deposited them in front of *Peppa Pig*, and were able to attack the scones ourselves.

'Don't get butter all over the place,' Jack scolded, as he dabbed his lips with a napkin then reached for the cardboard box again. Evelyn rolled her eyes but, I noticed, made sure to wipe her fingers on a tissue as Delia pulled up the chair directly opposite her and smiled.

'Your dear papa is being a great help today!' She turned to draw me into the conversation. 'We've been going through the papers from the room beside the library, Grace. I get so overwhelmed sometimes, thinking of how much I have to do, but Jack is right, it's just a case of taking one box at a time and seeing where it leads you.'

Jack selected a photo from the box, angling it so the light fell on it.

'It's all about knowing what to look for, really. Of course I'm strictly an amateur' – he gave the word the full-on faux French treatment – 'and I've told Delia, several times, that she might be better off getting one of those boffins from the university on board if she wanted. I'm sure those chaps would leap at the chance to go through this lot.'

'Arrah, who needs a load of strangers poking around.'

Delia reached over and tapped Jack on the back of his hand.

'I've had a few young fellas call out over the years all right, talking about PhDs and all sorts. But I couldn't be bothered with any of that. You'll do as good a job as any of them, Jack.'

'Yes, well...' Jack gave her an almost simpering smile. 'I have to say I have become rather passionate about the place. I might have mentioned my book? Well, I thought this might look very well on the cover.'

He handed me the photograph, taking care only to hold it by the edges.

'It's incredible, isn't it? How little has changed over the years.'

I could feel Evelyn's irritation at her dad's takeover of the conversation but when Jack handed the picture to me I felt my pulse quicken. Since the day of Isla's accident I had kept myself so busy I had been able to push what I had seen, or thought I had seen, in my bedroom to the back of my mind but I was still fascinated by Hollowpark and its history. Now here, finally, right in front of me was some of the information I craved. The black and white photo had yellowed with age but Jack was right: other than the absence of the cars out the front, it could have been taken last week. He picked up another picture and handed it to me, just as carefully.

'As *historians*' – Jack almost chewed the word, he was so proud of it – 'as historians we are blessed to have such rich source material here. Many of these Big Houses were neglected over the years, or changed hands so many times that the material got lost. But your relatives, my dear...' He inclined his head towards Delia. 'Well, they don't seem to have thrown anything away, do they?'

'Indeed and they didn't.'

Delia sipped her tea, a faraway look on her face.

'I cursed them for it too when I saw how much stuff they'd collected. But Jack's right, it'll really help with the tours if we can get this stuff catalogued properly. You really are a godsend!'

She looked at him over her gold-framed glasses and, remembering Patrick's romantic theories, I had to bite my lip to stop myself from giggling. But beside me, Jack's daughter didn't seem quite so amused; in fact Evelyn was looking decidedly bored as she reached for her handbag and pulled from it a couple of colouring books and a packet of multicoloured crayons.

'I think these two have had enough telly. Who wants to colour?'

To high-pitched squeals of 'me', Evelyn left the kitchen table and made her way to the other side of the room, laying the colouring books out on the low coffee table in front of the TV and ushering the children to sit down beside her. I should go and help her, I thought, I was, after all, being paid to mind Skye, but the prospect of rooting through the material in front of me was just too tempting. Jack noted my obvious interest and, with a proprietorial nod, handed me another sheaf of pictures. Pale figures stared out at me from across the decades. They were mostly staff members, I presumed, round-shouldered men holding horses by their bridles and the odd woman, bashful in front of the camera in full-skirted dresses and round, pinned caps. I picked up one photograph which must have been taken from the lawn and brought it closer to my face, searching for my bedroom. But all the windows were dark and I returned it to the pile, pausing for a moment before choosing my words carefully.

'Do you have any information on a woman called Deirdre? I think she was part of the original family here?'

'The ghost?' Jack smirked. 'I see you're familiar with Delia's work.'

'You leave my ghost alone!'

Delia, who had started to clear away the tea things, laughed, and I found myself blushing.

'Oh, I didn't mean—'

'Ah, don't worry about it.'

She smiled and came back to the table, resting her hand lightly on Jack's shoulder for a moment.

'That ghost paid for the plasma screen over there. I told you about the time we rented the place out for a film, didn't I? You'd be amazed how many people want to hear about things going bump in the night in a building like this.'

Jack looked up at her, his thin mouth twisting into a slight smile.

'Yes, but obviously the work our society is doing will be a lot more... historically accurate.'

'I've no doubt!'

Delia winked at me and then turned to continue

clearing up. Deciding that Jack was the type of man who liked explaining things, particularly to younger women, I swallowed down a few feminist principles and opted for an 'eager pupil' tone.

'So there really was a Deirdre then?'

'Indeed there was!'

Jack straightened his shoulders, all the better to lecture me with.

'We know quite a bit about her, actually. She was born around 1820, it was her grandfather who would have built the original house. I've made a good start on the family tree, so we know she did marry a Laurence Foster, who died soon after the wedding. Her cousin, Paul Fitzmahon, inherited the main house after her father died and she moved into the Gate House with her mother.'

'So she lost her home?'

Jack's answering tone was dismissive.

'Well, yes, you could put it like that, I suppose, but there was nothing unusual about it. The will stated quite clearly that the house was to go to the male heir. Deirdre was lucky to have a roof over her head at all.'

There was an extra sharpness to his words, and I was reminded of the fact that, when his own marriage had broken up, his wife had kept the family home.

'She seemed like a bit of a difficult woman, actually.'

'Really?' The phrase 'difficult woman' pushed all of my feminist buttons but, anxious to keep Jack talking, I kept my tone light.

'Oh yes.'

Jack's voice contained a definite sneer now.

'There are stories of her having cursed the place, that

sort of thing. All Chinese whispers, of course, but you can imagine how these things get legs. Deirdre was unhappy to leave the house, so the story went around that she decided anyone who mistreated the house would come to a bad end. All nonsense, of course.'

'If you looked after the house, it would protect you.'

Delia looked over at us from the sink, serious now.

'That was the story the family was told. My parents-in-law certainly believed it – that was why they were so anxious never to sell the place. "This house protects its own," that's what they used to say. They were determined it would never be sold, it was like a family member to them. They really believed that if you looked after Hollowpark it would look after you.'

Jack snorted.

'Old wives' tales. Deirdre would have lived through the Famine, so it's no surprise there were a few horror stories knocking around the place. I mean, she would have been shielded from the worst of it, but still, it was such a dreadful time, there was no need for ghost stories back then, reality was bad enough. A million people died in the space of a few years and a million more emigrated, there's no wonder people saw demons, or believed in fairy tales, or looked for some sort of unearthly explanation for what had happened to them. Even the name of the village itself lends itself to a bit of dramatic storytelling. Lios na hOíche.'

He paused and gave me a patronising smile.

'I don't suppose you speak An Ghaeilge, Grace?'

He gave the word for the Irish language several consonants more than I remembered from my school days and I found myself really bristling this time. Sure, I'd lived abroad for a while, but I'd grown up in Ireland and wasn't a complete ignoramus.

'Well, I know Oíche is night, so night village, something like that?'

'Not exactly.'

Jack was in full teacher mode now, the type of teacher who loved shaming his pupils for their lack of knowledge.

'The village is named after the plant, Belladonna – also known as deadly nightshade, or Lus na hOíche, in Irish. You might have seen it in the garden, with its quite distinctive purple flowers, shaped like little bells, and black berries, very poisonous.'

'Christ, yes.'

Delia pushed the door of the dishwasher closed and walked back to join us.

'One of the puppies ate some, once, the poor little mite was gone before we figured out what had happened to him. I hate the stuff. I've tried several times to root it out of the garden but it's in the maze, you see, it's all tangled up in the hedgerow, and no matter what I do I find that some of the seeds survive. The film crew were delighted when I told them about it, of course. Belladonna, it's practically Shakespearean, isn't it? But it's nasty stuff, if you don't respect it.'

'So – Lisheeha means Belladonna village?'

I hesitated over the words and Jack gave me what he probably thought was an encouraging smile.

'Nearly there! Lios Lus na hOíche would have been the original name. Lios is a fort, a ring fort usually, some sort of enclosure. But it got anglicised, of course, as most placenames did, to Lisheeha.'

'Belladonna Fort.'

I muttered the words under my breath and Jack narrowed his eyes.

'Well yes, technically. But it would never have been known as that, I mean...'

He droned on, meandering down a rabbit hole of etymology and linguistics from which I wondered if he'd ever emerge and I tuned him out, turning the words over in my head. Belladonna. The Belladonna Fort, the Belladonna Maze. And I thought of how Deirdre had been banished from her home, and how angry she might have felt about that...

'Do you know, I think I will be able to find it, if you give me a minute.'

I looked up. Jack pushed his chair back and headed for the door at the back of the kitchen, but as I had stopped listening to him some time before, I had no clue where he was going. Before I could say anything, however, Delia came back and took the chair opposite me.

'Let him off. He'd potter around the house all day if he could and what harm? How are the rest of ye doing?'

We glanced over to the far side of the room to where the kids' heads were bent over colouring books. Evelyn turned to us and smiled.

'They're doing great work over here. I'll give Dad a few more minutes and then we might make a move?'

'Sounds good.'

Delia pulled the box of photographs towards her again.

'I'll just get these tidied away and— Oh. Oh my word.'

She took a photo from the box and held it out to me, her hand trembling slightly. I looked at it, expecting another echo from a century gone, but was startled to see what, at first glance, might have been a photograph of Farrah Fawcett. It wasn't her, of course, but the bouffant hair, bright eye make-up and glossy lips made the woman look like a 1970s film star.

'Who's that?'

Delia reached out and gently stroked the over-made-up face with one plump fingertip.

'That's Paddy's grandmother, Ruth. Ruth Fitzmahon.'

I stared at the picture but couldn't see any resemblance to Patrick at all. In fact, underneath the garish make-up, the woman actually reminded me a little of Isla, not in looks exactly but in the width of her face, the strength of it.

'She was beautiful,' I told her daughter-in-law, who placed the photo reverentially down on the table and began to sift through the box again.

'She was, God rest her. Oh, and look at this...'

She handed me another picture, a small snapshot this time. It showed the same woman, now nestled into the arm of a tall man with long, bushy sideburns, who was laughing into the camera.

'That's my father-in-law, Patrick senior. Paddy's granddad. I can't believe it...'

Delia's eyes filled with tears suddenly and she wiped them away, sniffed and then smiled.

'The state of me! I just wasn't expecting to come across these today, that's all.'

She dipped in again and pulled out photo after photo, everything from family snaps to studio shots, bundled together seemingly at random with cuttings from newspapers and magazines. And there were plenty of those

– back in the 1960s and 70s it seemed that no Irish social page had been complete without a story about Hollowpark and its floating cast of characters. And then Delia picked up another snapshot and her face darkened.

'Ah. There he is. Yes.'

She stared at the photo for a moment then handed it to me without another word. For a moment I wondered why a picture of Patrick had ended up in the box, and from where he'd sourced the authentic 1970s gear. But it wasn't him, of course, the nose was slightly beakier, the eyes narrower. I glanced at Delia, who had fallen silent.

'Is that your husband?' I asked her.

She nodded. 'That's Rory.'

I squinted at the photo again. The young man was sitting on the edge of a chair, cigarette in one hand, drink in another. The photo had clearly been taken at another party, but then again, it looked like quiet nights in had been hard to come by in Hollowpark Hall in those days. My own mother would have fitted right in, I thought ruefully, taking a closer look at the photo. Actually, the man in the photo was younger than I'd first assumed, the open-necked shirt and brown leather jacket made him look like a baddie in a vintage cop drama but the face was of a boy barely out of his teens. He reminded me of something – and then the memory clicked into focus in my head and I almost laughed out loud. When I was a kid I was addicted to reruns of *Little House on the Prairie*, probably because life with Laura Ingalls's ma and pa seemed so much calmer than with my own. And there was a touch of 'Almanzo' about Rory Fitzmahon, in his wide smile and his mop of blond hair.

'He couldn't deny Paddy, anyway.'

It was a statement rather than a question, but I nodded anyway. Delia was right, Patrick was the spit of his father in many ways, in build, hair colour, even eye colour they were all but identical. But in other ways they differed. There was a cockiness about Rory that hadn't been handed down to his son; the father was a good-looking man all right, but looked far too aware of the fact. The picture had clearly upset Delia, and I handed it back to her gently.

'And when – when did Rory pass away?'

She started and then to my utter amazement gave what sounded very much like an amused snort.

'Pass away? Oh, darling, I'm sorry, did I give you that impression? Rory's not dead, sweetheart, he's beyond in England!'

'Oh!'

I flushed scarlet, mortified by my mistake. Delia and Patrick had mentioned Rory on a couple of occasions, but always in the past tense and I had assumed she was a widow. Delia replaced the photo in the box and sat back, folding her arms.

'Rory and I haven't lived together since Patrick was still in primary school, but he's still hale and hearty. Well, so Paddy tells me, anyway. We haven't exactly kept in touch, if you know what I mean.'

'Right.'

I was too embarrassed to ask any more questions but going through the photos seemed to have put Delia in a talkative mood.

'He was a gorgeous man, Rory, I mean you can see that from the snaps! But he wasn't exactly what you'd call the responsible type. I think I told you how bad with money he was?'

I nodded, thinking back to our first conversation in this kitchen, which seemed a long time ago now. Delia sniffed, and continued.

'Well, when I found out how much financial trouble we were in, I persuaded him, shall we say, that it would be best if he took off and left me here.'

Without thinking I glanced around the room, taking in the up-to-date fittings, the comfortable furniture and the high-tech entertainment equipment in the far corner. Delia sniffed again.

'You'll have to imagine how things were when he left, Grace. The place was in bits, there wasn't one bit of the roof that you could trust in a bad shower of rain, most of the plumbing was over a hundred years old – oh, it was all very well to have those fine parties here in the height of summer, but come winter we were all sitting around the one fire counting our chilblains. Rory would have sold up if he could, but I knew that wasn't what his parents would have wanted, and it would have been awful to let the house leave the family.'

'I can't believe he'd ever think of selling it.'

Evelyn looked over from where she was tidying up the kid's drawings.

'There have always been Fitzmahons at Hollowpark, I can't imagine it any other way.'

'That's right.'

Delia smiled at her.

'I couldn't have imagined it either, but there were times I didn't think we'd be able to keep the place at all. The amount of work that was needed to save it – ah, Rory just didn't have it in him. It was hard, manual labour. I was ripping off wallpaper, patching up leaks – I'll tell you, he was a great man for getting a party going but Master Rory Fitzmahon was not put on this earth to get his hands dirty. Besides, I wasn't going to build the place up just to let him put all the profits on a horse. So, we came to an arrangement. I had money from my own father, so I agreed to shoulder all the debt – and this place was creaking with it – and Rory signed the house over to Paddy, and in trust to me until Paddy turned eighteen. It didn't take much to persuade him, to be honest with you. Rory was no more a man for confrontation than he was for hard work. Besides, he was in a bad way with the drink at that stage too, he was a very different chap to the one in that photo. I believe the first thing he did when he got to London was to get checked into one of those clinics and I'm told he doesn't drink any more. But I don't ask too many questions. Paddy keeps in touch with him, I really don't want to know too much about him. I wish him well, but that's all in the past now.'

'But you are still married?'

I was aware of how nosy I was sounding but I was too fascinated by the Fitzmahon family tree to care. Delia nodded cheerfully.

'We are. To be honest, I don't really think about it any more but we are, yeah. It was simpler that way and it's not like I had a queue of fellas out the door waiting to keep Rory's side of the bed warm anyway. Ah no, once he accepted he had a problem there was never any question that I was the best person to stay here and look after Paddy and the house. There was no divorce in Ireland at that stage anyway, and even when it came in we didn't bother doing anything about it. I've a feeling, from the odd comment Paddy makes, that Rory has another partner now, so maybe he'd like to move on, but I haven't heard a word. And the place is in Paddy's name so it's not like there would be any row about inheritance or anything. It'll all belong to Skye one day, sure, so as long as I have my little corner of Hollowpark I'm happy out. Now!'

She glanced over at her granddaughter who, right on cue, started to whinge.

'These two won't want to be sitting around listening to us talking oul rubbish about the past.'

Evelyn looked at her watch.

'You're right, Delia, it's high time we got home. Do you know where my dad got to?'

'The library, I think.'

Delia stood up and stretched and I couldn't help noticing how tired she looked. No matter how blasé she appeared, it must have been an emotional afternoon.

'I'll get him,' I told her, and she looked at me gratefully.

'Would you, pet? And I'll help Evelyn get Eamon ready for home.'

'Sure.'

I made my way to the door at the back of the kitchen, then walked through and let it shut behind me. And was immediately plunged into darkness. I ran my hand along the wall, encountering heavy wooden panels and a good deal of dust, but no light switch, and was forced to fumble my way through. I'd been this way before, of course, Jack had led me through this shortcut to the main house on my first night at Hollowpark, but I'd been so flattened by tiredness that evening I had just stumbled after him, taking little notice of where we were going. Finally, my hand connected with a door at the far end of the corridor and I pushed against it for a moment before it creaked open and deposited me in the entrance hall.

'Jack?'

My voice echoed around the cavernous space, bouncing off the tiled floor. No response. The weather must have changed since we'd left the playground because the light coming through the front windows had dimmed even though it was barely four o'clock.

'Jack?'

My voice sounded hesitant, querulous even, and I coughed in an attempt to steady it before calling out again. There was no reason to feel nervous, after all this was my home now. I walked through this hall every evening, came down here from the bedroom every morning for breakfast and I should have been used to its size. For some reason, though, it felt particularly empty this afternoon. Maybe it was the fact that the front door was shut tight, maybe it was the rain I could hear beginning to tap against the large, draughty windows. Or maybe it was the fact that I knew I wasn't alone, but didn't know where Jack was, or how to find him. Or whether he could see me.

'Jack?'

Finally, an answer drifted towards me from behind the staircase.

'In here!'

My footsteps echoed dully on the stone floor as I passed through the hall and opened the wooden door that led to the library corridor. I called out again and this time Jack's voice led me, not to the library itself but to the dusty storeroom on its right-hand side.

'Come in!'

My nose started to prickle as soon as I crossed the threshold, assaulted by the thick dust that hung in the dim light. My eyes began to stream and, for a moment, it felt as if my body was warning me, telling me not to go inside. But that would be ridiculous. I swallowed, and then walked over to where Jack was standing by a bookshelf at the back of the room. It was even darker in here, the space lit only by a small lamp that stood on a side table and, as Jack beckoned me over, it was hard to make out his features, just the silhouette of his long, angular face.

'Grace! I'm glad it's you. I want to show you something.'

I wiped my eyes, wondering if I should dash upstairs and get my allergy medicine, but then Jack spoke again.

'I think I've found your Deirdre, come and look!'

A large, gilt-framed painting was balanced on a chair next to him. I walked over, but the room was too gloomy to allow me to see much and so I dropped to my knees to take a closer look. And then my breath caught in my throat as I tried to take in what I was looking at. She had no face, she was a woman with no face, she...

'Oh my God.'

I scrambled to my feet as Jack let out a loud, mirthless chuckle.

'Forgive me, didn't I warn you? Poor old Deirdre, not exactly in the best of condition, is she?'

'What happened to her – to it?'

I took a second to compose myself then bent over again to examine the picture, as much to avoid the smirk on

Jack's face as to see the details which were, quite frankly, upsetting. I could just about make out what could have been a woman's dress, a black gown which had been painted against a green background, but most of the rest of the painting was covered by whorls of water damage and the place where the woman's face should have been had completely flaked away. It was incredibly sad and not a little disturbing and I could feel Jack's hot breath on the back of my neck as he bent down to look over my shoulder.

'Yes, it's an awful shame. Must have been water damage, the roof is in a terrible state in parts.'

I reached out my hand and touched the surface of the portrait lightly. Close up, I could see a few more details, what might have been a white collar on the top of that dress, maybe a pale hand – but there was nothing left of her face at all. I stood up again, too quickly, my head spun for a moment and I reached out my hand to the chair to steady myself. Poor Deirdre. She had lost her home and now not even her image remained.

'Find her.'

The voice seemed to have come from behind me. I turned and then I saw her, framed by the doorway. She looked as solid as I did myself yet I instinctively knew, without checking, that Jack could neither see nor hear her. She was a tall, thin woman, maybe forty years of age, elegantly dressed in a slim black gown with a white collar. The same one she'd been wearing in the painting, maybe? Because this was Deirdre. I had never seen her face before but I knew her. And she knew me.

'Help her.'

Unable to move, I flicked a gaze towards Jack, but he had moved away now, bored of teasing me, and was leafing through a book on the far side of the room. My skin was crawling with fear, my spine a needle of ice, but I could not look away as Deirdre's eyes sought mine. They were blue eyes, or maybe grey, it was difficult to tell in the failing light, but they were looking directly into mine and I could feel my body grow even colder as she held my gaze. She wanted me, wanted something from me.

'Find her.'

Then Deirdre tilted her head slightly to one side, she was looking past me now and when she spoke again, her voice was so loud and so distinct I could not believe I was the only one who could hear her.

'Find her!'

'Gwace!'

And then she was gone. Skye's voice rang out from the main hall and I felt my heart give one solid thump as I fought to remain calm. Deirdre had not faded away, there had been no puff of smoke or disturbance in the air. She was just – not there any more, but she *had* been there and I was as sure of that as I was sure of the pool of cold sweat that had collected at the base of my spine.

'Where are you, Gwace?'

Skye's voice came again and I forced myself to walk out of the room and back into the entrance hall. The little girl ran towards me and I lifted her into my arms.

'I found you!'

'You OK?'

Evelyn, who was plodding along behind her, looked at me curiously.

'We came to find Dad – Eamon and I need to head home now. You don't look well at all, Grace, has something happened?'

I buried my face in Skye's hair for a moment, inhaling her favourite strawberry shampoo, the scent that told me she was still more of a baby than a little girl. Her plump arms tightened around my neck, she was sleepy now and in need of a cuddle. I didn't have to live here, didn't have to put up with this house and the darkness in its corners. But the Fitzmahons did, Skye did.

'Gwace OK?'

Skye lifted her head away from my shoulder and looked at me curiously.

'Are you sad, Gwace?'

'No, darling.'

I gave her a final squeeze, then placed her gently on the floor and wiped my eyes.

'I'm grand, Skye. It was just the silly dust making me sneeze, that's all.'

I took a tissue from my pocket and blew my nose then watched as Skye ran over to Eamon and began to make plans to see him in school. Evelyn went inside to fetch her dad and I leaned against the wall and took a deep breath, willing my heart rate to return to normal. Every instinct in my body was telling me to run, to leave this house and its secrets, to reach the end of the driveway and never look back and never ever return. But Skye needed me, the Fitzmahons needed me. Patrick needed me— I shook that thought away, the whole family needed me, that was what I meant. I took the little girl by the hand and we walked back through the entrance hall, airy now that the door was open, and stood and waited as Evelyn helped her son into her father's car and then climbed into the passenger seat.

'Bye, Eamon!'

I lifted Skye into my arms again, treasuring the weight of her as we watched the car drive off, Evelyn waving happily and Jack staring straight ahead.

'Find her.'

It had not been a request, I realised, but an order.

Chapter 24

1973

'Come to a party at ours?'

The words were so strange and so unexpected, he might as well have been speaking a foreign language and Catherine blinked at the boy, afraid to commit to an answer. Rory Fitzmahon appeared to be inviting her to a party, but that couldn't be possible, could it? Then again, everything that had happened that afternoon had been so unusual, Catherine wouldn't have been particularly surprised if he had gone on to say that the party was at Buckingham Palace itself.

And to think she hadn't even wanted to go to the shop for her mam that afternoon! Catherine had already received a drenching cycling home from school, and the last thing she had wanted to do was head back down to the village again just because her younger brother was a pig and had eaten all the sandwich bread. Proper mothers baked their own bread, Catherine had thought, sullenly, but had known by the look on her frazzled mother's face that she didn't dare give that sort of cheeky answer. So, with heavy sighs and dark looks at the leaden sky she had clambered back up onto her bike and headed back to Lisheeha again.

Her mother, of course, had followed her out to the gate, muttering 'seeing as you are there you might as well get...', so by the time Catherine was actually finished in O'Dwyer's – having waited to be served by Mrs O'Dwyer because everyone knew her husband had the habit of dropping the change on the floor by 'accident' when he was serving teenage girls, forcing them to bend over to pick up the coins – she was tired, cranky and carrying a plastic bag that was seriously overloaded. The bag split, moments after she'd hopped back onto her bike, sending her purchases flying all over the road and, worst of all, smashing open the can of Coke she'd bought out of her own money to soften the misery of the journey home. And then, as if it wasn't already the worst Wednesday in human memory, Rory Fitzmahon, bloody Rory Fitzmahon had walked past and seen her scrabbling in the dirt.

'Can I give you a hand?'

She had been so embarrassed, Catherine had briefly considered leaving the shopping on the ground, jumping back on the bike and not stopping until she got to Sligo, or Dublin, or somewhere far away from where Rory Fitzmahon was gathering up her collection of wizened carrots and, oh sweet Jesus, the special toothpaste her father used for his false teeth. But she couldn't even stand up because Rory was right there beside her, kneeling in the mud, picking up the bread, assuring her it wasn't that squashed actually and fiddling with her stupid useless bag to try and make it last the journey home. Like most of the girls in Lisheeha, Catherine had 'admired Rory from afar', which was a phrase she had read in one of her mother's romantic novels, and had even written 'Mrs Rory Fitzmahon' and C+R4EVA on her schoolbag, but she had always reckoned she had about as much chance of actually talking to him as she did of flying to the moon. Yet here he was, holding her bike and chatting away like he was some sort of a normal person. Close up he looked like a doctor, Catherine decided, a very young, very clean doctor from an American TV show, so good-looking and sure of himself that you'd probably thank him, even if he was after giving you terrible news.

And that's when he asked her.

'Come to a party, at ours?'

Catherine and her mother watched *Coronation Street* twice a week, so she knew that, in England, 'ours' meant a person's house. But that only made sense when it was a normal house like hers or Hilda Ogden's, it seemed mad to her that Rory was actually talking about Hollowpark Hall, a place so important it had a half page in the *Visitor's Guide to North-West Ireland* Catherine's dad got as a present one Christmas and kept on permanent display on the coffee table in the sitting room.

Rory, however, seemed to mistake her hesitance for a lack of enthusiasm, and tried again.

'Go on, it will be fun. I mean, the parents will be having the usual Hallowe'en bash, but I have a few friends coming over from London and we were going to do our own thing, you know? Bring a friend yourself, if you like. Bring a couple?'

'Well maybe...'

Catherine spent a moment running through a list of her friends in her head, but just as quickly dismissed them. What would Ciara, or Sandra or even Tracey say, she wondered, if she told them they'd been invited to a party at Hollowpark Hall? They'd squeal, probably, giggle definitely and then tell half the village. There was just no way Catherine could let that happen. She was fifteen, she hadn't even really been to a proper disco yet, just the ones the youth club ran once a month where leaders and parents stood around the walls, glaring at any couple that was brave enough to chance a slow set. Next year, maybe, Ciara's older sisters would grudgingly let her tag along with them to one of the nightclubs in Sligo or out in Enniscrone, but that would be nearly as bad as having a parent with you, any gossip would be back in Lisheeha before you got a lift home. And who would you meet there anyway, only the same lads from the youth club, pawing you and giving you a look as bad as Dirty Dwyer's. This party, though, at Hollowpark? It was way beyond anything Ciara, or even her older sister, could ever have imagined and Catherine knew the best thing was to keep it all to herself. If indeed she hadn't dreamed the invitation. But no, it had started to spit rain now but Rory Fecking Gorgeous Fitzmahon was still standing there, with his exotic question hanging in the air between them. Catherine took a deep breath, smiled, and answered him.

'Sure,' she said. 'Just me though. I'll be there.'

Chapter 25

2007

'Who's for crisps?'
'Meeee!'

The children's reactions were so immediate, and so enthusiastic, that both myself and Evelyn burst out laughing and I had to struggle to remain upright as they dived on me, covering me with sand and droplets of salt water.

'Hang on, hang on, plenty here for everyone!'

I reached into the picnic basket and brought out two bags, making sure they were the same flavour, then handed them over.

'Are your hands clean? Yes? Are you sure? OK then.'

Skye and Eamon flopped onto the picnic blanket and tore the bags open while, from her vantage point on a camping chair, Evelyn looked over at me and sighed happily.

'I told you this was a good idea!'

'You certainly did.'

She had tucked her own picnic basket under her chair and reached for it, extracting a flask and then handing me a cup of steaming coffee.

'You thought of everything,' I told her.

'Yes, well. There's no such thing as bad weather don't forget, it's—'

'Just bad preparation!' I finished as she rolled her eyes.

'God, am I that predictable?'

'Maybe. But you were right.'

The children were still nose deep into their crisps, so I sat back in my own chair for a moment and allowed myself just to sit, and look at the sea. When Evelyn had suggested a picnic on the beach on the last Friday of September I had been inclined to blame pregnancy brain for what, to me, sounded like a terrible idea. Sure, the weather had been surprisingly good for the time of year but it was still autumn, on the west coast of Ireland, not a time or a place that made me feel like reaching for a bikini. But, having no other plans on the day in question I'd agreed to go along with her optimistic scheme and we'd packed the kids, and what seemed like enough paraphernalia for a week-long camping trip, into Patrick's car and headed for Strandhill, a seaside resort around an hour from Lisheeha. Only to discover that Evelyn's idea had, in fact, been a brilliant one. Fair enough, we had needed fleeces more than we'd needed factor fifty sun cream, and I'd been reminded that Irish people are the only race I know who bring windbreaks rather than sunshades to the beach. But somehow it had all worked perfectly. The kids had paddled, and played chicken with the waves, and afterwards we'd bundled them up in warm layers and organised a sandcastle competition, all of which left them hungry enough to eat everything we had brought with us, even the carrot sticks which I'd optimistically packed alongside sandwiches and soft drinks.

'I had no idea how beautiful it would be.'

I let my head fall back against the deckchair, salt and hot coffee prickling my windburned lips. It was a glorious day, the white clouds fluffy in a blue sky, shards of sunlight occasionally breaking through to chase shadows down the strand and turn the sand from gold to gentle grey and then back again. There were a few other families on the beach but there was so much space it was impossible to hear them, let alone feel in any way crowded, and nothing further than my beloved but usually busy Greek beaches could be imagined. And the waves! It was easy, I thought, to understand why people walked by the sea when they felt under pressure, or used the sound of the sea to help them sleep at night. I closed my eyes, allowing my mind to drift further as the water washed against the shore, forward and back, forward and back, carrying my thoughts away with it.

'It's not exactly the Med,' said Evelyn as if she could read my mind, and I opened my eyes again, and shook my head.

'No. It's more beautiful.'

A couple darted past us, sleek as seals in black wetsuits, carrying surfboards under their arms. We watched as they jogged across the sand and into the water, not even wincing as the wavelets broke over their toes. They walked through the sea for a couple of paces and then, in unison, dived flat onto the boards, using their arms to power themselves out beyond the breaking waves. Then they turned, and waited and finally popped up onto their polystyrene vessels, allowing the rush of dark water to carry them back to the shore again. The movement was balletic and mesmerising, or at least it was until the man overbalanced and tumbled into the sea only to emerge after a moment, spluttering and laughing and wiping water from his eyes.

'I'd love to try that.'

Evelyn glanced at me.

'I'll teach you, if you like.'

She patted her stomach which was perfectly round now, and seemed an almost separate entity, just resting on her knees.

'I mean not at the moment, obviously. But next year.'

'You?'

My friend heard the note of surprise in my voice and gave a mock hurt laugh.

'Yeah, me! Me and Colm used to surf every weekend, back in the day. Sligo has some of the best beaches in Europe, you know! It's great fun. I haven't been out as much as I'd like since I had Eamon, but I'll take you next summer, let Colm mind the kids for the day.'

'God, that would be brilliant.'

And even as I answered her I realised I had just made a plan for the following year, without a thought, without any recognition that I might not still be in Ireland then. It would be six months, maybe more, before Evelyn would be in a position to take me surfing, did I really think I'd still be living at Hollowpark then? And more to the point, did I want to be?

The surfing couple had separated now, chasing their own individual waves, competing with the sea and not with each other. She was the more skilled athlete, popping onto the board with ease and sailing it gracefully back to the shore, but he was stronger, able to tirelessly capture and then harness wave after wave. It was beautiful to watch and this was a beautiful place to live. But was it home? Evelyn was watching the surfers too and the children, sated and sleepy, were playing quietly with their spades and I had a rare moment just to sit, and think and wonder.

I had been living at Hollowpark for over a month now and, for the most part my life had taken on an easy rhythm. I dropped Skye to playschool in the mornings and then had a few hours to myself, to meet Evelyn for coffee or go for a walk and I'd even started, tentatively, to run again, a hobby I'd enjoyed in my teens but hadn't had time to tackle in years. I'd pick Skye up after school and we'd have lunch and then play, in the grounds if it was fine or in one of Hollowpark's many rooms if it was raining. There was always something to do, draw pictures or play hide and seek, and in the afternoons we'd go for a nature walk or 'help' Patrick feed the cattle or visit Delia in her kitchen and watch her making scones and the day would fly by until it was time to drop Skye back to the Gate House again.

I enjoyed my time off, too: Delia was generous with her car and I often went to the cinema in Carrick-on-Shannon, or even as far as Sligo to look around the shops. It was the first time in years that I'd had this much time to concentrate on myself and, for the most part, I was enjoying it immensely.

When I wasn't thinking about the women. I focused on the waves again, trying to keep their faces from crowding my thoughts. The women. Deirdre and Catherine, I knew their names now. I hadn't seen either of them since the day Jack had shown me that awful, mutilated portrait but I often felt their presence, usually at night when I climbed that tall staircase and headed to my room. I knew if I had told anyone what was going on that it would have seemed bizarre that I had remained at Hollowpark under those circumstances, that I could sleep every night in a house where every floorboard played its own eerie tune and memories lined the corridors alongside the flock wallpaper. Yet I had stayed. I was staying for Skye, I told myself, she was such a lovely little thing and had been through so much, with her mother ill for much of her childhood and now laid up again, it would have felt almost unbearably cruel if I had abandoned her now. But I also had to admit I had other, less altruistic reasons. I had fallen under the spell of Hollowpark Hall, had grown to love its faded grandeur, its large airy rooms and long, echoing corridors. Those corridors should have terrified me, and, yes, sometimes I did feel uneasy within their walls and spent the hours after dinner watching soaps in Delia's cosy kitchen to delay the moment when I would have to return to my own lonely room. But despite all of this, Hollowpark had started to feel like home, and although I was sure I hadn't imagined the women, I was also convinced they didn't mean me any harm. I dreamed about them sometimes, dreams where I saw them walking through the maze together or standing in the window of the tower, their eyes searching the grounds. They wanted my help; of that I was certain. And I was curious to know why. So yes, I was staying at Hollowpark for Skye, but also for those women, who seemed to call out to me. And if a small voice was telling me I was staying for Patrick too, well, today it was quiet enough to be drowned out by the sound of the waves.

'Do you think Isla will want something to eat?'

Evelyn's question pulled my thoughts back from the sea, and Hollowpark and its many complicated residents. I shaded my eyes and turned to look along the length of the beach where a tall figure was walking slowly towards us, one arm still bound against her chest. When Skye's mum had asked if she could come on our little excursion, I have to admit I was initially disappointed, as I had hoped to spend the day gossiping with Evelyn and didn't want to have to be on my best behaviour around my employer. But Isla had turned out to be a great addition to the day, leading a game of I Spy in the car and helping the kids to build sandcastles far more elaborate than anything I could have designed. She had gone for a walk after lunch and now, as she drew near, it was clear the day had done her good too, her rosy cheeks and windswept hair making her look both incredibly like her daughter and well on the road to physical recovery. She reached the picnic blanket and lowered herself onto it and I could tell by the ease of her movements that she was also in much less pain than she had previously been.

'Mind Mummy's arm,' I warned Skye automatically as she snuggled into her, but Isla simply smiled.

'It's OK. The doctor was saying I could start using it a bit more, it's feeling much better. Honestly, I was almost tempted to go for a swim today, definitely next time!'

We sat for a moment, and then Evelyn yawned.

'I think we'd better hit the road, ladies. No point getting caught in the evening traffic, we'll made great time if we leave now.'

The children were too tired to put up much opposition and the next while was taken up with shaking sand off everything we'd brought, including the children, and packing the car. Evelyn insisted on taking the back seat with the kids to allow Isla more space for her injured arm, and we had barely left the strand before I could see three heads begin to nod in the rear-view mirror. Skye and Eamon curled into each other like kittens while Evelyn, arms folded on her bump, began to gently snore.

'Out for the count!'

I smiled at Isla, who grinned back at me.

'Can you blame them? They had a fabulous day, we all did. Thanks so much for inviting me!'

It seemed a strange thing to say, after all it was her husband's car I was driving and her daughter I had been minding, so I stayed silent for a moment until Isla sighed, and spoke again.

'We're so lucky you came to live with us, Grace.'

She looked down at her arm, still nestled in its sling.

'I don't know what we'd have done without you these past few weeks.'

'It was my pleasure,' I told her, meaning it. 'Skye is a little dote. And you've all been very good to me too, lending me the car and everything. Honestly, you've gone out of your way to make me feel welcome, I'm incredibly grateful.'

'That's lovely to hear.'

Isla smiled at me, then turned to look out of the car window.

'It could have all gone so wrong, after the accident. But I think – I really feel like I'm getting myself back together again, and a lot of that is down to you.'

'I'm delighted to hear it,' I told her, and fell silent again. Something about the warmth of the day, the silence from the back of the car, the happy tired buzz we were all feeling after the fun on the beach appeared to have left my boss in a talkative mood and I was happy simply to drive and listen.

'You do such lovely activities with her, the playdates and now this – you're really good at your job, Grace, you know that? Sometimes I think she's better off with you!'

'Ah now, don't say that.'

I checked my speed, then followed the signs that would guide me towards the road to home. Being Ireland, the sun had completely disappeared now, and a light rain was beginning to speckle the windows. It added to the feeling that we were alone in the car and when Isla next spoke, her voice had taken on a wistful quality.

'Oh, I'm a good mum, I don't mean that, I adore Skye. But I'm just not sure I could keep everything spinning the way you do. It has been hard for me to focus, these last few years.'

'You've been through a lot,' I commented, trying to sound as neutral as possible. The diminishing light lent the car the feel of a confessional, and although I wanted Isla to feel like she was being listened to, I didn't want her to be embarrassed later and feel she had told me too much. From the corner of my eye I saw her give one, slow nod.

'I have been through a lot. And I haven't been much use to Patrick or Delia either. I feel terribly guilty about it. They are powering along with the house; I mean, look at the playground, the amount of work Patrick has put into it. I feel like I haven't done a thing.'

'Well, when you're better…'

I paused. The fact of the matter was she was right. Delia and her son were running the renovation project and Isla, as far as I could see, was little more than a bystander. But it wasn't my job to comment on that – or even, let's face it, to have an opinion – so I cast around for something positive to say.

'Maybe some of your work would look good around the grounds? Those pieces you showed me were beautiful, maybe you could exhibit in the main hall, or the Great Room?'

'I don't know if Delia would like that.' Isla gave a dismissive laugh. 'They're not really her sort of thing.'

There was something so diffident about her response, so lukewarm, that I found myself struggling to overcome a surge of frustration. Sure, Isla had had a tough time and a nasty fall but she was well on the mend, she didn't have to be so bloody passive about everything. Delia was pretty much rebuilding Hollowpark brick by brick and Isla seemed happy just to sit around in her tower and watch her do it. And yeah, Delia could be bossy, but who could blame her? From what she had told me she'd been fighting for Hollowpark for most of her life, she was owed more than the minimal support she was getting from the woman who was, to all intents and purposes, her daughter-in-law.

I hesitated, then shot Isla a quick glance.

'Well you could try asking her? She might love to see the artwork, she has some really adventurous ideas for the house and the grounds. Anyway, it'll be your place one day, yours and Patrick's. You have the right to decide what's done to it.'

Isla's eyes connected with mine in the windscreen.

'I suppose you're right! Do you know, I've never really thought about it like that.'

She shifted in her seat and began to cradle her injured arm with her good one, rocking it gently from side to side. It was a movement I had seen before and it struck me that she was testing herself, to see how much she had healed and how much pain she could endure.

'I'm just not sure I'm the right person to make long-term plans about the house at the moment.'

I shook my head, not comprehending.

'But it's all going so well! Even in the few weeks since I've been here, the library is finished now, and the playground, Delia reckons you could be taking bookings for small weddings as early as the New Year...'

I bit my lip; aware I was starting to sound too involved. This was not my house, nor my family, it was none of my business. But I loved Hollowpark and, the fact of the matter was, I was starting to imagine a proper future there. Skye was still very young, she'd need a nanny for years, particularly if Patrick and Isla opened the house as a full-time venue. And, I thought as the car sped towards home, I really wanted to see how it all turned out, I wanted to see Hollowpark become the type of house I knew it could be. I loved the place, it was that simple.

This house protects its own.

And suddenly it didn't matter to me if that legend was real or if Delia had made it up and printed it in a crappy brochure to attract gullible tourists. I felt part of Hollowpark now, and I wanted to protect it too. But when Isla spoke again, her tone had changed.

'The thing is, Grace, something happened to me the day – the day this happened.'

She tapped herself lightly on her injured shoulder.

'I was so scared, that day in the tower. I mean, you were there, you saw how dangerous that fall could have been. And it was all my own fault, I tripped, I fell because I was afraid, and of what? Of some random person in the maze? It may not have been anything to do with Ethan at all, but it didn't matter because I was in such a bad place I ran anyway. I could have bloody killed myself, could have left Skye without her mum, because I was running from a shadow. But...'

Isla raised her good hand and fixed her hair behind her ear.

'The thing is, I didn't kill myself. I didn't die, I survived. The worst happened, or at least I thought it did, and I survived. I went back to the tower yesterday. The very thought of climbing those stairs terrified me, but I did it. And once I got up to my studio, saw my art, all of my belongings, I knew I couldn't afford to be afraid any more. And I came to a decision.'

She bit her lip.

'I'm going to contact my ex; tell him I want a divorce.'

I ignored the sudden jolt my heart gave at the words and offered her an encouraging smile.

'That's great news.'

'It is, isn't it? It has taken me a long time to feel like this, but my head is in a much better place now. I feel like the person I was before I met Ethan, I feel like myself again. And I'm strong enough to put an end to the marriage, for once and for all. I've contacted a lawyer in Sligo and we've started the process. Yes, it will mean letting Ethan know where I am and that thought terrifies me, but I am going to go through with it.'

I had left the dual carriageway now and was on the road to Lisheeha, and I sped up to overtake a tractor before answering her.

'I'm thrilled you are feeling better, Isla, it's great news. But I'm not sure what it has to do with Hollowpark? I mean a divorce is just paperwork, really, you'll get it sorted out and then you can really get on with things here, your art, and the house... You'll probably find it easier to work, even, when everything is sorted.'

Isla inhaled and then looked at me steadily.

'Well, that's the thing. You see, I'm not actually sure my life will be here at Hollowpark, at least, not long term. When I came to Ireland I was a mess, but I feel so much better now. I know you've heard the old stories, about the house sheltering its own? Well that's exactly how it felt for me. Hollowpark fixed me and it has been amazing to live here and to get that time to heal. But I need to get back on my own two feet now. And what happened in the tower that day, well, it was like the final push I needed. I feel stronger now than I have done in years, but I also want to test myself, you know?'

She nodded again, but slower, as if she was really speaking to herself.

'When it comes to my work, my art – Hollowpark is not the right place for me. I mean, the house is beautiful, and the countryside as well, don't get me wrong, it's idyllic, people would travel the world to visit it, I know they would. But it just doesn't... it doesn't inspire me. I'm an urban person, I need people around me, I need crowds. I miss smog, isn't that the most stupid thing you've ever heard? But I do, and the Tube, and loud noises. I want to hear cars drive by when

I'm falling asleep, I want to walk out my front door and buy oat milk, or Indian food, and swerve on the pavement to avoid strangers I'll never see again. I only did a year of art school before I dropped out to live with Ethan and I want to go back to university and finish my degree. I want to meet new people and have the confidence to go for coffee and talk to them and get to know them. Ethan took all that from me, and I want it back. Hollowpark is beautiful but it doesn't feel like home, nor like real life. I want Skye to grow up in a city, with friends all around her. Patrick wasn't always happy as a child, I know he goes on about the fields and the freedom but it wasn't all good, not all of the time. It was hard for him, being half Irish and half English, never quite sure where he belonged, changing his accent as he moved from one group to another. I don't want my daughter to have that confusion. Lisheeha is beautiful and I want Skye to spend her holidays here, I want her to know her granny and her heritage. But it's not my home. Ethan stole that from me, he stole London from me, and I owe it to myself to take it back. The solicitor says I'll get a good settlement, enough for a house in a decent area. I want to go home, Grace.'

And home, for Isla, was clearly not Hollowpark. Twilight had fallen while we were talking and, even though she was my employer and I had no right to fish for further information, the dim light lent me courage.

'And Patrick – does he know how you feel about this? He seems to really want Skye to grow up around here.'

Isla gave a vague smile.

'He'll be fine, you know Patrick, he's so easy-going. I mean, I'm only mulling it over myself really, I haven't discussed it with him but we have lots of options. It takes so much work to run a place like Hollowpark, maybe we'd be better off getting a manager in, or even selling it, who knows? I'm sure someone with a lot more money than we have could build a great hotel. Patrick will do whatever is best for everyone, he's one of the good guys.'

He is, I thought to myself. And my mind drifted back to that day in the playground and how enthusiastic he had been about Hollowpark and his plans for its future. How passionate. An image came into my head of that long bouncing stride and those mud-spattered wellies, and I just couldn't see Patrick Uprichard Fitzmahon shuffling along a crowded London street, having to duck around strangers and shorten his stride. And I knew I had no right to ask the next question but I did it anyway.

'Do you really think he'd go back to London?'

Isla shrugged. 'If it's the best thing for all of us, yeah.'

Her eyes caught mine in the windscreen and I suddenly felt as if Isla Fitzmahon could see a lot more in front of her than the road ahead. Then, from the depths of her handbag, came the chime of a phone. She pulled it out and read the text message.

'That was Delia, she wants us to come to her flat as soon as we get in. Says she has a surprise for us.'

I was so glad of the distraction that I didn't even wonder what Delia wanted, just put on a CD of nursery rhymes to gently wake the kids as we headed home to Hollowpark. The house that protected its own. And then I shivered as a sudden realisation hit me. What if there was someone living there who didn't have its best interests at heart, who didn't see it as home? Isla was singing now, jollying along the kids who were cranky following their nap. She was probably right, and if moving back to London was what was needed then she should follow her heart. But if Patrick followed, there could be no Fitzmahons left at Hollowpark, and what would Deirdre do then? Or what might she do to prevent that from happening?

I was being ridiculous, and I knew it, but that didn't stop my thoughts from churning as we reached the final bend for home.

Chapter 26

'A booking? But we're nowhere near ready.'

Patrick sounded more stressed than surprised, but his mother raised her hand to cut off his objections.

'Now before you go throwing cold water on it, Paddy, it's all organised. It's a family group and they don't want to stay in the house itself, they are going to camp.'

'Camp?'

Delia poured tea into the mismatched selection of mugs on the table while the rest of us busied ourselves locating milk and spoons. When we'd got back from the beach, dropping Evelyn and Eamon at home on the way, I had offered to take Skye back to the Gate House to let the adults talk. Isla, however, had insisted I was welcome to stay to hear whatever news Delia was so worked up about and, I had to admit, I was incredibly curious to find out what was going on. And so, pulling a chair up to the table, I handed Skye a slice of her granny's home-made fruit cake and settled her on my lap while Granny herself sank onto a kitchen chair and looked around triumphantly.

'It's a family reunion – they're flying in from all over the States. They're called the Mahonys, they've been tracing their roots and reckon their ancestors come from here.'

'Really?'

Patrick frowned.

'I didn't think we had any relatives in America.'

His mother shrugged.

'They're not related to the Fitzmahons, as far as I can work out, just some fella who worked here years ago. Anyway.' She sipped her tea before continuing. 'The woman in the tourist office sent me on the email. I didn't bother saying anything to ye because I assumed we wouldn't be anywhere near ready. But then he phoned me himself today, lovely man, Liam, his name is, and he says they will all be happy to rough it and just pitch their tents in the grounds. Honestly, I even gave him the name of the guesthouse in the village but he insisted, said it was Hollowpark or nothing. It's his fiftieth birthday, apparently, and you know how the Yanks are, they only get a few days' holiday a year and they want to make the most of it. He said they're used to being outdoors and they have all the gear, all we need to provide is hot showers and a kitchen and we're away on a hack.'

'But—'

Patrick attempted to interject again but was rewarded with a maternal glare.

'Now I know what you're going to say, Paddy, but it's sorted, I'm telling you. I'll move into the Gate House with ye for the weekend, and the visitors can have my apartment to cook and wash in. We'll do them a nice tour of the house on the first day and they're going to organise the birthday party themselves in the grounds. 'Tis the location they want, really, not anything else. And they are willing to pay top dollar for it.'

She reached into her apron pocket and took out a piece of paper that had been folded and unfolded several times.

'I didn't even give him a price, this is what he came up with, look!'

Paddy squinted at paper, and then a slow smile spread over his face.

'Right.'

His mother gave a smug grin. 'I couldn't say no to that now, could I?'

Her son shook his head. 'I don't think you could, no. And that's genuinely all they need? A place to camp?'

'Isn't that what I'm after telling you?' Delia nodded. 'I was thinking we could set them up in the field out the back here...'

She pointed out the kitchen window, beyond which lay a flat lawn which she had planned to turn into a kitchen garden but which was currently home to nothing more than a broken plastic swing set and too many weeds.

'They could pitch their tents there and have open access to this place for cooking and that. Then for the party we'll need a marquee, that sort of thing, and we'll set all that up on the front lawn.'

Patrick was enthusiastic now, nodding and clearly making mental notes about what needed to be done.

'Sounds great! How many are you talking about?'

'Around twenty-five.' Delia took another, longer, drink of tea. 'This Liam chap, it's his fiftieth, as I said, and then there's an uncle who is seventy and a few children, grandchildren, one baby, I think. A range of ages is how he put it. Honestly, he was a nice man, very reasonable. He said they go away camping together all the time, that it's their "thing".'

Delia didn't do the invisible air quotes, but I could hear them in her voice anyway, and had to hide a smile. It was lovely to see her so enthusiastic about the visitors, great to think that all the hard work she and Patrick had put in was going to come to fruition. I looked around at Isla, who was sitting next to me, but she seemed lost in thought, her eyes fixed on the far wall.

'Well I hope they'll have the sense to bring rain gear with them.' Patrick looked back at the printed email again. 'I mean it's one thing camping in thirty-degree heat in some national park in California, it's another...' His voice trailed off. 'Mum. You did see the date they are talking about?'

'I did.'

His mother sounded defensive. Patrick read the paper again and looked up at her.

'Mum, you can't be OK with this.'

'And why wouldn't I be?'

There were two spots of colour on Delia's cheek now. Even small Skye had fallen silent, the air in the kitchen twanging with tension.

'But Mam...'

He called her Mam when he was under pressure, I thought to myself inconsequentially. And then Isla reached over and took the paper from him, a quizzical expression on her face.

'I don't see what the problem is, Paddy. As you said yourself, they'll have all the rain gear and everything, it doesn't matter if it's cold. And a Hallowe'en party sounds like great fun, it'll be nice to have a theme, make it easier to plan...'

Hallowe'en. The word hung in the air for the moment. And then Delia turned to her son, and it was clear that at that moment there was no one in the room for her, but him.

'And are we to spend the rest of our lives being punished for something that had nothing to do with us? Christ Almighty, Paddy, Catherine Clancy was a brainless young one, I remember her from school, she hadn't the sense she was born with. Always running after some fella or another, she could have gone off with anyone that night, and probably did. I know her mother had half the country convinced someone did away with her but she would say that, wouldn't she? It was probably easier for Angela to believe the girl was dead than that she just left home and didn't bother coming back. There's no reason to believe that what happened to that little tart had anything to do with Hollowpark, yet we're supposed to go around in sackcloth and ashes like it was all our fault. Well, I'm sick of it! Sick of Angela and her cronies pointing at us every time we set foot in the village, muttering about Hollowpark as if we were in some way to blame. I'm not putting up with it any more, and if you want this to be a real, living business then you can't either. This is a serious offer, Paddy, serious money. It could fix the roof, set us up for the winter. For Christ's sake, don't let the actions of one stupid girl blight the rest of your life.'

Mother and son stared at each other. I suddenly felt very surplus to requirements and jumped up from my chair.

'I need to get this one changed.'

An exhausted Skye immediately started to grizzle.

'Want more cake!'

'You need a shower, darling, you're covered in sand...'

Before she could say any more, I bundled her out of the door. I needed to get away, this was a family matter, and I had no place in it, even though I had very strong views. On the one hand I could see Delia's point, she was a businesswoman, after all, and it would be foolish to turn down such a valuable booking. But a party on Hallowe'en night? Hadn't she even thought of discussing it with the others first? It had rained again while we had been inside and, not wanting to get Skye's feet wet, I led her back along the path to the main house rather than taking our usual short cut across the grass. When we reached Hollowpark I noticed that her sandal had come loose, and I bent down to tie it, surprised to find her unusually happy to stand still. It was only when I rose to my feet again that I realised that the little girl's attention was fixed on one of the bedroom windows, my bedroom window. And the pale face of the woman who was standing there.

'There's the lady,' said Skye quite conversationally. My back stiffened, all of the warmth of the day was gone now and my skin felt clammy, and cold.

'What lady, Skye?'

'The other lady who lives in the house, look!'

Deirdre's hand was on the curtain – my curtain – and she was staring straight out across the grounds. I had read the expression 'the blood drained from my face' before, but now felt its literal meaning; it was as if all of the liquid in my body had pooled in my legs leaving me both light-headed and leaden-footed, anchored to the ground. Skye was waving excitedly at the window but I could not move, could not reach for her.

Dry mouthed, I forced myself to speak. 'How do you know that lady, Skye?'

'She's the other lady who lives in the house!' Skye said again, throwing me a pitying glance. 'Daddy can't see her but you can, can't you, Grace?'

Yes, I could. I swallowed, and looked up again and this time Deirdre tilted her head until she was looking straight at me, her eyes dark, her hair pulled back so tightly that it gave her face a skull-like appearance. The white collar on her dress was the only relief against the blackness.

'Find her.'

And she was too far away, of course, for me to hear what she was saying but the words formed in my brain anyway, as distinctly as if she'd said them in my ear.

'Find her.'

And then Deirdre's gaze moved and settled on Skye again. The little girl had grown bored and was hopping from one foot to the other, wanting to go home. But there was a note of challenge on Deirdre's face now. Or was it a warning?

'Take care of my home.'

Willing myself to move, I grabbed Skye by the hand and tugged her across the gravel driveway, towards the path that led to the Gate House. I did not look back but the prickling of the skin on the nape of my neck told me that the woman was still at the window, still watching us.

'Take care of my home.'

And I was chilled now, chilled and anxious and, yes, frightened. I had felt all along that the women, that Catherine and Deirdre did not mean me any harm but Skye was involved now, she was a Fitzmahon and her mother, her own mother, was making plans for the house that were not in its best interests.

This house protects its own.

But what would happen to those who did not protect it in turn?

Chapter 27

Hallowe'en, 1973

'**C**hase us, Cathy!'

But Catherine Clancy, unsure and unbalanced in borrowed high heels, glowered at her younger brother and shook her head.

'Ah, go on, Cathy. Mam said you had to play with us!'

'Piss off, Bobby!'

'And I'll tell Mam you *cursed*...'

The little monster ran up to her and stuck out his tongue. Forgetting her heels for a moment, Catherine made a dive at him, and just about managed to stay upright.

'You little...'

'I'll tell Mammmmmyyyy...'

But Bobby had reached his friends now, on the other side of the lawn, friends who had liberated a pile of branches from somewhere and had turned them into weapons. A few 'stick 'em ups' later, Catherine decided it was safe to leave. She tiptoed across the grass, careful not to let her heels sink into the soft ground, and then turned at the edge of the lawn and looked back at the house. Hollowpark Hall looked incredible tonight, she thought, like something out of a film, a proper American blockbuster, not some soppy Irish yoke. The Fitzmahons always put a lot of effort into their Hallowe'en party but this year they'd gone all out, with fairy lights strung on the trees and turnips carved and arranged on the large stone steps at the front of the house. Catherine had never seen anyone go to the trouble of carving turnips before, but the effect was spectacular, with small candles flickering inside the hollowed out, grimacing faces. Hollowpark's annual party was supposed to be mostly for children, but there were plenty of adults around this evening as well, mams and dads who had dropped their kids to the festivities and stayed to have a nose around. Catherine didn't blame them. Lisheeha was the dullest place on earth and 31 October was the only night in the year when anything exciting happened there.

She moved across the grass again until she reached the edge of the lawn, then felt in the front pocket of her black jeans and pulled out a box of Carroll's cigarettes she'd found hidden under the passenger seat of her dad's car the day before. The smokes were squashed, and she rolled one around in her hands to straighten it up before looking up and out from under her fringe.

'Can I get a light, Rory? Thanks.'

He wasn't there, of course, but there was no harm in practising. Catherine hadn't, in fact, seen Rory Fitzmahon since the day he had issued that unexpected invitation outside O'Dwyer's, a day that was starting to feel more and more like a dream. But she had come to Hollowpark tonight anyway, in the hope she hadn't imagined their conversation. She lit her cigarette herself, then dropped the match onto the grass, trapping it under the sole of her shoe. Her mother had raised her eyebrows when she'd appeared downstairs that afternoon, wearing her new bell-bottom jeans that were so tight around the arse she could barely sit down in them and a pair of heels she'd borrowed from her cousin, and had looked extremely sceptical when Catherine had told her she was dressing up for Hallowe'en as 'a Bond girl'. But just as she was opening her mouth to complain Bobby pulled a bag of flour down off the kitchen counter, destroying both himself and the floor, and the resulting mess and confusion had meant all other confrontation was avoided. Catherine took a final drag from the cigarette, which she wasn't really enjoying, dropped it on the ground and wiggled one of her heels to try and put it out but the grass was too dry, and she ended up stamping on it to stop it from smouldering.

'Do you want a hand with that?'

A group of fathers, who were supposed to be helping with the games but were, in reality, helping themselves to the Fitzmahon's free beer, were standing a few feet away and a couple of them looked over at her, laughing in a most unfatherly way. One of them was Mr Sheehan from the school, Catherine noticed; he was looking at her arse too, dirty bastard. And him with two kids and another on the way.

'Perverts,' she muttered, just loud enough for them to hear, and she was satisfied to see Mr Sheehan redden, then turn away and begin to talk loudly about a match in the next parish. Catherine felt powerful for a moment and straightened her shoulders, ready to head to the real party and leave those eejits behind.

There was a shout from the lawn and her head snapped

round but it was only Bobby, his mask hanging off the back of his neck now, a bag of popcorn clutched in each sticky hand. He'd be fine, Catherine decided, he had forgotten all about her, she could head away. The only problem was she had no idea where she was supposed to be going. Rory's invitation had been so sudden, and so sophisticated, she hadn't wanted to ask boring questions about what time she should arrive and where they should meet, like some eejit who had never been to a party before. But the fact of the matter was, she *was* some eejit who had never been to a party before.

The teachers at school were forever saying that she 'lacked ambition', but Catherine Clancy always thought it was they who were short-sighted and couldn't see past 'being a good girl' and passing exams. Catherine had ambitions, all right, but they had nothing to do with knowing the square root of sixteen and the longest river in Connaught. The fact was, she wanted to get away from Connaught, all of Ireland actually, as soon as she could. Even Dublin wouldn't be far enough away; Catherine heard too many stories of girls getting a flat in the city and then running into or, God forbid, being asked out to dance by someone from down home. No, Catherine was going to go to London, or Manchester, or even America to work in an office with other women who wore high heels every day and didn't give a damn where you came from or who your people were.

She even knew how she was going to get there. Next year, after she'd done her exams, she was going to leave the convent and sign up for a commercial course in Sligo. Her parents would give out, but sure that was nothing new and there was nothing they could do to stop her anyway, once she turned sixteen. And as soon as she had a certificate to say she could type and file and do whatever else they taught in the college she'd be off, and no one would be able to stop her. After that, Lisheeha would only see Catherine Clancy at Christmas when she would arrive home with beautifully wrapped presents to show them all how well she was doing.

First though, she had a date with Rory Fitzmahon, or at least she thought she had. A sudden blast of wind rose goosebumps on Catherine's skin and she pulled her jacket tightly around her. It would be lovely, she thought suddenly, to have one of the girls here now, even Tracey, to reassure her that her hair looked grand, and try and figure out where they were supposed to be going. But all the girls Catherine's age were back near the Hall, pretending to be too old for the kids' party while actually stealing as many sweets as they could fit in their pockets and queuing up to get their fortunes told. For a moment Catherine longed to be back there, rooting out jellies from a bag that mostly contained monkey nuts and pretending that 'Gypsy Rose Lee' wasn't just Rory's mum in a purple scarf. There would be a few older girls around too, Mrs Fitzmahon always hired them in from the village on nights like this, and Catherine was sure if she hung around for long enough that one of them would liberate a bottle of vodka from Hollowpark's generous supplies. She'd heard Lisa O'Grady had had to take a week off school last year, she'd been so sick after her night's work.

But now she was being ridiculous. She had been invited to a proper party, there was no need to hang around with the others tonight. Catherine reached up and touched her hair, patting it down as smoothly as she could over her ears. It was so frizzy and dry, she usually just tied it back but tonight she'd borrowed her mother's rollers and created as sleek a style as she could manage, and, as she patted and smoothed, patted and smoothed, the actions lent clarity to her thoughts. Let Nuala and Tracey and the rest of them hang around the kids with their sweets and their nuts and their stupid games. She had been invited to a proper party and she was going to get there.

She turned and began to cross the wildflower meadow, moving slowly in her heels and hoping her ass was wiggling in a sexy, and not an 'I'm going to fall' sort of way. There was a crunching sound under her feet, and Catherine looked down to see small black berries littering the grass. Her dad would know what they were, she reckoned, but she couldn't ever ask him because she'd have to tell him where she had been. And then she stopped as a high hedge loomed over her. The Hollowpark maze. Catherine had heard about the maze, of course, had even read about it in her dad's book, but she had never seen it before. It was always off limits on Hallowe'en night because the Fitzmahons, it was said, were afraid one of the small kids would get lost in there. Looking up at it now, its leaves so dark they seemed to merge with the night sky, it was easy to understand their fears, and the thought of walking inside it made Catherine's stomach clench with fear. If she turned now, she'd be back with the others in minutes – and then she heard a giggle floating towards her on the night air, and after it, a louder snort of laughter. She put one foot inside the entrance to the maze and there was a smell of smoke now, and it wasn't cigarette smoke either but the other kind and the glamour of it, the sheer *boldness* of what lay ahead gave her courage and she moved forward again. She turned her head one last time to look at the entrance and for a moment she thought there was someone else in the maze with her. It looked like a woman, a woman the same age as her mam, a pale woman with her hair tied back, she was dressed up as a servant or someone from a very old film – and then she blinked, and the figure disappeared. A shadow, that's all it had been. And if anyone had been standing there on the edge of the wildflower meadow that night they would have seen only a flicker in the blackness as Catherine Clancy, fifteen years of age in her skin-tight jeans and her borrowed high heels, rose onto her toes and strode forward, with an assurance she didn't really possess, into the inky blackness of the Belladonna Maze. The leaves at the entrance rustled, and fell still.

Chapter 28

31 October 2007

'**I**'m comin' to get you!!!'

I screamed, then dropped to my knees, my hands clasped to my heart. The tiny ghost removed its head and peered at me in concern.

'It's ONLY me, Gwace. You don't have to be scared.'

'Thank goodness!' I let out an exaggerated sigh then drew Skye towards me for a massive hug.

'You had me fooled there for a minute! You look fantastic, my darling.'

'Like a real ghost?'

'Like a real ghost,' I agreed, releasing her, then standing up again. Isla, who was sitting at her work bench, now also furnished with a sewing machine, looked up at me and smiled.

'You like it? I'll have yours ready in a minute.'

'There's no hurry,' I told her, and walked to the window furthest from the door before leaning over, allowing the evening air to cool my face. I had been rushing around all day, all week, really, and this moment of stillness was glorious. Isla saw the expression on my face and smiled.

'It's going to be quite the night, isn't it?'

'It certainly is.'

She bent her neck and began to sew again, and I gestured at Skye to join me, lifting her into my arms and pointing out all the last-minute preparations for the party that were going on in the grounds below. The Mahony clan had flown into Knock Airport the previous day and had driven to Hollowpark in a fleet of rental cars and, despite mispronouncing their names Mah-HO-knee, had turned out to be as decent a bunch as Delia had predicted. Liam, whose birthday they were celebrating, had taken a brief look around the house and pronounced it 'phenomenal', and the rest of the family had taken their cues from him, pitching their tents, ordering food for elaborate barbecues and even describing the odd shower of rain as 'totally awesome' and 'just what they had hoped for' from their Irish holiday. Delia had, as planned, moved into Skye's room in the Gate House to free up her flat for the duration of their stay but I doubt Patrick and Isla had even noticed she was there, as she didn't seem to have slept in a week. She was like a steam engine moving around the grounds and house, dusting and tidying, mowing and organising and then starting at the beginning again, seemingly without the need for any fuel other than strong tea.

'I suppose you know about – everything. Why Patrick felt a bit funny about having a party here tonight.'

Isla bit a piece of thread and looked up at me. I shot a glance at Skye but her mother's question had been vague enough not to interest her. Still, I made a point of pointing out the fairy lights that had been strung all along the outside of the maze to distract the little girl before answering.

'About the girl who disappeared all those years ago? Yeah. Was Patrick... Is he OK about it all now? Has he sorted it out with Delia?'

'Sure.' Isla shrugged. 'That poor girl, it's incredibly sad. But I think Delia was right, actually. It was thirty years ago; they don't even know if anything actually happened to her here. She could have run away, they never found' – she mouthed the words – 'a body, even. She could have tried to hitch home and met someone nasty. Apparently she was the type, a bit wild. She was always talking about moving away, her friends said. There's no reason to believe anything actually happened to her here at Hollowpark.'

'I suppose.'

I kept my tone as level as I could. What Isla was saying made sense, of course, and Delia was right, they couldn't let what had happened over three decades ago decide everyone's future. But it was hard to be logical when you had met Catherine's mother and – I swallowed and looked out into the grounds again – when you had met Catherine herself, and knew how lost she was, how lost she felt. Delia may have been convinced that Catherine had run away but the truth, I knew, was much darker. The only problem was, I had no way of telling anyone without sounding like I had lost my mind, and that I was certainly the wrong person to be in charge of a three-year-old. Oh, Skye. I felt it again, that dragging sensation, and a cold prickling along my hairline. I had not seen Deirdre, or indeed anything out of the ordinary, since the day Delia had told us about the Hallowe'en party but I was frightened of her now, properly frightened for the first time. There was a darkness in this house and, even though I felt sure I was not its direct target, I could sense it all around me, in the long dark corridors and those large and dusty rooms where secrets were piled high in crumbling cardboard boxes. I had thought about leaving several times since that day, had even gone as far as to pack a bag and call the airport to enquire about flights. I had some savings and could have gone back to Greece, or to my parents' house in Dublin, or simply to a hotel somewhere to sit in safety and plan my next move. But all those options would have involved leaving Skye, and I just couldn't bring myself to do that. There was no question of telling her family what I had seen, they would have thought I was mad if I told them I needed to protect her from the ghost of the woman who had lived in their home almost two centuries before. And I simply was not prepared to leave her in the care of a new nanny who might not realise how closely she needed to be watched. And then there was Patrick. I swallowed, feeling the mixture of shame and, yes, excitement that swelled inside me now every time I thought about him. We hadn't really spoken since that day in the playground, other than to discuss Skye, and it was highly likely he had forgotten the conversation had ever taken place, and that I had imagined the connection between us. But I cared for him. I wasn't going to act on my feelings, I wasn't that sort of person, but I cared about what was going to happen to him and couldn't bring myself to leave Hollowpark without finding out.

And so I had stayed, keeping a light burning in my bedroom at night and my curtains shut tight against the darkness, and whatever else was outside. The preparations for the Hallowe'en party had helped, there was too much work for Delia and Patrick to cope with alone, and so I threw myself into helping them, spending all of my spare time cleaning and polishing and, in the process, exhausting myself to the extent that I was able to sleep for a few hours before getting up and throwing myself into working and Not Thinking again. I couldn't keep going like this, I knew it, couldn't keep running on adrenalin for much longer. But the party was coming, I would just get through this one night and then, finally, I would decide what to do.

'Earth to Grace?'

Isla's voice, coming from miles away, sounded amused. I turned to her.

'Sorry. Busy week, you know yourself.'

'Oh, I know.'

She snipped a piece of thread and pulled the dark material she had been working on out of the machine.

'You've all been amazing, I'm so sorry I couldn't have been of any more help. Here – try this on and see what you think?'

I walked across the floor, took her material and examined it, finding myself, not for the first time, in awe of her easy creativity.

'It's beautiful.'

'Well try it on then!'

I slid the velvet folds of the cape through my fingers, then slipped off my hoodie and let it fall to the floor. When the Mahonys had announced that we, the permanent residents of Hollowpark, were invited to their family party it had sounded more like an imposition than an invitation, especially when it was revealed we would all be expected to

dress up to go along with the Hallowe'en theme. Delia had
been particularly irritated – we had been killing ourselves
to get their party ready all week, and now they expected
us to, as she put it 'doll ourselves up' as well? And the
price of shop-bought costumes! But Isla, unexpectedly,
had come up with a solution. There was an old sewing
machine in one of the storerooms, she said, and bales of
material. If we gave her our measurements, she'd come
up with something decent for us to wear. The results were
nothing short of breathtaking. Skye's 'friendly ghost' outfit
would have made a Hollywood designer proud, while I
had been handed a fitted vampire's cape with scarlet lining
that could have taken me to the Met ball, let alone Liam
Mahony's fiftieth birthday barbecue. I drew the material
around me then walked back across the room. The evening
had arrived while I was in the tower, and the window had
become a mirror.

'I've put poppers on it, look.'

Isla gripped me gently around the waist, pinching in the
material to show me what she meant. The cloak, which
fastened at the waist and neck, was perfect, long enough to
cover my trainers yet fitted in such a way that would allow
me plenty of room to move around – or run around, if Delia
had her way. All I'd need underneath would be a plain black
T-shirt and pair of trousers and my transition to the world
of the Undead would be complete.

'It's gorgeous,' I told Isla. 'I hope I don't get it dirty or
anything...'

'Don't worry about that.'

She tossed her head in the direction of the main house.

'That material has been lying around for years, honestly

I don't think Delia and Paddy know half of the stuff that's over there. They'll need to do a proper inventory someday. I mean, look at this thing, it could be a trinket, could be a family heirloom, there's no way of knowing which.'

She was pointing towards a small ornament that sat on the window ledge and I walked over and picked it up to take a closer look. It was the little Sphinx I had noticed the previous day, it was nothing special to look at but I had been to Egypt on a package tour a couple of years ago and had retained a fascination with the place. Isla noticed my interest, and nodded at me.

'Feel free to take that for your room if you like, I'm sure Delia and Paddy wouldn't mind.'

Not for the first time, I noticed she had fallen into the habit of speaking about her partner and his mother as if they were the ones in charge of Hollowpark, and she was only a visitor. But that wasn't any of my business, so I dropped the little ornament into the pocket of my cloak, and changed the subject.

'How's the arm?'

Isla was sorting through another pile of material now and looked up and nodded at me.

'Yeah, not too bad actually. The physio said I could do some gentle movement now, so I took the sling off last night. It's feeling OK, I'll see how tonight goes.'

From outside the window came the tinkle of broken glass that told me the caterers had arrived. Even from up here, I could sense that Delia's stress levels were soaring.

'I'd better get going. Will I take Skye with me now?'

Isla looked vaguely around the room.

'That would be great, I want to tidy up here. Could you

get her something to eat? And I might just see you at the party, would that be OK?'

There was a steady hum rising from the grounds of Hollowpark now, the sound of partygoers arriving, boxes being unloaded and the smell of roasting meat drifting towards us on the night air. I needed to go, I thought suddenly, and pulled at the material which suddenly felt far too tight around my neck.

'Hey!'

Isla looked at me, laughing.

'Take it easy. There's a knack to it, look...'

'No, I'm fine.'

I pulled the cape off then folded it over my arm as carefully as I could, still moving at speed.

'Come on, Skye. Say goodbye to Mummy, now.'

The little ghost put her hand in mine and chattered excitedly about the party as we headed down the stairs and out into the grounds again. Alongside the fairy lights, Patrick had hung a *No Entry* sign at the entrance to the maze, saying he had no desire to rescue drunken Americans from it at midnight. It was the smart thing to do, of course, but I was no tourist. I thought of the stone angel, and how many Hallowe'en nights she had seen, and how good it would be to sit with her for a moment and draw breath. And then I pushed the thought out of my mind.

'Bye, Mummy!'

The little girl turned and waved up at her mother, who had come to the window of the Tower and was gazing out over the grounds. But she wasn't looking at the house, nor indeed at her daughter. Instead, Isla was staring into the distance, towards Lisheeha and maybe even beyond that again, to the sea and the coast somewhere far away from here. *This house protects its own.* And right now, Isla had never looked so separate from it.

'Bye, lady!'

It took a moment for me to process what Skye was saying and then I saw the shadow behind Isla, the pale face, the triangle of white at her throat. Deirdre, too, was watching over her home.

And then it was seven o'clock and we were, as Delia pragmatically put it, as ready as we would ever be.

As her grandmother had taken up residence in her bedroom, I had brought Skye over to the main house to get ready. I dropped her ghost costume over her head and she stared at herself in the bathroom mirror for a moment, then flung herself at me, her tiny body vibrating with excitement.

'This is going to be a BWILLIANT party!'

It didn't have to be, I thought to myself grimly. Uneventful would do nicely. I spent a few minutes practising ghost noises with Skye – her final 'wooooOOOO' was so effective she actually scared herself, and had to bury her head in my shoulder for a few minutes to recover – then brought her back down the hall to my room to get changed myself. When Isla had asked what I wanted to dress up as at the party I had picked 'vampire' for the simple reason that I knew I had a pair of black jeans and a T-shirt in my wardrobe, but now I'd actually seen her cape I decided I should put in a bit more effort. I had already thrown on the palest foundation I owned, a pot I used in winter when my annual Greek tan faded, so I rifled through my small make-up bag again and unearthed some black eyeliner and a deep red lipstick I'd got free with some moisturiser and had never been brave enough to wear. I opened my small hand mirror and dusted on some face powder to make me even more ashen faced, then ringed my eyes with black liner and, as I was starting to enjoy myself now, gave myself a pair of exaggerated eyebrows as well. In the absence of gel I used conditioner to slick back my hair then applied the lipstick and sucked in my cheeks, giving what I hoped was a vampirish leer. The little ghost shrank from me nervously, so I gave her a broad smile and then tickled her until she collapsed into giggles.

'It's only a game, silly!'

And that was all it was, wasn't it? A game to entertain a few visiting Americans, to make sure they had a good weekend and spent plenty of dollars, and maybe even tell their friends how they should all come visit Hollowpark too. I gave one final twirl in front of the mirror and felt the Sphinx in the cloak pocket bump against my hip. I would leave it there, I decided. It was going to be a long and busy night and it felt good to have something to anchor me.

Delia had hired party planners to help with the preparations, then fallen out with them and done most of the work herself anyway, but despite the tension behind the scenes, the result was nothing short of spectacular. The lawn in front of the main house was crammed with stalls, a fortune-telling booth, a table for apple-bobbing, a face-painting station, even an outdoor pool table. In fact, Patrick's mum had created a Hallowe'en atmosphere Steven Spielberg himself would have been proud of – if I'd looked up to see Skye fly across the moon on a magic bicycle, I don't think I'd have been particularly surprised. A massive barbecue had been set up near the gravel path and tables were laden with salads, meat and carefully selected vegetarian food while a marquee housed a bar serving everything from draught Guinness, which the Yanks took photos of, and fizzy lager which they preferred to actually drink.

Skye kept a tight grip on my hand as we wandered around, visitors in our own home for the evening. Two men in their twenties perched George W. Bush masks on top of their heads as they attacked the pool table, their formal shirts, chinos and deck shoes making it impossible to guess whether the masks were ironic, or a heartfelt tribute to the real thing. Lynette, Liam Mahony's ferociously thin but surprisingly down-to-earth wife, was radiant in a green flapper dress and was passing around cocktails as if she were in a New York apartment and not a muddy field in the west of Ireland. There were Americans everywhere, munching crisps, eating sweets and loudly proclaiming everything to be very awesome indeed.

'It's like magic!' Skye breathed and I nodded in silent agreement. Wooden effigies of witches and wizards had been placed at intervals around the grounds, each one holding a wooden bowl of what the partygoers no doubt called 'candy', and I grabbed a handful for myself and Skye as we continued our tour. Sweets didn't cause either tooth decay or weight gain on 31 October, everyone knew that. Besides, Skye's buddies in the village would be going from door to door tonight collecting treats and it didn't seem fair for her to miss out just because she lived in a more isolated spot. A couple in their forties dressed as Woody and Jessie from *Toy Story* passed us, bickering about how much he'd had to drink but they had the good sense to shut up and even pretend to be frightened as my tiny ghost waved at them. We were out of the formal garden now and into the area of wildflowers Delia referred to as the meadow but there were traces of the party here too, with arrows reading *Haunted House* and *Transylvania* pinned to the trees and, even though I knew it was all part of the celebrations, I couldn't help doing a double take when I passed a large cardboard tombstone sticking out of the grass. The Americans seemed to have had a word with the weather, too, because the night was perfect, clear and dry and just cold enough to be atmospheric while still allowing us to remain comfortably outside.

'Hi, guys!'

We turned to see a miniature Darth Vader and a large pumpkin stroll across the grass towards us.

'You look terrific!'

I reached across to give Evelyn a kiss on her orange cheek.

'Well thank you for inviting us! This fella couldn't sleep last night with the excitement.'

When I had, with Delia's permission of course, invited Evelyn and her son to the party, my friend had leaped at the chance, admitting she was dying to have a look at both the Yanks and the big celebration the village had heard so much about. The locals in Lisheeha were divided over the Hallowe'en party, she told me, with the older residents, most of them friends of Angela Clancy, feeling that it was in appalling taste while the younger residents, many of whom hoped that any upswing in fortune at the Big House would trickle down to the rest of the village, were adamant that the Fitzmahons had the right to do whatever they wanted with their property, and that it was time to move on from whatever had or hadn't happened at the house more than three decades before.

Darth Vader aimed his light sabre at the ghost, who ducked, and began a game of tag, causing all four of us to turn away from the maze and head back in the direction of the main house. The children joined a queue for popcorn while a woman, whose face I vaguely recognised from school drop-offs, although she wasn't usually wearing devils' horns, walked past us with a tray of sparkling wine. Evelyn reached out and grabbed a glass.

'A half a glass won't kill me this close to the end, will you join me?'

I shook my head. 'I never drink on the job.'

'Fair enough.'

Evelyn had spotted an empty picnic table and we walked towards it, followed by the children who had been given cartons of juice. I sat down opposite her as she sipped her drink, then looked at me over the rim of the glass.

'So, it's going well then? The party?'

I nodded. 'I think so. Delia and Patrick have worked incredibly hard this last month, but it looks amazing and the Americans are delighted. I'm so happy for them!'

Evelyn replaced her glass on the table before continuing. 'And how's Isla these days?'

'Oh, she's doing pretty well. I mean, she can't really work yet, but she's got most of the movement back in her shoulder, and she's in much better form. She's really excited about tonight, too.'

Not even Evelyn's orange make-up could disguise her sceptical expression.

'Is she? I wouldn't have thought all this was her thing.'

'Mmm.'

I took a moment to look around at the scene that was unfolding around me. Spooky sounds blared from speakers attached to the trees and the partygoers had gathered in groups, shouting to be heard over the creaking of doors and the clanking of chains. I had already seen an unsteady witch whose green complexion appeared to owe more to the free bar than her costume and, somewhere behind me, an overexcited child had started to scream. This was certainly a posh barbecue, fuelled by bubbles and organic burgers, but it was still essentially a party in a field and no, I couldn't imagine it was the quiet, refined Isla's idea of a good night out. I didn't need to spell out what I was thinking, though, because Evelyn was still talking, almost to herself.

'I've known Patrick all my life, you know. He was friends with my older brother in school, and you know how small Lisheeha is, we ended up in the same group sometimes. I had a bit of a crush on him when I was younger, I have to admit!'

She giggled and looked over at the children to make sure they couldn't hear what she was saying.

'He's a great guy and a hard worker and I know how much he loves this place. And Isla seems lovely, don't get me wrong, I really enjoyed spending time with her that day on the beach and I know she's talented, I mean, I've seen her work. I can't draw a straight line, I'm in awe of people who can be creative like that. But Dad has been filling me in on some of the plans for Hollowpark and to be honest with you, Grace, I'm not sure if she realises the amount of work that's involved? It'll have to be a real team effort, there is so much left to do to get this place to where they

want it to be. It's just not very her, do you know what
I mean?'

'I do...'

I paused, the desire to talk to her almost overwhelming
me. It had been a long time since I'd wanted to unburden
myself to a friend but then again, it was a long time since
I'd had a friend who I knew would really listen to me. But
then Evelyn grimaced and replaced the glass on the table.

'Ugh, heartburn. Nature's way of telling me I've had
enough, I suppose! Look, don't mind me, that's the first sip
of alcohol I've had this year, I'm just talking bollocks. I just
thought—'

'I need the toilet!'

Skye's voice sang out from the opposite side of the table
and Evelyn's answering grin seemed tinged with relief.

'I bet you do, my love! I was just thinking that myself!'

We gathered the children and made our way towards the
house, leaving all talk of Isla behind with the unfinished
champagne. There were Portaloos dotted around the
grounds, but I used my insider knowledge to lead my friends
to a bathroom near the library which I knew Delia had left
unlocked for the senior Mahonys. Once we'd sorted out
the kids, we used the loo ourselves and, as we were leaving,
heard a peal of laughter coming from the far end of the
corridor. Evelyn looked at me quizzically.

'Oh, that's the movie!' I explained and motioned at her
to follow me. 'Liam Mahony wanted a place inside for the
kids to go if they were tired, or for later when the adults
want to let their hair down.'

I pushed open the door to the library, which looked
completely different this evening, with sofas and chairs

pulled into the middle of the floor, all pointed towards a giant plasma screen TV which had been hired from Sligo for the evening. Three children and a bored-looking teenager were lolling on bean bags, light from the movie *Hocus Pocus* flickering onto their faces. Skye tugged at my hand.

'Can me and Eamon watch the movie?'

'I guess so.'

I looked at Evelyn who gave an easy shrug.

'Suits me! I'll watch them for a bit, take the weight off the pumpkin!'

It was probably for the best, I thought to myself, feeling my sudden need to unburden myself to Evelyn recede in the bright light of the movie screen. Besides, I should be helping out more; I hadn't seen Delia in over an hour and should probably check if she had some jobs lined up for me. As Evelyn settled herself on the sofa, I told her to call me if she needed me and then turned and headed back down the corridor and out into the evening again. The temperature had dropped a few degrees and I pulled my cloak tighter around me and then screamed, as a werewolf reared up out of the darkness from the bottom of the stone steps.

'Got ya!'

Patrick pulled off the furry, long-nosed mask, roaring with laughter. It was a great disguise, but he hadn't bothered changing the rest of his clothes, I noticed, and was still wearing his ancient wax jacket and muddy, farm-stained jeans and boots.

'I see Isla wasn't able to persuade you into a costume?'

He grinned and tucked the wolf mask under his arm. The long nose drooped towards the ground, the toothy grin now saggy and gaping.

'That's the whole point of a werewolf, isn't it?'

He picked up the mask again and waggled its nose at me.

'Just a poor ordinary chap like myself, going about his business and then when the time is right...'

Patrick pointed over my shoulder to where the moon was almost full in the clear sky, casting a blue light over Hollowpark and its occupants. We stared at it for a moment in silence, and then he touched me lightly on the elbow.

'How's it all going, anyway? Mum has been keeping you busy.'

'Yeah.'

I smiled, but said no more for a moment, aware as always of the thin line that divided me from my employers and how a casual remark could be taken as criticism, no matter how good my intentions were. Then I continued, keeping my voice cheerful.

'I've just left Skye with Evelyn and Eamon, actually. They are watching a movie and I was going to see if Delia needed a hand.'

'Oh, she'll be fine.'

Patrick turned, and pulled his mask onto one of the stone orbs that topped the pillars on each side of the steps, leaving a bodiless werewolf grinning out into the darkness. The effect was so ridiculous I couldn't help laughing and he grinned back at me, the skin at the corner of his eyes crinkling. He looked tired, I realised, but then again, we all did. It had been a hell of a month, and now that energy from the partygoers was crackling all around us I was only too aware of how hard we had worked, the effort we had put in to make it happen.

As if reading my thoughts, Patrick jerked his head in the direction of the lawn.

'We deserve a bit of a break too. Why don't we grab a drink, check out how it's all going?'

I shook my head. 'Oh, I'm sure Delia—'

'Come on, Mum will be fine, she's in her element, bossing people around. Here...'

A table had been set up at the edge of the gravel, bearing the handwritten sign *Magical Potions*. Patrick darted across to it and returned, moments later, with two brimming goblets.

'Evelyn can watch Skye for a bit.'

He handed me the 'potion' which, when I sipped it, turned out to be a really delicious, dark red wine. I paused then, remembering what I had said earlier to Evelyn about drinking on duty, but as if reading my mind, Patrick waved away my concerns.

'Honestly, Grace, you're off the clock, you're a guest at the party now, same as the rest of us. Evelyn has both our numbers if she needs us. Go on, you deserve it!'

I hesitated, then took another sip of the wine which was rich and incredibly moreish. Patrick was right, I decided, I had been invited to this party as a guest, after all. The werewolf's head grinned after us as we wandered across the lawn, goblets in hand. Cheers erupted from the pool table as we walked past. It was just gone eight o'clock but the partygoers were getting rowdier and I found the sensible side of my brain checking out the food tables to make sure there was enough soakage to go around. The non-sensible side meanwhile had another sip of wine. It was even colder now too and I lifted my hood up over my head. It fitted perfectly, a tribute to Isla's skill. Patrick looked around at the festivities.

'It's really working out, isn't it?'

I could hear the note of uncertainty in his voice and was reminded, given the history of the house and the date, of the risk he had taken allowing the party to go ahead tonight at all.

'It really is,' I reassured him. 'The Yanks are having a ball, and the house looks brilliant. Would you do it again? Now you see exactly what it involves? Would you be willing to do other gigs like this one?'

We had reached the edge of the lawn now but kept walking, through the wildflower meadow, my cape making swishing sounds as it caught the long grass.

'Absolutely.'

Patrick nodded, suddenly serious.

'The camping wasn't really something I thought of before but now I see it in action it makes perfect sense. We're only a couple of hours from Dublin, I think we can really capture the family market. There's the playground, of course, I could organise pony rides too, maybe set up a proper pet farm. I mean, it's fantastic really, I had thought we'd have to finish the house before we even thought of paying guests but this way we might be able to open up much sooner and make some proper money too. I'm going to investigate buying some permanent tents as well – there are a few companies that provide them, for glamping, like at the big festivals. You can charge a small fortune for them!'

'Sounds brilliant,' I agreed, energised by the obvious excitement in his voice. I assumed Isla had told him she was weighing up her future at Hollowpark but he was certainly showing no evidence of it this evening. We passed the sign for the playground and I wondered for a moment what it would look like in the dark, its swings dangling empty in the moonlight. I had felt so close to him that day – but Patrick kept walking straight ahead and I followed him, lifting my cloak to allow myself to keep pace. A huge cardboard skeleton was dangling from a tree and he shook its hand solemnly as we walked past.

'I remember when you only got this sort of stuff in the States,' I told him. 'It's so cool to see it here. I was in San Francisco one Hallowe'en and I kept taking pictures of the houses, it was so unusual to see them decorated. But you can get everything in Ireland now.'

Patrick stopped, then pulled a bottle of red wine from his inside pocket and waved it in my direction.

'Top-up?'

'Oh, I shouldn't.'

But it was clear to both of us that my objections were merely for show and he cupped his hand around mine to steady it as he refilled the goblet.

'So, San Francisco?' He replaced the bottle in his pocket then took a long drink. 'That sounds exciting. When were you there?'

'About seven years ago,' I told him. 'Just for a couple of weeks, between jobs. But it's a fantastic place, have you been?'

'Never been to the West Coast.' Patrick shook his head. 'Never been anywhere worth talking about really. You've had an amazing life, Grace.'

I snorted. 'Amazing? I'm a twenty-nine-year-old nanny, I can't see what's amazing about that!'

'Don't put yourself down!'

We started walking through the meadow again, more slowly this time, our hands on the goblets blue in the moonlight. Patrick took another drink before continuing.

'I never really travelled after university, too busy coming back here in the summers and then working in London. Went on the odd stag weekend, or a ski trip with the guys, but nothing adventurous. But look at you! You've seen the world, you're brilliant at your job – your parents must be incredibly proud of you.'

'They certainly are not!' I thought of my mother, and sighed. 'They were horrified when I told them I wasn't going to university, especially my mum, she thinks I'm wasting my life, doing this.'

I took another sip of wine which was dark, and spicy, and nothing like the local vino I was used to drinking in Greece.

'Dad works in advertising; Mum spends his money. She didn't like changing my nappies much, she can't imagine why I would want to do that for other people.'

My cloak snagged on a root and I bent over to release it. I was starting to feel quite fuzzy now, the hood adding to the feeling that I was cut off from the real world. I'm not normally a big drinker, my job involves too many early starts and no one in their right mind wants to mind kids with a hangover but I was enjoying how I felt that evening, buzzed, relaxed. Not drunk, but tipsy, still largely in control of myself but in a fluid way. I felt distanced from my day job, from my family, even from little Skye. I loved her but it was nice, for a while, to only have myself to look after. And to be with Patrick on this clear, magical night. And then a chill fell over me and I pulled my hood back from my face to see the maze looming over us, lights twinkling like shards of ice around the entrance. Patrick looked at me, devilment on his face.

'Have you ever been in here at night?'

I shook my head. 'I thought it was out of bounds?'

Patrick drained his glass then stuck it, too, into his jacket pocket.

'For strangers, not us. Come on, it'll be fun. Really get us into the Hallowe'en spirit!'

And before I knew what I was doing I had followed him inside. The darkness in there was almost total, the light from the moon blocked by branches overhead. Patrick strode ahead and, when I hesitated, reached back, and tugged at my sleeve.

'Come on, just for a minute.' Then he rounded a corner and disappeared. I paused for a moment, not sure whether or not I should follow him, wondering whether I was imagining the energy crackling between us, a feeling exacerbated by my hazy sense of being cut loose, weightless, out of time. Maybe I was being ridiculous, this was Skye's dad, my boss, for God's sake, and he was probably just letting off steam after a hard month.

Or maybe he felt the same way I did. The drink and the darkness were dragging feelings to the surface I had been fighting to ignore. I had to admit it, to myself even if to no one else, I had fallen for Patrick Fitzmahon, fallen hard. And that could only end in disaster. To hell with the ghosts, I thought suddenly, this was the reason I should leave Hollowpark Hall. I was the ultimate cliché, a nanny with a crush on the daddy, and it was embarrassing really, that was the truth of it. I was an embarrassment and I should leave now before we got too deep into the maze, and whatever lay inside it. But I didn't leave, instead I followed Patrick around the corner. He had disappeared, and I began to move more quickly, following the leafy path until it divided, suddenly, in two. Heart hammering, I stopped dead, trying to force my head to clear, my mind to focus. This was ridiculous, I had been through here many times, I knew the way – but it was all very different in the darkness. I reached out a hand to try to steady myself but it plunged through a gap in the hedgerow and I almost stumbled, small berries crunching underfoot as I struggled to stay upright. And when I finally stood straight again, all thoughts of Patrick disappeared because there she was, waiting for me. Catherine Clancy. And she was blocking my path.

How to describe a ghost, when her reality was right there in front of me? In the dim light of the maze Catherine was grey but she shimmered, too, lit from within by a silvery light which was just strong enough to illuminate her face but did nothing to break the darkness around her. She was dressed in black, as always, and this time I could see she was wearing high-heeled shoes, 1970s' style wedged heels that were hovering inches above the mud. I was not tipsy any more, but terrified, and my earlier impression that I had nothing to fear from this girl, this apparition, had completely disappeared. This was not a reflection, nor a vision, Catherine was here, right here in front of me, and she wanted me or wanted something from me. Acid from the wine burned in my stomach but my throat was bone dry, leaving me unable to make a sound. And then Catherine Clancy tilted her head to one side and spoke to me.

'Find me.'

Chilled breath puffed towards me and I recoiled as it hit my cheek. The movement seemed to anger her because she reached out then and grabbed me by the hand, her touch ice cold and burning. I could not look away as her eyes opened wider and then wider, and then the flesh shrank back from her face and there was no face at all there now, just hollows and bone and black emptiness where her eyes should have been, and where her mouth should have been and then that cavity opened to emit a scream—

'Grace?'

Patrick's voice tugged me back to the world, saved me. I turned and ran, pushing my way through the leaves, not daring to look back, not caring as my cloak snagged on the branches, running and slipping and sliding until I finally made my way to the entrance of the maze where he was standing, small lights glinting all around him, a lazy smile on his face which disappeared when he saw me.

'Hey. Are you OK? I'm sorry, I just thought it would be fun—'

'I need to get back to Skye.'

I pushed past him, not wanting him to see the fear on my face or the tears in my eyes.

'Sure, but—'

'I just need to get back, OK?'

And I meant it, too, as I began to jog through the night. I needed to get back to Skye , to make sure she was okay, I had been wrong to leave her with Evelyn, wrong to leave that little girl anywhere out of my sight on this night when the very air at Hollowpark was thick with menace, and I was aware of nothing, anymore, but fear.

Chapter 29

Hallowe'en, 1973

Catherine Clancy had always wanted to taste red wine. Her mam bought a single bottle of white every year to drink with the Christmas dinner. It was called Blue Nun and when Catherine was small she had somehow thought it formed part of the religious aspect of the day, like going to mass or putting the candle in the window to guide the Holy Family. Each Christmas, Catherine begged her mother for a taste but, last year, when she had finally relented, the 'Blue' Nun had turned out to be a straw yellow colour, cold and acidic, and Catherine had to drink two full glasses of Club Orange to get rid of the aftertaste.

She had always assumed red wine would be different though, fruity, like Ribena maybe only richer, and definitely more glamorous. And so, when she reached the middle of the maze and saw Rory pouring from a bottle, she accepted the glass he handed her without question.

'Good girl,' he said, admiringly, and Catherine wondered if he knew what age she was, and decided not to tell him. Not yet, there was no need. There were four others in there with him, all boys, or maybe she should call them young men, who had travelled to Hollowpark from England for the weekend and were sitting on a wide stone plinth, passing a bottle of whiskey around and smoking hand-rolled cigarettes. The angel above them had a disapproving look on her face which reminded Catherine of the head nun in her school and made her smile. Disappointingly, the red wine turned out to be almost as cold and sour as the stuff her mam bought, but Catherine managed to keep her lips from puckering and instead tilted her glass towards Rory in a way she had seen someone do on TV. He raised his in return and she felt a burning sensation inside her that had nothing to do with alcohol and everything to do with having followed her heart this evening, and having made the right decision.

Rory introduced her to his friends, but she couldn't get the names fixed in her head, they were names out of books – Charlie and Alfie and Clive – and their owners all looked the same, they had longer hair and a confidence to them, a sheen that made them very different to the local lads. In any other circumstances Catherine would have been afraid to speak in front of them but she wasn't afraid tonight because Rory was at her side, staring at her as if everything she said was fascinating and he was genuinely thrilled she had come. He told the other lads the story of how they met but made it sound funny, not pathetic, like she had been a damsel in distress and not a mortified schoolgirl. Then he planted a kiss on her cheek, so quickly she didn't have time to be nervous and his friends didn't laugh the way the boys in town would have. Rory sat up on the plinth then and made space for Catherine to sit beside him and after a while he put his arm around her. The others were all talking now, laughing and joking about people Catherine had never met and places she had never been but that didn't matter because Catherine Clancy was happier than she had ever been before, sitting close beside Rory Fitzmahon with his hand gently stroking the tip of her shoulder.

Her head was spinning now, her insides dissolving, and she didn't understand the jokes swirling around her but laughed at them anyway. There were more cigarettes, and the end of the bottle of wine and then someone pulled out a naggin of whiskey and offered it around – that was another drink Catherine had never tasted but she sipped at anyway, when her turn came. One of the others said it had grown cold. Catherine hadn't noticed but she supposed it had, and it started raining too, so Rory suggested they go back to somewhere called the Gate House. Catherine felt sad, then, because she wasn't sure if she was invited and she really didn't want to go home. But then Rory looked at her and said, 'That's OK, isn't it? You will come?', and he lifted her down from the plinth, and he took tight hold of her hand and didn't let it go as he led her through the maze, his fingers intertwined with hers, his thumb gently caressing the centre of her palm.

Chapter 30

2007

'I won't keep you too long.'

Liam Mahony, fifty years of age today and rich enough to mark the occasion by bringing a planeload of his extended family across the Atlantic, rapped his fork against his glass and smiled, and I lifted Skye into my arms. Anyone watching would have thought I was helping her to see over the heads of the crowd but in reality, I just wanted to keep her close to me and to feel her warmth. I had collected her from the movie a few minutes before to find both Evelyn and Eamon sleepy, and ready for home. But Skye, hyped up on sugar and the novelty of the party, was still wide awake so, after plastering on a smile and saying goodbye to our friends, I brought her back to the lawn, where the Americans had gathered to listen to their father. I didn't give a damn about Liam Mahony's birthday any more, but I was desperate to be surrounded by people, and this seemed as good a place as any to catch my breath and to make an escape plan.

'Honestly, it'll just take a few minutes!'

Mahony had the perfect teeth of an American businessman and the gentle authority of a man who never had to work too hard to be listened to and, despite my disquiet, I found myself listening properly to what he had to say.

'You know, I'm not actually sure I can put into words how honoured I feel to be here this evening and how much it means to have you all gathered around me today.'

Standing on the other side of the crowd Patrick caught my eye and gave me a concerned look. I hadn't spoken to him on the way back from the maze, other than to say I'd left Skye for too long and was anxious to get back to her and I knew he was worried he had done something to upset me. But I couldn't bring myself to tell him what had happened in there, at least not until I had figured out how the hell I was going to get away.

'Lolly?'

The little girl was bored now, wriggling in my arms, and I placed her gently on the ground beside me, then unwrapped a sweet and handed it to her, less worried about her teeth than the need to keep her happy until I figured out what to do next. I touched her lightly on the head and she smiled up at me, then took a doll from her pocket and began to play with it, slurping happily at the same time. Liam Mahony was still talking. I couldn't quite figure out if he was in fancy dress or not, he was wearing a tweed outfit with matching cap that could have been a nod to his ancestry, or could have been the latest in American off-duty millionaire wear, but he wore it well and stuck his hands deep in his pockets as he finished thanking family and friends and reached what seemed to be the focus of his speech.

'When I stand here today,' he said, looking around for a moment. 'When I stand here, I am thinking of my great-grandfather and trying to imagine how he felt the last time he saw this place, and if he knew where he was going, and that he would never see it again.'

Liam paused and despite the turmoil in my brain I found that he was beginning to draw me in to his story. He seemed to really mean what he was saying, he wasn't just spinning a line to impress his relatives or, indeed, his Irish hosts. He was, in fact, struggling for composure and his wife pushed her way through the crowd towards him and then grasped his hand, her long, pink-tipped fingers slim and tapered in his solid paw. She was wearing a ring that I suspect could have funded Hollowpark for the best part of a year but when I looked at them, I got a sense of solidity and real affection rather than extravagant flashiness. Liam smiled at her and cleared his throat to begin again.

'When I decided to trace my roots, well, it was the ultimate cliché, I guess. Just another middle-aged American going through a crisis. Better for my marriage than a sports car, I guess. Or any of the other options I hear men of my age opt for.'

He paused to let the crowd laugh and, as they obliged, I took a quick look around at them. I had already been introduced to Liam's daughters, two tall, golden-haired women who had their father's height and their mother's chiselled features yet failed, somehow, to be as good-looking as either of them. But they looked rich, and well-groomed and happy. One of them had brought her husband, who at over six foot four who could have made serious money working as a stunt double for The Rock, and was rendered even more attractive by the dark-haired baby he had strapped to his chest in a posh carrier. Beside him stood Liam's uncle, who was also celebrating a birthday and took occasional neat sips from a cut-glass tumbler of whiskey. They might claim to be fond of 'roughing it', but the Mahonys clearly drew the line at drinking out of plastic cups and most of the other adults in the crowd were drinking champagne from Waterford Crystal flutes. Most had made a serious effort with the fancy dress, too: there were the Bush twins, of course, a couple of zombies and a Dracula who had made much more of an effort with his make-up than I had. And then Liam's voice took on a more serious tone and I tuned in once again to what he was saying.

'It was pretty easy to trace our roots back to here, hey, we're called Mahony, so there had to be Irish in there somewhere – although I know you guys wince every time we say it!'

He glanced at Patrick who shook his head and forced a laugh.

'And when I dug a little deeper, I found out more about the location of the house and that was good news too, you know? Yeats country, Joyce country – you know, for a while I thought I was going to find a Nobel winner in the family, or at the very least that one of you guys would write a blockbuster and I'd be able to retire on the proceeds!'

He looked around at his family, who tittered again, while his daughters gave him an affectionate eye-roll.

'But then I had to find out why my family left this place.'

His voice dropped even further and I thought to myself that he could have been a DJ or made a serious living voicing radio advertisements. Holidays, used cars or stairlifts, I'd buy anything Liam Mahony was selling.

'And that's when I learned about Ciarán O'Mahony.'

Liam said the name perfectly this time, or as accurately as his accent allowed, and I felt that all of Hollowpark appreciated the gesture.

'Ciarán was born here, his father was groundsman at Hollowpark, but the house changed ownership and the family fell on hard times. Ciarán, like so many others before him, emigrated to the United States in 1849, and those of you who know your Irish history will know the type of situation he was fleeing, and why he had to get away from here. He was a young man, but he had already suffered the terrible loss of his first wife and their baby daughter.'

Liam paused, and pinched the bridge of his nose with his thumb and finger in a gesture that seemed completely genuine.

'I can't imagine the pain that must have caused him, yet in a terrible way, I have to be grateful for that loss, because if it hadn't happened then Ciarán would never have married again, and started the family that was to become our family. We are lucky, too, that he was an educated man, and left behind some letters that were later donated to a university here in Ireland. I've been able to use them to piece some of his story together.'

Liam paused, took a sip of his drink and then continued.

'He was a good man, a hard-working man, and he built the business that was eventually passed down to my grandfather, and laid the foundations for the wonderful life we all enjoy. But his story started here at Hollowpark, and it was rooted in sadness and loss. It must have taken exceptional bravery for Ciarán to have gone through what he did, and to find the strength to leave, and survive, and prosper.'

Liam paused, then dug in his pocket for some paper, and again for a pair of gold-framed spectacles.

'I've brought some lines of his with me and I hope you don't mind me reading them. This is from a letter Ciarán wrote to his father, just after his second marriage.'

The night was utterly still, even the leaves in the trees seemed to have fallen silent and it was as if the house and its grounds had paused to hear what he had to say. Liam placed the glasses on the end of his nose, and read, in that same, mesmerising tone.

'"Hollowpark was never ours, but it was home to me. The house fell on bad times, as did we, but I had a friend here, who helped me to escape to a land where I could find a future. Deirdre Fitzmahon told me once that Hollowpark protects its own. She offered that protection to me, and I hope and pray that she found her own peace and comfort, as I did."'

Liam removed his glasses and looked up at us again.

'Ciarán's first wife was called Mary, and their baby was Kathleen. I don't know much more about them but I feel, very strongly, that we should remember them now on this night that is bringing us so much happiness.'

He raised his glass and as the others joined him in the toast I glanced upwards towards my bedroom window, not surprised to see that black dress, the flash of white at her throat. As Deirdre Fitzmahon's angular face looked down at us, I suddenly knew that whatever was happening in this house, whatever had been building, was going to come to the surface this night. Anxiety rose inside me and I looked down, but Skye was no longer at my feet.

'Skye?'

Liam was still talking and I whispered the name, then began to pick my way through the crowd, my eyes searching for that small white costume.

'Skye?'

And I was saying her name now, and saying it loudly, not caring about disturbing the party, I just wanted to find the little girl who was out there somewhere, lost and alone.

'Skye?'

Some of the others heard me calling and they turned their heads towards me and even Liam looked up from his letter and turned in my direction.

'Is everything OK, miss?'

'I just can't find…'

I couldn't continue, my heart was thumping so loudly it had knocked the breath from my lungs, and in the silence one of the George W. Bushes lifted his mask and jerked his thumb towards the meadow.

'That's the little ghost girl, right? I saw her a few minutes ago, she looked like she was heading to the maze.'

'But she's not supposed to wander off on her own!'

I was running now, and he shouted his answer after me.

'She wasn't on her own though, she was with some older guy.'

The cape, that bloody cape was flapping around my ankles now and I grabbed the folds of material and bunched them around my waist as I continued to sprint across the lawn, the grass slippery under my trainers.

I heard heavy breathing and then Patrick caught up and fell into place beside me.

'I heard you shouting – what's wrong?'

'Skye... can't find her...'

I was running too fast to continue and besides, I feared if I said anything else I would burst into tears and then I would be of no use to her. 'She's with some guy' – Jesus, what had I done? Isla, the day she had fallen, had thought she had seen a person in the maze – could it have been her ex-husband after all, come back to find her? Had he come to take her daughter instead? That precious little girl – I tripped and almost fell but Patrick caught me before I hit the ground.

'We'll find her.'

But the look on his face belied the reassurance of his words. Berries crunched under my feet as I began to run again, berries, belladonna, deadly nightshade... the words swam into my brain. Those small, shiny things – Skye wouldn't eat them, would she? She had grown up at the Hall, had been taught the dangers – but this night was all about sweets, there were bags of them everywhere, trails of treats. What if she mistook the berries for yet another surprise?

My mind skittering, I only stopped running when I reached the maze and saw that the *No Entry* sign had been pushed aside. The garland of fairy lights still twinkled in the leaves and my heart dipped even further when I realised how attractive they would have been to a little girl...

'Skye?'

We both shouted her name and then dived forward,

Patrick just slightly ahead of me. The edge of his jacket flapped behind him and I resisted a sudden surge to hold on to him and let him pull me along, but I could not, would not fall to pieces now, this was my fault, I had to be strong. He stopped suddenly and I ran into the back of him, my head thumping off his shoulder.

'Sorry, wrong way,' he muttered and pushed past me to start running again. But we were both panicking now and took a second wrong turn, and then a third, where was she?

'Skye?'

But our words were trapped by the thick hedges and bounced back at us.

'Come to Daddy, Skye!'

And then miraculously, beautifully, came the soft echo of the word.

'Daddy!'

Patrick stopped dead, grabbed my wrist.

'Did you hear it?'

And I did, and I heard it again. We turned, and followed yet another leafy passageway and my heart sank when we rounded a corner and discovered we had doubled back on ourselves and were back at the entrance to the maze again. And then it didn't matter, because we saw, under the fairy lights, the small white costume.

'I'm here, Daddy!'

There was no panic in the small voice as we ran towards it. Patrick burst out of the maze and swept up the little figure in his arms.

'Dad!'

But this time it was his voice and not Skye's that called out to his father.

Chapter 31

Hallowe'en, 1973

The rain began to fall more heavily as they exited the maze, and the grounds of Hollowpark had emptied. Catherine wasn't quite sure how long they had been inside, but it must be very late now because all of the small kids had disappeared and the noise coming from the main house indicated that what was left of the party had moved inside. There was no one in the meadow to see the small group of teenagers dart across the grass, towards the path that led to the Gate House. Catherine was surprised to find that building both smaller and colder than she had expected but it didn't matter, because one of Rory's friends lit a fire in the grate, causing the others to crack jokes she didn't understand about 'Dib Dib Dib' and 'Being Prepared'. Within moments they were all sitting on an ancient, sagging sofa, Catherine nestled into Rory who had his arms tight around her.

The wine was gone and so was the whiskey but somebody produced vodka and that was OK, lots of girls in the school drank vodka and it didn't taste too bad if you swallowed it down without thinking. When Catherine passed the bottle back to Rory he took it out of her hands then bent closer and kissed her, properly this time. And she kissed him back and somehow, knew exactly what to do.

Things happened in flashes, after that. Another cigarette was passed around and Catherine inhaled deeply, realising too late that it didn't contain ordinary tobacco. But she would have looked like a baby if she complained so instead she drew the sweet, spicy smoke deep into her lungs and pretended to enjoy it when her face and lips grew numb. Another flash, and she was sitting on Rory's lap and now it seemed that the others were gone and they were alone. Her shoes were missing and so was her jacket but that didn't matter, she was warm and safe and Rory was kissing her and everything was going to be OK.

'Will we turn in?'

The old-fashioned phrase dissolved any slight hesitation she might have been feeling. Catherine loved the way Rory talked, it was so romantic, so respectful, and she kissed him again before they rose from the sofa, then followed him up the stairs. She should have been nervous, she supposed, the nuns had warned her about boys like him and, Jesus, her mother would have been scandalised if she knew what was happening but despite all their warnings and their scare stories there was something so right about how she was feeling that it couldn't be a bad thing to do, not really. There was something that she had to tell him though, and she paused as he walked through a door into what must have been a bedroom, tugging on his sleeve to make him listen to her.

'Rory.'

'What, darling?'

Oh, that voice.

'I'm only fifteen.'

'Ah.' And then he pulled her closer to him, and there was no break, really, before the kissing started again.

Chapter 32

2007

'Rory Fitzmahon. It's lovely to meet you properly.'
Prop'ly.

The man rose from the sofa and I walked over and shook his outstretched hand. In the harsh light of the Gate House kitchen the resemblance to Patrick was striking. Rory Fitzmahon's hair was still thick, although grey rather than sandy, and his brown eyes undimmed by age. He spoke like Patrick too, that light upper-class accent that was neither Irish nor English and marked them out as not quite native to either country.

Patrick himself, who was taking milk from the fridge, looked over at me.

'Did Skye fall asleep OK?'

'Yeah, she's grand.'

I took a seat at the kitchen table and accepted the cup of tea that was handed to me. I could have done with a brandy, actually, but I didn't think that more drinking on the job would have been a good look that evening. Oh sure, Patrick had said all the right things, that Skye had only been gone for five minutes and that it was unsurprising she had run off, given the excitement of the evening and the number of things that were in the garden to explore. But even if Patrick didn't blame me for not keeping an eye on her, I blamed myself. I had been so distracted by Hollowpark and its ghosts and even Liam Mahony's bloody history lesson, that I had taken my eye off my little charge and although nothing had happened to her, anything could have. Her grandfather had been walking past the maze, he said, when he had seen what he thought was a white sheet blowing past and something, some long-buried parental instinct maybe, had caused him to take a second look. And thank God he had.

I sipped my tea and closed my eyes for a moment, wondering how long I could stay without seeming rude, craving solitude, and decompression. Skye had gone to bed happily, exhausted after her day and unaware of the fuss she had caused, but I still felt sick every time I remembered looking down and not seeing her there. My nerves were still jangling from what I'd seen in the maze too, and I needed to be on my own, to process what had happened that evening and to decide what I was going to do.

'I can't believe how good this place looks!'

'It's comfortable, yes.'

Patrick raised his eyebrows.

'But wait until you've seen what we've done to the main house. Mum has been working like a trojan.'

'I don't doubt it!' Rory sipped his tea before continuing. 'I was... very touched when you invited me over.'

Patrick replaced the milk in the fridge and then picked up his own mug of tea. He hesitated for a moment, as if

considering settling down beside his father on the small
sofa, then apparently thought better of it and opted for the
kitchen chair beside mine. He looked exhausted, I thought,
which increased the similarity to his father. Rory Fitzmahon
looked healthy, well rested and younger than his years. Tired
and drawn after the scare, his son seemed to be catching up
with him in age.

'Yes, well.' Patrick gave a fleeting smile. 'I didn't expect
you'd take me up on it tonight! You could have called. But
it's good to see you, Dad. I thought it was about time you
saw what we were doing with the place. After all, it was
your home too.'

They seemed to have forgotten I was there, and,
completely shattered by the day's activities and then the
fright with Skye, I wondered if I could get up and leave
without attracting attention. But Patrick had positioned
his chair between me and the door, so I settled instead for
trying to make myself small and unnoticeable as father and
son continued to talk.

'I got a flight at short notice – I tried phoning the house
but no one seemed to be picking up.'

'Ah, OK.' Patrick nodded. 'The only landline is in Mum's
kitchen, and the Americans have set up shop there for the
weekend. You could have tried my mobile.'

'Oh, I can't stand those things.'

Rory ran his fingers through his hair, making him more
like his son than ever.

'And how is your mother?'

'She's good, yeah.'

Patrick shifted uncomfortably on his chair and Rory shot
him a suspicious glance.

'You did tell her you had invited me? Paddy, she—'

'And who is she? The cat's mother?'

There was a whirl of fresh air from outside and Delia walked into the kitchen. She was dressed for the evening's festivities in a bunny onesie, complete with a fluffy white tail and a pair of ears which waggled as she spoke.

'Well, Rory Fitzmahon.'

She pushed her hood back and patted her hair back into place. After the hard work she had put in that day she must have been exhausted but, with her eyes sparkling and her head held high, I'd actually never seen Delia looking better.

'Delia.'

The word hung in the air and then the older man unfolded himself from the sofa and crossed the kitchen floor towards her. They stood stock-still for a moment, regarding each other, and then he grinned, and enfolded her in a hug. The embrace only lasted for a minute before Delia pulled away, but she was smiling, and not quite her usual brisk self as she ushered her husband back to his seat.

'I suppose my darling son invited you over?'

Patrick gave her a bashful look.

'Are you really cross, Mum? It just felt weird to have done so much to the house and not let Dad see. I didn't know he was coming tonight, though, I would have warned you if I had.'

Delia poured herself a cup of tea and walked back to the table.

'Well, I would have liked a bit of notice but – lookit, you're here now, Rory, and it's good to see you looking so well. Did they make ye tea? Did you see the party?'

'They did, and I did.'

Rory grinned, and I felt more like an intruder than ever as Patrick looked from one parent to another, a look of soft happiness on his face.

'And what do you think of what we've done with the place?'

'It's wonderful.'

Rory shook his head, as if in disbelief.

'My God, Dee, just seeing the place so full of life again – I feel like I've gone back forty years. And you didn't mind, I mean, on Hallowe'en...?'

He glanced at me, the stranger in the room.

'You were OK with having a party tonight, given the date and everything?'

Delia nodded briskly. 'It was time to move on, Rory. We should have done it years ago, probably. Hollowpark is about the future now, Patrick and his family.'

Patrick was smiling broadly now.

'That's right, and I can't wait for you to meet Skye properly, Dad, and Isla, of course. Actually, where is Isla? Have you seen her, Mum?'

Delia shook her head. 'No, I don't think I've seen her all evening. Wasn't she with you?'

Patrick felt in his pockets and then withdrew his phone and dialled but was rewarded only by a buzzing noise coming from upstairs. He left the room and returned, moments later, a second phone in his hand.

'She must have gone off without it. I'll go and check the tower, won't be a moment.'

He left, and I rose too, muttering about leaving them all to catch up, but Delia placed her hand gently on my arm.

'There's no need to rush off, Grace, you've been working hard all day. Why don't I get us something to eat?'

She was nervous, I realised, which was probably not surprising, given that this was the first time she had seen her husband in over twenty-five years. And he was, after all, still her husband. In fact, the usually solid Delia looked, for want of a better word, quite flustered all of a sudden. Ha! Patrick might have been convinced that Jack Sheehan had designs on his mum but, by the looks of things, she herself looked far from ready to move on from her marriage. Rising from my chair, I helped her make a round of sandwiches and another pot of tea and the busywork seemed to calm her because by the time we had carried the food over to the table she was back to her old self again, asking Rory about his journey, and talking about relatives whose names I wasn't familiar with.

'I was thinking,' she said, cutting a slice of home-made apple tart and putting it on his plate. 'That maybe, when things are more settled—'

'I can't find her!'

Patrick burst through the door, a puzzled expression on his face.

'I can't find Isla anywhere – are you sure none of you have seen her?'

We shook our heads and I unspooled the evening in my mind, thinking about Skye's little adventure, then back to my walk through the maze with Patrick and beyond that again, to our ramble around the grounds with Evelyn and Eamon. And no, I hadn't seen Isla since we left her in the tower, and that had been – I checked my watch – over five hours ago, now. Surely – and then, even as my mind ticked over practical things, the colour leached from the room. The others were still talking, discussing where Isla might have gone, but my head was swimming now and I had to grab onto the sink to stay upright. I was outside the scene looking in, the same way I had been in Greece all those weeks ago, but I was definitely not sleeping now, I was wide awake and my heart was hammering.

This house protects its own.

It was Hallowe'en night, the night when the curtain that divides our world from another is gossamer thin and I knew beyond all doubt that Deirdre Fitzmahon was here, and that she was watching us. And I knew too that Isla Fitzmahon had been making plans to leave Hollowpark, plans that could result in the house passing from the Fitzmahon family for ever. Plans that would cause Deirdre to hate her. Could ghosts hate? Could spirits do harm? I needed air. The others, now deep in conversation, did not notice me leave but the sense of menace I had been feeling all evening had expanded, filling my lungs and my mind. I needed space...

And then Catherine Clancy was by my side.

'Help me.'

I felt the icy coldness of her hand in mine, and followed her out of the door.

Chapter 33

The Mahony party had entered a celebratory phase, the solemnity of Liam's earlier speech forgotten. Loud music blared from the tree-mounted speakers and his guests had scattered across the lawn drinking, chatting and some even dancing in small excited groups. A woman dressed as a farmer, complete with straw sticking out of her sleeves, tried to shove a glass of wine into my hand as I passed but I swerved past her, then pulled my long black cloak tight around me and dragged my hood over my head. Isla was in trouble, I knew it, and I needed to find her. I began to jog, but no matter how fast I moved the grey glistening figure of Catherine Clancy remained just ahead of me and within minutes we had reached the maze. It was in darkness now, fairy lights extinguished, the *No Entry* sign firmly replaced.

'Find me.'

A breath of air tickled my cheek and then she was gone, and I was alone. I felt a moment of utter loss and sheer helplessness and then something burrowed its way under the cloak and sniffed at my ankle. The little dog emerged and looked up at me, his head cocked.

'Good boy. Good boy.'

Saying the words out loud steadied me a little. The dog gave a sharp bark then scampered ahead of me into the maze and, not stopping to think about my own fears or indeed my own safety, I plunged in after him. The darkness in here was almost total, my only guide the snuffles of the tiny animal. If I fall now, I thought, if I injure myself then no one will think to come and look for me – and then that thought disappeared as we rounded a final corner and found ourselves at the centre. The stone angel gazed down on me, unworried, unchanged. Instinctively I looked up to where the tower should have been, but the sky was ink black, the moon obscured by cloud and the tall stone structure was completely hidden from view. The little dog whined, then jumped up onto the plinth that held the tall stone angel and gave two sharp barks. There was a moment's silence and then, so faint I wasn't sure I had heard it, a scuffling sound. The dog barked again, and afterwards came the faintest of cries.

'Help me!'

I dropped to my knees and pounded the plinth but it was solid, unyielding. The little dog was barking and whining frantically now, and I slid my fingers along the edge of the structure but every corner was smooth. And then the dog barked again and when I looked up he was launching himself at the angel, flinging his tiny body against her white stone wings. I stood up and ran my fingers over the stone and then I found it, a bump, a tiny lip where one wing joined her body. I pushed and the wing gave way with a sudden jerky movement, but then stuck fast again. I pounded at it then but the gap was too small, my hand too thick and I realised, with a sudden, sickening sensation, that my grunts of effort were the only sounds remaining in the clearing, as the cries for help had disappeared. And then I felt a thump against my thigh, and reached into the pocket of my cape to pull out the Sphinx, its shine dimmed but its weight substantial. I hurled the ornament against the stone, the base fitting neatly between wing and body and struck it again and again until I suddenly I heard a click, deep underneath me. Dropping to my knees I noticed with a gush of relief that a crack had appeared along the edge of the plinth, creating what looked like a panel in the previously smooth structure. I pushed it, felt a slight give and then tugged it towards me and the panel slid suddenly backwards, releasing a rush of warm, stale air from the cavity behind. Reaching my hand in as far as it would go I connected with damp material and then clammy skin, and I pulled the bundle towards me as gently as I could, holding my breath as Isla slid onto the soft boggy ground. Her face was bloodied from a wound on her forehead and one eye was almost obscured by a bruise but she stirred as I drew her close to me and spoke in a rasping whisper.

'You found me.'

And then her eyes rolled backwards and what little colour there had been in her cheeks disappeared. Kneeling down, I rolled her into the recovery position, moving her as gently as I could, and as I touched her back my fingers connected with a long, smooth, hard object which had become entangled in her clothes. A bone, white and smooth as an angel's wing. I looked back then into that dark terrible space and saw more bones, a pile of tattered clothes, the sightless gaze of a skull. I had found both of them.

Chapter 34

I had found both of them, but had I been in time? Kneeling on the soft, damp grass I called Isla's name, then shook her gently on the shoulder but she seemed to have lapsed fully into unconsciousness and her pulse, when I checked it, was weak and thready. I grasped her by the shoulder and began an attempt to lift her but it was impossible, she was a bigger woman than I was and completely immobile and besides, there was no telling what extra damage I could do by moving her now. I needed to find help, as quickly as possible.

'You'll stay with her, boy? Good boy.'

The dog gave me a sharp, reassuring woof as I laid Isla as gently as I could on the grass, made sure her airway was clear, then turned and darted from the maze. The party seemed to have increased in volume even in the few minutes since I'd been inside and as I darted back through the merry and excited crowd, I decided it wouldn't be worth asking one of the Americans for help, it would take longer to explain what was going on than it would to find Patrick. And then from out of nowhere a heavy rain began to fall, soaking my cloak and causing it to cling to my legs, and I was both out of breath and close to tears by the time I burst through the door of the Gate House.

'Isla – in the maze...'

As quickly as I could, I explained to Patrick what had happened and he dived for his phone to call 999.

'I think – I think she's dead...'

'You wait for the ambulance. I'll go to her.'

He sprinted through the door and, as it closed behind him I sank onto a kitchen chair, my legs suddenly useless, and turned to Delia.

'She was in the plinth, Delia. I've never seen anything like it, it was like a grave. There were bones in there!'

Delia stared at me. Then she blinked and slowly, as if emerging from a dream, she turned to her husband.

'What have you done, Rory Fitzmahon?'

Rory stared at her, confusion and what looked like fear written on his face.

'What do you mean, Delia? I've never met Isla. I – I don't know what you're talking about.'

Delia's voice was steel.

'Oh, I think you know damn well what I'm talking about.'

'But, I...'

The old man – he was an old man, I could see that clearly now – began to shake and when he put his teacup down on the saucer it rattled alarmingly.

'Jesus, Delia, you can't think—'

'She's a beautiful woman, Isla. A bit old for you, I would have thought, but maybe your tastes have changed?'

Rory dropped his head into his hands and his next words emerged like a wail.

'I've done nothing...'

From outside the house came a sudden scream, and then laughter. The party was still going on, despite the weather, but it seemed very far away now. Rory lifted his head again, his face stricken.

'I don't know – I've done nothing – I didn't touch her, Delia, I swear, I didn't do anything to her.'

'Oh, for God's sake!'

In three strides Delia had crossed the small sitting room floor. She reached out and slapped her husband's cheek but he didn't even flinch, just sat and stared at her.

'It's over, Rory, don't you see? I've protected you for long enough.'

'Gwace?'

A blonde head peeked through the door to the hallway. I ran to Skye, but Delia was closer and reached her first, sweeping the child into her arms.

'Did we wake you? I'm sorry, my pet. Come to Granny, now.'

She walked back to the table then sat down heavily, tucking the child onto her lap.

'It's too late, Rory, I covered for you for a long time. But if you've hurt Isla – I can't hide what you did any more.'

Skye's blue eyes grew even wider, but she was too tired, or maybe too bemused by what was happening to say a word as her grandfather flailed.

'I don't know what you're talking about – cover for me? Jesus, Delia, I don't know the woman, I didn't touch her!'

'Yeah, just like you didn't touch Catherine Clancy all those years ago.'

'But I didn't—'

'I covered for you then, Rory.'

Delia's voice was low but her words were sharp as shattered glass.

'I covered for you then, Rory, but I can't do it any more.'

Chapter 35

Hallowe'en, 1973

'I'm only fifteen.'

'Ah, I see.'

Rory kissed her again and then he pulled back, put his index finger under her chin and lifted it softly until he was looking into her eyes.

'You silly girl.'

Catherine saw a flicker of something – could it have been anger? – in his expression and she flinched and buried her face in his shoulder.

'Are you cross with me?'

Even as she said the words she was annoyed with herself at how weak they sounded, how childlike, but Rory simply pushed her away slightly and shook his head.

'Cross? No. It's just I thought... Oh, look, it doesn't matter what I thought. Let's get you home, eh?'

'I can't go home!'

Shame, fear, guilt – layers of emotion surged inside her and suddenly Catherine was unable to stop the tears from flowing. He was so lovely but fellas got angry, didn't they, when things didn't go their way? And of course he wanted her to leave now but oh God, she was a mess, she couldn't let her mother see her like this...

'I can't go home!' The words came out as a wail. Rory opened his mouth as if to say something but then shook his head.

'I'm too tired for this love, I'm going to bed. Stay, go, I really don't care.'

Over his shoulder Catherine could see a bed, covered by a rumpled quilt, that suddenly looked like the most inviting place in the world. Maybe if she could just lie down for a minute, maybe then her head would clear and she could make her way home and sneak in before her mother ever knew she was missing. If she was just able to rest, for a little while, then everything would be OK.

Catherine couldn't remember going to sleep, but she must have done because when she woke she saw Rory's golden head on the pillow beside hers and felt, for a moment, extraordinarily happy. And then scenes from the hours before rushed into her head, bringing with them waves of remorse and guilt and fear, fear of what Rory would think of her now, of what her mother would say, and the waves were in her stomach now, churning inside her and she knew she was going to be sick. She crept from the room, hand clasped to her mouth, her head spinning so fast she could barely see where she was going but she was wearing her clothes, she realised, that was something to be thankful for but oh God she needed to get to the bathroom now, where was it? It was OK, it was here, she had made it... She flung open the door and dashed inside and then her foot caught on a trailing towel and Catherine felt herself falling, her head hitting the sink with a crack she was just able to register before everything disappeared.

Chapter 36

2007

'You filled that poor girl full of drink and you killed her, Rory Fitzmahon.'

I felt as if I had been glued to my chair. All of my professional instincts were telling me to reach out and take Skye from her grandmother's arms, but she was clinging to the little girl now, speaking to her husband in a voice that was low, but dripping with venom.

'You killed Catherine Clancy, all those years ago. And now Isla. Did you get a taste for it? Was that it? Is that why you did it again?'

Rory's face was grey, and he stammered as he tried to speak.

'I d-don't know what you're saying, Delia. Catherine Clancy? I didn't even have—'

He threw his granddaughter a glance but the little girl, although wide-eyed, didn't seem to understand the conversation.

Rory shuddered, as if disgusted by the conversation.

'I didn't, you know. She was only a kid, just fifteen! As

soon as she told me that I couldn't get away from her fast enough. You know all this, Delia, I told you at the time. We fell asleep and when I woke up she was gone. You said yourself she had probably just run away, that she was that type of girl. That's what I told the guards – that's what *we* told the guards.'

'But maybe you killed her?'

Delia was speaking in a low, sing-song voice, presumably designed not to disturb the child, but the effect was incredibly chilling.

'Grace said she found bones, did you kill Catherine, Rory? And hide her body in the maze? Maybe that's why you were so keen to get away—'

A sudden hammering at the door made us all jump. I walked over to find Patrick and a stunned-looked Liam Mahony, holding Isla between them.

'She's conscious.'

Wordlessly, Rory stood up to make space on the sofa and we watched as the men laid Isla gently down. Patrick placed a cushion under her head, then rose to his feet.

'I need to keep watch for the ambulance.'

'I'll come with you.'

Liam Mahony, too, was heading for the door.

'There's a lot of excited people out there, they've all been drinking. I'll make sure they clear some space.'

As the kitchen door shut behind them, however, Isla moaned and struggled into a sitting position.

'No! Get away from me!'

I stared at Rory, but the old man was slumped against

the wall and looked too frail and shaken to pose a threat to anyone.

'Get away from my child!'

And then I realised it wasn't Patrick's father Isla was speaking to, but his mother.

Chapter 37

1973

Everything was dark but there was water on her face now and someone was shaking her and tapping her on the cheek and she was being lifted up now and somehow, she was standing.

'Come with me.'

The pain in her head was so violent and so sickening Catherine could barely open her eyes but her arm was around the someone's shoulder now and she was walking forward.

'Careful on the stairs.'

There was a terrible taste in her mouth and she was afraid to say anything, but the someone's voice was kind so Catherine allowed herself to be led down the stairs and out of the house. It was still dark outside, and the cold air on her face felt good, for a second, but then she felt terribly sick again and found that she was shaking.

'I want to go home.'

'You will, pet. We'll get you home.'

'My mam is going to kill me.'

'No, she won't. Follow me now, pet.'

The 'pet' sounded like something her mam would say and the thought gave her comfort so Catherine forced her eyes to open, and squinted at the person who was being so very kind. It was Delia Quinn, from the chemists' shop. How strange! What was she doing here? Delia had been working at the party last night, Mrs Fitzmahon often hired girls from the village, but surely the party was over now, it was very late. Oh Jesus, her mother was going to kill her...

'I want to go home.'

'Your mam is here, love, she came looking for you.'

Mam was here? Catherine's stomach lurched, and for a moment she thought about turning and running, but then a wave of exhaustion hit her and she started to cry. Mam was here, she'd look after her. Delia was walking across a meadow now and she quickened her pace, trying to keep up. Mam was here, and Catherine really wanted to see her. Sure, she had been stupid, but that was OK, wasn't it? She'd made a mistake. Her mam would be cross for a bit but then she'd look after her, she always did in the end. She hadn't even had sex, there was no chance she was pregnant or anything, so she couldn't be in that much trouble. She'd gone drinking and stayed out late but she was going home now and everything would be OK, Mam would give out but she might make her a cup of tea then and even put a hot water bottle in her bed...

Catherine had been so wrapped up in thinking about home that she hadn't noticed where Delia was leading her. But then the huge stone walls of a tower loomed up in front of her and she stopped dead in her tracks.

'This isn't the way to the house. You said my mam was here. Where is she?'

Delia turned and gave her an encouraging smile.

'She's waiting for you in here. She didn't want to go to the main house, there was no point in getting the Fitzmahons involved in all of this. You don't want to get Rory into trouble, do you? Follow me now and it'll all be all right in a minute.'

Delia heaved the door at the bottom of the tower open and Catherine's nose wrinkled as she followed Delia inside, an empty vodka bottle clanking against her foot as she stepped into the lobby. It looked like there was more than one place at Hollowpark where you could have a secret party. It was a perfectly round space, lined with wooden panels and a set of stone steps rising up in the middle and Catherine walked towards them, confused.

'Is Mam really here?'

'She is love, over here.'

Delia didn't go near the steps, instead she walked towards one of the wooden panels and gave it a sharp tug. Catherine gazed, open-mouthed, as the dusty wood slid smoothly aside, revealing a cavity in the wall.

'I just want to show you something first, come on! It'll only take a minute. Just take a look.'

'But I want to go home...'

Catherine was confused now, and not a little frightened, but Delia knew this place like the back of her hand, she had been working up here for years, surely she knew what she was doing? She walked forward and peered into the dark space as Delia nodded encouragingly.

'Go on, just take a look, honestly you won't believe it.'

'But where is—'

But Catherine didn't have time to finish her question, as the blow on the back of her head sent her staggering, and then pitching forward into darkness.

Chapter 38

2007

Isla lifted her hand to her head and touched the bruise around her eye. She was staring, not at Patrick's father but at his mother, and at her little girl who was sitting in Delia's lap, tightly clasped in those strong, tanned countrywoman's arms.

'Why did you hit me, Delia? Why did you put me in that place?'

The arms tightened around the little girl, who shifted uncomfortably, but was unable to move.

'Get away from her...'

But as Isla's voice rose, Delia took one arm away from the child then reached into the pocket of her ridiculous, childish outfit and took out a knife, its blade gleaming in the harsh kitchen light. I knew that knife, I thought, dully. If I looked across I would see its brothers on the kitchen block. I had seen Delia use it many times to prepare meat for stewing, twisting her wrist back and forth to separate the fat from the lean. She looked down at the blade and then over at Isla.

'Don't come near me.'

I moved forward on my chair but even that slight movement made Delia snarl, and with a flick of her wrist she positioned the knife under the little girl's throat. Skye began to sob, silently, but stayed perfectly still, as if she somehow understood what was happening to her.

'Don't come near.'

Isla groaned, and then her head flopped forward onto her chest. Rory, the nearest person to Delia, seemed paralysed with shock and fear and I knew the only thing I could do was keep Delia talking, distract her in some way, until help arrived. I forced myself to relax back into my own chair and spoke to her, as calmly as I could.

'You don't want to hurt Skye, Delia, you know you don't. And why would you do this to Isla?'

'She was going to sell my house!'

'I'm sure she wouldn't do that—'

'She would!' Delia gave a short, mirthless laugh. 'She wants to leave, to take them all away from me, to take my house away from me. I couldn't let that happen, not after everything I've done to keep Hollowpark. She was never the right person for this place, she was frightened of it, didn't understand it. Hiding herself away in that stupid tower instead of working down here, with me, where she belonged. I knew from the start she would never settle here.'

And suddenly I felt the presence of other women in the kitchen too; I could not see them but they were there, the women of Hollowpark who had come to me and asked me for help. And then I understood everything.

'You killed Catherine Clancy.'

'I did it for Hollowpark.' Delia spat out the words. 'None

of you understand how important this house is, how hard we have to work to save it. I love it, I always loved it. This is where I was always meant to live, I knew it, growing up in the village, it was all I ever wanted. I love every stick and stone of it and it loves me!'

She looked over at me, eyes blazing.

'Rory's mother used to pay us girls to come up here and polish the silver, or pass around drinks at her bloody parties. I didn't need the money but I came here anyway, just to be close to the place, to get to know it. All I could ever think of was living here one day, restoring the house, loving it the way it should be loved.'

She snorted.

'The Fitzmahons didn't have a clue. And Rory?'

She tossed a dismissive glance towards the frail, diminished figure who was now seated on the kitchen floor, his head in his hands.

'It might as well have been a slot machine for all the heed he paid it. It was a grand place to bring his fine friends, but he didn't love it, not the way I did. Hollowpark protects its own, you know. And I always knew I belonged here.'

'You killed Catherine,' I said again and Delia nodded, but the hand holding the knife did not move.

'I was working here that night – helping to serve drinks. That was my station in life, wasn't it, Rory? That was all I was good for, back then.'

She shot a look in her husband's direction.

'It was three in the morning and we were running out of glasses in the main house, so they sent me over here to see if there were any spare.'

She looked around the Gate House kitchen.

'I walked straight in here and the place was filthy, but there was no sign of Rory, or of anyone else.'

As Delia continued to speak it was as if the years had rolled away, and I could almost see the empty bottles, smell the overflowing ashtray.

'And then I went upstairs, and I found her in the bathroom.'

Skye was drifting back to sleep now, cuddled into Delia's soft costume and her grandmother kept her voice low as she continued.

'She had been sick everywhere – good Christ, Rory, what were you thinking?'

'I don't know.' The man by the wall shuddered. 'I don't know, I wasn't thinking.'

'She was only a child.' Delia snorted. 'She had fallen against the sink and hit her head. I thought she was dead, when I saw her, and maybe it would have been easier if she had been. But she was still breathing, so I woke her up and brought her downstairs. That little slut…'

She looked down at her granddaughter for a moment, as if hoping the little girl hadn't heard the word, before continuing.

'We had been seeing each other for a few months at that stage, Rory and me. I loved him, and I loved Hollowpark. This beautiful place. I just couldn't understand it – why would he mess with a little tart like that? And what if she was pregnant, or if he chose her over me, what would happen to the house then, the family? Catherine Clancy knew nothing about Hollowpark, that little bitch could have sold it out from under them.'

Delia's voice took on the light, sing-song tone again.

'I said, oh come through here, pet, we'll get you sorted out, I'll clean you up, no you won't get into trouble, just follow me. I knew all about the passageway, you see, it leads from the tower straight to the heart of the maze, it was designed by the people who built this house, as an escape route. I had been working at Hollowpark for quite some time by then, I'd had plenty of time to look around. I'd found a map in the library. So many books in there, so much information, if you care enough about the place to read them.'

Her eyes were glassy now, her voice soft and she could almost have been back at her own kitchen table, I thought, regaling us with stories of long ago.

'Mrs Fitzmahon thought I came up here to clean, to earn money – I didn't need her bloody money. My father could have bought and sold the Fitzmahons, back then. But I needed to learn more about this place. So I came here to work, and I worked hard, but I was learning too, going through all of the books I could find, reading all about Hollowpark. I was the only one who cared enough to learn its secrets. Rory didn't have any real interest in the place, none of them did, they didn't deserve it. So I found the passageway and, that night, I brought Catherine there. She didn't take much persuading, she would have gone with anyone, that one. "Oh look, your Mummy is in there, just lean in now…"'

A wave of nausea washed over me as she continued.

'I gave her a little push, just a little push, and then slid the panel shut behind her. And that was that. It's a sheer drop, they would have used a ladder, I suppose, years ago, or a rope to help them climb down, but there's nothing there now, and no other way out other than through the plinth in the maze. Even then you have to know the trick to opening it. It's so clever. You know, people around here' – she almost spat out the words – 'people around here didn't always respect those who live in Hollowpark so the men who built the house must have wanted to give themselves a little way out, in case they ever needed it. But somewhere over the years the passageway was forgotten about. Until I found out about it.'

Delia gave a pleased smile, creating a sickening echo of the woman I thought I had known.

'After I closed the panel again, it was just a matter of scattering leaves and dirt around the ground, making it look like it hadn't been disturbed. The guards even searched the tower the next day but I knew they'd never find her. Nobody knows Hollowpark like I do.'

Rory Fitzmahon was staring at his wife, a look of absolute confusion on his pale face.

'You said Catherine had run away!'

'I said she had run away.' Delia sneered. 'I told you I had found her in the bathroom, and that she was so ashamed of what had happened between ye that she ran away. And you believed me, Rory Fitzmahon, because it suited you to believe me. When the guards came around looking for her I covered for you, I told them I'd been with you the whole night and that was that.'

She turned to me again.

'I cleaned up in here, too, there wasn't a trace of the little slut by the time I was finished. Rory's friends headed back to England the following morning and they never heard a thing. There was no internet in those days, there was no way the story of one stupid little girl would make the news over there. So all I had to do was play my part, pretend to be all embarrassed that I'd been caught spending the night with the lord of the manor, beg the guards not to tell my parents. The sergeant had a teenage son himself, he felt sorry for us, I think, and it never went any further. Catherine was gone all right but there was no reason to believe it had anything to do with us, and they never found a body, of course. So the next time Rory came home, I was waiting for you, wasn't I, darling?'

Patrick's dad cringed under the weight of her words as she smiled at him, then turned back to me.

'He thanked me, for helping him with everything, and we were together again, the way we should have been all along. And when we found out Patrick was on the way, well, it just made everything even more perfect. We got married and I looked after them all, Rory and Patrick and Hollowpark, and his parents too when the time came. I was a great wife and a great mother.'

Poor Patrick, I thought suddenly, as she continued, looking down at Skye.

'And I would have been a great grandmother to this one too.'

Skye jerked suddenly in her sleep and Delia looked from the knife to Isla, and back again.

'Except she's not my grandchild, is she? You were going to take everything from me, Isla, my home, and my son, and hand everything to a girleen who isn't even my blood—'

'She's mine!'

Her eyes springing open, Isla launched herself from the sofa and tugged at Delia's arm, twisting it until she screamed and the knife fell from her hand. And Skye fell from her arms too but I leaped forward, you can always count on nannies in a crisis, and caught her before she hit the floor. And then the kitchen door opened and I heard Patrick call out and, from behind him, sirens drifted towards us on the night air.

Chapter 39

'I'm so sorry you got mixed up in all of this, Grace.'

Isla gave me a tired smile. We were in the hospital, not in the canteen this time but a bright single room at the end of a long, quiet corridor. It turns out you don't need expensive health insurance to get a private room, you just need to be the victim of an attempted murder who unwittingly discovers the body of a long-missing girl in the process. There had been camera crews outside Hollowpark when I left that morning, with serious-faced reporters staring into their lenses and telling their viewers a story of which they only knew a small portion. Remains had been discovered at Hollowpark Hall, and a woman was in hospital following a serious assault. Another woman was being held for questioning. The details had sounded quite straightforward when I heard them on the car radio. But of course, they weren't straightforward at all.

'I owe you my life. Again.'

Isla's head was bandaged and she was deathly pale, but her eyes were clear and her voice steady. Patrick, who was sitting on the opposite side of the bed to me, reached out and touched her hand.

'Take it easy, Isla. You know the doctors are keeping an eye on your blood pressure.'

'It's OK, Patrick. I want Grace to hear everything. God knows what people are saying down in the village.'

'Well, yeah.'

I looked away, shifting uncomfortably on my hard hospital chair. I had dropped Skye off at Evelyn's house that morning and, despite her attempts to stay calmly supportive, my friend had been practically twitching with the desire to hear all the details of what had happened at the party after she and Eamon had left. Evelyn was my friend, and prepared to be patient with me, so I could only imagine how hungry for information the rest of the good citizens of Lisheeha were, especially those who were friendly with poor Angela Clancy who had finally, after thirty years, opened the door of her house to a solemn-faced guard who informed her that he had some news, and asked if there was anyone who could sit with her for a while. So yes, there were a lot of people out there looking for information about what had happened at Hollowpark Hall. And I was one of them.

Isla sighed, and looked at me.

'I'm not sure where to start, really. With the tower, I suppose. You see, Saturday night, while you were all at the party, Delia came up and told me that my husband... that Ethan had come to Hollowpark, and that he had taken Skye.'

'Jesus!'

I was unable to hide my surprise and Isla gave a brief, clearly painful nod.

'Yes, she had found out everything, you see, or thought she had.'

Isla coughed, and Patrick offered her water, but she waved it away, looking irritated.

'I need to keep going, OK? Grace needs to know.'

Then she turned to me again.

'She came up to the tower, not long after you and Skye left actually, and told me I was needed urgently downstairs. She was breathless, she looked genuinely scared, I had never seen her look like that before. She told me Ethan had turned up and had taken Skye and was going to take her back to England. It didn't make sense, of course, he couldn't have done anything of the sort, but I wasn't thinking straight, I panicked the minute I heard his name. So I followed her down the stairs and, when we got to the bottom, one of the wooden panels on the wall was open, like a sliding door, it was the most extraordinary thing. I must have walked past those panels a hundred times and never really noticed them before. Delia was very excited, or anxious really. She told me Skye was in there and that I had to go and look for her. I was confused, but all I could think of was Skye so I walked inside and then I felt this blow to the back of my head and I remember falling forward, and hitting the bottom, and I must have passed out then.'

Isla was frighteningly pale now, but seemed determined to finish her story.

'It was pitch dark when I woke, I was lying on the ground, my head was throbbing and I couldn't catch my breath, the air smelled vile, old and stale. I thought I was blind, for a moment, but it was just that there was no light, no light at all. I must have been very far underground. I felt around to see if I could find my way back to the tower but it was useless, it had been a sheer drop and the walls were smooth, there was no way of getting back up there. So I turned around and crawled forward and when I reached out my hands I found a little passageway. It was very narrow but I felt I had no option, really, other than to move forward. I was so cold, I knew I had to keep moving if I had any chance of surviving. My head was bleeding, too, and I was so dizzy, I might have passed out again, I've really no idea how long I was moving for. And then I felt the passageway rise up in front of me and then I hit what felt like a wall of stone. It was horrendous, Grace.'

She reached over the white bedsheets and clasped my hand tightly and I returned the pressure as she took up the story again.

'I felt like I was in a grave, and that's what it was, really, a tomb. I tried to turn around and go back the way I came but I was totally lost, totally disorientated by then so I just started to scream. I thought I was going to die, Grace, I would have died. Until you came.'

My mind was racing, sifting through the information, trying to make sense of it.

'How did Delia – how did she know how to lure you in there? How did she even know about your husband?'

Isla withdrew her hand and gave me a weak smile.

'A stupid mistake on my part. The guards came to see us this morning, they've been very helpful. They contacted Ethan last night and he was able to tell them part of the story. It looks like Delia found out what my real name was. It was on a stack of invoices relating to the sale of my work, I had all the paperwork stored in the tower. I thought I had been careful but I guess she must have been snooping around and found it. I don't think she was looking for anything in particular, not at that stage, but I guess she just wanted any extra information she could get about me. I knew all along, you see, that she didn't like me but I had persuaded myself that I was just imagining it.'

She bit her lip.

'That's what happens, you know, when you're in an abusive relationship. Ethan had spent so long telling me I was paranoid and stupid that I lost all faith in myself, in my own judgement. So I didn't trust my own feelings about Delia either. But looking back, I was right all along, she had been undermining me for a long time. Those noises in the house, when I was trying to work – I wouldn't be surprised if she was behind them, if she was trying to test me, to see if I was really committed to Hollowpark. That was the only thing that was important to her, the house, and who would take care of it after she was gone. So, she must have searched the tower and she really struck gold when she found those invoices. After that it all fell into place for her, I suppose, thanks to Google. Ethan's parents had put our wedding notice in their local paper, so she found us there, with a photograph and everything, and after that she found his firm. She knew then I'd been lying about who I was. And that must have driven her crazy, she was so obsessed with Hollowpark, and who was going to look after it. She had never really trusted me, I don't think, or believed I was the right person for the house. And then she had the proof she needed. '

We all lapsed into silence for a moment, Isla and Patrick because they were clearly exhausted and me out of a growing sense of shame. My face reddened as I remembered Delia's barbed asides about Isla, the times she commented on how tired she looked and how much time she spent in the tower. Comments, I now realised, which had been designed to paint a picture of a weak woman who wasn't really worthy of Hollowpark. I remembered too that first morning, when Isla had thought Skye was missing and Delia had winked at me over her shoulder, drawing me into her confidence, belittling a mother's very real fears. I had thought she was being supportive, at the time, trying to calm down an overly anxious woman, but the truth, it appeared, was much darker.

Isla took up the story again.

'Then somehow – and we're still not sure how – Delia found out that I was thinking of moving back to London. That must have tipped her over the edge.'

I looked over at Patrick, thinking how horrendous it must have been for him to hear those things about his own mother, but he was stony faced and stared at the floor as Isla continued.

'I could have died in that awful place, Grace. I was slipping in and out of consciousness, I don't think I had long. And then you came. You saved my life. But what I don't understand...'

I stared at the floor, anticipating the question.

'How in heaven's name did you know where to find me?'

'I...'

I shook my head, then mumbled something about having read about the secret passageway between the tower and the plinth in a book in the Hollowpark library. I'd have to come up with something better than that, there would surely be official questions I'd have to answer down the line and I didn't think the guards would be too willing to accept a small dog or indeed Catherine Clancy's ghost as the source of my information. But both Patrick and Isla were too exhausted right now to interrogate my explanation and besides, I had a few questions of my own.

'Was Ethan really there?'

Isla shook her head, but then started to cough again and this time Patrick took over the story.

'No. He's an absolute shit and I wouldn't put anything past him but he was in London working all week, and he can prove it. But Delia had been in contact with him all right.'

He didn't call her 'Mum', I noticed, as he continued.

'They'd had quite the little chat. He painted a very different picture of what had happened with Isla, of course, claimed she had just walked out on him with no notice.'

He looked directly at me and bit his lip.

'And when Delia mentioned Skye and how old she was, they figured out that Isla must have been pregnant when she left him.'

I wasn't surprised to hear it, but Patrick looked so bereft I had to look away, and after a moment Isla took up the story again.

'It was because I was pregnant that I finally left Ethan. They confirmed it, that day at the hospital, I had thought I just hadn't properly recovered from the miscarriage but it turned out that Skye was on the way. And I just couldn't do it, Grace, I couldn't bring a baby into that mess of a marriage. So, I walked away.'

She turned to her partner.

'You've been the best dad in the world to her, you know that.'

I should have felt like a stranger in that room but instead

there was a strange sensation of it being the three of us against the world, puzzling everything out, so I chanced one final question.

'Why do you think Delia tried to put the blame on Rory? For taking you, I mean?'

Isla shrugged. 'She panicked, I guess. She must have thought I'd just disappear, the way poor Catherine Clancy disappeared, so when you told her you'd found me she needed a story and he was there. It might have worked, too, if I had died. Rory was a man with a history of addiction, who had left his own home under a cloud and gone to England. It would have been his word against hers, and it wouldn't have looked great for him.'

'Mum was always good at thinking on her feet.'

Patrick looked devastated, and I folded my arms around myself and held on tightly, reminding myself that it was not my place to walk over to him, to comfort him.

'Dad suspected something awful had happened, all those years ago.' Patrick's voice was grim. 'We had a long chat about it last night after they took Delia away. Dad said he always felt there was something strange about the way the Clancy girl disappeared. But Mum – Delia – kept telling him it had nothing to do with him, that she had just run away and it was easier for him, I think, just to go along with her. But I suspect that's why he left Hollowpark in the end – he knew deep down he hadn't done the right thing by her.'

'What's going to happen now?'

Patrick gave a slight shrug. 'I don't know. Delia is in Dublin, in the Central Mental Hospital. There will be an investigation, I suppose, and a trial at some stage but it won't be straightforward.'

Isla shifted herself up higher on her pillows.

'And we'll go back to the UK, as soon as the police allow it. I was thinking of leaving anyway, you know that, Grace. There's no way I can stay here now, not after what happened. I can't let Skye grow up here...'

Her eyes filled with tears at the mention of her daughter and I saw Patrick's hand reach for hers again across the white sheet.

'I'm so sorry my mum did this to you.'

Suddenly I couldn't stay in that room any more. I scraped my chair backwards and muttered something about ringing Evelyn, then left before Patrick and Isla could see the tears in my eyes. I made it as far as the car before climbing inside and allowing myself to burst into loud, hot sobs. They were tears of exhaustion, of course, and of distress; it was going to take me a long time to process what had happened at Hollowpark the night before. But deep down I knew I was crying for myself too, and for a future I had stupidly allowed myself to dream about.

I rested my head on the steering wheel and began to berate myself, silently. Just what the hell had I thought was going to happen, anyway? That we'd all live happily at Hollowpark, Patrick and his family in the Gate House and me chastely in the main house, thinking about him, reading too much into every conversation and blowing every stray glance out of all proportion? Living for every moment we could spend together – oh God. I had been such an idiot. I was That Nanny, the one mothers warned each other about. I had fallen in love with my boss... and I did love him. I loved Patrick. I stopped for a moment and allowed my mind to drift back to that hospital room and his white strained face, imagined, for a moment, a different outcome where I walked over and took him in my arms – oh, for Christ's sake. Where was Isla in this scenario? I sat back and banged my head gently against the headrest. I was being beyond ridiculous. Patrick had a partner and a child and they were all going to go back to live in England and Hollowpark would be rented, or sold, and I would find another job and another place to live. Maybe they'd even ask me to work for them in London but, even as that thought crossed my mind, I dismissed it out of hand. As fond as I was of Skye and, let's face it, Patrick, my life with them belonged here and I couldn't imagine trying to mimic that anywhere else. No, I'd go back to my old agency and tell them I was looking for a new position, and they'd sort me out. That was what I did, that was what I always did.

More hot tears sprang from my eyes but this time I reached up my hands and roughly scrubbed them away. I would move on and some day in the future I'd be able to think of Skye, and Isla and even Patrick with affection, and nothing more than that. That day was not today, but it would come, I had to believe it. I blew my nose firmly, then reached into my bag to find my parking ticket. I would get going, I would make plans. There was a new text message on my phone and, when I blinked away my remaining tears, I saw it was from Isla.

Grace, I owe you everything. I won't forget that.

I knew she was telling the truth. But what she didn't know was that she was taking everything too.

Chapter 40

January 2008

'You'll think about what I said?'
     'Of course I will.'
'C'mere, so...'
Evelyn stepped forward and enveloped me in a hug.
The baby in the sling on her chest squawked, and we both
giggled and jumped backwards.
     'Probably best not to kill her with kindness. But you will
think about it?'
     I nodded at her. 'Absolutely.'
     'That's all I can ask.'
     Evelyn hesitated and then her face darkened.
     'I hear Delia is still in hospital?'
     'Yeah.'
     I looked at her, but didn't say any more. I had already told
Evelyn as much of the story as I could without betraying
the Fitzmahons' confidence and I knew that she, along with
everyone else in the village, was finding Delia's arrest hard
to process. Delia had lived in Lisheeha all of her life, she
was part of the place and it was hard for any of them to

think of her as a killer. And then I noticed my friend was suddenly close to tears.

'Grace? There's something I need to tell you.'

She dropped a kiss on her baby's head then looked up at me and began to speak quickly, as if afraid if she stopped she wouldn't be able to start again.

'I've been thinking about what you said, about how Delia hated Isla and knew she was thinking of leaving here and, oh Christ, Grace, I think that's all my fault! I overheard you two talking, that day in the car when we were coming back from the beach. It's not like I was deliberately listening, I swear, but you know what it's like when you are dozing, I was just, like, aware of the words, I thought you were chatting openly, I didn't think it was a secret or anything. But I was talking to my dad a few days later and he was going on about Hollowpark as usual and I said something like, oh I'm not sure if they are making long terms plans, I don't know if Isla is in it for the long haul. I swear to God that's all I said, and it went out of my head the next second, but it could well be that he went off and said something to Delia after that. I feel absolutely terrible.'

'It's not your fault.'

I reached over the baby's head and gave my friend's shoulder a gentle squeeze.

'You can't blame yourself, Ev, none of us can. Delia did this, nobody else. Jesus, I've been torturing myself too, thinking of signs I should have picked up on, the way Delia acted towards Isla, asking myself if I should have stepped in. Honestly, if there was a medal for beating yourself up I'd win gold. But she did what she did, there was no one else involved. You should probably tell the guards what you just told me, it will be useful information for them, if the case ever comes to court. But nobody will think badly of you, I promise. It's all a horrible mess, we're just lucky everyone came out of it OK.'

'Yeah.' Evelyn wiped her eyes and gave me a brief smile. 'Yeah, I suppose you're right.'

Then she placed her hands over the baby's ears, and roared, 'Eamon! Skye! We're going!'

The two children, who were halfway up the playground climbing frame, pretended not to hear her and she winked at me and roared again.

'Or maybe I'll find some other children to bring to the movies?'

'The movies?'

Eamon's head spun round so fast, his mother chuckled.

'I thought that might grab your attention. Yes, love, the movies! But we have to leave now.'

She opened her car door, then lifted her little daughter out of the sling and placed her carefully in her car seat, clicking it into place.

'And treats?'

Skye and Eamon left the playground and ran to our side, gazing up at her hopefully.

'For good children, yes, I think so. Are ye good children?'

'Yes!'

The good children in question dived into the back of the car and settled themselves into their own seats on either side of baby Aileen. The infant blinked, and then regarded them placidly, not making a sound.

'You're sure you don't mind all this?'

I followed my friend around to the driver's side as she climbed in.

'Three is a lot to take on for the night.'

'Ah, the little one is a doll.' Evelyn glanced into the back seat of the car, maternal pride written across her face. 'And Eamon has been asking for a sleepover for weeks, honestly, he's easier to mind when he has someone to play with. And he's really going to miss Skye when she goes...'

Her smile dropped suddenly and her eyes filled once more with tears.

'Jesus, what am I like? Bloody hormones, I cry at everything these days, toilet roll ads on the telly, everything. Honestly, don't mind me! It'll be lovely to have her, that's all, and I'm sure you have plenty to do up at the house.'

'Yeah.'

I kept my answer short, aware that my own tears weren't far away. Then a sudden sprinkle of rain made me look up, and I stepped away from the car.

'Ring me if you need anything, OK? And I'll see you in the morning. Bye, Skye!'

'Bye!'

The last thing I saw as the car bumped away down the driveway was the little girl's excited wave. I pulled the hood of my jacket over my head and turned to begin the walk back up to Hollowpark. It was a typical Irish January day, grey, overcast and miserable, and the house looked bleaker than usual, its sandy stone darkened to a flat beige in the full afternoon light. Those sunny days of early autumn felt very far away.

We had all been questioned for weeks after the events of Hallowe'en night, Patrick, Isla and me. Even the Mahonys had had to tack a few unexpected days onto the end of their trip and I suspect they ended up seeing more of the local garda station than the west of Ireland beauty spots they had been expecting. But by the start of December we had all been allowed to get back to some sort of normality. Having drafted in one of the neighbours to look after the animals – an act that I suspected owed more to the farmer's curiosity about the events at Hollowpark than any sense of charity, but which was welcome nonetheless – Patrick and his family had headed to France for Christmas, to a house belonging to one of his schoolfriends. They told me I was welcome to stay on in the Gate House, but I decided to head to Dublin instead, preferring even the irritating presence of my mother to weeks alone in Hollowpark. And in fact I suspect my dad, having heard about the events in Roscommon, had had a word, because she was kinder to me than usual. Dad solved another mystery too, when he told me over Christmas lunch that he had asked a colleague of his, from his firm's west of Ireland branch, to drop into Hollowpark Hall in the early days of my employment and find out how I was getting on. The place had seemed deserted, he told me, and she had left again without speaking to a soul. She had taken a little detour, however, and had told my dad she saw some beautiful gardens, and a stunning maze. So that was who Isla had seen that day, I realised, another part of the puzzle clicking into place.

After that, I'd had a surprisingly restful Christmas. I had taken long walks by the sea, watched a lot of TV, drank more wine than usual because I didn't have to get up with a small child in the morning and basically did everything in my power not to think about Hollowpark and its residents

– the living and the dead. But now it was the second week of January, the greyest time of the year, and I had come back to Roscommon to help Patrick pack up the family's belongings. Isla was already in London, completing the purchase of a flat. She had received an early divorce settlement from Ethan – it was amazing, Patrick told me with a wry smile, how generous Isla's soon to be ex-husband had become when he learned how his name had been used in an attempted murder – and Patrick had brought Skye back to Ireland to say goodbye.

The phone in my pocket buzzed as I reached the large stone step at the top of the house and I took it out to see a text from Patrick. Ignoring the jolt I felt in my stomach every time I saw his name on my phone – it was barely a jolt any more, I told myself firmly, little more than a ripple, in fact – I opened the screen and read the brief message.

Do u have a measuring tape tnx

He texted like a thirteen-year-old girl, I thought to myself, then smothered a smile – barely a ripple, Grace, remember? – and texted my reply.

Sure. Where do you need it?

Tower. I'll come down.

No need, I'll bring it up.

Then I jogged to my room, grabbed the tape measure from my sewing kit and made my way back out of the house and across the grass. The afternoon had settled into that midpoint between raining and not raining and a damp mist was hanging over the grounds, and I was sweating in my raincoat by the time I reached the tower and climbed up the stairs. I patted my hair down when I reached the top, then gave up trying to tame the frizz as a bad job and pushed the door open. Patrick, who was chipping plaster from the large wooden table in the centre of the room, looked over at me and smiled.

'Hey there. Thanks a million for coming up.'

'It's fine.'

Still slightly out of breath – from the climb, I assured myself, just from the climb – I walked across the room and handed it to him, our fingers brushing slightly as I did so. My heart gave a sudden double beat and there was no point in blaming it on the stairs this time, but Patrick simply thanked me, then walked over to where Isla's remaining sculptures were lined up against the wall and dropped to his knees.

'The specialist movers are coming in the morning, I need to give them exact measurements. Could you give me a hand for a moment? If you don't mind.'

'Sure.'

I took the other end of the tape measure and kneeled beside him while he muttered figures and scribbled them down on a piece of paper. Our heads were almost touching and when he was finished I rose to my feet quickly, not wanting him to see how flustered I was. Just a ripple, Grace, remember? Not a jolt. But I still had to fight to keep my voice steady.

'Is there anything else I can help you with?'

'I think I'm OK now.'

Patrick rose to his feet, clutching his back dramatically.

'Old age catching up with me! Was Skye happy to go off with Evelyn?'

'Was she what!' I grinned, my mood immediately lifting as I thought of the little girl. 'She was thrilled. She's really going to miss Eamon though.'

'I know.'

Patrick paused, then walked across the room to where a plastic cool box was standing under the window. He reached inside and took out a pair of familiar green bottles.

'Would you like a beer?'

'Ah no, I'm fine, I have so much to do, I—'

But he shoved it into my hand anyway.

'Ah, go on. I was going to bring a flask of tea, but I found these in the kitchen, they must have been left over from the American party. Seems like a shame to let them go to waste.'

I grinned at him, but accepted the bottle with a nod.

'Well, if you put it like that. I've heard beer can go off really quickly if you don't drink it.'

'Exactly what I was thinking!'

Patrick opened my drink, then his own, then walked over to the table and hopped up onto it. It was the only piece of furniture left in the room, I realised, and after a moment I followed him over and perched awkwardly on the edge. Patrick took a long drink and then exhaled.

'I'm nearly finished here anyway. The movers will be here tomorrow morning and I have most of Skye's stuff packed in the Gate House. Our flight is at two in the afternoon, she'll sleep in her new bedroom tomorrow night.'

He paused, and I searched around for something friendly to say but came up with absolutely nothing so we sat in silence for a moment before he took another drink and turned to me.

'I really appreciate your support these past few weeks. You've been amazing, Grace – oh shit. I'm sorry, that was a terrible pun!'

His groan broke through the awkwardness I had been feeling and I reached over and mock slapped him on the shoulder.

'It was appalling, but I have heard it before! I was only doing my job, though.'

'It was a bit more than that.'

Patrick put down his beer bottle and used his hands to shift himself further into the centre of the table, leaving his long legs dangling off the edge. He was sitting closer to me now, I realised, but assumed he hadn't noticed. We were just friends, I reminded myself, friends who had been through a lot and were now just hanging out, decompressing, having a beer. Except there wasn't even the width of the bottle between us. The sky outside had darkened further, it would be raining properly soon and the light in the tower had grown dim. Patrick glanced at me.

'I mean it though, I don't think we would have got through these past few months without you. It meant so much to have someone around who knew us, who knew Delia...'

His voice trailed off and I took another drink, then looked at him.

'Have you seen her?'

'No.'

The word was a sharp inhale.

'I spoke to her doctor yesterday. They have her on this new medication, they say she's taking to it really well, that she's very calm. I suppose I should go to visit her, but I just can't bring myself to do it. I keep thinking back to that night, and what she did to Isla. And she was going to hurt Skye...'

His voice faltered and it was all I could do not to reach for his hand. Instead I took another sip of my drink, and remained silent. I was a good listener, everyone said it, and if listening was all I had to offer Patrick then he could have as much of my silence as he needed. After a moment he ran his hand through his hair in the way I couldn't believe I had once found irritating, and sighed.

'I'll go up to see her soon, I suppose, at least I should. It's just too much to think about at the moment, with everything else that's going on. I'm just trying to take things one step at a time, you know? Get Skye's things sorted out, get her settled.'

He paused, then gave a flicker of a smile.

'And what about you, Grace? Have you thought about what you want to do next? You know you're welcome to stay here as long as you want, the last thing I want is for you to feel you're being kicked out of your home on top of everything else.'

'I have, actually.'

I took another sip of beer, feeling a slight and not unwelcome fuzziness. I had been running around all day, it was nice to stop, and to have someone ask about me.

'I just had a chat with Evelyn, and she's had a pretty amazing idea. There's a redundancy offer on the table in her job and she's seriously thinking of taking it and opening a creche in the village. She reckons there's definitely a market for it, you know the playschool only caters for pre-schoolers. She says there are loads of new families in her estate with new babies. And she was wondering...'

It had seemed fanciful, when Evelyn had mentioned it to me earlier, but the more I thought about it the more sense it made.

'She was wondering if I wanted to work for her – well, work with her really. Run the childcare side of things, while she ran the business.'

'Wow!'

Patrick's face lit up in a way I hadn't seen in many weeks.

'That's amazing! You'd be brilliant, too. So, you'd stay here? In Lisheeha?'

'Well yeah!' I was smiling now too, feeling more enthusiastic about Evelyn's plan by the second. 'I went back to Dublin for Christmas and it was fine, but it's not home any more. I've loved living around here so – yeah! Yeah, I actually think I might do it!'

'That's fantastic, Grace!'

Patrick turned his head fully, and held my gaze for a moment. And suddenly the gap between us was both tiny and yawningly wide at the same time and I knew I had to move the conversation along.

'So, how's Isla doing?'

I felt a dull ache when I asked the question, like pressing a bruise to find out if it was healing.

'She's really good, actually.'

Patrick nodded, and took another sip of beer.

'In fact she's amazing. I mean, I always knew she was

strong but to see how she was able to cope, these past few weeks – I'm completely in awe of her.'

'That's great,' I told him, and realised with a thud that the bruise had not healed at all. I should go, I told myself, but didn't move.

'And Skye? Do you think she's OK about the move?'

Patrick shrugged. 'I'm not sure. We've tried to make it sound like an adventure, you know? A new bedroom and a new school. And every so often we think she's totally on board with it, and then she'll turn around and say something like "Will Eamon still be in my class?" and it turns out she hasn't really understood at all.'

'You'd be surprised at how quickly kids adapt,' I told him, and wondered if I could have sounded more like a dull, boring nanny if I tried. But Patrick nodded as if I'd said something profound.

'That's what Isla says. And she can come back here for the holidays. I'm going to miss her so much, but Hollowpark will always be her home.'

It was definitely a jolt, and not a ripple this time. I looked at him, frowning.

'What do you mean, you're going to miss her? You'll be with her, won't you? In London?'

'God, no!'

Patrick returned my look, clearly surprised.

'Didn't you know? I'm staying here, Grace. Isla and I – we're not together any more.'

And it was a good thing I was sitting down, I realised, because I knew if I was standing, my legs would not have supported me.

'You're not?'

My answer came out as a whisper, and the room was very dark now and that space between us was very, very small.

'No.' Patrick gave me a direct look. 'It has been over for a while. Before everything with Delia happened, actually, but we hadn't really talked about it then.' He gave a soft chuckle. 'You know the whole story, Grace, you're probably the only person who does, outside of Isla and me. When she came to live here and when Skye was born, I really thought we could make a go of things, as a family, and we did, for a while. I loved the baby so much, and I thought that would be enough for the three of us. But once Isla was well, once she had recovered from everything Ethan had done to her, it was clear she was never going to be really happy here. There was a time I thought I'd move away with her, if that was what she wanted. But our relationship wouldn't have survived it. We had a lot of time to talk over Christmas. After everything that happened, there was no point in being anything other than honest with each other.'

I began to fiddle with my beer bottle, tearing off the label to avoid meeting his gaze.

'And you'll keep seeing Skye?'

'Absolutely. I adore that little one. I'm her dad, no matter what any bloody birth certificate says. London is only an hour by plane, we'll make it work. She'll always have a home here.'

My hands were suddenly shaking so much the bottle nearly slipped from my fingers so I put it aside and then rested my hand in the space between us.

'And you'll stay in Hollowpark.'

'Yes.'

Patrick's voice had deepened and now his hand was on the table too, his little finger millimetres from mine.

'I'd like to try and carry on with the plans to open it up, if I can. I got an email from Liam Mahony the other day, you remember the American guy? Turns out he'd like to invest in the place. I couldn't really take it all in, you know what Americans are like, it was all about "reaching out" and "giving back" and something about his ancestors. But he'll be back in Ireland in a few months and we are going to meet up then. It could solve a lot of problems, having proper money to spend.'

'That's fantastic!'

I was genuinely pleased; I'd really liked the handsome American whose birthday hadn't quite gone according to plan.

'Yeah.' Patrick smiled. 'He had a few conditions though, as you'd expect. Nothing outrageous. But he thinks the Gate House should be turned into a proper standalone holiday let and he wants to rename it. You remember he told us about Ciarán O'Mahony, the guy who emigrated? He wants to call it Kathleen O'Mahony Lodge, after his child who died.'

'Wow.' I felt the air around me shift and settle as I thought of the name, and all it represented. 'I think that's a gorgeous idea.'

'Isn't it!'

Patrick's smile flared, and then faded just as quickly.

'I mean, don't get me wrong, getting a business up and running here won't be easy. A lot of people in Lisheeha are very angry about what happened, and I can't blame them. But I hope I have some friends left too.'

'You do.'

I wasn't aware either of us had moved but somehow the edges of our fingers were touching now and I found myself wondering how such a small area of skin could create so much heat.

'People will support you.'

'Do you think so?'

Patrick's finger was stroking mine now, it was the slightest of touches but it sent tiny darts of electricity crackling through me.

'Yeah, I'm sure of it. People around here love Hollowpark, they'll have your back.'

'And do you think I'm doing the right thing, Grace?'

And then Patrick's hand was covering mine and we sat like that, motionless for a moment, before he turned to me, and pulled me gently towards him.

'Is this the right thing?'

I wasn't sure which question I was answering but my kiss seemed to tell him everything he needed to know.

Epilogue

The Next Day

Hollowpark's large wooden door stood slightly ajar and I pushed against it and walked into the entrance hall. The draught I created sent a pile of brochures fluttering to the floor and I picked one up and looked at it, then shoved it into my pocket. Delia's brochures, they would be useless now, or maybe worth a fortune, who knew? There may well be tourists out there who would be attracted to, rather than repelled by, a house with such dark secrets.

I walked across the floor, my footsteps echoing on the flagstones. The future of Hollowpark Hall was still far from certain but at least now I knew I was going to be around to find out what happened. I had dropped Patrick and Skye at the airport earlier that afternoon and would stay in the Gate House that night, then pick him up when he returned. And after that Patrick and I... I paused, and let the words settle in my mind, almost tasting them. No, I didn't know what the future held, but there was a 'Patrick and I' in it, and for the moment, that was enough.

Right now, however, I was planning a bath, an early

night and one of Hollowpark's stash of Agatha Christies. I pushed open the door at the back of the hall, turned in the direction of the library and then felt my heart thump when I saw its door was ajar.

'I'm so sorry! I didn't mean to startle you.'

Jack Sheehan had aged since I had last seen him. He was stooped and looked far frailer than he had been before and I was reminded of how many people loved Hollowpark and just how much damage Delia had caused to all of them.

Evelyn's dad attempted a smile.

'I parked around the back – I had a pile of documents I wanted to return, I hope you don't mind.'

I shook my head. 'Of course not. And I'm sure...'

It wasn't my place to say it, but I felt the need to offer him some comfort.

'Maybe Patrick will still want you to work on the archive, when things settle down.'

'Oh, I doubt that.' Jack's face darkened. 'I feel so guilty, you know. The passageway from the tower, where that poor girl was found – I should have known about it. I called myself a historian, but I hadn't a clue, really, what I should have been looking for. It's no wonder Delia didn't want proper researchers wandering around. She must have hidden everything interesting, and just passed on to me what she wanted me to read. She had me right where she wanted me; I would have published some stupid pamphlet about the place and the real story would have stayed hidden for ever. Isla could have died.'

His eyes filled with tears, and he stared straight ahead for a moment, then made a visible effort to straighten his shoulders.

'We all have a lot to thank you for, Grace. And, oh yes! I want to show you something!'

I followed him into the body of the room, my nose prickling as usual as the cloud of dust rose to meet me. There was an A4-sized brown envelope lying on a wooden, leather-topped table and Jack picked it up and handed it to me.

'That painting you were interested in? Deirdre Fitzmahon? One of the members of the history society has a background in art history so I took a photograph of it to show him.'

I opened the envelope as he continued to talk, and a sheet of paper slid into my hand.

'He'd need to see it, of course, but he reckons the original painting would cost a fortune to restore, I'm afraid. Says it looks like water damage, and years of neglect. But he looked it up in one of his books and he thinks he might have found a photo of the original. Look – he printed this out to show you.'

I turned over the page in my hand. The thin printer paper was shiny on one side and as I angled it towards the light to see it properly, I realised that, although this was the first time I had seen her picture, I knew her face as well as I knew my own. There she was, Deirdre Fitzmahon, daughter of Hollowpark, protector of this house and of the many generations of women who passed through its doors. There was her dark hair, drawn back from her calm, intelligent face, there were those confident blue eyes. And there, at her feet, was a small terrier who sat, head cocked, looking out at me.

'He's called Prince,' said Deirdre and when I glanced up she was standing a few feet away from me, framed by the door. She was smiling. It was the first time I had seen her smile and I smiled too, as the little dog nuzzled her hand.

'Good boy.'

Deirdre reached down and scratched him on the top of his head, between his ears, just the way I knew he liked it.

'You'll look after the place now?'

I nodded, and then they both turned and walked away, melting into the shadows of their beloved Hollowpark.

This house protects its own.

This house that I too now called home.

Acknowledgements

Thanks to my agent Sara O'Keeffe and editor Rosie de Courcy who believed in *The Belladonna Maze* from the very beginning.

To Bianca Gillam, and all at Head of Zeus for your enthusiastic support.

To Emma Rogers for your beautiful cover design.

To the team at Gill Hess, it's always a pleasure to work with you.

To Professor Margaret Kelleher and Dr Richard McMahon, thanks for your invaluable advice – all errors and omissions are my own!

To Caroline Stynes, valued first reader and friend.

To my friends in the writing world, in particular Jane Casey and Liz Nugent, I could not have kept going without your support. And to the wider crime writing community, please let me stay in the gang!

To Catherine Ryan Howard, for the DM that changed everything.

To booksellers everywhere, for the huge effort you made to keep the industry going during COVID-19.

To Rive Droite for many years of friendship and encouragement.

To Andrew Phelan for your belief in this story.

To Patricia Phelan and Maisie Malone, two wonderful women, in memory. Because of the pandemic, we couldn't mark your passing in the traditional way but you are remembered every day.

Finally, this book is dedicated to my sons, Conor and Séamus Phelan. All of the hard work is for you.